High Praise for Jill Shalvis

"Count on Jill Shalvis for a witty, steamy, unputdownable love story."

—Robyn Carr, *New York Times* bestselling author

It Had to Be You

"Engaging writing, characters that walk straight into your heart, and a town you can't wait to revisit make this touching, hilarious tale another heart-warmer worthy of Shalvis's popular series." —*Library Journal*

"A winner...Readers will laugh out loud as they rush to turn the pages." —*RT Book Reviews*

Always on My Mind

"Charming and engaging...Shalvis's fans will devour the two friends' introspective and passionate journey to love."

—*Publishers Weekly*

"Shalvis adds another steamy, sassy episode to her popular Lucky Harbor series." —*Booklist*

"Full of the warm and crazy characters who make up her tiny town, *Always on My Mind* has a sexy and tangled story that will put readers on the edge of their seats." —*RT Book Reviews*

Also by Jill Shalvis

A Little Bit of Luck

♥

2-in-1 Edition with *It Had to Be You*
and *Always on My Mind*

Jill Shalvis

FOREVER

New York   Boston

It Had to Be You and *Always on My Mind* are copyright © 2013 by Jill Shalvis

Cover design by Daniela Medina. Cover copyright © 2022 by Hachette Book Group, Inc.

Forever
Hachette Book Group
1290 Avenue of the Americas, New York, NY 10104
read-forever.com
twitter.com/readforeverpub

It Had to Be You and *Always on My Mind* originally published in 2013 by Forever. First 2-in-1 edition: November 2022

Forever is an imprint of Grand Central Publishing. The Forever name and logo are trademarks of Hachette Book Group, Inc.

The publisher is not responsible for websites (or their content) that are not owned by the publisher.

The Hachette Speakers Bureau provides a wide range of authors for speaking events. To find out more, go to www.hachettespeakersbureau.com or call (866) 376-6591.

ISBN: 9781538723630 (mass market 2-in-1)

Printed in the United States of America

CW

10 9 8 7 6 5 4 3 2 1

It Had to Be You

Chapter 1

Some things were set in stone: The sun would rise every morning, the tide would come in and out without fail, and a girl needed to check herself out in the mirror before a date no matter the obstacle. To that end, Ali Winters climbed up on the toilet seat to get a full view of herself in the tiny bathroom mirror of the flower shop where she worked. Ducking so that she didn't hit her head on the low ceiling, she took in her reflection. Not bad from the front, she decided, and carefully spun around to catch the hind view of herself in her vintage—aka thrift store—little black dress.

Also not bad.

She'd closed up Lucky Harbor Flowers thirty minutes ago to get ready for the town's big fundraiser tonight, where they were hopefully going to raise the last of the money for the new community center. Earlier, she'd spent several hours delivering and decorating Town Hall with huge floral arrangements from the shop, as well as setting up a display of her pottery for the auction. She was excited about the night ahead, but Teddy was late.

Nothing unusual. Her boyfriend of four months was perpetually late but such a charmer it never seemed to matter. He was the town clerk, and on top of being widely beloved by just about everyone who'd ever met him, he was also a very busy guy. He'd been in charge of the funding for the new community center, a huge undertaking, so most likely, he'd just forgotten that he'd promised to pick her up. Hopefully.

Still precariously balanced, she eyed herself again, just as there was a sudden knock on the bathroom door. Jerking upright in surprise, she hit her head on the ceiling and nearly toppled to the floor. Hissing in a breath, she gripped her head and carefully stepped down. Managing that without killing herself, she opened the door to her boss, Russell, the proprietor of Lucky Harbor Flowers.

Russell was in his mid-thirties and reed thin, with spiked blond hair, bringing him to just above her own almost-but-not-quite, five foot five. He was wearing red skinny pants and a half tucked–in red-and-white checkered polo shirt. These were his favorite golf clothes, though he didn't golf, because he objected to sweating. He was holding a ceramic pot filled with an artful array of flowers in each hand.

Ali took in the two arrangements, both colorful and cheerful, and—if she said so herself—every bit as pretty as the pots, which were hers too.

"What's wrong with this picture?" Russell asked.

She let go of the top of her head. "Um, they're all kinds of awesome?"

"Correct," Russell said with an answering smile. "But

they're also all kinds of waste. No one ordered these, Ali."

"Yes, but they'll look fantastic in the window display." An age-old argument. "They'll draw people in," she said, "and *then* someone will order them."

Russell sighed with dramatic flair. The flower shop had been his sister Mindy's until two years ago, when he'd bought it from her so that she could move to Los Angeles with her new boyfriend. "Sweetkins, I pay you to make floral arrangements because no one in Lucky Harbor does it better. I love your ceramic-ware and think you're a creative genius. I also think that genius is completely wasted on the volunteer classes you give at the senior center, but that's another matter entirely. You already know that I think you give too much of yourself to others. Regardless of that big, warm heart of yours, *you* make the arrangements. *I* run the business."

Ali bit her tongue so she wouldn't say what she wanted to. If he would listen to her ideas, they'd increase business. She was sure of it.

"And speaking of the shop," he went on, "we need to talk sometime soon. Um, you might want to fix your hair."

She turned her neck and glanced in the mirror. Eek. Her wildly wavy hair did need some taming. She quickly worked on that. "Better?"

"Some," Russell said with a smile, and put the flowers down to fix her hair himself. "Where's your cutie-pie, live-in boyfriend?"

Two months ago, her apartment building had been scheduled for lengthy renovations, and Ali had needed a place to stay. Teddy had generously offered to share his place. He was like that, open and warm and generous. And fun. There hadn't been a lot of that in her life. And then there was the pride of being in a real, adult relationship.

So she'd happily moved into his beach house rental, and suddenly everything she'd ever dreamed of growing up—safety, security, and stability—was right there. Her three favorite S's. "Teddy's late," she said. "I'll just meet him there."

Russell peered at her over the top of his square, black-rimmed glasses. "Don't tell me that Hot Stuff stood you up again."

"Okay, I won't tell you."

"Dammit." He sighed. "The sexy ones are all such unreliable bitches." He hugged her. "Forgive me for my complaint about the fabulous arrangements?"

"Of course. What did you want to talk about?"

A shadow passed over Russell's face but he quickly plastered on a smile. "It can wait. Come on, I'll take you to the auction myself. I want to get there before all the good appetizers are gone."

"How do you know there'll be good appetizers?"

"Tara's cooking."

Tara Daniels Walker ran the local B&B with her sisters, and she was the best chef in the county. Definitely worth rushing for.

Russell drove them in his Prius. Lucky Harbor was a picturesque little Washington beach town nestled in a rocky cove with the Olympic Mountains at its back and the Pacific Ocean at its front. The town itself was a quirky, eclectic mix of the old and new. The main drag was lined with Victorian buildings painted in bright colors, housing cute shops and a bar and grill called The Love Shack, along with the requisite grocery store, post office, gas station, and hardware store. A long pier jutted out into the water, and lining the beach was a café named Eat Me, an arcade, an ice cream shop, and a huge Ferris wheel.

People came to Lucky Harbor looking for something, some to start over and some for the gorgeous scenery of the Olympic Mountains and the Pacific Ocean. Ali was one of those looking for a new start. The locals were hardy, resilient, and, as a rule, stubborn as hell. She had all three of these characteristics in spades, especially the stubborn as hell part.

They parked at the Town Hall building at the end of the commercial row, and found the place filled to capacity.

"Look at all the finery," Russell said as they walked in, sounding amused. "For that matter, look at us. We're smoking hot, Cookie."

"That we are."

"Not bad for a pair of trailer park kids, huh?"

Ali had grown up in a rough area of White Center, which was west of Seattle. Russell had done the same but in Vegas, though he'd made himself a more-than-decent living in his wild twenties as an Elvis impersonator. About ten years ago, he moved to Lucky Harbor with his sister. Ali actually hadn't ever lived in a trailer park, but in a series of falling down, post–WWII crackerbox houses that were possibly even worse. Lucky Harbor was a sweet little slice of life that neither of them had imagined for themselves. "Not bad at all," she agreed.

They entered the hall to the tune of laughter and music and the clink of glasses. Ali caught a fleeting glimpse of Teddy working the crowd, gorgeous as ever in a suit and good-old-boy smile, which he flashed often. His light brown hair was sun kissed from weekends golfing, fishing, hiking, and whatever other adventures he chose. Extremely active and fit, he'd try anything that was in the vicinity of fun. It was one of the things that had drawn her to him.

He caught sight of her and smiled, and Ali's heart sighed just looking at him. She called it the Teddy Phenomenon, because it wasn't just her—everyone seemed to respond to him that way.

But then she realized he was smiling at the pretty server behind her, who then turned and walked into a wall. Ali shook her head and sipped her champagne. She got it. It was his job, pleasing the public. And he did have a way of making a girl feel like the most beautiful woman in a crowded room.

Mayor Tony Medina took the stage and tapped on the mic to get everyone's attention. A financial advisor, he'd been mayor for coming up on two years now, having taken over when the previous mayor, Jax Cullen, had stepped down from the position to concentrate on his first loves—his family and carpentry.

"Good evening, Lucky Harbor!" Tony called out. "Thanks for coming! Let's all raise our glasses to our very own Ted Marshall, who worked incredibly hard at raising the funds for our new community center."

At that, the crowd whooped and hollered, and Russell nudged Ali. "You worked hard too. Where's your credit?"

"I don't need credit," Ali said, and she didn't. She'd assisted by running car washes and other donation drives to help Teddy behind the scenes, where she was content to stay.

"As you know," Tony went on, "the town council promised to match the funds raised tonight. So without further ado, we're adding a total of *fifty thousand dollars* to the pot tonight."

Everyone cheered.

Teddy hopped up onto the stage with the mayor, hoisting a very large aluminum briefcase. He'd worked damn hard at getting this rec center built for the town, and it was within his sights now. Looking right at home, he smiled. "The build is an official go," he said into the mic. He opened the briefcase and showed off the fifty thousand, neatly stacked and wrapped in bill bands. Obviously it'd come straight from the bank for the reveal, but the crowd ate it up anyway.

After the ceremony, Ali went looking for Teddy. She needed a ride home, not to mention it'd be nice to see her boyfriend. She circled the large room twice to no avail, and then finally headed down the hallway to the offices to check there. She could see the light under Teddy's door, but to her surprise it was locked. Lifting a hand to knock, she went shock still at the low, throaty female moan from within. Wait…that couldn't be…

And then came a deeper, huskier moan.

Teddy.

Ali blinked. No. No, he wouldn't be with someone else…in his office…

"*Oh, babe*, yeah, just like that…"

It was Teddy's sex voice, and Ali got really cold, and then really warm, and she realized she had far bigger problems than finding a ride home.

* * *

Ali woke the next morning, alone. A sympathetic Russell had driven her home. In the dark, she'd paced the big house for a while, steam coming out her ears.

When Teddy hadn't shown up, she'd called her very soon-to-be ex-boyfriend, *twice*, but there hadn't been a return call. She did, however, now have a waiting text:

> *Babe, this isn't working. It's not you. It's all me. I just need to be alone right now. FYI, our lease ended on 5/31. So no worries, you're free to leave right away.*

Ali stared at the words in shock. She hadn't had caffeine yet so her brain wasn't exactly kicking in, but she was pretty sure he'd just broken up with her—by text—and that he'd also rendered her homeless.

Ali pulled up the calendar app on her phone. Yep. Yesterday had been May thirty-first. Flopping back on the bed, she stared up at the ceiling, trying to sort her tumbling emotions.

He'd beaten her to the break up, and after last night, hearing him in the throes and calling someone else "babe," she'd *really* needed to be the dumper not the dumpee. "Damn," she whispered, and sat up.

You're free to leave right away.

Magnanimous of him. And also a vivid reminder. Men came and went. That was the way of it for the Winters women. She'd nearly forgotten that it was a lifetime goal of hers to not perpetuate this pattern, that she needed to be more careful.

She'd remember now. And while she'd like to lie

around and plot Teddy's slow, painful death, and maybe wallow with a day in front of the TV and a huge bag of popcorn, she had work to do. She had to get back to Town Hall and take down the floral designs and collect whatever ceramics hadn't sold at the silent auction.

Then she apparently needed to figure out her living situation.

Still stunned, she showered and dressed in jeans and a sweatshirt for loading up boxes and then headed out. The rental house she'd shared with Teddy was high on the cliffs on the far north face of the harbor. It was isolated and not easy to get to, but she didn't mind the narrow road or being off the beaten path. The house itself was old and more than a little creaky, but full of character. Ali loved it and loved the view, and after a childhood of city noises, she loved sleeping to the sound of the waves hitting the rocks.

Normally, early mornings were her favorite part of living in Lucky Harbor. Cool and crisp, the sun was just peeking over the rugged mountains, casting the ocean in a glorious kaleidoscope of light. Beyond the surf, the water was still, a sheet of glass, perfectly reflecting the sky above. A brand new beginning. Every single morning.

Never more so than this morning...

She parked in front of the Town Hall. The place was locked, but Gus the janitor let her in. Mumbling something about getting back to his work, he vanished, and Ali began lugging the heavy floral arrangements out of the building, down the steps, and into her truck by herself. Then she carefully packed up the pottery that hadn't been sold and took that out as well. With every pass she made, she had to walk by Teddy's office, and each time her emotions—mostly anger—coiled tighter and tighter. Her mom and sister had the quick fuses in the family. Ali had always been more of a slow burn, but today she'd gone straight to red-hot ticked off.

When she was finally finished, she searched out Gus again, finding him indeed very busy—kicking back in the staff room watching a ball game on his phone. In his thirties, six feet four and big as a tank, Gus hadn't shaved since sometime last year. He looked like a tough mountain man who belonged on a History Channel show hauling logs—except for the tiny kitten in his big palm.

"Aw," Ali said, softening. "So cute."

At her voice, Gus startled, and with a little girl–like squeal, fell right out of the chair. Still carefully cradling the unharmed kitten, he glared at Ali. "Christ Almighty, woman, make some noise next time. You scared Sweetheart here half to death."

Sweetheart had her eyes half closed in ecstasy. "Yes, I can see that," Ali said wryly, reaching out to pet the adorable gray ball of fluff. "I can also see how very hard the two of you are working back here."

She couldn't tell if Gus blushed behind the thick, black beard, but he did have the good grace to at least look a little bit abashed as he lumbered to his feet. "I wanted to help you," he said, "but I had Sweetheart in my pocket, and the boss told me twice already not to bring her here. But she howls when I leave her home, and my roommate said if I didn't take her with me today, she was going to be his Doberman's afternoon snack."

"Sweetheart's secret is safe with me," Ali said. "I just need to get into Teddy's office for a minute."

Gus scratched his beard. "I'm not supposed to let anyone into the offices."

"I know," Ali said, "and I wouldn't ask, except I left something in there." She'd made Teddy a ceramic pot. It was a knotty pine tree trunk that held pens and pencils, and she'd signed it with her initials inside a heart. There was no way she was leaving it in his possession. He didn't deserve it. "Please, Gus? I'll only be a minute."

He sighed. "Okay, but only because you guys are always real nice to me. Teddy knows about Sweetheart, and he didn't rat me out." He set the sweet little kitten on his shoulder, where she happily perched, and then led the way to Teddy's office. There he pulled out a key ring that was bigger around than Ali's head, located the correct key by some mysterious system, and opened the office door. "Lock up behind you."

"Will do," Ali said, and as Gus left her, she went straight to Teddy's desk.

No knotty pine pot with the little heart she'd cut into the bottom. She turned in a slow circle. The office was masculine and projected success, and the few times she'd been here, she'd always felt such pride for Teddy.

That's not what she was feeling now. In fact, she sneezed twice in a row at some unseen dust, annoying herself as she looked for the pot. She finally located it in the credenza behind the desk, shoved in the very bottom beneath a bunch of crap. It was the shape of a Silver Pine tree trunk, every last detail lovingly recreated down to the knots and rings around the base. For a minute, Ali stared at the pot she'd been so proud of, shame and embarrassment clogging her throat. Swallowing both, she grabbed it, locked the door as she'd promised, found and thanked Gus, and left.

In her truck, she drew in a deep breath and drove off. It was a Winters's gift, the ability to shove the bad stuff down deep and keep moving. Teddy wasn't even a five on the bad stuff meter, she told herself.

As always in Lucky Harbor, traffic was light. At night, strings of white lights would make the place look like something straight from a postcard, but now, in the early light, each storefront's windows glinted in the bright sunlight.

Things stayed the same here, could be counted on here. She thought maybe it was that—the sense of stability, security, and safety—that drew her the most.

Her three S's.

At least until last night...

She put in her shift at the flower shop, worrying about how light business was. She brought it up to Russell at lunch, gently, that she felt she really had something to offer here, the very least of which was a website. But Russell, equally as gently, rebuked her. Like his sister Mindy before him, he was a technophobe. Hell, even the books were still done by hand, despite their bookkeeper's urging to update their system. Grace Scott, a local bookkeeper, had given up on changing Russell's mind, but Ali was going to bash her head up against his stubbornness, convinced they would make a great partnership.

On her break she used her smartphone to fill out as many online applications for apartments as she could find. By six o'clock, she was back at the beach house, hoping not to run into Teddy. She didn't, which was good for his life expectancy. Even better, the front door key still worked. Bonus. She had a roof over her head for at least one more night.

In the kitchen, she tossed her keys into the little bowl she'd set by the back door to collect Teddy's pocket crap.

Out of curiosity, she poked through the stuff there: a button, some change, and…two ticket stubs, dated a week ago for a show in Seattle.

A show she hadn't gone to.

She stared at the stubs, then set them down and walked away. Something else niggled at her as she headed into her bedroom, but she couldn't concentrate on that, because she was realizing that Teddy had been working 24/7 for weeks. And before that, he'd been sick and had slept in a spare bedroom. They hadn't actually slept together in…she couldn't even remember.

Which meant that Ali had been very late to her own break up.

At this, her heart squeezed a little bit. Not in regret. She tried really hard not to do regrets. It wasn't mourning either, not for Teddy, not after hearing him cheat on her. It was the realization that she'd really loved the *idea* of what they'd had more than the actual reality of it.

Sad.

She stripped down to her panties and bra before it occurred to her what the niggling feeling from before was. Reversing her tracks, she ran barefoot back to the large living room.

The house had come fully furnished, but Ted had always made the place his own, thanks to the messy, disorganized way he had of leaving everything spread around. Running shoes hastily kicked off by the front door. Suit jacket slung over the back of the couch. Tie hanging askance from a lamp. His laptop, e-reader, tablet, smartphone, and other toys had always been plugged into electrical outlets, and when they weren't, the cords hung lifeless, waiting to be needed.

Not now. Now it was all gone, even his fancy, highfa-
lutin microbrews from the fridge. Everything was gone,
including *her* iPod.

How she'd missed that this morning, she had no idea,
but facts were facts—Teddy had moved out on her like a
thief in the night.

Detective Lieutenant Luke Hanover had been away from
the San Francisco Police Department for exactly one day
of his three-week leave and already he'd lost his edge,
walking into his grandma's Lucky Harbor beach house to
find a B&E perp standing in the kitchen.

She sure as hell was the prettiest petty thief he'd ever
come across—at least from the back, since she was wearing nothing but a white lace bra and a tiny scrap of
matching white lace panties.

"You have some nerve you…you *rat fink bastard*," she
said furiously into her cell phone, waving her free hand
for emphasis, her long, wildly wavy brown hair flying
around her head as she moved.

And that wasn't all that moved. She was a bombshell,
all of her sweet, womanly curves barely contained in her
undies.

"I want you to know," she went on, still not seeing
Luke, "there's no way in hell I'm accepting your breakup
message. You hear me, Teddy? I'm not accepting it, because *I'm* breaking up with *you*. And while we're at it,
who even does that? Who breaks up with someone by
text? I'll tell you who, Teddy, a real jerk, that's who—
hello? *Dammit!*"

Pulling the phone from her ear, she stared at the screen
and then hit a number before whipping it back up to her

ear. "Your voice mail cut me off," she snapped. "You having sex in your office while I was in the building? Totally cliché. But not telling me that you weren't planning to re-sign the lease? That's just rotten to the core, Teddy. And don't bother calling me back on this. Oh, wait, that's right, you don't call—you *text*!" Hitting END, she tossed the phone to the counter. Hands on hips, steam coming out her ears, she stood there a moment. Then, with a sigh, she thunked her forehead against the refrigerator a few times before pressing it to the cool, steel door.

Had she knocked herself out?

"It's just one bad day," she whispered while standing in the perfect position for him to pat her down for weapons.

Not that she was carrying—well, except for that lethal bod.

"Just one really rotten, badass day," she repeated softly, and Luke had to disagree.

"Not from where I'm standing," he said.

Chapter 2

At the unexpected male voice, Ali's heart leaped into her throat. She whirled and stared in shock at the guy standing in her kitchen. Reacting without thinking, she grabbed the key bowl off the counter and flung it at his head.

He ducked, and the bowl bounced off the wall behind him, shattering into a hundred pieces. As ceramic shards tinkled to the tile floor, he straightened, dominating the kitchen as he turned to her, eyes narrowed.

"Who the hell are you?" she demanded, heart thundering.

"Oh no, you first," he said, arms crossed, looking impenetrable and imposing. "Why are you throwing shit at me?"

Wishing like hell that she had clothes on, she was surreptitiously reaching for the coffee mug on the counter—another of her creations—to pitch at his head when he lunged and wrenched the mug from her hand. "Stop with the target practice," he said, oozing dangerous levels of testosterone.

He was tall—six feet, at least—and built like he was very familiar with a gym or physical labor. And while he stood there in the middle of the kitchen as if he owned the place, she took in other details. Sharp eyes. *All the better to see you with, my dear*, she thought half hysterically, feeling a little bit like Little Red Riding Hood must have when she'd been trapped by the big, bad wolf.

His hair was dark brown and tousled, as if he couldn't be bothered with a comb. His T-shirt was stretched across broad shoulders, his jeans sitting low on lean hips. And his cross-trainers made no noise when he took a step toward her.

All the better to catch you with, my dear…

He didn't look like the big, bad wolf, she told her panicky self. Nor did he look like an ax murderer who broke into homes and tortured women in their undies—not that she was sure what an ax murderer might look like. Snatching the dish towel off the counter, she attempted to cover herself since her Victoria's Secrets weren't hiding much of her secrets.

The maybe–ax murderer's gaze wasn't leering, though he was definitely taking in her body, and she forced herself not to squeak as he snatched her sweater off the back of a chair and held it out to her, mouth hard.

All the better to eat you with, my dear…

Heart in her throat, she didn't reach for the sweater. She was afraid to. Instead, she eyed the block of knives two feet over on the counter, wondering if she could possibly get to them before…

He shoved them farther away.

Dammit. "You're trespassing," she said, proud of her steely voice.

"No, that would be you."

Clutching the towel for all she was worth, she shook her head. "I live here." Although technically, thanks to Teddy, that wasn't quite true anymore. "And if you don't go, I'm going to call the cops."

He didn't go.

Ali knew exactly one self-defense move, and she went for it, risking everything to step into him and jerk her knee up.

But he moved so fast she didn't have to time to get him in the family jewels. She didn't even have time to blink before she was helplessly pinned against the counter by a tough, sinewy body.

"Stop," he said in her ear. Then, as if nothing had happened, he stepped back from her, once again offering her the sweater.

This time she took it, dropping the tiny, ineffective dish towel and diving gratefully into the long garment, wrapping it around herself so that she was covered from her chin to her thighs.

Better.

Or as better as she could be with the stranger watching her carefully. He stepped back a little farther still, giving her some badly needed space. His expression was carefully neutral, but his body language spoke of a deadly tension that she didn't want to further provoke.

"So," he said calmly, propping up the doorjamb with a broad shoulder. "You break in?"

Was he serious? He certainly looked serious. Not to

mention stoic and controlled, which set her nerves crackling.

His eyes were blue. Ice blue. She only noticed because she was watching him closely for any sign of aggression. His face might have been classified as devastatingly handsome, but it could also have been carved in stone, his expression dialed to an intimidating pissed off.

But she was pissed off too. And more than a little bit scared. Sure, she'd grown up in a tough neighborhood, but this guy was light-years ahead of her in badass experience. He had attitude written all over him, and a day's worth of stubble darkening his jaw. Though his hair was cut short, some of it managed to fall across his forehead, which didn't soften his appearance. She doubted there was anything soft about this man. "I didn't break in," she said. "I live here."

"That's impossible."

"How would you know?" she asked.

"Because I own the house."

Still leaning against the doorway, Luke gave the woman standing in front of him a long look that usually had bad guys running like hell.

But she wasn't running. Instead she met his gaze with wide, hazel eyes, making him wonder about the glimpse of fierceness he'd seen when she'd been leaving that phone message. He ached for peace and quiet, and she was clearly the opposite of peaceful and quiet—so he needed to show her the door.

"You own this place?" she asked. "You're Luke Hanover?"

"Yes."

She didn't relax. "I'm going to need to see your ID."

That was usually *his* line. And for a woman standing in little more than a lightweight peach sweater, she had balls. Except what she really had was an acre of creamy, smooth skin and that mind-warping sweet, curvy body. He pulled out his wallet and showed her his driver's license. "Now you."

She blinked once like an owl, her hazel eyes not nearly as hostile now as she shoved some of her wild hair from her face. "I'll have to get it out of my truck," she said. "I left my purse out there."

The cop in him winced. But this was Lucky Harbor not San Francisco, and people felt safe here. And yet he knew better than anyone that shit happened everywhere. "I had this place rented out to a single male through a management service," Luke told her. "No B and E experts or half-naked women were on the lease." He'd really counted on finding the place empty and was prepared to facilitate that by whatever means necessary, because he needed that few weeks of peace and quiet in the worst possible way.

"Teddy didn't tell me until a few hours ago that he hadn't re-signed the lease," she said.

"Teddy," he repeated. "The 'rat fink bastard' you were yelling at on the phone?"

She nibbled on her lower lip. "So you heard all that, huh?"

Yeah, he'd heard it and had suddenly appreciated his long dry spell in the women department. "Where's Marshall now?"

"Moved out." Turning from him, she climbed onto the barstool, and for one brief glorious second, the sweater raised, flashing him another quick peek-a-boo shot of those hot, little panties before she settled. She really did have a world-class ass. And a wedgie.

"He never mentioned he wasn't re-signing the lease?" Luke asked.

"No. Hence the rat fink bastard part."

That nearly got a genuine smile out of him. It would have been his first in weeks, but he bit it back. Because in truth, there was nothing funny about this. He'd come to Lucky Harbor to be alone.

He *needed* alone.

It'd been years since he had been here. After inheriting the house from his grandma, he'd kept it rented out. He'd done so purposely, even though he'd spent some of the best times of his life here while growing up. The cliffs and water had been a teenager's haven and so had the pier and arcade. Back then, he hadn't cared that the house was inconvenient to get to or isolated. He cared even less now. In fact, he liked both of those things.

The property included a rickety set of stairs down to the beach and its own small dock. The huge, old house was equally rickety. He hadn't thought of selling it though, not once. He couldn't, not without far more guilt than he was equipped to handle.

He was glad for that now, because he'd needed out of San Francisco after his life had detonated. On his last case, he'd been part of the unit that had been tasked with gathering evidence against Senator Robert Daniel-son, who was accused of murdering three young women over the course of a year.

From the beginning, the evidence had been shaky at best: a few emails, texts, and phone calls between the senator and the women. A handful of questionable expenses. But Danielson was respected, and, by all accounts, also a decent guy. During four months of investigation, not one person had said a negative thing about him other than the guy worked too hard. Eventually, due to lack of evidence, the case against him had been dropped.

Two days later, the senator's pretty, young aide, Isabel Reyes, had floated in on the tide of the San Francisco Bay.

The senator had been found only an hour after, hanging from the rafters.

The press had gone ape-shit that no one had seen this coming, questioning the integrity of everyone involved with the case, including the judge, the DA, and the entire investigative team—which Luke had led.

He still felt sick about Isabel Reyes's death. He couldn't get past his gut feeling that he *should* have known. Disgusted with the job, the system, and most especially himself, he'd put in for all twenty-one days of the vacation he'd accumulated and left the city, hoping to find his sanity. He'd come here to Lucky Harbor, planning to sleep for at least a week and then maybe have some pizza and catch a few games, and then sleep for another two weeks. He'd wanted to do that free of other people, especially recently dumped-by-text renters.

"Okay," he said, "so Marshall's gone, and you're…?" He paused for her answer, thinking that the only acceptable response would be "leaving now."

"I have a place to move to," Hazel Eyes said.

Thank God.

"Probably." She paused. "Hopefully. Soon as I hear back from the applications I put in today, I'll know more. Not that this is your problem, of course." She hopped off the barstool, and Luke told himself that the reason his body tightened was relief that she was on the move. He wasn't going to have to forcibly remove the sexy, crazy, naked lady from his house.

But instead of gathering her things and going, she walked to the refrigerator and pulled out some ingredients. "You like turkey?" she asked.

He blinked at the quick subject change. "Yeah."

"Your stomach's growling." Quick as lightning, she put together a thick turkey sandwich with some fixings and handed it to him.

"Thanks," he said in surprise.

"No problem." Moving to the counter, she stared out the window.

The hem of her sweater covered her ass, even most of her thighs, hugging her curves for all it was worth. Her legs were long, toned. *Bare.* Working at not imagining running his hands up their entire length, he shoved in a big bite.

Still looking out the window, she set one foot on top of the other and cocked a hip, silent.

"I think there are boxes in the garage," he said, trying to be helpful. Hell, he'd even carry her shit out for her, no problem.

More silence, which was normally *his* thing. He was good at it too. But when she finally spoke, the words stabbed him.

"Dumped and made homeless in the same day," she said softly. "That's got to be some kind of record for pathetic, right?"

Luke let out a breath, pushed the now-empty plate away, and tried to harden his already stone heart. That his ex-renter had screwed her over wasn't his problem. He was temporarily off duty from solving other people's problems. Sure, she'd had a tough break, but the cold, hard fact was that lots of good people got screwed over every day of the week. He couldn't care right now. He hadn't slept in days, and he was going to pass out on his feet if he didn't get horizontal in the next five minutes. "Look, stay tonight. It's not that big of a deal."

She didn't move from her perch. "Thank you, but no. I'll be okay."

Luke followed her gaze to the ancient Toyota truck parked at the curb. He'd been a detective long enough to know exactly what she was thinking—she was going to sleep in her truck. "Seriously. Stay one more night."

She turned and looked at him then, eyes bright with pride. "Don't you dare feel sorry for me."

He had a sister. A mom. He knew how to swim through the shark-infested waters of a woman's psyche without getting injured. "Are you kidding?" he asked. "I feel sorry for me. The sandwich was great, and I'm not much in the kitchen. Even if I was, I'm too tired to go to the store for stuff. If you leave now, I'll go hungry tomorrow."

She stared at him for a long moment. Luke didn't have to work at looking genuine, because he'd spoken the utter truth.

"You won't be sorry," she finally said. "Or hungry." And then she vanished down the hall.

Luke didn't like to disagree with a pretty woman, but he had a feeling she was going to be dead wrong on at least one of those points.

Chapter 3

Luke followed his unintentional houseguest to the master bedroom.

His grandma's old room.

Clamping down on the memories, he stopped in the doorway, happy to note that it didn't look like his grandma's room. There were clothes and shoes and bottles and jars of stuff everywhere. It looked like a girl-bomb had gone off.

"Did I tell you that I love your house?" Sexy-Crazy-Nearly-Naked Tenant asked, coming out of the attached bathroom.

But she was no longer nearly naked. She'd buttoned up and added a pair of jeans. Her feet were still bare though. Her toes were painted sky blue, with little daisy decals on the big toe.

And he had no idea why he was checking out her toes. None.

Twisting up her hair, she sailed by him and out the bedroom door, once again leaving him to follow after her.

"So you filled out some apartment applications?" he asked.

"Yes." She walked into the kitchen, where she grabbed a watering can from beneath the sink and filled it.

"Any background checks?"

"No. Why?"

"I ran one on Marshall before he moved in here," he said.

She stared at him. "You did?"

He nodded. Being a detective, he often dealt with the dregs of society, the bottom feeders and the ones who'd sell their own mother's soul to the devil. In Luke's world, trust was not a given; it was earned. "If I'd known you were living here, I'd have done one on you too."

"Oh." Her voice was different now, which had him taking another look at her. She'd dropped eye contact and was biting her lower lip.

Ah, shit. She had something to hide. "Would that have been a problem?" he asked.

"No. Nope, not at all."

He raised a brow.

"Really," she said.

"The search program I have on my laptop is pretty intense," he said.

"Intense, like…you could see my third grade teacher and when I stopped believing in the Tooth Fairy?" she asked. "Stuff like that?"

"Yeah," he said dryly. "Stuff just like that."

"Fine. Do it."

"What's your name?" he asked.

"Ali Winters. Ali with an 'i.'"

He pulled his laptop out of his duffle bag. "Let's see what comes up."

"Sure." She shifted back and forth on her bare feet while he worked. He hadn't been kidding; this program was pretty damn invasive. It came in handy when he was hunting down suspects. Not so handy for running a background check on cute, hazel-eyed houseguests, because he was bound to find out far more than he needed.

The basics began to spit out, including a list of her previous known addresses, her age, job history, public records, etc. Ali-with-an-i was twenty-six, and her listings for previous addresses were fifteen deep, most in and around White Center and Burien, both just below Seattle. A longer look told him that ten of them had been before the age of eighteen.

She'd been questioned by the police a handful of times, thanks to being related to a Harper Winters—her sister—who'd been arrested for petty theft and assault after stealing a Peeping Tom neighbor's binoculars and beating him over the head with them. And then again when her mother—Mimi Winters—had threatened a lowlife ex's life by chasing him down the street with her car.

Ali herself had steered clear of any arrests. She'd gone to a junior college and worked as a singer in a casino/hotel lounge and at a flower shop.

"Is it bad?" she asked, leaning over his shoulder, seeming torn between wanting to know and not wanting to know.

He craned his neck and looked at her. "You're a singer?"

"Not even a little bit. I gave up the singing job when

I got jumped by a Cher impersonator for forgetting the words to that 'do you believe in life after love' song. But I got to keep my clothes on, and the tips were good. Plus I got my associate's degree with no student loans." She moved into the living room and began to water the plants scattered throughout the big, open space. There were several large ceramic pots on either side of the couch and beneath the picture windows. Several smaller pots were scattered around on shelves and the coffee table.

This was new. Luke's grandma had been warm and funny and bossy as hell, fiercely loving all who crossed her path—except plants. Plants she'd killed with just a look, including the supposedly invincible cacti. "Where did these come from?" he asked.

"Me," Ali said. "This house is so wonderful, all old and filled with character and charm…" Her smile was a little wistful. "But it needed…life. Besides feeding you, I'll take care of the plants."

"They're your plants."

"Hmm."

Hmm? What did *hmm* mean?

"Your yard's a mess," she noted casually. "You've got smooth douglasia and piper's bellflower out there, and they're being choked to death by the red willow-herb. And the Indian paintbrush…do you have any idea how hard it is to grow that?"

"I'm not looking for a gardener. Or a tenant," he said, seeing where this was going. He rubbed the ache between his brows. "I'm not looking for anything or anyone, just some peace and quiet." Which wasn't to say that he didn't want a woman. He wouldn't mind that, though it'd be fourth on his list after sleep, food, and more sleep, but yeah, he'd absolutely take a warm, sexy, naked woman under him. Over him.

However she desired…

But not this woman, no matter how attractive he found her. Because this woman had a set of eyes that had so much life and emotion in them, he'd drown in her.

The house phone rang, and they both looked at it. "Is that your personal line?" he asked. "Or Marshall's?"

"Well, it started out Teddy's," she said. "But I use it too."

He gestured for her to go ahead and answer it then, since it couldn't be for him. Few if any knew he was here. Certainly not his commander, who was still pissed off that Luke had taken time off in the middle of the media shitstorm. And not his parents or his sister, Sara.

The only people who might know—his two closest friends, Jack and Ben—were working. Jack, right here in Lucky Harbor as a firefighter, and Ben, off saving the world. Somewhere.

Ben, who'd suffered his own unimaginable losses, would have known to leave Luke alone, but not Jack. Jack would sniff him out sooner rather than later, but Luke wanted to have his head on straight first, because no one saw through him like Jack did.

Ali had answered the phone and was frowning. "You're looking for who?" she asked. "Detective Lieutenant Luke Hanover?" She slid Luke a long look.

People usually had one of two reactions when finding out that he was in law enforcement: They either wanted to see his gun and be shown some self-defense moves, or they ran like hell.

Ali's reaction was somewhere in between, but Luke

didn't care. What he cared about was not having anyone know he was here. He shook his head with a "hell no" look. He had no idea how whoever was looking for him had gotten this number but he was *not* here.

"How did you get this number?" she asked whoever was on the phone.

Luke liked the question and wondered at the answer.

"Uh-huh," she said, still looking at Luke. "I see."

Luke pointed to himself and shook his head, his message implicitly evident: He was *not* here.

Ali gave him a sweet smile and then lifted a single finger, indicating that she needed a minute.

Luke gave her his best intimidation stare—which was completely wasted on her because she turned her back to him.

"Yes, of course," she said into the phone. "I understand why you'd want to speak to him."

Okay, they were done here. Luke strode toward her, intending to physically remove the phone from her hand, but then she surprised him again by holding him off with a hand to his chest. "However," she said, "you're mistaken about Detective Lieutenant Hanover being here…uh-huh…"

She was getting an earful, he could tell. Ignoring the hand still on his chest—which was shockingly difficult to do—he motioned for her to hang the fuck up.

"Uh-huh…"

Again he reached for her, and again she pressed on his chest. "Hmm," she said, reminding him he still had no idea what that meant. "Well, as I mentioned, he's not here. Don't call again." She hung up and looked at Luke. "Interesting."

"A reporter," he guessed.

"Yes."

He let out a breath. "Thanks."

"No problem," she said. "I've got lots of practice dodging callers. I honed the skill with bill collectors and various other annoyances for my mom. Had it down to a science before I knew my multiplication tables."

Luke braced himself for the inevitable questions that most anyone else would have asked, but she surprised him yet again.

"I'll get that phone line shut down for you before I go," she said.

"Thanks. Ali—"

Someone knocked at the door, and he swore.

"I'll get it," she said. She started to head out of the kitchen, but stopped to look at him. "I take it you're still not here?"

"Correct."

She looked at him for a beat, her eyes softening just a little before she vanished. He had no idea what that meant, but a minute later he heard the front door open.

"Mr. Gregory," she said, an obvious smile in her voice. "Everything okay?"

In the kitchen, Luke swore again. Mr. Edward Gregory was the closest neighbor, a disarmingly sweet-looking old man who was actually about as sweet as a rattler.

And once upon a time, for about three minutes, he'd been married to his grandma—which made him Luke's biological grandfather. Not that Ali could possibly know that since he sincerely doubted Edward would have mentioned him. Luke hadn't exactly done anything to be proud of in his grandfather's eyes, unless one counted getting his sister sent to prison at age eighteen, and then two years later, letting his grandma die alone.

Luke and Edward hadn't spoken in a while, a long while. And for now, he intended to keep it that way.

"Do you need help with the pot I started for you?" he heard Ali ask.

What the hell?

"No, I'm good," Edward said. "I'm heading over to the senior center to take the whole crew to the buffet special."

Luke glanced out the kitchen window. Parked behind Ali's truck was a big, white van with SENIOR CENTER DIAL-A-RIDE across the side. His grandfather was old enough to be in the damn center himself, or at least close to it, but apparently he was driving for them instead.

"I saw an unfamiliar truck in the driveway," Edward said. "Wanted to make sure you were okay."

Luke's truck was two years old. No one here in Lucky Harbor would recognize it except Jack, but Edward Gregory was a wily, old fox. And Ali was clearly kind and caring and all kinds of gullible. She'd probably fall for it hook, line, and sinker and let the old man in.

And wouldn't that just make Luke's day, having the confrontation that had been brewing for a decade, on top of everything else.

"Oh, aren't you sweet," Ali said. "But I'm just fine, Mr. Gregory. Thank you so much for asking."

Was she actually protecting Luke? It'd been a while since he'd found himself in this position, *needing* help, and he didn't know how to feel. He settled for uncomfortable and off balance.

"You still having problems with that kitchen plumbing?" his grandfather asked.

"Nope, it's behaving now."

Luke looked into the kitchen sink. Yeah. She was definitely protecting him. It was totally clogged. And suddenly, so was his throat. Christ, he was tired. Tired and messed up.

Ali and his grandfather continued to chitchat for what felt like ten years, but in reality was only a few minutes, with Edward continuing to angle for an invite in, turning on the charm full power.

But Ali held her own, laughing and keeping things light, while remaining utterly firm. And in another minute, the front door shut, and she was back.

Luke looked at her. "You deal pot to the geriatric crowd?"

She stared at him and then laughed. She laughed so hard she had to put her hands on her knees and double over. Finally she straightened and swiped at her eyes. "Oh my God, I needed that." She got herself under control with what appeared to be some effort. "No, I don't deal pot. I teach a weekly ceramics class at the senior center." She shook her head at him. "You are such a cop."

Guilty. "A detective."

"So I heard."

The damn reporter.

"A *lucky* cop too," she went on.

His life was such complete shit that he had no idea what she could possibly be talking about. "Lucky?"

"With your neighbors," she said. "Growing up, my neighbors were career arsonists and loan sharks." She shrugged. "The arsonist was nice enough, but if I left my dolls out, he'd set their hair on fire."

"And the loan shark?"

"He wasn't crazy about little kids," she said. "He used to tell me and my sister that he was going to sneak into our place one night and sell us on the white slave market, and then retire off his portion of the profit."

Jesus. "How old were you?"

"I don't know, twelve maybe. He never got the chance. When my mom found out what he'd said, she threw a lamp at his head. That straightened him out pretty quick."

Luke wasn't into civilians taking matters into their own hands, but in this case, the vigilante justice worked for him. "*Good.* And thanks for your help."

She smiled. "I figured you didn't want to socialize."

"No."

"So maybe it's fate that I'm here."

Fate? He'd call it bad luck. "I don't put much stock in fate." He believed in making his own path—even if that way was to fuck up a few times before he got it right. He never blamed something as intangible as fate for his screwups.

He blamed himself.

She stared at him for a moment, her eyes soft, as if maybe she felt sorry for him, of all things. "That's okay," she said. "I believe enough for the both of us."

Well, hell.

He tried to shake it all off, but his eyes were gritty from the exhaustion. "I'm hitting the sack." He walked away and took the stairs down to the basement.

It'd been years since he'd been down here, but not much had changed. The walls were a midnight blue with the galaxy painted on the ceiling. Pluto was still a planet. The door was covered in late '90s radio station stickers, a virtual time capsule to Luke's teenagehood.

Not that there was a lot to the time capsule. His parents, both doctors, had never put much stock in sentiment. They believed in higher education, hard work, and harder, tough love. And the cause, always the cause.

Right now that meant being in Haiti. Back then, it'd been Doctors Without Borders, which had left Luke and his older sister, Sara, more often in the care of their grandma up here in Lucky Harbor than at home in San Francisco.

Which had worked for Luke.

He'd had a lot of good times in Lucky Harbor, the best times of his life. His first climb. His first ski. His first boat race. His first jump off the pier. His first kiss. And given that Candy Jenson, a senior to his freshman, had also taken his virginity, he'd had just about every possible first here.

Good memories.

At least until several years later, on one particularly stupid night when he'd been with the girl of his dreams. They'd parked up at Pigeon Point to "stargaze," aka have sex, in her daddy's truck. They'd been doing just that when his sister had called him. Twenty years old to his eighteen, Sara hadn't bothered with Luke all that often, but that night she'd been drinking and had needed a ride home.

Luke had still had two condoms left. He'd told his sister to give him a little bit.

But Sara hadn't waited. She'd driven home drunk, blasting through a stop sign and killing an old man crossing the street.

Though Sara had never blamed him for her two years in jail, Luke still hadn't forgiven himself, and their relationship had been strained ever since.

And then his grandma had died two summers later. Again, he hadn't been the direct cause, but close enough.

He'd not come back to Lucky Harbor since.

The stack of boxes against the wall suggested that at some point this room had gone from housing a teenager to housing extra crap. His grandma Fay had never been able to throw anything of his or Sara's away. She'd been the only sentimental one in the entire family.

Luke took a long look around and nudged the first box with his toe, eyes locking in on a lump of clay—the stupid snowman he'd once made at summer camp. It was missing an eye and a chunk of its head, but his grandma had cherished the thing, which had sat on her desk as a paperweight for as many years as he could remember.

Her desk was still upstairs in the den, but it was empty now, available for whichever tenant wanted to use it.

Luke stared at the snowman, reluctantly acknowledging the damn ache in his chest before shaking his head and heading straight for the bed. Kicking off his clothes and shoes with equal carelessness, he sprawled onto the mattress.

His last conscious thought was the image of Ali standing in his kitchen in nothing but her sexy bra and panties and that smile, the one that told him he was in a whole shitload of trouble, whether he liked it or not.

And for the record, he didn't like it.

Chapter 4

Ali heard the door shut from the depths of the house, and then nothing.

Just silence in Luke's wake.

She cleared up the shards on the floor from the ceramic pot she'd thrown and let out a long breath. Luke Hanover was a force. A big, edgy, enigmatic force.

And a cop. A detective lieutenant.

Good Lord.

Her mom loved men, *all* of them, but one thing she'd always imparted to her daughters was a general distrust of men of the law. Ali's growing up years had been like living through a season of *COPS*, and she still tended to twitch when she heard a siren. Though she'd twitched at the sight of Luke for an entirely different reason.

In light of the fact that she was just dumped and therefore temporarily uninterested in anyone with a penis, this was deeply disturbing.

Luke was a good-looking guy, she told herself. Any

woman would react. It was the way he carried himself—the sharp gaze that missed nothing and a calm, controlled demeanor even after finding a half-naked woman
in his house. Although, there'd definitely been something
in his expression suggesting a tension that had nothing to
do with her. The earful she'd gotten from the reporter had
confirmed this. Luke had clearly had a week far worse
than hers, especially since his had involved dead people.

Clearly Luke dealt with more stress and responsibility
on any given day than Ali had ever managed. She felt bad,
but at the moment, she had her own problems.

Big problems.

Roof-over-her-head problems. She could stay here
tonight, but she had every other night to worry about. Letting out a shaky breath, she lifted her chin. It was what
the Winters women did, they faked their bravado. Then
they told themselves everything was going to be okay. "It
is going to be okay," she said out loud to convince herself, because that would make it so. "It's really going to
be okay."

But she had no idea how. She didn't charge the senior
center when she taught there, and Lucky Harbor Flowers
was slower than usual this season. Russell kept talking
about his dream, which was to follow his ex-boyfriend
Paul to Las Vegas. And that meant closing the shop.

Unless she could suddenly convince him that she could
run the shop in his absence, things were going to go bad
for her.

Her phone buzzed. It was Leah Sullivan, pastry chef
and Ali's closest friend in town. "Hey," Ali said, going for
chipper.

"You okay?" Leah asked.

"Yep," Ali said. "Totally okay."

Leah, a wanderlust soul, was friendly and curious and funny as hell. She seemed to have a knack for recognizing bullshit. "You're lying."

"A little," Ali admitted.

Leah sighed. They hadn't been friends that long, Leah was only in town to run her grandma's bakery while the older woman recovered from knee surgery, but some things didn't take any time at all.

"Men are scum," Leah said. "Even cute Ted Marshall apparently."

"How is this already news?"

"There was a sighting of Ted carrying boxes into a rental duplex. So you're still at the house?"

"Yes," Ali said, not mentioning that she was only staying for one more night. She didn't want to worry or burden Leah, who'd just recently come back to Lucky Harbor after a long stretch away. She worked in the bakery in the same building as Ali, which was how they'd become friends. But Leah was only here to help her grandma, and was staying in her grandma's tiny place. Leah would insist Ali join them, but Ali wouldn't impose.

"I've got fresh éclairs," Leah said. "Excellent breakup food."

"Definitely. I'll come by later," Ali said and clicked off. She could go to her mom's and sister's. White Center wasn't that far, a couple of hours, and Mimi and Harper would welcome her with open arms. But she'd left them and come here for a new start, to make something of herself, dammit.

She had other friends, but no one close enough to barge in on. Pensive over the realization that her life wasn't exactly going in the carefree, fun direction she'd hoped, she finished watering the plants. It was quiet in the house in spite of the big, brooding guy in it. Eerily quiet. She put the watering pitcher back under the kitchen sink and then sagged a little in the silence.

She didn't have to leave right now, but the fact remained that this was *his* home now.

Not hers.

She had no real home. This wasn't exactly a new feeling, but she hated that unsettled spot in her gut, and her fingers itched for a clump of cool, wet clay, which always soothed her. She might have gone out to the garage, where she'd set up a little workstation for herself, but the house phone rang again. She answered to another reporter and gave the same spiel that she'd given the first, but more firmly.

She'd seen something in Luke's eyes, a hollowness that she understood. Clearly he'd escaped to Lucky Harbor for some peace and quiet, and she was willing to fight for it for him. It was the least she could do to earn her keep.

Ali woke up on Sunday morning to a silent house. Luke's truck was still out front, so she assumed he was still sleeping.

She didn't have that luxury. She had a class to teach at the senior center and a life to figure out.

First up: breakfast. If her life was going to hell in a handbasket, well then she was going on a full stomach. In the kitchen, she pulled out the makings for two omelets. She cooked and then inhaled one while standing on the back deck. From here, she could see down the steep stairs to the house's private dock below, which jutted out into the water. She stared at the churning swells, lost in thought.

And worry.

And anxiety.

And lingering temper.

A movement caught her eye. There was a wiry-looking guy trying to get into the bushes along the side of the house. He had a camera in one hand and a cell phone in the other, which he was waving wildly about, trying to shoo something.

Narrowing her eyes, Ali moved closer. "Who are you?" she demanded.

He'd disturbed a few bees, and they were on him. The guy dropped to the ground, losing both his camera and his phone. "You have kamikaze bees!"

Clearly not a local. "Where are you from?" she asked.

He came up to his knees, gingerly looking around. "Are they gone?"

There was still one circling his head. "Yes."

"Whew." He let out a breath of relief and reached for his things. "I'm looking for Detective Lieutenant Luke Hanover. I just want a picture—"

That was all she needed to hear. She grabbed the hose that she'd coiled yesterday after watering the yard and nailed him.

"Hey!" He curled over his phone and camera to protect them. "*Hey!*"

She lowered the hose. "You're trespassing."

He stared at her like she was a loon. "You ruined my things! I'm going to call the cops!"

"Do that," she suggested. "And be sure to tell them you

were on private property trying to get a picture to sell to the media when you accidentally ran into the sprinklers."

"I'm not leaving," he said. "Not until I talk to the owner of this house."

Ali lifted the hose again, and he squeaked and then ran off. "That's what I thought," she said, and dropped the hose.

Feeling a little better, she went inside and wrapped up the second omelet and put it in the fridge with a note to her tall, dark, and attitude-ridden landlord:

Luke,
I made you a kick-ass omelet. Thanks for letting me stay the night.
Ali
P.S. I hosed the paparazzi scoping out your back deck so I doubt he'll be back today.

It took her a moment to find her keys, since she'd thrown the key pot at Luke. They were under the table. Grabbing them, she headed out to her class. It was surprisingly hot already, which might have sent anyone else scampering back inside, but Ali was made of sheer, one-hundred-percent resilience.

Or so her mom always said.

Outside, her truck didn't want to start. It was a morning thing, something the two of them had in common. "Come on baby," she coaxed, patting the dash with love. "Do it for me." The sweet talk worked, the truck roared to life, and they were off.

Lucky Harbor tended to roll up its sidewalks at dusk, and they hadn't yet been unrolled. The sleepy town was just coming to life, with little to no traffic on the streets and the shops not yet open for business. The pier was quiet too, the arcade dark, the Ferris wheel still against the morning sky.

On the outskirts of town stood a large, one-story building that had once been a small Army outpost. The barracks had been converted to apartments and then into a senior center.

Inside, Ali was greeted by Lucille. She was somewhere between sixty and one hundred, had a tendency toward velour sweat suits in eye-popping colors, and had a heart of gold. She also had an ear for gossip. She ran the local art gallery and the town's Facebook page with equal enthusiasm. Recently she'd expanded her social media platform to include Pinterest as well. She came out for all of Ali's classes because she had a crush on the men at the senior center, at least the ones who were "still kicking" as she liked to say.

Lucille smiled sympathetically at Ali. "You okay, honey?"

"Sure," Ali said. "Why?"

"I heard about your breakup. It's on Facebook."

Ali stared at her. "Who put it on Facebook?"

"Me." At least she grimaced. "I'm sorry. I heard it from the grapevine, so I wanted to get Ted up on our list of eligible bachelors." She patted Ali's hand. "Don't give him another thought. A man like Ted Marshall isn't ready to be tied down is all. Not your fault."

Ali hadn't wanted to tie him down. She'd wanted...well, she didn't know exactly.

Liar, liar, pants on fire. She knew.

She wanted to be loved.

They entered the big rec room for class and found the usual gang, ex-postmaster and currently a professional hell raiser Mr. Lyon, ex–truck driver and current geriatric playboy Mr. Elroy, and ex–rocket scientist and current ringleader Mr. Wykowski—all of them decades north of their midlife crises. Mr. Gregory was there as well because he'd just driven them back from the breakfast buffet and was helping everyone off the Dial-A-Ride van.

Ali had kept a few of the floral arrangements from the town auction. She unloaded them, setting them around the place so that the seniors could enjoy them. Then she started class. They'd been working on miniature animal statues. It was a thing of Ali's. When she'd been a little girl, she and Harper had sometimes been left alone for long periods of time while Mimi had been at work, and it hadn't always been safe enough to go outside to play. Ali would mix flour, salt, and water together into a homemade clay, passing the time creating palm-sized animals.

The seniors enjoyed it. Leah's grandma Elsie was there, working meticulously on a cat. Mr. Lyons created a lump that he claimed was a grizzly bear. "Top of the food chain," he said. "Like me. Why aren't I on your list of eligible bachelors? I'd kick ass on that list."

Mrs. Burland, a former teacher, smacked him upside the head. "Watch your language."

Mr. Elroy, who'd been watching the exchange and sliding his dentures around some, grinned at Mrs. B. "I'm making an elephant," he said. "Want to see its trunk?"

Mrs. Burland reached over and flattened Mr. Elroy's elephant with one smack of the palm of her hand.

Mr. Wykowski chuckled. "No worries. His trunk didn't work anyway."

After class, Ali dashed to her truck beneath a sizzling sun. The temp had risen and so had the humidity, and it took forever for her AC to kick in. While she waited, she realized that Teddy still had a presence in her vehicle and that rankled. She ripped down his pic from the dash, yanked out his Coldplay CD, and grabbed his sunglasses from the console. She thought about how beloved Teddy was here in Lucky Harbor—of course no one knew that he was a two-timing jerk—and gave brief thought to tossing his stuff in the trash.

It would be extremely satisfying, but she just couldn't do it. So she let out a breath and headed to Town Hall. Hopefully Gus was around today too, and she could drop everything off in Teddy's office so she wouldn't have to look at it—or him—ever again.

There were cars in the lot, but not Teddy's Lexus. Others cleaning up from the celebration, probably, and maybe some hard-working government employees putting in overtime. Ali shoved Teddy's things into her purse and took a moment to peek into the rearview mirror. Her hair had soaked up the humidity, frizzing into what now closely resembled a dandelion. Nothing she could do about that, because she'd run out of her drugstore defrizz a week ago. But she could wipe the mascara from beneath her eyes and apply some watermelon gloss, whose label promised to bring forth some serious shine and sexiness. After the past few days she'd had, Ali could have used some fortitude and strength to go with it, but she was pretty sure she wasn't going to get that from a lip gloss. A good stiff drink, maybe…

Later, she promised herself. A glass of something strong, a bath, and a serious pity party for one. But for now, she patted down her hair the best she could and grabbed her purse.

Teddy shared an assistant with several other city workers. Aubrey, who was tall, willowy, and beautiful, was standing behind her desk, frowning at her computer while still looking beautiful. And on top of that, *her* shiny blonde hair wasn't the slightest bit frizzy.

"Ali," Aubrey said in surprise, "what are you doing here on a Sunday?"

"I was just going to ask you the same thing."

"Work." Aubrey gestured to her computer, where a Skype screen was open to reveal another woman.

Bree Medina, the mayor's wife.

Bree was in her early forties, though she looked a full decade younger. She was an interior decorator to the rich and famous, and was one cool customer. Ali was glad Bree was not there in person, because in person she had a way of making Ali feel like a bargain-basement special. Plus, Bree's perfume made her sneeze. In fact, just thinking about it made her nose itch.

"Sorry," Ali said. "I didn't mean to interrupt. But I've got some things of Teddy's that I forgot to drop off yesterday." She left out the part about stealing her pencil pot back. No need to present herself as a Level Five Crazy Ex. "Can I leave it all in his office?"

"I can't let you in there," Aubrey said. "It's against the rules. But I can take it for him."

"It's not work related," Ali warned her, leaving

out details on purpose. People loved Teddy, she got that. But that's not why she kept quiet about their breakup. She kept quiet because she didn't want to be pitied.

There was an awkward silence.

"What is it?" Bree asked. "The ex-boyfriend box of crap?"

So they did know.

"Facebook," Aubrey said. "Lucille knows all."

"I have to go," Bree said. She looked at Aubrey. "I'll be in the office on Monday with the new office chairs we talked about." And then she clicked off.

Aubrey quit Skype and looked at Ali. "I knew you two lived together, everyone did, but the general consensus was that you two were just friends. At least that's how Teddy always made it sound." She pulled out her keys. "You can leave everything on his desk, but I did *not* let you in there."

"Never saw you."

And so Ali found herself in Teddy's office for the second time in as many days, which was two more times than she'd been here all month. Teddy had been far too busy for far too long. It burned deep that she'd let it happen, that she'd let him put her on the back burner without a thought.

Why had she done that? Why had she accepted less from him than she deserved? Because he was the golden boy? Because she'd gotten herself infatuated with the idea of a relationship?

She sat in his big, leather chair, set his things on his desk, and eyed the blotter scribbled with Teddy's familiar scrawl. *Call CPA. Order cards. Email reports.*

Huh. No *Screw over Ali* anywhere on the list.

She grabbed a new sticky note and let out the beast:

ASS.

She set the note front and center on his desk, next to the things from her truck. She studied her handiwork a minute and decided it wasn't quite enough. She added a few more thoughtful sentences on what she thought of his skills as a boyfriend, and finally feeling marginally better—and grateful that Mrs. Burland wasn't here to smack her upside the head for her language—she exited the office.

Aubrey was no longer at her desk, which was just as well. Ali wasn't sure if she could muster a smile as she exited the building.

Of course it was still hot. Once again Ali made her way to her truck and cranked on the AC, which was making an ominous grinding sound. Today would be a great day for it to break.

She wasn't sure where to go next. She didn't want to crowd Luke in his own home after he'd been so generous by letting her stay an extra night. The flower shop was only a half block away. She could grab her paycheck. Russell would probably be in his office in the back, watching Bravo, yelling at whatever *Real Housewives* show was on. She could spend some time online and see if an available apartment had come up.

With that decision made, she got out of the truck, into the sweltering day, and walked over to the flower shop. The old Victorian building had long ago been divided into three storefronts: the flower shop, Leah's grandmother's bakery, and an old bookstore that had been closed all year.

Most of the other downtown buildings had been renovated in the past decade, but not this one. It needed a major overhaul, but Ali loved it. The place had quirks and its own charm and character in spades. The flower shop was on the left, painted pastel yellow with white trim. The wood floors creaked and the lights always flickered, but to Ali, those things gave the place personality. It felt like her home away from home.

If she had a home...

Russell wasn't here, and as she moved through the front room, she inhaled the familiar scent of flora and tried to relax. She went through the available rentals again, lowering her expectations, trying to find something that would work. There were two, but one was subletting a room in some guy's house, and that felt a little sketchy for a woman. The other was on the outskirts of the county, far more remote and isolated than even the beach house. Not ideal...

She looked around Russell's office, which held a tiny desk, two filing cabinets filled to overflowing, and enough room to stand.

Nowhere to sleep.

Knowing she'd stalled as long as she could, she got up to go and opened the top desk drawer to grab her paycheck. But Russell hadn't written it, and one glance at the balance scrawled in his checkbook told her why. He was short again. He'd left her an envelope with half of what he owed her in cash, and a note that he'd get her the rest by the end of the week. Oh boy.

Things were going to be okay.

But she didn't know how. She moved to the office window and looked out. She could see the pier from here.

The Ferris wheel was turning. The trees lining the street were swaying. She knew if she opened the window, the breeze would be scented with an intoxicating combo of sea salt, pine trees, and hope.

She craved that. The fact was Lucky Harbor gave off a quiet serenity and strength, and she craved that too. She'd grown up in smoky, noisy, colorful lounges and bars. Mimi Winters had a long work history, from waitress to "dancer," and then back to waitressing when it got too hard on her body. She might not have been all that good with money, but she was good with love. Some would argue too good, as she'd rarely met a man she didn't fall for. But when there'd been trouble—and there *had* been trouble—Mimi had always come through for her girls, and together they'd handled whatever had come up.

Ali had gotten good at handling things, real good. This was just another of those times. Needing to connect to someone who loved her, she pulled out her cell phone and texted both her mom and sister with: *Missing you, how's things?*

Harper replied right away. *Got a hot date with Lenny. Remember Lenny? He's hot as ever and running his dad's plumbing business now.*

Mimi's response was just as fast. *Ali-gator! Miss your pretty face! Gotta run, caught some OT to help cover rent. Oh and I'm taking an online business class that's gonna change everything, you'll see.*

In Mimi's world, there was always something that was going to change everything. And the thing was, Mimi honestly believed it. Optimism was one of her most endearing qualities, but it also left Ali as the only realistic one in the family. She looked in her envelope again and worked some fancy math before texting her mom back. *Got some extra this month. I'll send.*

Mimi's response was immediate: *You're an angel. What would I do without you?*

Exactly what Ali worried about.

Luke woke up with a start, heart thundering in his chest, the vision of a drowned Isabel Reyes crystal clear in his head. Her hair had been floating behind her in a terrible parody of beauty, eyes open in permanent terror, skin so pale as to be translucent.

He'd been there when they'd pulled her body from the water, but he'd seen plenty of dead bodies before. It wasn't the image haunting him now so much as the failure to save her.

It was pitch black in the room, but he didn't need a light to remember where he was. In hell. He sat straight up. It was dark outside. He'd slept all day.

Scrubbing his hands over his face, he let his wits catch up with him. He would've rolled over and closed his eyes to take the rest of the sleep he still needed, but his stomach rumbled in protest. Damn. He reached for his phone and saw he had messages. No big surprise there.

His commander, wanting him to get his ass back to San Francisco in one week, not the three Luke had asked for, because "vacation time was for pussies"—not to mention that it left him dealing with the "media shitstorm" on his own. His mom, reminding him that sometimes things happened for a reason. His dad, telling him to work through it and stay strong. Last was Jack's message, suggesting that Luke not read the news or turn on the TV.

So of course Luke went straight to the browser app on

his phone and brought up the news. Yep, the media storm was still raging, with people blaming the DA and the entire SFPD.

And Luke, of course.

That was okay. Luke blamed Luke too.

He was starving. He slid off the bed and staggered up the creaky stairs and into the kitchen. He could drive into town, but he'd have to get dressed, and plus, he had no idea where he'd left his keys. He rarely did. Without turning on the light, he pulled open the refrigerator door.

He had no idea what he was expecting. He hadn't yet stocked any food. He hadn't thought that far ahead. Hadn't thought of anything other than getting away to hear himself think.

Or better yet, not think.

But there was bottled water, milk, eggs, cheese, luncheon meats, apples, oranges, and—hitting the jackpot—beer. A plate on the middle shelf had a colorful note stuck right on the top of it, from Ali.

He'd nearly forgotten about her.

Curious, he pulled out the plate. An omelet. He'd have preferred pie, but this looked good.

Hell, who was he kidding? *Anything* he didn't have to cook would have looked good to him. He nuked the plate, and then wolfed down the omelet where he stood. He was moving to the sink when he heard a whisper of a sound.

Footsteps.

Luke reached for his gun before remembering he was unarmed and in his boxers. Christ, he needed more sleep.

"Hands where I can see them, dick breath," a female said, and then the overhead light was slapped on.

Turning slowly, Luke came face to face with Ali standing in the kitchen entryway with an umbrella in one hand—aimed in his direction like a sword—and the other hand still on the light switch.

Clearly, she'd been in bed sleeping. Her hair was wild, like an explosion in a mattress factory. Her eyes were huge in her pale face. She wore a thin, white wife-beater tank top and sweatpants that were so big they were slipping off.

She lowered the umbrella and hitched up the sweats. "I thought we had an intruder."

"We do," he said. "*You.*" To distract himself from the fact that she was very braless, he eyed her stance. She wasn't new at protecting herself. "Dick breath?"

"Sorry, I was trying to sound tough." She shoved a hand through that crazy hair, looking a little bit wild and a lot off her game, and yet, he thought, there she stood ready to defend his house.

The first person on his side in a good long time.

Firmly ignoring the odd feeling in his gut, he shook his head. "Bad idea, coming up on a pissed-off, hungry, exhausted cop like that."

"I didn't know it was you," she said. "And you're not a cop right now. You're on leave."

He could have told her he was *always* a cop. "What if I'd shot you?"

"Would have ruined my whole day," she said in a tone that told him her day had been shitty. Then her gaze ran over him, and he knew the exact second she registered that all he wore was boxers because her breath caught audibly.

She was aware of him as a man. Ted might have dented her heart but he hadn't broken it.

"Is that a gun in your shorts," she asked softly. "Or are you just happy to see me?"

Chapter 5

Ali worked at not swallowing her tongue, as Luke—after a speculative, edgy look—turned and vanished down the hall without responding to her question.

Good Lord, the man wore nothing but boxers like no one else. She'd known he was good looking, but she hadn't known he had acres of hard sinew that bunched and flexed with his every move.

And she had no idea what she'd been doing baiting him like that. She certainly hadn't expected to feel scorched by heat just from looking at him. The man was drop-dead sexy, that was for sure.

Equally for sure was relief that he hadn't responded to her. It'd been a rhetorical question anyway, one uttered only because her brain had clicked off at the realization that he was half naked. But before she could reboot, he was back, wearing low-slung Levi's, shrugging into a shirt that he didn't bother to button. He had that whole dangerous, brooding air going on, spilling testosterone and bad boy vibes all over the place.

It did something very unwelcome in the pit of her belly. And lower. She cleared her throat. "I found two possible rentals today."

He didn't speak.

Good to know where she stood. Probably he was so thrilled and overjoyed that he *couldn't* speak.

He went to the fridge.

"One's on the outer edge of the county," she said. "In the Highlands. The other's a room from the guy who owns the hardwood store. Anderson something."

"No," he said.

"No?"

"The Highlands is a bad neighborhood. And you're not renting a room from Anderson. Hell no."

She stared at him, but he was head first in the fridge. "You still hungry?" she asked. "I can make you something." She moved over there just as he turned to her. She tried to nudge him out of her way, her palms settling on his chest, absorbing the heated, hard strength of him.

He didn't budge.

She pushed a little harder and this time he stepped back. "Thanks for the omelet," he said.

"Want another?"

"Sure."

She pulled out the eggs, cheese, broccoli, and a red pepper. Grabbing a pan, she turned on a burner. "Oh, I almost forgot. I have something for you."

His gaze went hooded, and she felt herself blush. She wasn't sure what he thought she might be offering, but given what she'd said about the gun in his boxers, it was probably far more than she'd meant to offer.

"There," she said, gesturing with her chin to the envelope on the kitchen table. It was the cash equivalent of three nights' worth of rent. Last night, tonight, and hopefully tomorrow night as well.

Optimism. Guess her mom wasn't the only Winters with that particular trait after all. The fact was that she'd hoped to get into a place tomorrow, but he'd just shut down her two current options.

He didn't make a move for the envelope, a fact Ali ignored as she began cutting up the pepper and grating cheese while he just stood there looking rumpled and sleepy and on edge. "Ironic, don't you think?" she asked.

"That you're more at home in my kitchen than I am?"

"The fact that we're complete strangers, and yet we've already seen each other in our underwear."

"Yeah." He stole a piece of cheese and popped it into his mouth. "I noticed that *you* didn't hand me a sweater like I did for you."

She smiled. Her first of the day. Maybe of the week.

He actually smiled back, which had to count for something, especially since he had a pretty great smile. She flipped the omelet and then a moment later transferred it to a plate, placing a few small broccoli spears on top before handing it to him.

He stared down at the broccoli. "I don't like broccoli."

"Why not?"

"Because it's green."

"When was the last time you tried it?" she asked.

"I don't like it," he repeated, as if this answered her question.

"Eat around it."

He stood there eyeing the offending vegetable like it was a bomb, and then his stomach grumbled loudly.

"Eat."

Kicking out a chair, he sat. "Thanks," he said around a mouthful. "I hate to cook."

She smiled. "My mom always said I should know how to feed a man. She says most women assume a guy's most critical body part is considerably lower than his stomach, but they're wrong. She says it's a man's stomach that does his thinking for him, not—" She broke off and felt herself flush. "Anyway, cooking is how she caught all her boyfriends."

"Was your dad one of those boyfriends?"

Ali's dad lived in Tacoma, and last she'd heard, he was a bartender. By all accounts, he was an effortless charmer who meant well, but she knew him as the guy with all the unfulfilled promises. Long gone were the days where she'd wait by the phone for the call he'd promised, but the memories still made her ache a little bit. "He didn't stick around. The first boyfriend who did was a dentist." She let out an involuntary shudder. "He was a pincher."

"A pincher?" Luke asked.

"Yeah." She opened and closed her first finger and thumb together a few times to demonstrate. "Whenever we annoyed him, he'd pinch. Always where the bruise wouldn't show too. Hurt like hell."

Luke didn't show much in expression or body language, and he had a way of staying very still. But his eyes had gone hard, pissed off on behalf of a young girl he'd never known.

"Your mom let him touch you?" he asked.

"Oh, we didn't tell her," Ali said. "She liked him so much, it would have killed her. But one day we were shopping and she saw a bruise on my sister in the dressing room."

"I hope she kicked his ass," Luke said.

"She took a baseball bat to him." Her smile faded because Mimi had cried for a week when he'd moved out. "She didn't bring another guy home for a long time after that."

"Good." Hooking his bare foot in a chair, he pushed it toward her. "Sit with me."

She put the pan in the sink and sat, shaking her head when he offered her a bite.

"So you learned to cook so you could catch a man?" he asked.

"No. I learned to cook because I like to eat," she said, "not because I want a string of boyfriends. Because I don't." Not until she figured out how to pick them anyway. She watched Luke work his way carefully around the broccoli. "Broccoli has almost as much calcium as milk," she told him, amused. "It gives you strong bones."

His gaze slid to hers, and she felt her face heat again. He had strong bones. And as they both knew, a few minutes ago, he'd had one particularly strong boner to boot. But mercifully he let the comment go.

Setting down his fork, he opened the envelope she'd left on the table, staring in surprise at the cash she'd carefully counted out. "What's this?" he asked.

"What I owe you for a few nights' stay. I prorated what I was paying monthly. I hope that's okay."

He was quiet for a full sixty seconds, and when he spoke, his voice was low. "I got the impression you were hard up for money."

"Not that hard up."

He looked at her for a long moment, then set the envelope back on the table and pushed it toward her with one finger.

She slid it back. "I pay my debts."

"How much does it leave you?" he asked.

She felt a small smile curve her lips. "Worried I won't have enough to find another place?"

"Hell yes."

She laughed softly. "Don't be. I'm not your responsibility." She wasn't anyone's responsibility and hadn't been in a long time.

He went back to eating. When a tiny piece of broccoli found its way on his fork, he gave it a look, but shoved it in his mouth.

She waited, but he just shrugged.

"Don't overwhelm me with praise or anything," she said dryly.

He flashed a quick grin. "It's good," he said. "Really good. You're holding up your end of the bargain." His smile faded. "But I'm not taking your money, Ali."

Bossy alpha. She got up and loaded the few dishes into the dishwasher, trying to pay no attention to the silent man behind her. Hard to do when he rose and put his dish in for her.

A *neat*, bossy alpha.

"You should go back to bed," she said softly. "You look beat."

He gave her a long look, which she decided was best

not to decipher, before walking away, leaving her alone with her thoughts.

Ali didn't sleep well and got up before dawn. With several hours before she had to be at the shop, she quietly made her way to the garage. She pulled on an apron that said Florists Do It with Style. Retrieving fresh clay from her storage bin, she worked it for a few minutes, trying to lose herself.

From the other side of the garage door, she heard a car pull up, but it didn't really register until the doorbell sounded. Startled at the early hour and pissed that another reporter might have found Luke, she wiped her hands on her apron and left the garage, moving quickly through the house to the living room. Prepared to kick some ass, she opened the front door, shocked to find two police officers standing there, flanking Teddy.

"Are you Ali Winters?" one of the cops asked.

"Yes, yes, it's her," Teddy said impatiently.

"Is something wrong?" Her heart dropped. "My mom? My sister, Harper? Are they okay?"

"This isn't about your damn family," Teddy said in disbelief. "It's about the fact that you stole that money to fuck me over. You're *that* pissed at me, that you had to try to ruin me?"

Ali shook her head in confusion. "What?"

"Ma'am," one of the cops said, "we need to bring you down to the station to ask you some questions."

Her heart stuttered to a stop just as someone came up behind her. Luke. She could feel the warm strength of him at her back.

"What's the problem here?" he asked calmly.

"Who the hell are you?" Teddy demanded.

Luke ignored him and waited for the officers to speak.

"We have a situation in regards to a theft that occurred at the town offices over the weekend," the first cop said. "A briefcase of money went missing from Ted Marshall's office."

Ali felt the horror fill her—they thought *she'd* stolen the money?

"It didn't go missing," Teddy said. "She stole it to get back at me for breaking up with her."

"Hey," Ali said, "*I* broke up with *you!*"

The officer went on as if neither of them had spoken. "The missing cash was from Friday night's town auction. According to several eyewitnesses, you were the last one in his office."

"Twice," Teddy said. "You were let into the office first by Gus on Saturday and then again by Aubrey on Sunday. Christ, Ali, how could you do this to me? I thought we were friends, at least."

"Friends don't sneak out in the middle of the night," she said, hating that they had an avid audience soaking up the exchange. "And I didn't steal anything." She recognized one of the cops. He'd been in the shop to buy flowers for his girlfriend. She spoke directly to him. "I've *never* stolen anything. Not once in my whole life."

Well, except she had. She winced. "Okay," she said, "so maybe one time I took a lip gloss from the drugstore, but I was twelve and stupid and my mom made me take it back. I had to work there for free for a whole day to make up for it. I haven't stolen anything since."

The second cop was rubbing his temple. Men did that a lot around her. Apparently she gave good headache.

"You have to believe me," she said. "I didn't take any cash. How much is missing?"

"All of it," Teddy said tightly. He was wearing khakis and an untucked, white button-down shoved to his elbows. He looked like he'd walked right out of a *GQ* ad, but instead of feeling her heart sigh, it hardened. The dreamy quotient of Teddy Marshall had run out.

"So you just showed up here to accuse Ali?" Luke asked him.

Teddy stared at him. "Seriously, who the hell are you?"

"Detective Lieutenant Luke Hanover."

"My landlord?"

"*Ex*-landlord," Luke said.

Ali's stomach was somewhere in the vicinity of her toes, so she couldn't process the exchange of testosterone at the moment. "So what now?" she asked the first cop.

"You come to the station for some questions, ma'am."

"Even though I didn't do it?" she asked.

"Yes, ma'am."

"Ali," she managed. "You keep saying *ma'am*, and I want to look over my shoulder to see who you're talking to. Why can't you just question me right here?"

"That's not policy, ma'—"

At her glare, he wisely swallowed the "ma'am" part.

"Look, Ali," Teddy said, clearly attempting to soften his voice. Once upon a time that might have charmed her, but not today. "You're pissed at me," he said. "I get that. So just give us the money back, and we'll all go to our separate corners. No harm, no foul."

"I don't have the money; I didn't take it!"

When the two cops just looked at her, she let out a breath. "I didn't."

"Go through her stuff," Teddy said wearily. "There isn't much. It shouldn't take long."

Luke put a hand to Teddy's chest, halting his forward progress. "No one's searching her *or* the premises," he said, still calm but with one-hundred-percent authority. "Not without consent or a warrant."

Ali turned and looked at him for the first time. He was in black board shorts, still damp enough to cling to his body. No shirt. Bare feet. A towel was slung over his shoulder, his hair wet and uncombed.

He'd been in the water, she realized, swimming or maybe on the paddleboard she'd seen leaning against the back deck. She wasn't sure if she was grateful for his intervention or pissed that he clearly thought she needed the protection from a search due to what they might find.

"I didn't do it," she told Luke. "They can search."

"Good." Teddy pushed his way in through the door. "Where's the stuff you took out of Town Hall, Al?"

"I brought the floral arrangements to the senior center yesterday," she said. She pointed to her purse and the box of small ceramics on the foyer bench. "That's all that's left from the auction."

Teddy reached for the box, but the first cop stopped him. "It can't be you, Marshall, sorry," the cop said, and grabbed the box.

Ali heard all her things clink together. "Careful—"

She broke off when he pulled out the pine tree pencil pot.

"What the hell?" Teddy said incredulously. "You gave that to me." He turned to Ali, brows knit together. "You stole it out of my office?"

"*Took back*," she corrected. "I took it back because you didn't deserve it."

"You *stole* it. Where's the money, Ali?"

"I didn't take the money!"

The first cop pulled something out of the pot.

"Jesus," Teddy said as they all stared at a bank bill wrapper, the kind that was used to hold together a stack of money, exactly like the bill wrappers that'd been used on the auction money.

He whirled on her now, eyes furious. "*Where's the money?*"

"I…" At a loss, she shook her head. "I didn't know that was in there."

The cops looked at each other, faces impenetrable, their entire demeanor shifting from fairly relaxed to on guard and far more alert.

"Oh no," Ali told them. "This isn't what you think. That bill wrapper must have been in there when I took the pot."

"So you admit to taking the pot, ma'am?" the first cop asked.

"Well, yes, but…" She trailed off at their expressions. Clearly, they thought she was full of shit. She didn't dare turn to look at Luke to see if he felt the same. "I didn't steal the money," she said, suddenly feeling very small and very alone. "I didn't."

Teddy blew out a breath and shoved his fingers through his hair. "What now?" he asked the two cops.

"Do we still have your permission to search the premises?" one of them asked her.

"You don't need her permission," Teddy said. "I shared this place with her. It's half mine. *I* give you permission."

"Wrong," Luke said with that same steely authority in his voice. "You no longer live here or have rights to the property."

Again, Ali didn't know whether to be touched or upset. She went with upset. "Search," she said. "Please. You'll see…"

They started with the living room and kitchen. Luke stood by, watchful. Impassive.

Not Ali. Her thoughts raced. Why was Teddy was acting so sure that it'd been her? Had he set her up? And what was the motive for that? Did he think that would keep her quiet about what he'd been doing in his office that night? "Where was the money in the first place?" she asked.

"In my locked bottom desk drawer," Teddy said stiffly. "As you very well know."

"I *don't* know," she said, just as stiffly. But she'd gone through his desk looking for the pencil pot. Had there been a locked drawer? She didn't think so. "You sure you locked it?"

"Yes."

"*Sure* sure?"

"Jesus! Yes!"

But Ali knew that expression and defensive tone. *He wasn't sure.* "You're lying about being sure," she said. "What else are you lying about, Teddy?"

Both officers straightened and gave him a long, appraising look. He raised his hands. "Hey, *I'm* the wronged party here! I put the briefcase in the bottom drawer to keep it locked up until the bank opened so I could deposit it. Hell, it was all just for show to begin with. Most of the money that had been actually collected was in electronic form. But we wanted to display cash that night to make it look impressive and to encourage more donations. I had it in my bottom desk drawer. I just…"

"What?" asked one of the cops.

Teddy sighed. "Okay, so maybe I can't remember if I locked the drawer. I was in a hurry."

"Doing what?" Ali asked, knowing damn well what—just not who.

"It's not pertinent," Teddy said.

The cop looked pained, and the look he gave Teddy said he didn't appreciate being put in the position of having to push. "It's pertinent. What did you do directly after putting the money in your bottom desk drawer?"

Teddy opened his mouth, and then closed it. After a long pause, he sighed again. "Melissa Mann."

"What?" the cop asked.

Teddy sighed. "I was doing Melissa Mann."

There was a beat of stunned silence.

Melissa Mann was a local manicurist, fun and sweet and pretty. She worked at the Hair Today salon a few doors down from the flower shop. Ali absorbed the hit and stared at Teddy.

Surprisingly, he had the balls to meet her gaze, an apology there behind his lingering temper. "I'm sorry, Ali. But we'd been over for a while."

That was not even close to true, but she didn't dispute it. Because dammit, he meant for him. It'd been over for him, and she'd not paid close enough attention to notice. But hell if she'd admit to being stupid.

"So you had Melissa in your office," the second cop said, "with the money."

"Yes," he said. "Apparently money is an aphrodisiac."

Ali felt the snarl catch in her throat and thought about how satisfying it'd be to wrap her fingers around his neck, but the witnesses were problematic. If she was in trouble for a crime she hadn't committed, she could imagine how much trouble she'd be in for murder.

A hand settled on her shoulder. Luke's. Clearly she'd projected the murderous urge...

Teddy took in the touch and narrowed his eyes.

"And afterward?" the first police officer asked him.

Teddy was still eyeing Luke's hand on her shoulder. "I gave Melissa a ride home."

"You gave her a ride home," Ali repeated slowly. "Let me see if I have this right. You stood up your girlfriend, dumped fifty thousand into your desk, maybe forgot to lock the drawer, had sex with Melissa, and then gave her a ride home and left the money there."

Ted grimaced again. "Listen, I realize that makes me look bad."

"Actually," Luke said, "it makes you look like a douche."

Teddy flushed an angry red. "Which still doesn't make me a thief."

The cops moved on to check the rest of the house, including the bedroom Ali had been using. They went through her drawers, which was embarrassing enough, but then the closet. One of the cops pulled out the *Fun 'N Pleasure* bag that she'd gotten as a gag gift for her birthday from her sister. "No," she said quickly. "Wait— That's not mine—"

Cop number two pulled a Catwoman costume from the bag and then a massive, eye-popping neon-pink vibrator.

Teddy gawked at the sheer size of the thing. "You have a vibrator?"

"It was a gag gift," Ali said, sure she was as pink as the vibrator.

Still standing stoic and steady as ever, Luke eyed the items without a word.

"You have a vibrator," Teddy repeated in disbelief. "Is *that* why we hadn't had sex in two months?"

Once again Luke's hand settled on Ali. Just as well since there were two—no *three*—cops watching. So she didn't go for Teddy's throat, a fact she considered a real feat of restraint.

But it wasn't restraint at all. It was burning humiliation, anger, and something else.

Terror.

And that terror was tripled when the cops finished searching both the house and her truck. Though they didn't find the money, they took her downtown anyway.

Chapter 6

Luke stood in the center of his living room, which looked like it'd been tossed by a couple of thieves.

Hurricane Ali.

He didn't know what to make of the fact that she'd been caught with the bill wrapper. Nor did he know what to make of her being taken to the station for questioning.

But he did know one thing. Marshall—he refused to think of him as *Teddy*—had rubbed him the wrong way.

Still, this wasn't his problem. He didn't know Ali from Adam. What he *did* know was that he didn't want to get involved. He was on break from getting involved. In spite of what his commander wanted, he had nineteen days left on his leave, and he planned on using every single one of them to do jack shit. He was looking forward to it.

But for reasons he couldn't explain, he couldn't dispel the image of Ali at the station, sitting in an interrogation room, in trouble.

He'd always believed in the system. He'd had to. It was what had made his job so important to him. Take down the bad guys and let the courts keep them down—that had been his life, his entire reason for being.

But then that very system had failed him. And he'd failed too. He'd failed the people who believed in the system. And now he was taking a break from people so he couldn't fail again.

Which in no way explained why, instead of putting the house back together, or hell, going back to paddleboarding, he ended up in front of his laptop.

He'd already done that basic search on Ali, but he hadn't gone far. He picked up where he'd left off. Her mother had a record: two arrests for assault and battery, one, apparently, for the baseball bat incident Ali had told him about. Both times the charges had been reduced, and Mimi Winters had been let out on time served. Ali's sister, Harper, had a record as well, for indecent exposure.

Nothing for Ali. Though going back further, he caught a few additional times where she'd been questioned, one for an incident involving her science teacher, who'd allegedly been sexually inappropriate with his students. Christ, he hoped she hadn't been one of them. Leaning back in his chair, Luke stared at his screen. He already knew that she was protective, loyal, and tough as hell. Now he also knew that she'd grown up knee-high in shit, and yet somehow she appeared to come out of it with a sweet kindness that was to-the-bone genuine.

And she *was* innocent in regard to the money. He felt it deep in his gut.

He researched Ted Marshall next. There'd been the basic search done when Marshall had applied for the lease, but Luke went deeper without remorse, because something wasn't right.

The golden boy had certainly sailed through life so far. He'd been raised here in town, was captain of the football team, and had gone on to the University of Washington, graduating with a degree in political science. He'd not gotten into law school, so he'd come back to Lucky Harbor. He paid his bills on time, golfed, and had a fantasy football team that did pretty well. He'd been pulled over three years ago in Kent with a hooker in his car, but the story had later been amended to describe the woman as being an "exotic dancer." Marshall sat on several charitable committees in Lucky Harbor, and as the town clerk, no one had a single negative thing to say about him. He was well known and well liked.

Luke was experiencing bad flashbacks from the whole senator nightmare. Not that Marshall was a secret stalker and murderer. No, Luke suspected he was exactly as he appeared—a guy for whom things either came easy or not at all, because he was just on the wrong side of lazy.

Which also told Luke something else. Marshall wasn't the thief either. He didn't have it in him.

So the question was, did Marshall really believe Ali had taken the money? This was a tough one because there'd been something in the man's eyes, something in his tone, that hadn't rung true to Luke.

He'd been lying.

But about what exactly?

Luke made a call to Sheriff Sawyer Thompson. Sawyer had run wild in his youth, only a few years ahead of Luke. Their paths had crossed professionally on several occasions, most notably when Luke had helped

Sawyer track down one of his perps in San Francisco not too long ago.

They bullshitted back and forth for a few minutes, and then Luke asked about Ali.

She was still being questioned. Having the bill wrapper in her possession looked bad, real bad, Sawyer said, but it wasn't enough evidence for an arrest. He said that a toe ring had been found in Marshall's office couch, and it didn't seem to belong to anyone who had business being in Marshall's office.

Or to Melissa Mann.

Luke hung up and chewed on that for a few minutes. *Not your problem*, he told himself. But he was still mulling it all over when his cell rang.

"How's the brooding going?" Sara asked.

He frowned at his sister through the phone. "I'm not brooding."

"Of course you are. You're a professional brooder."

Luke pinched the bridge of his nose. "Did you call for something in particular or just to piss me off?"

"Well, fun as it is to piss you off, I did call for a reason." But then she hesitated.

Shit. "What?" he asked. Sara had come out of prison determined to fix her life. Luke had done whatever he could, paying for rehab—twice—sending her to school—also twice—and finally sitting in the crowd with pride and relief when she'd eventually graduated with her teaching credentials. She now worked with troubled kids in an alternative high school in the Bay Area, and he couldn't be more proud of her.

But she was still a colossal pain in his ass. "You okay?" he asked.

"Yes. I just…"

"Whatever you need, Sara. You know that."

She sighed, sounding exasperated. "Okay, stop expecting me to be in trouble every time I call."

He felt a twinge of guilt, but there'd been years when that had been true. Not that he wanted to remind her. "I don't do that."

"Yes, you do," she said. "But this time, *you're* the one in trouble."

"Me? I'm fine."

"Really? Is that why you took off for Lucky Harbor— *Lucky Harbor*, Luke, where you never go anymore? You ran away from the press. What was that?"

"I needed a vacation," he said.

"Is that it? Really?"

"Yes," he said, trying to assuage the worry he heard in her voice. "I told you, I had three weeks of leave that I was going to lose if I didn't use."

There was a beat of silence, as if she was trying to assess the truth from two hundred miles away. "Don't make me come up there," she finally said. "Because I totally will."

"I'm fine," he said, relieved she'd backed down. "I'm just…relaxing. Hanging out."

"Good. Then you can also give grandpa a hug for me."

"Sara—"

"He's old, Luke. And getting older. Do it for me."

The doorbell rang. *Saved by the bell.* "Gotta go." Luke clicked off and walked through the house, looking out the window at the white Dial-A-Ride van in his driveway. *Ah, Christ.* He opened the front door and faced the entire gang of Lucky Harbor's biggest troublemakers: Lyle Lyons, Cecil Elroy, Joseph Wykowski.

And their ringleader, Edward Gregory.

Edward and Luke's grandma had divorced in the '70s, when Fay had founded the local historical society to preserve the buildings that made up Commercial Row, and then insisted on running it herself. Back in the day, Edward hadn't gotten the memo about women's rights, not to mention exactly how strong willed and stubborn a Hanover could be. He'd stood firm, and Fay had dumped him.

Edward had moved out, eventually buying the house next door, saying he'd done so to spite Fay. But everyone knew it was because he hadn't gotten over her.

Or her death.

Or Luke, seeing as he'd caused it…

Luke leaned against the doorjamb and waited, because whatever this was, it was going to be good.

Or really, really bad.

"Took you long enough to answer the door," Mr. Lyons said, leaning heavily on his cane to peer inside, and then let out a low whistle at the mess. "Holy smokes, boy. You haven't outgrown that party animal stage yet?"

"He didn't do that, you idiot, the cops did," Mr. Wykowski said. "They tossed the joint looking for the dough."

Edward didn't speak. They hadn't been face to face in years, hadn't seen each other since Fay's funeral. "What's up?" Luke asked.

"We called Edward to drive us over here to see you," Mr. Wykowski said. "On account of I lost my license last year and these yahoos are blinder than bats."

"Hey," Mr. Elroy said, glaring at him. "You're the one who tried to drive down the pier and ended up nose first inside the deli. You smelled like pickles for a month."

"I turned at the wrong place. Big deal, we all make mistakes." Mr. Wykowski waved this off as he turned to Luke. "Ali's still at the police station."

"I know."

"Thing is, Ted Marshall's sort of the golden boy around here. Hell, he had the senior center redone last year so we could open up more rooms, and he single-handedly raised the money for the Dial-A-Ride van. He makes sure there's money in the budget for Edward's pay. People love him and trust him. If he says Ali stole the money, everyone believes him. You know what I'm saying?"

"No," Luke said. "Just because someone's a good guy doesn't mean what he says is gold. There's a justice system."

Which he knew better than anyone didn't always work.

"Listen," Mr. Lyons said, "we watch *Law and Order*. We know shit happens. And shit's happening."

"Ali's our ceramics teacher," Mr. Elroy said. "She also gets library books and reads to us. We need to help her. We're all she has."

"And you want me to do what exactly?" Luke asked.

"We figure since she's been staying here, that makes her yours too."

"It's not like that," Luke said.

"What is it like?" Mr. Elroy asked, and every one of them looked at Luke through rheumy, but sharp-as-hell, eyes.

Yeah, Luke, what was it like? She'd come along when he'd wanted to be alone, and she'd gotten his entire house torn up in the search for the fifty large. But the landline hadn't rung in a full twenty-four hours. Ali, whose damn life was circling the drain, had amazingly managed to scare everyone off and give him a chance at his peace and quiet.

In spite of himself, he wanted to help her in return. Not that she wanted his help. The envelope of cash she'd tried to give him was still on the table. Broke as shit, she'd still given it to him, because that was the right thing to do.

It'd been the pride flaring in her eyes that had slain him. She *needed* to pay her way. He was an ass, but not that big an ass to squelch the life that she projected with every single breath. He might be standing in the darkness, wallowing, weighed down by the things he saw on his job, but she wasn't like that. She was light.

And yet she was at the police station right now being questioned.

Alone.

He told himself that she was used to shitty circumstances. Hell, it appeared she was used to shitty men too. Her father, the pincher...him. She was used to taking care of herself and others.

And he had no idea why that got to him. But it did. *She* did.

"You still with us, boy?" Mr. Elroy asked. "Now's not the time to go all silent and cranky on us."

Luke hadn't been called "boy" in a damn long time. And few other than Sara dared to call him on the silent and cranky. "Ali's just being questioned," he said.

"What if she needs bailing out?"

"She doesn't."

"But if she does?"

"You could do it," Luke said.

"Yes, and we would," Mr. Wykowski said. "But…" He glanced at Edward, who still said nothing, gave away nothing. At seventy-two, he looked as fit and healthy as Sara and Jack had reported and pretty much the same as always—as if he'd just swallowed a lemon.

"We don't have very much," Mr. Lyons said. "We pooled our available cash together from what was left of our social security for the month, but it's not much. We had a poker game a few nights back, see, and normally I'd have taken the pot—"

Mr. Elroy coughed and muttered "bullshit" at the same time.

Mr. Lyons glared at him. "—But I had a little bad luck."

"That's not what happened," Mr. Elroy said.

"Yes, it is," Mr. Lyons said.

"No." Mr. Elroy shook his head. "Eileen Weiselman knew she had a losing hand, so she flashed you her tits to distract you into folding, and you lost. We all lost."

"Okay, look," Luke said, rubbing his temples where he was getting a stress headache. "Ali isn't a thief. I'm sure it's all a misunderstanding that will get worked out."

"But you can't just let her sit in jail while it does," Mr. Wykowski said, horrified.

"She's not in a jail cell. She's being questioned. Big difference. And unless she's charged and arrested—which they won't do without just cause—she won't need bailing out."

"See," Mr. Elroy said, "that's good information. I didn't know that. It's why you need to be in charge of this situation."

"I'm not in charge," Luke said. "Of anything."

"But she's down there with *hardened* criminals," Mr. Lyons said. "You can't let her sit there with them."

Luke sincerely doubted there were any hardened criminals in Lucky Harbor. The daily police reports read like something right out of Mayberry: an elk walking down Main Street, a drunken and disorderly at two a.m., high school punks running over mailboxes. "This isn't up to me," he said. "You know that, right? They're just following procedure."

They all looked deeply disappointed in him. And then Edward spoke for the first time, uttering only two words. "Get it."

Mr. Lyons nodded and used his cane to navigate back to the van.

Edward just stood there looking at Luke.

Luke ignored them all and thought about Ali. He'd meant what he'd said, she was no thief. She'd probably give a stranger the shirt off her own back. The thought reminded him of what she'd looked like without a shirt in his kitchen, yelling at Marshall's voice mail.

Vibrant. Fierce. *Sexy.*

But she was also sweet and warm. And vulnerable.

And she was sitting in the police station. *Shit.*

His cell vibrated. He looked at the screen. His commander. With a long, slow inhale, he connected. "Hanover."

"Got a death threat this morning." Commander Craig O'Neil's voice was gruff and as commanding as his title. "Aimed at all of us. Just wanted you to know."

"Great," Luke said. "I'll start working my way down my bucket list."

"How about instead you just get your ass back here."

Not a question but a statement. Actually, more like a direct demand. "I'm on vacation," Luke reminded him.

"You're not, you're working a fucking case. Sheriff Thompson called me to make sure I didn't mind sharing you. What the hell?"

Thanks, Sawyer. "What did the threat say?"

"It said 'die pigs.' But he misspelled 'die,' used a Y. *Dye* pigs just doesn't have the same impact. But watch your back just in case."

"Will do."

"How long are you really going to be?"

"Didn't we just do this? Three weeks."

"Goddammit." The commander went quiet for a moment. "How about one?"

"I'll get back to you." Luke disconnected.

"Work problems?" Mr. Wykowski asked.

Luke didn't answer. Mr. Wykowski was a nice guy, but he was close friends with Lucille, which was a lot like being close friends with a PA system. Whatever he told Mr. Wykowski, he had to be willing for the entire county to hear. If he mentioned the threat, it'd be on Facebook in five minutes flat.

Mr. Lyons made his slow way back up the driveway, cane in one hand and in the other…an apple pie.

"Homemade," he said, waving it back and forth beneath Luke's nose. "We got it off of Betsy Morango, who made it for her granddaughter. We have to let her in on the next poker game now, but anything for Ali."

"You can't bribe me with pie." Before he'd finished the sentence, his stomach grumbled loudly in a plea for the pie.

The men grinned.

"We all know you're a pie ho," Mr. Elroy said.

Mr. Lyons had two plastic forks tucked neatly into his breast pocket. He took one out and scooped up a bite of the apple pie. "Oh yeah," he murmured, licking the fork. "Good stuff."

Just the thought of it was making Luke's damn mouth water.

Edward was still looking at him steadily. Intensely. Luke had no idea what his grandfather's angle was on this, but one thing he did know: There *was* an angle. "If I agree to step in here, you nosy-bodies have to agree to something too."

"What?" Mr. Lyons asked.

"Ali needs a place to stay until she gets an apartment. You have lady friends." Again he met Edward's gaze. "Surely one of you knows someone looking for a room-mate. She cooks. She does her own dishes. She's…" Not quiet. Not easy to ignore. "Cheerful," he finally said, hoping that sounded like a compliment. "She'd be a good roommate for anyone."

Except for him.

"She can stay with me," Mr. Elroy said, and waggled his brow.

Luke wrestled with his conscience and lost. "No." *Christ.* "Never mind. I'll find her a damn place myself." He reached for the pie, but Mr. Lyons held it close.

"Almost forgot, I need another favor," Mr. Lyons said.

Luke gave him a look. "I'm a little busy working on the first one right now."

"This one can wait until you get Ali home safe and sound. Roger Barrett needs to hire you. He's got a prob-lem. He misplaced his '67 GTO."

"He didn't misplace it," Mr. Wykowski said. "He lost it in a poker game to Phillip Schmidt two years ago, remember?"

"Yes," Mr. Lyons said, "with the caveat that when the old geezer died, he had to give it back to Roger. Phillip's been six feet under for six months now, and his grandson Mikey 'The Doper' Schmidt still says he hasn't 'located' the GTO, which is bull-pucky. He's just not done driving the piss out of it."

"You realize that car's no longer PC," Mr. Elroy said, disapprovingly. "It's a gas guzzler."

"Gas guzzler, smuzzler," Mr. Lyons said. "It's a beaut. They don't make cars like that anymore. God rest Pontiac's soul."

Luke shook his head. "And the GTO is my problem why?"

"Because you're the problem-solving guy," Mr. Lyons said.

"Says who?"

"Your grandpa says that's what you do best."

Luke met Edward's gaze. Edward still didn't speak.

"So you're going to help Ali, right?" Mr. Lyons asked.

Luke could smell the brown sugar and baked apples. He needed that pie. *The hell with it.* He snatched it. "Yeah. I'm going to help her." He snagged the other fork out of Mr. Lyons's pocket. He took a big bite and nearly died and went to heaven. "Sawyer said the cops aren't done talking to her yet, not until around two."

Mr. Lyons blinked. "You were already going to help her," he said all accusatorially.

Luke took another big bite. "Yeah."

Mr. Lyons narrowed his eyes. "And Roger? You'll help Roger too?"

"Yeah, but *only* because Phillip Schmidt was the idiot who built that monstrosity on northeast bluffs. It blocks access to the beach from that side of the harbor, so he calls the cops on the kids that have to trespass to get to the water."

Mr. Lyons smiled. "You're a good boy. You're going to be good for Ali. I take her classes, you know, both the ceramics and her floral-design class. They help with my arthritis. She deserves better than to be treated like a common criminal."

Luke turned to Edward. "So what's your interest in this?"

"Oh, he takes Ali's classes too," Mr. Elroy answered for him. "We all do." He smiled. "We love her."

Luke was having some trouble with the image of his tough, stoic, impenetrable grandfather taking ceramics and floral design.

Not to mention—what the hell was floral design?

Chapter 7

Ali had a recurring nightmare that changed in details, but at the core it was always the same—she was alone.

Terrifyingly alone.

Sitting on a chair in some chilly room at the police station, her nightmare had gone live.

There'd been lots of questions. *Had she been angry when Teddy had broken up with her? Angry enough to want to frame him?* Because apparently her messages, both the voice mail and the sticky note, indicated a vengeful woman.

Did she know that if she turned the rest of the money in right now that charges would be reduced, possibly dropped? Because apparently she was holding it hostage somewhere.

Did she know that the sticky-note message could also be construed as an actual threat? She didn't know how calling someone an ass who was an actual ass had become threatening, but okay. Fine. Lesson learned.

She'd said maybe she needed an attorney, and one of the cops brought her to a phone. She stared at it in rare indecision. This was new, being on *this* side of the phone call. She'd been on the other side, several times, the first being when her mom had been arrested for property damage after she'd taken that bat to her boyfriend's car. What the cops hadn't known was that Mimi had been aiming for the guy's head.

The second time had been when Mimi had set fire to a different boyfriend's wardrobe. Her mistake had been in using the bonfire to have a party. Mimi had tried to plead temporary insanity on that one, but no one bought it. There was nothing temporary about Mimi's rage whenever she got cheated on.

Both times Ali and Harper had bailed Mimi out using the secret cash stash taped to the bottom of their couch, which was accumulated from her mom's tips. Over the years, that stash had ebbed and flowed, depending on various needs. Christmas. School field trips. Mimi's breast augmentation. And then the second surgery to remove the implants after they'd begun to leak.

Then Harper had taken her turn one year and had gotten arrested for indecent exposure after she'd pulled off to the side of the road to pee in the snow.

Ali still liked to tease Harper about that one.

She could call them, either of them. They'd be here in a blink, their tip stash in tow on the chance that she did indeed get arrested. But Ali wasn't going to call them. She hadn't been arrested—yet—and even if she had, she wasn't going to have them spend their hard-earned money on her.

Besides, neither her mom nor her sister was qualified

to offer legal advice, and then there was the embarrassment factor, which on a scale of one to ten, was at an
eleven right now.

She *should* call Ted, because oh, did she have things to
say to Ted. She stared at the phone some more. Luke. She
could call Luke. He'd probably know what she should do.
Except she wasn't his problem.

And she needed an attorney, not a detective.

She knew exactly one attorney: Zach Mullen. They'd
gone to high school together, and skinny, geeky Zach,
the PlayStation master of their neighborhood, had always
been the smartest guy she knew, despite his huge crush on
Harper. He'd graduated from UNLV law school last year,
but it'd been months since she'd talked to him. Had he
passed the bar?

She called him and was so grateful to hear his soft,
friendly "yo" that she nearly collapsed. "Zach," she said.
"Tell me you passed the bar."

"Okay, I passed the bar."

"No, really." She lowered her voice and crossed her
fingers. "Did you?"

Zach huffed out a laugh. "Barely, but don't tell anyone
that part."

Thank God. "So you're a real lawyer?" she asked,
needing to be sure.

"Yep," he said. "A real, bona fide lawyer. I work for
a hotel in Seattle in their legal department, though this
week I'm in their Los Angeles office. Mostly fact gathering, but they pay bank so—"

"Okay, that's great," she said quickly. "Listen, I have a
side job for you. How fast can you get to Lucky Harbor?"

There was a beat of silence. "Lucky Harbor?"

"Yes. I…sort of need some legal advice."

Zach might be a sweetheart, and he looked like a good wind could blow him over, but he was also sharp as a tack. "I'm in L.A. until the day after tomorrow," he said. "I've got a late-night flight back into Seattle, and then I'm all yours. What do you need, Ali? Anything."

"I need you."

Ali was eventually released with the caveat that she not leave town. A few minutes later, she was standing on the sidewalk in the bright sun, staring in surprise at the tall, silent Luke, who'd been waiting for her. "Why are you here?" she asked.

"Later. You've got other issues." He pointed at the two women holding up FREE ALI signs in front of the courthouse.

Her mom and sister.

"Ali!" they cried at the sight of her and rushed over. Dropping her sign, Mimi grabbed Ali in close and hugged her tight. "Oh, Ali-gator! Did they violate any of your rights? Because honey, you have rights, lots of them."

"I'm fine, Mom. All my rights are still intact."

Mimi was wearing white capri leggings and a sparkly gold lamé top. Her gold hoop earrings matched the wide strip of bangle bracelets up one arm and was the same color as her spiked sandals. Her face was creased with worry as she tried to pat down Ali's gone-wild hair.

Ali pulled free and turned to Harper, who was wearing Daisy Dukes and a halter top, her hair and makeup bar-ready. She'd come straight from work and probably raced through the two-hour drive out here.

"Zach called us," Harper said. "Told us you might need moral support until he could get here."

"And moral support means picketing the courthouse?"

"Hey, it works on TV," Mimi said. She smiled up at Luke. "My baby has no manners. I'm Mimi Winters, Ali's mama, and this here's her sister, Harper."

Luke reached out to shake her hand. "Luke Hanover."

Because Mimi was looking at Luke with a speculative are-you-going-to-marry-my-daughter gaze, Ali quickly said, "Luke's helping me out with a place to stay."

"Aw!" Mimi kissed him on the cheek. "Aren't you the sweet one?"

"Mom, I'm paying rent," Ali said.

Mimi cupped Ali's cheek. "Of course you are." She sent a look Luke's way. "She's stubborn, this one, can never accept a helping hand." She looked around. "Where's Teddy? I swear, I don't care how hot he is, I'd like to castrate him. I've got a perfectly good pair of pliers in my purse to do it with too. Should've packed scissors, but the pliers'll be more painful. I'm thinking one slow twist and his doodle will snap right off…" She mimed the motion.

"Mom!" Ali quickly looked around. If a sticky note had constituted a threat, she couldn't imagine what packing pliers with the intent to twist off a guy's…*doodle* would mean.

"Just sayin'," Mimi murmured.

"Well stop just saying," Ali said. "And castration would mean cutting off his…other parts, not his…" She gestured vaguely, not daring to glance at Luke. "Doodle."

"Honey, he deserves to be castrated for accusing you of stealing money. You wouldn't steal money. You wouldn't steal anything." Mimi lowered her voice to a whisper and leaned in close. "You don't still steal lip gloss, right?"

"No!" *Good Lord.* "And no castrating. I've got this handled. I'm sorry you made the drive out here, and I appreciate the support, but you should both go back to work. I'm fine."

"We were going to wait until dark and TP Teddy's new place," Harper said. "Where's he living now?"

"I don't know," Ali said, her second lie of the day. "But no TPing!" She was in enough trouble. "Everything's going to be fine."

"You promise?" Mimi asked. "Do you swear by the tip jar, baby? Because we need you."

"Yes," Ali said, crossing her fingers behind her back. "I swear by the tip jar that everything's going to be fine."

Mimi hugged her again, and she smelled like her favorite body spritz and long-past, sweet memories. "Love you, Ali-gator."

Ali held on for an extra minute and closed her eyes. "Love you too, Mom."

Mimi kissed her cheek and then turned back to Luke. "It was very nice to meet you, Luke."

"You too, Mrs. Winters."

"Oh, please. Call me Mimi. When are you coming home, baby?" she asked Ali.

As she'd been told not to leave town, she was pretty sure it wouldn't be any time soon. "I'll let you know."

"Next weekend? 'Cuz they're filming a new reality show down the street. Something about men and their tools and the women who love them. You could help us get on TV."

"Would love to," Ali said. "But I'm working."

"The weekend after then," Mimi said. "For my surprise birthday party."

"Mom," Harper said, exasperated. "You said you wanted it to be a *surprise*."

"I do. I want to be surprised by both my daughters throwing me a party with friends and flowers and balloons and lots of decorations."

"I don't think you're getting the concept of *surprise*," Harper said.

"And maybe a piñata," Mimi went on, "but with good stuff in it. Too bad men can't fit into piñatas…"

"*No men* in piñatas," Harper said. "That's a different kind of party altogether."

"Fine," Mimi said. "But I still want the balloons and flowers. And Ali."

"I'll be there," Ali promised, and watched them get into Harper's car. The engine coughed, emitted a bunch of smoke, and then leaped into gear.

"You crossed your fingers," Luke said.

"What?"

"When you promised her that everything was going to be fine."

Ali turned away. "She needs to think that everything is going to be fine."

Luke pulled her back and looked at her for a long moment. "Cell phone."

"What?"

"I need your cell phone."

She passed it over, watching as he programmed his number into it.

"For the next time you're faced with one phone call,"

he said. Luke looked into her eyes and let out a long breath. "Look, don't read more into this than it is. If you need me, you call."

"That simple?" she asked.

He shrugged, which she took to mean that he really had no idea, but he'd still do it.

"I wasn't going to call you," she said. "You're on vacation."

"I'm also not getting involved, but neither is working out so well for me."

Her mind had been going one hundred miles per hour since the cops had shown up at the door that morning. The adrenaline was wearing off, leaving her exhausted and far too shaky and emotional to deal with this. Horrifyingly close to the edge, she chewed on her lower lip and ordered herself not to lose it. "Why did you come?" she asked.

"You needed a ride."

Her chest squeezed even tighter. "You're not worried I'm going to steal something from you?"

"Stop," he said, his voice far too gentle for her fragile state of mind. She swallowed the lump in her throat and told herself she was just tired. This was out of control. She was out of control. It was just that for once, she wanted her life to move in a direction that *she* directed. With a sigh, she looked away. Life around her appeared to be maintaining the status quo. There was the usual early evening, low-level traffic. People were just getting off work and heading to the gym, the grocery store, the pier…home.

Ali had no idea where that would be for her tonight.

All she wanted was a hot shower and then to go to bed

and not wake up again until this whole unbelievable situation had resolved itself. Or until she was old and gray. Whichever came first.

Luke was looking her over. She was still wearing her apron. She had a streak of dried clay across one arm and on one foot. And given the look Luke aimed at her face, she had some there as well. She lifted her chin.

With a small twitch of his lips, he hitched his head in the direction of his truck. He opened the passenger door for her and waited until she pulled her seatbelt across her body before he hit the lock and shut the door. He walked around the front of the vehicle, his stride long-legged and easy. No rush.

When he slid behind the wheel, he put the key in the ignition but didn't start the engine. There was a beat of silence, and then he turned to her, one hand on the back of her head rest, the other on the dash.

She did her best to appear as though she hadn't just been sitting in an interrogation room for hours being questioned about a crime she hadn't committed. But as it turned out, the pretense was far too much for her overloaded emotions, and she closed her eyes, trying to disappear into the seat. If she disappeared, then he couldn't see her fall apart.

"You okay?" he asked.

Her throat tightened further, and she shook her head. Nope. Not okay. Not even close. "Don't," she said.

"Don't what?"

"Don't be nice to me right now. I'll lose it."

With surprising gentleness, he pushed the hair from her face, then clicked open her seatbelt.

It was all the invitation she was going to get, and all the

invitation she needed. Turning to him, she burrowed in as steady, strong arms closed around her. He stroked a hand down her back, and she pressed her face into the crook of his neck, soaking in the warm comfort he offered.

It was the safest and most secure she'd felt in far too long, and she wasn't sure she was going to be able to let go.

"Ali."

Afraid he was going to pull away before she was done soaking him in, she squirmed a little closer. "Please, not yet."

A rough sound escaped him, and he tightened his grip. "It's okay. I've got you."

Thank God. For just this one second, someone had her. She didn't have to be strong all on her own. She exhaled a long, shaky breath and concentrated on dragging more air in. After a few beats, she realized he smelled amazing, guy amazing, and that her lips were pressed against his throat. Suddenly it wasn't just comfort she was feeling, but a whole boatload of other things too, with arousal leading the pack. Extremely aware of the big, warm hand moving up and down on her back, she wondered—did he feel it too?

And then she had a bigger problem. Her face was still pressed up against his warm skin, and—look at that—every time she moved, her mouth slid over him.

He hadn't shaved that morning, probably not yesterday either, and his skin was rough with stubble. Deliciously rough. And then there was his scent...Yum. She could no more have stopped herself from doing it again as she could have stopped breathing.

In reaction, Luke let out a low, very male sound that called to the most female part of her.

Which answered her question. Yeah, he felt it too.

He said her name again, his hand coming up to cup her jaw, his fingers weaving their way into her hair, tightening as if to draw her away from him.

But he didn't.

Shaken, she inhaled a deep, uneven breath. Her breasts brushed his chest. The first time was accidental. The second time was all her. So was the third, and her entire body got all warm and tightened. What would it be like to have such a man belong to her? To belong to him? To kiss that mouth, feel it open under hers, feel it on her?

The temptation was too much, and her lips slid over his throat yet again. It still wasn't enough. She needed to taste him.

Don't do it...

But her day had been complete shit, her brain was full—*too* full—and there was no room in it for logic. None. So she did it. She ran her tongue along the column of his throat, and then because that was so good, she let her teeth sink into him a little bit as well.

A rough groan escaped him. Pulling her back, he searched her gaze for something, though she had no idea what. Probably her sanity.

Too late, she could have told him. She'd lost it.

Whatever he saw, he shook his head.

He was going to pull back. She could feel it in the sudden tautness of his muscles. She gave him her best sex kitten look, but the truth was she wasn't exactly a sex kitten on the best of days, and this was definitely not one of those. But something in his eyes warmed. Still half expecting him to push her back into the seat, she was surprised when he instead pulled her up against him.

"Playing with fire," he murmured. "And one of us is going to get burned."

She managed a nod. Yes, and yes. And for the record, the person getting burned would be her. She was already burning up, from the inside out. A full-blown inferno, and he'd barely touched her. She hadn't even realized until now how badly she wanted him.

Moving slowly, clearly giving her plenty of time to stop him, Luke cupped the nape of her neck, gliding his thumb along the sensitive skin there. Then he slowly leaned in.

She met him halfway, pathetically eager, but she couldn't help herself.

Luke let out a half groan, half low laugh that seemed to be aimed more at himself than her. He shook his head again and brushed his mouth across hers.

When she murmured for more, demanded really, he did it again, and then finally he deepened the connection, parting her lips with his, kissing her deep and hot, banishing every worrisome, unhappy thought from her mind. When they broke for air, he ran his tongue over her bottom lip before gently sinking his teeth into it, just as she'd done to his neck. Heat and desire licked through her like flames, and her fingers curled into his shirt. She wasn't ready to stop, wasn't ready to come back to reality.

He said her name in a silky, rough whisper, covered her mouth with his again, and as before, there was no more thinking.

Hell, there was no more air. There was nothing but this, and she strained to get even closer, thwarted by the console between them. She couldn't help it. Whether merely walking into a room or picking her up from jail, he had a way of commanding her attention. He was steady as a rock, steely. Edgy. Dangerous.

His kiss was all those things too. And he was a master at it, his big hand still gently caressing her neck, liquefying her bones with each delicious stroke of his tongue to hers. His other hand slid down her back, settling low on her spine, holding her still as he plundered.

Completely caught up, she held on tight, working to get closer still. Hell, she'd have crawled inside him if she could. He cupped her ass, and her hips arched to try to meet his in a movement as old as time, but she couldn't get to him. She heard her own soft mewl of frustration, and then he was slowing them down, pausing to rest his forehead against hers. "Damn," he said, stroking the pad of his finger over her wet lower lip. "Did *not* see that coming."

"Didn't see what coming?"

"You."

Chapter 8

♥

Ali had no idea how it'd happened that she'd ended up trying to climb Luke's body, but she blamed his mouth. One hundred percent. "I'm over men," she said out loud so that she might hear it and have it sink in.

Luke didn't say anything to this. He just looked at her with the same intense expression on his face that he'd worn when he'd kissed her, which made her want to beg for another kiss. Instead, she bit her lips to keep them to herself. But as it turned out, she wasn't good at holding her tongue. "It's nothing personal," she said, "but as a whole, men haven't proven themselves all that reliable." She paused. "No offense."

"None taken."

"It wasn't going to be a hardship," she said, "to be over men."

He gave her an almost smile. "Hence the vibrator?"

She felt her face heat. "Okay, that really was a gag gift.

And it's not like sex isn't…enjoyable or anything. It just tends to lead to bad decisions on my part."

"I can respect that," he said. "But for the record, sex, when it's done right, is a hell of a lot more than *enjoyable*."

Her body was still tingling from his kisses, so it wasn't much of a stretch to believe that he could make sex far more than *enjoyable*.

"One more thing," he said.

She looked into his deep blue eyes.

"Not all men will disappoint you," he said. "I don't mean me. Because I will absolutely disappoint you. But we're not all assholes, Ali. I can promise you that."

She held his gaze, the man who'd let her stay in his house, the man who'd come for her no questions asked, not even "are you guilty?" Which meant that already he'd done more for her than most of the men in her life. She was still staring at him when her phone rang.

"Ohmigod, Ali," Aubrey said. "They brought you in for questioning? Why? How? *What the hell happened?*"

"Well," Ali said, "apparently after you let me into Teddy's office, I stole the fifty big ones."

"Did you?"

"No!"

Luke reached over and hit END, disconnecting her call.

Ali stared at him. "Why did you do that?"

"You shouldn't discuss the case with anyone," he said. "And especially don't joke about stealing the money."

"But that was Aubrey, Teddy's assistant."

"I don't care if it was the Easter Bunny."

"She's nice. She's the one who let me into his office the second time. She…" Ali broke off, her mind suddenly racing.

"She what?"

Ali met his gaze. "She asked me to make sure to never tell anyone that she'd let me in."

Luke's eyes were sharp. "You're friends?"

"Not the go out and share sushi kind, but yeah. It's more the 'your dress is pretty, where did you get it' sort."

Luke shook his head. "Was that in English?"

"We're friends," she clarified.

"You know they found a toe ring in Marshall's couch?"

"Yes," she said. "The cops asked me about it, but it wasn't mine."

"And it's not Melissa's either. So whose is it? And is the owner fifty thousand dollars richer this week?"

She shook her head. "I don't know." She'd been going over and over this in her head until it spun. "I saw the money at the auction like everyone else. The next day, I cleaned up the hall and carried out all the floral arrangements. Then I remembered the pencil pot I'd made Teddy, the one sitting on his desk. For some reason, I couldn't leave it there, so I went in to take it back. But it wasn't on his desk."

"Where was it?"

She paused, remembering how embarrassed she'd been to find it buried. "In his credenza."

Luke blew out a breath. "You went through his things?"

"Yes, but I never saw the money. I grabbed the pot and left. I didn't know the bill wrapper was there until the police found it, and I sure as hell don't know where the money is. I'm thinking Teddy framed me."

"Is there any reason that he'd want to stop the building of that new rec center?"

"I can't imagine why. It's his baby, a feather in his cap. And he likes feathers in his cap." She shook her head. "I've never seen him lose it like he did this morning. He was…"

"Scared," Luke said.

She nodded. "Yeah. I think he really believes I stole the money."

"It does have a woman scorned feel to it."

She didn't say anything to that, not wanting to know if he thought her capable of being that scorned woman. "I'm meeting my lawyer tomorrow."

"Who?" Luke asked.

"Zach Mullen." She watched as he pulled out his cell phone. "He's an old high school friend," she told him. "What are you doing?"

"How old is he? He looks twelve." Luke showed her the screen. He'd brought up Zach's Facebook profile, where indeed his pic revealed a young-faced Zach, clearly fresh from a haircut, since he had a ring of pale skin across his forehead and the tips of his ears. His latest status update—from an hour ago—indicated he was at a sports bar in L.A.

Hooters.

"He's there for business," she murmured. "You're pretty quick with the research. I know you went back to your laptop. What else did you find out about me?"

He just looked at her.

"Come on," she said. "You're an off-duty detective, and I got taken from your house for questioning on the missing fifty thousand. What else did you dig up about me?"

Luke shrugged. "A few things."

"Like what? That I hated elementary school so much I used to hide at the park and my mom had to take off work and come find me?"

"You were a decent student though," he said. "And you took dance."

"I loved dance," she murmured. "But I quit early; I had no coordination."

He slid her a look. "Or you were worried about the cost."

Or that...

"You moved around a lot," he said. "There's a few gaps in the known addresses."

She slid down a little farther in the seat. Yeah, there'd been gaps, which matched her mom's gaps in income, when they'd bunked on friends' couches here and there. "Sometimes my mom would lose jobs if she couldn't keep certain hours. Or...whatever."

He nodded, no judgment on his face. And, thankfully, no pity. She hated going back there in her mind, but she hated even more that he knew so much about her. "What else?" she wanted to know.

"You applied to transfer to several different state schools, even getting into a few of them," he said, "but you didn't go. No word why, though I can guess."

She felt a horrifying burning behind her lids. "You're thorough," she managed.

He shrugged.

Ali wasn't sure what that meant, but decided she didn't want to know.

"Tell me about Zach," he said.

"We went to high school together. He's a good lawyer."

"Yeah?" He slid her a look. "How long has he been practicing?"

Ali hesitated.

"How long, Ali?"

"He just passed the bar."

His mouth tightened. "You need someone who knows what they're doing."

"Zach does," she said. She hoped. "And it's not like I've been arrested."

But you could be... She knew he was thinking this but thankfully it went unsaid.

"Where to, Ali?"

She knew she should come up with a plan, but suddenly she couldn't speak.

Reaching out, Luke pulled something from her hair.

Dried clay.

He let his fingers linger, then tucked a strand of hair behind her ear. "I've already asked," he said very quietly, very seriously. "But I'm going to ask again. Are you okay?"

She had no idea, but she suspected no. No, she wasn't okay, not even a little bit. She'd been unceremoniously dumped, made homeless, and could be arrested at any moment. It'd been a craptastic week.

But hell if she'd say it. *Couldn't* say it, really, since the lump in her throat had grown to the size of a regulation football. So she nodded instead, acting perfectly okay...But she could feel the heat and strength of him, and for one shocking moment, she wanted to crawl into his lap and lay her head down on his shoulder. She wanted to burrow in and feel his arms close around her again. She wanted to feel the brush of his rough jaw as he pressed it to hers and whispered silly little nothings in her ear, like "you're going to be all right."

But he didn't do any of that.

Because he didn't want to be involved. She suspected it was his greatest wish to just be left alone, which, of course, was pretty much the opposite of her wish. "You can drop me at the B and B," she said.

"Stay with me," he said softly. "But you should understand that there are things you don't know about me."

"Are you an ax murderer?"

"No."

"You beat up old ladies?"

"No. Jesus, Ali."

"Do you call your mom every once in a while?" she asked.

Something came and went in his eyes. The very slightest glimmer of amusement. "Yes."

"Then I know enough," she said.

"You don't know that there are death threats being lobbed at me."

This had her taking a beat. "Seriously?"

"I think it's probably just the average, run-of-the-mill nutjob news junkie, but I can't be sure."

"That's okay," she said. "There's something *you* don't know about *me*." She smiled proudly. "I'm a three-time, sharpshooter Lucky Harbor Arcade champion."

"You're an…arcade champion."

"*Three* time," she repeated. "Missed that in your research, didn't you? I can shoot all my ducks in a row, ask anyone. Ask Lance, he runs the ice cream shop next to the arcade. I beat him just last week on a break."

Luke laughed softly. "Well in that case…"

She smiled, but his faded and he shook his head. "This isn't a joke, Ali."

"As I'm all too well aware," she said quietly. "Look, thanks for the accommodations. I'll pull my weight, I promise."

He looked a little taken aback at the statement. Did he do all the giving in every aspect of his life? If so, it made her ache for him, because she understood. That she'd found this common ground between them felt both unsettling and comforting.

She was going to have to get over that. And him.

Chapter 9

Luke drove up the narrow road toward his grandma's house, the rocky landscape made up of skyscraper-tall granite boulders that had been pushed here twenty thousand years ago, during the last Ice Age.

His passenger stared out her window at the rocks, as still and quiet as the surface of the water in the harbor far below.

This was unusual enough, but there was an element to Ali's silence that worried him. She was giving off a sadness, a sense of loneliness that made him ache for her.

He'd seen her with her family, who maybe rivaled his own family for the crazy quotient. But it was clear that she loved them with everything she had.

He understood that too.

"Thanks," she finally said softly, "for coming for me."

She hadn't called, and that got to him too. She hadn't wanted to be a burden. She'd asked him if he was worried she'd steal from him. The thought had never crossed his mind. She had the face of an angel, but that wasn't why he trusted her.

It was her eyes.

Christ, those eyes.

And bastard he might be, he wasn't usually wrong about people.

"You've done a lot for a perfect stranger you found squatting in your house," Ali murmured. "Or maybe not so perfect when it comes right down to it…"

"Perfect is overrated," he said. "And you're welcome, but I didn't do it just for you."

She turned to him. "No?"

"No."

"Then…why?"

There were two spots of color on her cheeks, and he wasn't sure if it was pride, temper, or intense curiosity. But any of it was hugely preferable to the brief sheen of tears he'd caught before, which had struck terror in his heart in a way that taking down hardened criminals never had. It was now his sole goal to keep her from crying. To that end, he answered her question more lightly than he would have otherwise. "Because the geriatric gang was going to drive me crazy until I did."

"My seniors?" she asked, shocked. "Why?"

Her seniors. He paused, really not wanting to go there. He thought about omitting, evading, or even out-and-out lying. He had no problem with any of that when it suited him, but for some reason, he had a problem with it now, with her. So he drew a deep breath and concentrated on the road. "Edward Gregory is my grandfather."

She stared at him. "Mr. Gregory, the Dial-A-Ride driver? He's your grandpa?"

"Yeah. He was married to my grandma Fay a million years ago for about ten minutes. When she left him, she changed her name—and my dad's—back to Hanover. My dad's their only kid."

"And he lives next door to you."

"Next door to my *grandma's* house," he corrected.

"Which is now *your* house. So he made you come check on me?"

"He was worried about you."

"And you?" she asked.

Again, he answered lightly. This time for *him*. "I was worried I'd never get any peace if I didn't do as they asked."

There was a long silence from the passenger seat, with Ali studying each passing tree as if it held the secrets to world peace.

He sighed. "Yeah, okay. I was worried too."

She said nothing to this, and he glanced at her. "You okay over there?"

"Just trying to picture you as someone's little grandson."

"Hard to believe, I know. But I wasn't always thirty and jaded as hell. I actually had a childhood, a lot of it spent right here in Lucky Harbor, in fact."

This got her. She turned her head and stared at him. "Are your parents here in town?"

"No, they raised me in San Francisco, mostly. They're doctors, both in Haiti now. When I was younger and they traveled, which was just about all the time, my sister and I came here to my grandma Fay's."

She shook her head. "Still trying to see you as a little boy, having fun, playing in the sandbox."

He smiled. "I was more of a blow-shit-up kind of kid. And believe it or not, I do know how to have fun."

Again she met his gaze, and the air seemed to crackle around them.

"Hmm," she said.

That damn "hmm" left him tempted to pull over and show her *exactly* how much fun he could be. But that would be a mistake.

Showing her anything over and above what they'd already done would be a mistake. Still, he was shockingly tempted, and he let her see that when he looked over at her.

Color bloomed in her cheeks again. "You're a distraction," she said softly. "I don't need a distraction. I need to do some problem solving."

"Are you going to ask me for help?"

"No," she said. "You're not getting involved."

Maybe if they both kept saying it, it would be true. "Right," he said, wanting to drive this point home. "I am definitely on a break from getting involved."

"Because of your last case."

"Among other reasons."

She fell silent, and he was a big enough jerk to be grateful.

"It wasn't your fault," she finally said, quietly. "What happened to that woman…Isabel Reyes."

"She might feel differently, if she could say so," he said with a lightness he didn't feel.

The typical late afternoon wind was kicking up as they made the last hairpin turn to the top of the cliffs. The water wasn't quiet now. The sun shimmered on it, lighting up the whitecaps as if they were a million bursts of fire.

Once upon a time, Luke would have been out there on

that water with Jack or Ben, stirring up shit in one form
or another. Now he was asking for trouble of a different
kind altogether by bringing Ali back to the house.

"The news accounts I've read say that the prosecu-
tion's evidence got tossed out," she said. "And we both
know that once they set the senator free, it was out of your
hands."

The knife in his chest twisted a little bit. She was looking at him. He could feel the weight of her gaze.

"Must be a terribly helpless feeling," she said softly.
"When something like that happens, and there's nothing
you can do to stop it."

"Yeah."

"Why do you do it?"

"The job?" He shrugged. "Someone's got to. And I'm
good at it. Usually."

"You didn't fail her, Luke. The senator did. *You* didn't
fail anyone."

"You're wrong there," he said. "I've failed plenty."
He'd failed his sister. His grandma. And no matter what
Ali said, he'd also failed Isabel Reyes. He pulled into the
driveway, turned off the engine, and got out of the truck.

He came around for Ali but she was already sliding
out, and they headed up the walkway in silence.

Before he could open the door, Ali stopped him with a
hand on his arm. He felt the zing of her touch all the way
to his soul.

"You manage huge amounts of responsibility," she said
quietly. "You face so much, every day. I think you're
amazing, Luke. I also think a part of why you want to
be alone is because you're feeling vulnerable right now.
You're afraid you're going to fail someone else."

And if it was her, if he failed her in any way, it would kill him.

"Luke?"

"No," he said.

She was standing there in her muddy apron and wild hair, looking at him with those big, soft eyes that said she thought he was a hero.

But a hero wouldn't want to push her up against the door and kiss her.

"You haven't failed me," she whispered.

Fuck it, he thought, and giving in to the need swamping him, he backed her up to the door and kissed her. It didn't take more than a single heartbeat for her to wind her arms around his neck and kiss him back.

"*That's* why I need to be alone," he said when they broke apart, breathless. "We have a chemistry problem."

"Yes. I think you're right." She wobbled, and Luke slid an arm around her as he unlocked the front door, noticing he wasn't all that steady either. "Food or shower?"

"Both." She was still looking a little shell-shocked at their combustibility. "Shower first."

He led her inside, blocking the view of the still-trashed living room, standing there until she'd gone straight into the bathroom. Then he turned and faced the destroyed house. Shaking his head, he moved back to shut the front door just as Jack pulled up.

Jack was a firefighter and ran the local fire station. He was still in uniform, complete with the radio at his hip, and he carried a bag of food. They'd been best friends, brothers really, since the summer after sixth grade—which meant there were no formalities.

"You're an asshole," Jack said.

Guy code for *good to see you, man.*

Jack came to San Francisco at least once a month, almost always staying with Luke. They'd seen each other two weeks ago, when Jack had come down to go sailing on a friend's boat. "Right back atcha," Luke said. "How's your mom?"

Dee Harper was fighting breast cancer and, by all counts, winning the war but it was costing her. And Jack as well.

"She's doing better, much better," Jack said, and started to walk right on in, but Luke shoulder-checked him.

"What?" Jack asked.

Luke took the food. "Thanks for dinner. Add it to my tab." Before he could shut the door, Jack stuck his steel-toe, big-ass boot out, blocking it.

"The size of your tab could feed a third-world country," Jack said.

Actually, the reverse was true, but Jack had a selective memory when it suited him. He also had the whole laid-back ski bum vibe going, but the truth was, beneath the deceptive playfulness, Jack Harper was anything but laid back and easygoing. Maybe he made his way through women like some men went through socks, but he worked every bit as hard as he played.

Luke peeked in the bag. "Orange chicken and spicy beef?"

"And fried rice, just in case the main course doesn't clog our arteries properly." Jack was trying to see past Luke into the house, his sharp eyes missing nothing. "Damn. They really did make a fucking mess."

"What did you know about the missing fifty K?"

"I'm too hungry to talk; I'm wasting away as we stand here. I need to eat. In front of the game."

"The game's not on."

"Yeah, it is."

"It's not on in *here*," Luke said.

"The game's always on at your place."

Down the hall, the shower went on, and Jack's brow went up.

Luke blew out a breath. "Ali Winters."

"She's here?" He grinned. "You were holding out on me." He pushed past Luke and headed into the messy living room. He shoved the cushions back onto the couch and then dropped onto it in a big, lazy sprawl. "Where's the remote? I've only got half an hour before I have to be back at the station."

"You're not staying."

"Aw, come on. It's been forever since I've gotten to see you be an idiot with a woman. Don't ruin my fun."

"I'm not an idiot with women."

"You're a complete idiot with women, and I'll prove it: *Tina Rawlings*."

"Tina Rawlings was when we were *sixteen*," Luke said.

"Yeah, you had sex with her at the lagoon and got caught by her boyfriend. He beat the shit out of you."

"Because he and his entire baseball team jumped me."

"Bowling team," Jack corrected. "It was the *bowling* team, and *I* could've taken them with one arm tied behind my back."

"Hey," Luke said, "some of us didn't get our growth spurt until college."

Jack laughed. "Whatever helps you sleep at night, man. So you and Ali…?"

"No."

"Sure? Because I don't think you have to worry about the bowling team these days. You're not in bad shape."

"I'm not getting involved." How many times was he going to have to say that? He'd come to Lucky Harbor to lose himself for a little while. *Not* to share the place with a woman who made him ache like crazy and had the singular ability to make him want to both howl at the moon and run like hell.

The phone rang, and Luke stared at it like it was a striking cobra.

"You going to get that?" Jack asked.

"Fuck no."

The machine clicked on, and a woman's voice said, "Ali-gator? Just checking in on you—"

"You still have an actual answering machine?" Jack asked. "Man, it might be time to upgrade the place from the 1980s…"

Luke strode to the machine and picked up the phone. "Ali's in the shower, Mrs. Winters."

"Luke!" She sounded pleased to hear his voice. "You were going to call me Mimi, remember?"

He let out a breath. "Right. Mimi…"

Jack went brows up again. Luke ignored him. "I'll have her call you," he said to Mimi.

"You're a sweetheart, Luke. Thank you."

"Wow," Jack said when he'd hung up. "Look at you, not getting involved."

Luke flipped him off and snatched the remote from Jack's hand.

"Figured you'd want the 4-1-1," Jack said. "If you kick

me out now, you won't get to hear it. But hey, if you're not getting involved…"

"Tell me."

Jack grinned. "Lucky for you, I work with a bunch of little girls."

"You work with a bunch of firefighters."

"Who all gossip like girls. The money's still missing, as you know, and actually there's a reward going out on it, but Ali isn't the only one they hauled in. They questioned Ted Marshall further. And also Melissa Mann. You remember her, right? She said—"

"That Marshall was screwing her and he can't remember if he locked the drawer with the money," Luke said.

"Damn, you stole my thunder. Seems Golden Boy's keeping secrets. Melissa said the police searched the office and came up with a woman's toe ring deep in the couch that doesn't belong to her."

"Or Ali," Luke said.

"Okay," Jack said, irritated now. "If you already know everything, why did you ask?"

"Because gossip is usually based in fact," Luke said. "Got anything else? Maybe something on the admin, Aubrey?"

"Nothing on Aubrey. But Melissa did say she believed that Teddy and Ali were just roommates. Which means Ted had a good thing going. They're going to question everyone who was in the office on the night of the auction, but there's a few problems."

"Like?"

"Teddy isn't talking about any other possible indiscretions. And apparently that whole wing of the building was a revolving door. Several people were back there using the quiet hallway for phone calls, and people were going through on bathroom runs. The janitor had a thing with the caterer in the treasurer's office, one door down from Marshall's office. Reportedly even the mayor's wife was seen slipping out of the hallway storage closet just past the bathroom. Go Mr. Mayor."

Luke stared at him. "Are you telling me that place saw more action than the rest of us saw all year?"

"Speak for yourself." But Jack's grin faded. "The fact is Ali's the one who got caught with evidence. And there's a lot of pressure on Sawyer to make an arrest. She's also the only one with an obvious motive."

"Circumstantial evidence," Luke said. "And people don't need a motive to steal cash."

"She stole a ceramic pot because she'd made it for her boyfriend who'd just dumped her by text," Jack pointed out. "Hello motive."

"She didn't know there was evidence to a crime in it."

"We both know that's weak, Luke."

"I know. And I know something else too, it's not Marshall either. Yeah, he's into politics, but he's a piggy-backer, not a big-plan sort of guy. He doesn't have the stones for this."

"So…what? He was framed?"

"I'd bet on it," Luke said. "And somehow Ali got caught in the middle—" He broke off at the sound of bare feet padding down the hall.

Ali appeared. She'd showered and changed faster than any woman Luke had ever known. She was in sweats and makeup-free, wet hair piled up on top of her head, with wavy tendrils framing her face. She headed straight to the kitchen and headed back with a carton of ice cream from Lance's shop.

Luke felt a small smile play around his mouth as she ate right out of the container with a wooden spoon. Ali Winters might be down, but she wasn't out for the count.

She scooped another big bite, and her expression finally relaxed. Until she saw the mess of the house. That wiped the smile right off her face. "Oh no. Oh Luke, I'm so sorry."

"Don't worry about it," he said. "It's seen worse."

"This is true." Jack rose off the couch. "Way worse. We were what you might call wayward teenagers."

Jack had the same height as Luke, but more bulk to his muscle tone. Of the two of them, Jack also possessed the charm, which had gotten him out of more trouble than Luke had ever managed to get into. Jack flashed all one thousand watts of that charm at Ali now.

"Jack Harper. I've seen you around, but we've never been introduced," he said, holding out his hand to Ali, smiling his "reassuring" smile. It was number three in his arsenal, behind his "you can't resist me" and "I want you" smiles. "I'm the best friend, by the way. The better-looking, far more fascinating one, I should add."

"Ali Winters," she said, looking a little dazzled, which made Luke roll his eyes. "Nice to meet you." She glanced at the mess again, but Luke stepped in her way.

"I've heard a lot about you," Jack said.

"I'm sorry," she said, glancing at Luke. "I can't say the same."

"Not surprised," Jack said. "Luke's not exactly a big talker."

"No," Ali said faintly, a slight blush coming to her cheeks. "He's not."

There was nothing in Ali's tone to suggest that they'd spent some time in Luke's truck kissing like their lives had depended on it, but Jack knew him better than anyone else on the planet. Proving it, his gaze shifted from Ali to Luke. "Also, he can never find his keys and he snores," Jack said.

"Thanks, man," Luke said.

Jack smiled at Ali. "Hope you're hungry; I brought Chinese. Ben, my cousin and the third musketeer, would've brought a loaded pizza. He's on government assignment right now, and I'm just superstitious enough that I won't eat a pizza until he's home. You need anything else?"

Clearly surprised to be asked, Ali blinked. "No, thank you." Her voice sounded funny and gave Luke a very bad feeling.

Jack didn't miss it either. Jack didn't miss much. "All right, I'll get plates," he said very gently, waiting until he was behind her and out of her peripheral vision to send Luke a steely look.

One thing the two of them had always shared was a hatred of seeing anyone mistreated or taken advantage of. Jack loved Luke, but the message was clear—*don't hurt her more than she's already been hurt.*

When Jack vanished into the kitchen, Ali moved to the couch, head averted. There might even have been a muffled sniffle.

Oh, Christ. Luke had faced down countless gangbangers, armed felons, and drugged-up perps. He'd faced the worst humanity had to offer, but he'd never gotten the hang of dealing with a woman's tears. Sucking it up, he sat next to her.

She stiffened.

Ignoring that, he reached for her ice cream, thinking to set it down for her, but she surprised him with an elbow to the gut.

"What the hell?"

She hugged the ice cream to her chest. "I told you not to be nice to me right now!"

"I'm not nice. I'm never nice. And Jesus, remind me to never try to separate you from your ice cream again."

Jack reappeared, paper plates and napkins in hand as he took in the scene. "Bad time?"

"Yes," Luke said.

"No," Ali said, and glared at Luke.

Jack nodded in approval. "Keeping him in line. That's good. He needs that."

Luke shot Jack a look, which Jack ignored as he plopped down on the couch right between them. The big oaf actually bounced Ali nearly to the floor and half sat on Luke as he settled in. He took the ice cream from Ali—and didn't get elbowed, Luke couldn't help but notice—and then handed out plates. They divided up the food, with Jack taking the last eggroll.

"Hey," Luke said.

"It'd go straight to your ass," Jack said, and popped the eggroll into his mouth. "No one wants to see that."

Luke ignored this. They were both fit, but extremely competitive. Maybe Jack could kick his ass on a run, but Luke totally had him on the water and the boards.

When Ali finished her food, she pushed her plate away. "Okay, let's hear it."

"Hear what?" Luke asked.

"Whatever information you two have that I don't."

Jack sent Luke a look, and Luke turned to Ali. "Look, at this point it's all really just speculation…"

"I'm not some dainty flower, Luke. Spit it out."

Jack grinned at her. "We're going to be great friends, you and I."

"As my friend then, tell me," she said. "Tell me what I'm missing."

"It's about Marshall and his office," Luke said carefully. At the first sign of tears, he'd shut the hell up. "And what else might have occurred there that night."

"I already know what happened," Ali said. "He screwed Melissa on the couch and then screwed me by claiming I stole the money."

"Yes," Luke said. "But the toe ring tells me that in all likelihood, Teddy had more than one woman in his office. And maybe one of those women got greedy. Problem is, the sheriff's department is getting a lot of pressure to make an arrest. Hard to do when the hallway outside his office was Grand Central Station that night." And then he told her about the comings and goings.

Ali stood and paced the room, stepping around the mess of things all over the floor. "So are they checking out Gus, and the caterer, and everyone else, including Mr. and Mrs. Fancy Mayor?" she asked.

Luke nodded. "Yes."

"But I'm the only one who got caught with any sort of evidence," she said quietly.

Luke rose and made his way to her. "We're going to figure this out."

Jack gave him a look at the "we."

"How?" Ali asked.

"We put the evening together like a puzzle," Luke said. "One piece at a time."

"There's a lot of pieces," Ali said, and crouched down to begin picking up.

Luke pulled her upright. "I'll get the mess later," he said. "As for the pieces of the puzzle, we'll figure it out."

Her expression showed her doubt and gave him a pang right in his gut.

Apparently in Jack's too, because he stood as well. "No one's going to leave you to fry for something you didn't do," he said quite intensely.

Ali managed a small smile. "Thanks. I owe you both."

"No, you don't," Jack said, and kissed her on the cheek. "'Night."

Luke followed him to the door.

"*Don't* sleep with her," Jack said quietly. "She needs comfort and a friend. And—" he continued before Luke could utter a word, "don't give me any bullshit like you're not her friend because you're not getting involved. You're as involved as I've ever seen you."

Chapter 10

The next morning, the sky was dark and mottled, the clouds tumbling against each other, threatening rain. Instead of putting himself out on the water on a board to be bait for a bolt of lightning, Luke put on his running shoes.

It started to sprinkle as he ran along the rocky beach, but he didn't mind. It kept him cool. The air was salty from the ocean and also scented with pine from the trees. And in spite of the weather, the mountain chickadees were still out singing in force, "cheeseburger, cheeseburger," sounding like The Chipmunks on crack.

It made him hungry.

On the way back, he slowed at the Schmidts' summer beach house, remembering his promise to the Geriatric Gang to locate Roger Barrett's GTO. He walked around the front of the house and took a look through the glass panel across the top of one of the two garage doors.

Yep. There was the '67 GTO.

With a shake of his head, he knocked on the front door. No answer.

He knocked harder.

Two minutes later, the door was opened by Phillip Schmidt's twenty-two-year-old grandson. Mikey was wearing a bright Hawaiian-print shirt with red and green parrots on it, unbuttoned over a pair of sunshine-yellow boxers. His sun-kissed blond hair hit his shoulders, and he had on small, round, purple-lensed John Lennon sunglasses, a laid-back, surfer-dude smile, and held an unlit joint pinched between his fingers. "Oh shit," he said at the sight of Luke and turned to run.

Luke reached out and grabbed him by the back of his shirt. Mikey, as thin as a pipe cleaner with eyes, ran in the air for a few beats before Luke gave him a little shake and dropped him back to his feet.

"Dude," Mike said, rolling his shoulders, "I have rights."

"Yes, but smoking pot isn't one of them."

"It's called Maritime Law, man. They can't tell you what to do in the ocean."

"You're not in the ocean, and I don't give a shit about your pot. I'm here about the GTO in the garage."

"My grandpa won it in a poker game. Sweet, right?"

"Very. But it's not yours."

"Says who?" Mikey asked.

"Roger Barrett."

"Aw, man, that guy's a hundred and something years old. He can't see past his own nose, and anyway, he's a little cuckoo for Cocoa Puffs." For emphasis, Mikey made the crazy sign, twirling a finger by his ear.

"He's seventy and sharp as a piranha's eyetooth," Luke

said. "Plus he had Lasik surgery. Roger can see better than both of us put together. And he's got one finger on his 'oops I've fallen and can't get up button' to report the GTO as stolen. Get it back to him today."

"Can't. I have, like, plans."

"Cancel them," Luke said.

"No can do. Candy James is coming over today. I'm going to get laid, man. She is one hot piece."

"If you don't return the car, *you're* going to be the hot piece, Mikey. In prison."

Mikey sighed. "Harshing my buzz, dude."

Luke held out his hand. "Keys."

Mikey mopily grabbed a set of keys on the foyer bench and slapped into Luke's palm. "It's on empty."

Of course it was. Luke started to walk out, then turned back. "You work for that cleaning company that takes care of Town Hall, right? The night shift?"

"Yeah. Why?"

"You ever see anyone there in the offices late at night?"

"Sometimes. People are, like, working hard to keep their jobs, man."

"How about recently?" Luke asked.

"You mean as recently as when your girlfriend stole the money from Ted Marshall's office?"

"Ali isn't my girlfriend, and she didn't steal the money."

"Ted Marshall's a pretty good guy, man. He wouldn't lie."

"Have you seen anything helpful? Anyone else in the office with him, for instance?"

"Maybe I don't feel like telling you."

"You feel like going to jail?"

Mikey let out a dramatic sigh. "The cops already asked me this. I told them I didn't see anything."

Luke crossed his arms over his chest and eyed Mikey over the tops of his sunglasses.

After all of three seconds, Mikey broke eye contact. "If I get fired from another job, my dad's gonna gut me."

"You keep stealing cars, and your dad is the least of your worries. Talk to me, Mikey."

"Okay, so normally when I go in, everyone's gone. Twice this past week, Marshall was working late. Only he wasn't working, you know what I mean?"

"No."

Mikey hesitated. "I don't think I should say, man. He's never snitched on me. I don't want to snitch on him."

"You're not snitching. You're helping me solve a crime so that an innocent woman doesn't get blamed for it."

Mikey sighed. "He was in his office, in his chair, with some hot chick bouncing on him."

"You know her?" Luke asked.

"Hello, she was *naked*, man. Hot as hell. My eyes never got higher than her ass. But maybe she had blonde hair. Maybe. I dunno. She was a real screamer though, if that helps. She kept going 'harder, baby, harder,' which didn't make sense, because she was on top and—"

"Have you seen him working late since?" He was grasping at straws here, and knew it.

"If that was 'working' then I want his job," Mikey said.

When Luke just looked at him, he let out a breath. "No, I haven't seen him"—Mikey used air quotes—"*working late* since."

"Thanks." Luke turned to go.

"If you let me keep the car, maybe I'll remember something else."

"How about this," Luke said. "If you remember something else, you tell me. Fast and quiet. And then—"

"You'll get me the car back?"

"No. But I'll let you live."

Mikey blew out another breath, and Luke left. He filled up the GTO, and because it was dirty and the interior reeked like weed, he also drove it through the car wash and got a pine tree air freshener to dangle from the rearview mirror. Thirty minutes later, he was handing the keys over to Roger Barrett. "Good as new," he said.

Roger couldn't wait to sit in it. Gleeful as a kid in a candy shop, he made Luke join him and cranked up the music.

Neil Sedaka.

They sat there, the windows rattling with "Breaking Up Is Hard to Do," sipping sodas. Just when Luke was thinking he needed a sharp stick with which to poke out one of his eyeballs, Roger turned to him. "About your girlfriend, that cutie patootie from White Center."

Luke didn't bother to sigh. "Ali. And she's not my girlfriend."

"Well, whatever you kids are calling it nowadays then," Roger said. "Friends with benefits?"

Luke choked on his soda.

"You know, Ted Marshall's a good man, right? He takes care of Lucky Harbor, and he gives back. But Ali's good people too. She goes to the senior center. My sister's there. Ali takes the time to sit with her, talk to her, get her involved in the activities. If Ali stole that money...Well,

I just wanted to say that I know she must have had a real good reason."

"She didn't steal it," Luke said.

"I'm just saying…"

A few minutes later, Luke left for home, once again jogging through the morning chill. He took the streets this time, his running shoes hitting the damp ground. He'd meant to steer clear of all Lucky Harbor business. He'd definitely meant to stay clear of Ali.

He'd failed at both.

Ali had had a crappy day. Leah had tried to get her to go out tonight but she wasn't in the mood. Instead, she was in the kitchen licking brownie batter from a wooden spoon like her life depended on it when Luke wandered into the kitchen.

"I smell chocolate," he said, looking hopeful.

He was wearing sexy-as-hell jeans and a white, long-sleeved shirt that was snug across his broad shoulders. He looked even better than the chocolate. "Brownies from a box," she told him. "Comfort food."

"What's wrong?"

She shook her head and reloaded the spoon with more batter.

Taking her wrist, he brought her hand up to lick the spoon in the same spot she'd just licked.

It gave her a hot rush. So did Luke shifting closer.

"Tell me," he said.

She shrugged. "People kept coming into the shop to see the girl who stole the money. And you were right—word is they're getting ready to make an arrest."

"And you're afraid it's going to be you."

"Well, who else at this point?" she sighed. "Russell's taking two days off and keeping the shop closed. Even he's planning for me to be in jail." She needed to get to the bottom of this now. Determined, she set down the spoon, grabbed her keys and purse, and turned to the door.

"Where are you going?" Luke asked, slapping his pockets, turning in a circle, clearly searching for his keys in the universal bewilderment of men everywhere across the planet. "Ali—"

"Table," she said.

"What?"

"Your keys are on the table."

"Damn, you're good." He scooped them up. "Where we going?"

"To be proactive."

"Yeah? Where's this proactive thing taking place?" Outside, he took her elbow and redirected her to his truck.

"I don't need help, Luke. Not with this."

"Think of me as a wingman," he suggested, and opened the passenger door for her.

Since he was standing there blocking her escape, looking big and bad and absolutely unmovable, she got in. "If you're just the wingman, why are we taking your truck?" she asked.

"Wingmen always drive. Where to?"

"The Love Shack." The local bar and grill was the only nightlife in the entire county.

"I have liquor in the house," Luke said.

"I want to talk to Gus. He told the police he'd holed up with the caterer."

"So?"

"So the caterer was Tara Daniels Walker, and she's

very married. But Tara's assistant—Callie—dated Gus a few months back and then broke up with him. Loudly."

"What makes you think he's lying?"

"*Someone's* lying," she said. "If it's Gus, why? What's he covering up? Something for Teddy, or himself?"

"Okay, I like the way you think," Luke said, "but this has trouble written all over it. I talked to Mikey Schmidt today."

"The stoner guy?"

"He cleans Town Hall at night. He caught Marshall with a maybe blonde the other night."

She glanced at him. "Melissa?"

"He couldn't say. I need a favor, Ali."

"Sure. Anything."

The look he slid her was pure heat, and she flushed at the thought of doing *anything* for him. *That's not what he'd meant*, she told herself firmly. Get a damn grip.

"When we get there, let me lead." He parked in the parking lot between the pier and The Love Shack, catching her before she could jump out of the truck. "Wait," he said. His phone was ringing. Holding onto her purse—clearly a man who knew how to slow down a woman—he punched SPEAKER on his phone, which was still lying on the console. "Hanover," he said shortly.

"Oooh, so official," a woman said. "Odd, for a man on vacay."

"I'm…" He glanced at Ali. "Busy. You okay?"

"You mean, do I need you to save me?" the woman asked. "Never fear, little brother, I do not. *I'm* trying to save *you*."

Luke's sister, Ali thought with way more relief than she should have felt.

Luke's brow knit in annoyance. "I'm fine, Sara. Just—"

"Busy," Sara said. "Yeah, yeah, I get it. I heard about you and the cute florist."

Luke stared at the phone, and Sara snorted into the silence. "You were seen kissing her in your truck on Main Street in Lucky Harbor, Luke. What did you expect? Anyway, you've got some reporters here who want—"

"Tell them no," he said with steel. "Tell them to stay away from you or I'll get restraining orders. Tell them—"

"Got it, Ace. I can handle this. What are you doing?"

Luke tightened his grip on Ali's purse when she tried to break free. "Working."

"Liar," Sara said. "You never answer the phone when you're working. It's the cute florist, right? Tell me about her."

Luke pinched the bridge of his nose. "I'm hanging up now."

Sara laughed at him. "I'll start. Her name's Ali. Jack says she's pretty. Maybe I should get a few days off work and come up to get a look at her myself."

Ali felt a warm fuzzy flow through her, which was rudely chased away by a blast of reality by Luke himself.

"It's work," he repeated.

Work...

"Uh-huh," Sara said, sounding amused. "Love you."

Luke punched END and looked at Ali. "Ready?"

Oh, yes. She was ready. She was ready to leave his truck. *Alone*. "I'll handle this," she said.

"Never hurts to have backup, Ali."

"I won't be more work to you."

He gave what might have been a very small sigh. "You

don't know my sister," he said. "If I'd told her anything else, she'd drive up here and butt in."

She unhooked her seatbelt.

Behind her, Luke did the same. "Let me do the talking."

Over her dead body.

"Listen," Luke said, going for reasonable. His mistake, because it'd been a while, but he should have remembered that angry women were never reasonable. "You're looking pretty riled up. You need to—"

Ali slid out of the truck and headed to the bar with purpose.

"Go in low profile," he finished. "*Shit*," he muttered behind her when she didn't slow down. He followed her inside and watched as she walked right up to the bar where Gus was sitting with a few other guys over beers.

Luke nodded to the guy behind the bar—Ford Walker, co-owner of the place, ex–world sailing champion and all-around good guy.

"Can I have a minute?" Ali asked the janitor.

The big guy smiled down at her. "Hey, Ali. Luke. Heard you two were a thing now."

"Remember the other night?" Ali asked him.

"When I let you into Marshall's office? Yeah." His smile faded. "I'm sorry you got caught."

"I didn't steal the money," she said, looking like steam might start coming out of her ears. Or her hair. The hair was pretty wild today, but he liked it.

He liked *her*. Way too much.

"Right." Gus nodded adamantly at her. "You didn't steal the money."

"Can you tell me who else you saw in the hallway that night?" Ali asked.

"Well," he said, scratching his beard, "just as I told the police, it was hard to keep track. That hall was busy as hell."

"Could you give it a shot?"

"Sure. Mrs. Medina wanted to see the Lost and Found, which was in the storage closet. Then, while I was waiting on her, Ella came in to make a phone call in private. Only she ended up yelling at her sister, so it really wasn't so private at all."

"Ella?"

"From the post office. And then Aubrey came in to see why people were in the office to begin with, and she got all up in arms about it. And then there was Ted himself…" Gus blushed a bit at that. "But I suppose you've already heard…"

"That he had Melissa in there?" Ali asked politely.

Gus downed his drink. "Yeah. I didn't know, Ali. I swear it."

Gus's mountain-sized friend snorted.

Luke agreed. As the janitor, nothing happened in that building that Gus didn't know about.

"And you," Ali said to Gus, "you were there with Callie, right?"

Gus went very still, only his eyes sliding to the giant next to him. "Uh, who told you that?"

"It's what you told the police," Ali said calmly. Except she wasn't calm at all. Her eyes gave her away. Was Luke the only one who could see it?

Gus's friend set down his beer and glared hard at Gus. "You were with Callie?" he asked. Actually, it was more of a shout.

"Now, now, Buddy," Gus said quickly, raising his hands. "In all fairness, you did say you two were just friends, so—"

Buddy punched Gus in the mouth. "In all fairness," he said.

Luke grabbed Ali and hauled her back just as the two men tumbled to the ground, Gus's long legs taking out the two men on the other side of him.

"Hey!" one of them yelled. "You spilled my drink!" And then he jumped into the fray too.

His friend dove in as well, and pretty soon beers and fists were flying in a full-out bar brawl. Ford hopped over the bar to break it up, and Luke helped him separate the idiots from the idiots.

Afterward, Ali was staring at him. "Wow," she said.

"What?"

"You just waded into the flying fists and yanked them apart like it was no big deal, like you didn't even notice the danger."

He could have told her that it was no big deal. He'd been in a lot worse danger than a damn bar fight, but she was looking at him all impressed, and it was kind of nice. He led her outside, where they ran into a woman going in.

Aubrey.

In a navy blue suit, looking elegant and chic, hair perfect, she looked startled to see them. "We got cut off on the phone," she said to Ali.

"Yeah." Ali slid Luke a glance. "Sorry about that. Listen, careful in there. It's crazy tonight."

Aubrey took a look at the bar's entrance. "What's going on?"

"A little fight," Ali said.

"Seriously?" Aubrey pulled out her phone. "Did you call the police?" She turned to Luke. "Aren't *you* the police?"

"It's handled now," Luke said. "How often do you work late?"

"A lot." Aubrey gave him a wary look. "Why?"

"Just wondering if you've ever seen anyone else late in Marshall's office."

Aubrey was quiet for a beat. "You're on vacation, which means you're not a cop right *now*, right?"

"Right," he said. *Cop rule numero uno: be able to lie your ass off right to anyone's face.*

"So this isn't official or anything."

"Absolutely *not*," Luke said without hesitation.

Aubrey nodded, then glanced apologetically at Ali. "I think it's possible that Teddy's been seeing someone else."

"Besides Melissa and me?" Ali asked.

"Yes."

"Who?"

"I don't know," Aubrey said. "I'd have told you before, but until you came into the office the other day, I really thought you and Ted were just roommates."

Aubrey entered the bar, and Ali, looking a little deflated, fell silent. Luke took her hand. "Come on."

That she let him lead told him it was time for more ice cream. So he took her to the pier and bought her a triple cone from Lance at the ice cream shop. Then he took her hand again. At this time of night, the pier was quiet, and once they walked past the arcade and Ferris wheel, they had the night to themselves. They walked in silence to the very end and stood there looking out at the ocean, lit by a streak of light from the moon. Water slapped rhythmically against the pylons. The sound always calmed Luke, and next to him, Ali let out a soft sigh.

"That got me nowhere," she finally said, leaning against the railing, licking her cone like she meant business.

He tried not to stare and failed. Christ, he wanted her to lick him like that. "We knocked on some doors," he said. "We shook things up."

She turned to face him. "And now what?"

He stroked a finger along her temple, tucking a strand of hair behind her ear for the sheer pleasure of touching her. Then he leaned in for a kiss. She tasted like chocolate and trouble. Big trouble. "We wait for the dust to settle."

"We?"

"Yeah. We." He let his hand fall from her. "But—"

"Yeah, I know." She pushed away from the railing and started walking back to his truck. "It's a short-term 'we.'"

Chapter 11

♥

It was two in the morning before Ali got Luke's kitchen back together. She was heading to do the den next when she got her usual daily check-in text from Harper: *Made good tips tonight! Next time you come home, dinner's on me.*

Ali managed a smile. Exhausted, dusty, and a little sweaty, she swiped her forehead and texted Harper back. *Sounds good. How's Mom?*

The money you put in her account made her day. You okay? You don't sound okay.

You got not okay from sounds good?

It's in the tone…

Ali rolled her eyes. *I'm fine…'night. Sweet dreams.*

Don't let the bed bugs bite!

It was an old mantra, and it made Ali smile again as she went back to cleaning up. Two hours later, she'd worked her way to the living room, and it was a disaster. Besides Luke's things, her own pottery was still un-wrapped and scattered on the floor.

After the bar brawl, Luke had once again told her to ignore the mess, that he'd get to it in the morning. "Get some sleep," he'd said, and had vanished into the basement to presumably follow his own advice.

But Ali couldn't sleep, and she couldn't ignore the house anymore. When she'd first seen it, she'd felt sick to the bone. The place was a mess, mirroring her own life. But it was *her* life and not Luke's. *She'd* brought this disaster to his home. And since she had, it was important that she clean it up.

She'd already straightened the bedroom she'd been using and had packed up her stuff while she was at it. She'd tortured Luke enough with her presence. When she was done here, she would go to the Lucky Harbor B&B, and then to the first apartment that was ready, and hope to God her Visa could handle the weight.

It would be okay.

She'd always been spectacularly good at denial, at not looking back, at keeping one foot in front of the other. Nothing about that had changed. She'd landed on her feet before, and she would do it again. Knowing it, she took her first real deep breath since...

Since too long to remember.

At a whisper of sound behind her, she whirled around to find a heavy-lidded, tousled-looking Luke in the doorway, hands braced over his head on the jamb.

"What, no umbrella this time?" he asked.

She relaxed her hold on a ceramic pot. "You nearly got this upside your head."

A ghost of a smile crossed his face. He'd clearly come straight from his bed. He was wearing only a pair of black basketball shorts, disturbingly low on his hips, putting all his hard muscles directly in her line of sight. If she touched his abs, she'd find them rock hard. She knew this because during their kiss in his truck, she'd copped a feel.

And there. That. *That* was what her mind had kept going back to all these past hours while she straightened up. Their kiss. How he'd tasted. How his mouth had slanted over her own, his tongue gliding along hers…She didn't have to think about the heat they'd generated; she was sweating just remembering it. "Sorry if I woke you," she said, surrounded by the disaster she'd brought to his door. Averting her face, she concentrated on righting the books.

He didn't say anything, so she turned back and found him still looking at her, his own gaze hooded. Sleepy. And something else, something that made her throat burn.

Dammit.

"Thought I told you I'd get to this in the morning," he said.

"It *is* morning."

Padding barefoot into the living room, he headed to the coffee table. Its big drawer had been dumped onto the floor. Crouching, he began tossing the things back inside.

"Luke, stop."

He didn't stop.

"This was my doing." She caught his arm. "I've got this."

His eyes held hers, not at all sleepy anymore, his muscles beneath her fingers corded. Warm. Then he went back to work. He finished the drawer and looked around, frowning when he saw the box of her pottery still scattered. He reached for the first piece, a miniature lion that she'd created last year, when she'd first come to Lucky Harbor. It represented courage. *Her* courage.

Luke stared down at the lion for a long moment, then very gently ran the pad of his finger over the mane. "It's amazing. It looks so real."

"Thanks."

"You sculpted this?"

She nodded.

"Then painted it?"

She nodded again.

He looked at her collection of animals sprawled out carelessly, toppled over like carnage. "These must have taken you a long time."

"Years." She shrugged at his questioning gaze. "My mom used to work a lot of nights. After my sister would go to bed, sometimes I'd stay up." Waiting for Mimi to come home. "It was something to do."

"Each piece means something to you," he said.

"Yes."

"What does this lion mean?"

"I made him when I first moved to Lucky Harbor." She paused. "He's my...roar."

A small smile crossed his lips. "You already have courage in spades, Ali." He grabbed a piece of the packing paper, then very carefully rolled up the lion as if it was the most precious thing in the world.

Ali opened her mouth, but then, unable to speak, closed it again.

Without another word or glance her way, as if he knew how painful this was for her, Luke reached for another piece of her pottery. An owl. He held it up to her.

"To remind me to try to be wise," she said softly. "No stupid decisions."

"Like sex."

Okay, that hadn't been exactly what she'd meant, but it didn't matter. Her body was reacting to the way he'd said "sex," and a shocking heat of arousal washed through her. She swallowed hard, but nodded.

Another smile. He rolled up the owl and set it carefully in the box with the lion. Over and over again with each piece, the whole time showing a respect for her things in a way the police hadn't.

Ali never really expected much from the men in her life. That way it wasn't a surprise when they didn't come through. But Luke kept surprising her, and it was unexpected to say the least.

He was unexpected.

An hour later, dawn broke. Shortly after that, the sun slanted in the huge picture windows, casting them in gold. "Done," Luke declared, tossing aside the broom in his hands.

They'd been quiet so long that she jumped. "The garage—"

"Was already a mess," he said. "Leave it. Go to bed, Ali. Get some rest."

She looked at the boxes and bags lined up in the hall. Her things.

His gaze followed hers. "You packed," he said flatly.

"Yes."

"Where are you going?"

"The B and B," she said. "Just until something pans out."

He stepped closer. "Why?" he asked.

She took in the high angle of his cheekbones, his strong jaw, the column of his throat. His broad shoulders were stiff with tension. He was holding back, and it was costing him.

"Ali, why?"

"Because…" His hands went to her hips. God, he was beautifully made, all tough, sinewy lines and smooth skin, which she knew would be heated to the touch. And oh, how she suddenly needed to touch. She lifted her hands to his chest. "Because…"

His eyes pinned her, his sheer force of personality making her go weak in the knees. And that wasn't all. He wanted her. There was no question; the proof of it was pressing into her belly.

And at that realization, she got weak in a lot more places than just her knees. But she didn't go weak for a man anymore, no matter how much she wanted to learn her way around his body and satisfy them both. Indulging herself—just for a minute—she let her hands roam.

Oh yeah, warm to the touch. *Hot* to the touch, really, his muscles smooth and hard. She could feel his heart beating beneath her hand, steady as a rock, flowing through her fingertips to mingle with her own pulse. He held himself very still, his big body just barely brushing hers. He didn't want to take advantage, she knew that. Sweet.

Except he wasn't sweet. And she wasn't feeling so sweet either. She was feeling dangerous as she kissed one corner of his delicious mouth. And then the other. Just a taste, she promised herself. "I'm going," she said, "because of this." And then she kissed him again, not just a taste.

Beneath her fingers, his muscles jerked, but he didn't make a move. That's okay, she had her own moves. She skimmed her hands up, around his neck, into his silky hair, and then fisted it, pulling his head closer to hers.

With a rough groan, his hands tightened on her, thumbs splaying across her stomach, rubbing her own heated skin. Pulling back a fraction of an inch, he looked down at her, his gaze dark and full of desire. It was irresistible and so was the way he watched her, his body seeming to shudder when she pressed more closely against him.

And then he kissed *her*, his tongue tracing the curve of her lips until she allowed him entry. He hooked his fingers in the hem of her tank top, slowly drawing it up, exposing her inch by inch.

Dipping his head, he looked his fill. Drawing a long, serrated breath, he slowly traced the lines of her ribs with his fingertips before cupping the curves of her breasts.

She loved the way he seemed to tremble when he touched her. Or maybe that was *her* doing the trembling from the feel of his palms searing her skin. He had a way of driving every thought from her head. Everything, except for need.

And right then, in that moment, the only thing she needed was him. "Luke."

Lowering his head, he put his mouth on her breast, taking the peak between his teeth, flicking it with his tongue before tugging gently.

He tightened his grip on her hair, and she cried out before she could stop herself.

"Stop me, Ali."

Was he kidding? Her nails raked across his back for more, making him inhale sharply.

"You're not ready for this," he said against her skin. "For me."

If she were any more ready, she'd be in flames. "Not your call, Luke."

With another groan, he pressed his forehead to her shoulder. "Then I'm not ready for you," he said. "I can't give you what you want, Ali."

"I don't want anything." But the magic spell was broken, and she stepped back, pulling her tank down, entangling her hands together to ensure she kept them off of him. "I'm going to go."

He blew out a breath, and then shook his head. "The B and B is in high season. They're charging tourist prices."

She knew one of the owners; Maddie, the middle sister, came into the shop weekly to buy flowers for the inn. Ali thought she would give her a good deal, but he was right—it was still going to be out of her price range. "Fine," she said, "I'll go stay with my mom and commute from there."

"Have you seen gas prices?" he asked. "That's a stupid idea. And you're not stupid."

"Stop it, Luke."

"Stop what?"

"I'm not staying here just because you suddenly feel sorry for me."

"Okay, then stay so we can have wild, up-against-the-wall sex," he said.

Her breath caught. She wasn't even sure what wild-up-against-the-wall sex would feel like, but she had a feeling she'd like it. A lot. And yet she knew that he was merely trying to rile her up so she wouldn't do something awful, like cry. "I'm not a pity case."

"I don't have the capacity for pity," he said. "Hell, Ali, stay here because…I need you."

Stunned, she stared up into his face, which was cast in

granite. Apparently she'd met her match in stubbornness. "You *need* me," she repeated doubtfully.

As if on cue, the phone rang, shattering the early morning quiet. He pointed to the phone and then to her. *See? Need you.* And then he vanished down the hall without another word.

The phone rang again.

Ali looked at it, weighing the price of the B&B along with the danger to her bank account against the price of staying here and endangering something even more fragile—her heart.

No contest on which decision would cost her the most. And yet she headed to the phone and used her apparently pent-up frustration getting rid of yet another reporter looking for Luke.

Chapter 12

Zach showed up that afternoon in a suit that emphasized his beanpole body, a messenger bag strapped across his chest, and thick black-rimmed glasses on his nose. His jet-black hair was in spikes. His eyebrow piercing glittered as he scooped Ali in for a big hug.

Zach's familiar ease faded when she introduced him to Luke. Oh, his warm chocolate eyes were friendly enough, but reserved, as the two men sized each other up.

Luke was his usual steely intense self as they shook hands, and Zach reverted to geeky awkwardness, though he maintained eye contact. Ali gave him credit for not peeing his pants.

"So you're licensed in the state of Washington?" Luke asked him.

Ali gave him a long look. "Luke…"

"Yes," Zach said, and pushed his glasses higher on his nose. "I'm licensed in Washington."

"How many trial cases do you have under your belt?"

Ali grimaced. "*Luke*."

"If Ali gets arrested, and if the case goes to trial," Zach said, "this would be my first solo. But we both know even if it gets that far, as a first-time offender she might end up with restitution over time served. The record would be the worst part."

"Might isn't good enough," Luke said. "And how about the fact that she's innocent?"

"Of course she's innocent," Zach said simply. "It's Ali."

Ali smiled at him, sent Luke a hard look, and brought Zach to the kitchen table, where they discussed the case at length. Zach asked questions that might have had her head spinning, except he had a way about him. Sweet. Calm. It allowed her to concentrate on the task at hand, telling him all they'd learned about the comings and goings the night of the auction.

Zach looked over his notes. "So you took your pencil pot back without looking inside it."

"Yes, except it wasn't exactly mine. It was his, a little bit."

"How little?"

"One hundred percent."

Zach looked up from the iPad, expression wry. "You mean you stole it."

"Well, if you want to get technical, yeah. I stole it. I guess I shouldn't admit that to my attorney, right?"

Zach smiled gently at her. "You can tell me anything, Al. I'm not a cop." He slid a silent Luke a long look. "And the only cop in the room is off duty."

So Zach had done his own background search.

Whatever Luke thought about being baited by Zach, he kept it to himself. He was good at that.

It was a lesson Ali would be well served to learn herself.

The next morning, Luke was woken just before dawn by a text from his commander.

Need you back for internal review on Reyes case. There's prep work the size of the California debt. Stop with the small town PI shit and get your ass back here.

Luke thumbed his way to the browser and searched for the latest reports. It wasn't pretty. The first article he pulled up called the SFPD a complete failure. Luke tossed the phone aside and tried to tell himself he didn't give a damn. But he did. Only a week ago, his job had been everything to him, his entire being wrapped up in the reputation and ego of it. That had been who he was.

Now, far from San Francisco, he didn't feel like that same guy.

He'd lived the fast-paced, adrenaline-rushed job for years, and he'd thrived on it. But he wasn't thriving anymore. It wasn't the danger he faced on the force, or the darkness of the things he saw, or the slogging knee-deep through shit on a daily basis.

He missed life here.

He'd left Lucky Harbor, exiled himself really, and not looked back. And in doing so, he'd cut himself off from the happiest times of his life. In coming back, he underestimated the pull that the wild, hauntingly beautiful, resilient Pacific Northwest had always had on him.

Now there was something else pulling at him as

well—the equally wild, hauntingly beautiful, resilient Ali Winters.

Rolling out of bed, he pulled on swim trunks. Out back, he balanced his board on his head and took the steep stairs down to the water.

The harbor was quiet. By the time he'd set the board in the water, the sky had lightened from black to purple. The water was icy cold and would clear his head.

Or kill him.

He pushed off and began paddling. And then there was nothing but the sound of his board skimming through the water, the occasional splash of a zealous fish, and the chirping birds that were waking with the dawn.

Alone.

Quiet.

It was the closest to heaven that he could imagine. He paddled out past the pier and harbor and into the open water. He pushed himself hard, until his heart pounded and he couldn't catch his breath. It felt good. Here, in the zone, he couldn't think, couldn't obsess, couldn't regret.

An hour later, muscles quivering, he stopped, panting as the sun beat down on him. He cooled down by making his way back slowly, enjoying the early morning. As he entered the harbor again, he passed the pier and the Ferris wheel, and saw a female jogging along the water's edge. She was built like a Victoria's Secret model, and her long blonde hair flowed behind her.

Melissa Mann.

Shading her eyes with her hand, she took him in, a wide smile crossing her lips. "Well, look who the tide dragged in," she purred as he slid up on the beach and got off his board. "Heard you were back," she said, "and looking for trouble." She waggled a brow and gestured to herself. "Meet trouble with a capital T."

He had to laugh. She was right. She *was* trouble with a capital T. The very best kind of trouble. "How's the salon going?" he asked.

"Running it now," she said proudly. "Come by sometime. I'll give you a buff and shine." She smiled. "On the house."

He smiled too, knowing that they both understood he wouldn't. "Heard you were at the auction the other night."

"I was. Everyone was." She cocked her head and studied him a moment. "You've got quite a cop face on, Luke. Why don't you just ask me what you want to know?"

"You're sleeping with Ted Marshall."

Melissa laughed. "Somehow, I don't think that's jealousy I hear." She was still smiling. "You've been gone a long time. There's a new dog in town. He's a thoroughbred, but a dog is still a dog."

"And by dog you mean…"

"Just what you think. Ted's single and enjoying the life. Maybe our…enjoyment was mutual a few times."

"He had a girlfriend."

"Ali Winters? He always said that they were just roommates."

"That doesn't bother you?"

"What, that he's really only exclusive with his own dick?" She smiled again and shrugged. "He's actually pretty careful. He's got political ambitions. He likes it that everyone likes him. Plus, it's not like I'm looking for a relationship. He's a good guy, not to mention hot. And he always springs for dinner first."

"On the night of the auction, did you see anyone else with him?"

Melissa gave him another smile. "I don't kiss and tell, Luke. You know that."

He ignored the reference to the one and only night the two of them had shared, back when they'd been nineteen and drunk as skunks on the pier behind the Ferris wheel. "Did you even see the money?" he asked.

"Nope. He did put a big briefcase in the bottom drawer of his desk though. I saw that."

"He lock it?"

"The police asked the same thing. I don't remember either way."

"After," he said. "What happened after?"

"Aubrey came in, and she got *all* pissed off, asking Ted what he'd have done if someone had seen us." She rolled her eyes. "Like he's running for president or something."

"Then what happened?"

"We left separately. He insisted on that. He really does like to keep his private life private."

Which was tough shit, because "Teddy's" life, private or otherwise, was about to be blown wide open. "Thanks, Mel."

She smiled. "Was I helpful?"

"Yes."

She looked him over for a long beat, taking in his wet gear. "If you need anything else, Luke, you look me up."

He smiled at her, but he wasn't going there. He had a different woman on his mind.

Back at home, he got out of the water, carried the paddleboard up the stairs, and leaned it against the deck. He looked up at the house. Today was day two of Ali's enforced leave, thanks to Russell's taking off to Vegas, and Luke had no idea what she might be doing. Not that it mattered, of course. It didn't. Not in the slightest.

Shit. It mattered. It mattered a whole hell of a lot.

He grabbed the towel he'd left for himself on the deck. He was rubbing it over his wet head when he realized he could hear voices coming through the kitchen window. Glancing in, he saw Ali at the island cooking something that smelled amazing and had his mouth instantly watering. On the other side of the island, cozied up on one of Luke's barstools, sat Zach. Ali was listing off characteristics of Leah Sullivan, and why Zach should ask her out.

"She's funny," Ali said, "and has a great personality—"

Zach groaned. "Great personality? That's the kiss of death right there."

Ali's eyes narrowed. "What does that mean?" she asked in a tone that would have had Luke changing course pronto.

But Zach apparently wasn't versed in the *Don't Go There Department*. "You know," he said. "When you say someone has a great personality, it means that they're...*not* hot."

"Wow." Ali shook her head. "And here I thought you were better than the rest of your gender." She shrugged. "Your loss, because Leah's *totally* hot."

"Yeah? How hot?"

"Forget it, you've ruined it."

"Aw, man." Zach wasn't in a suit today. Instead he wore skinny-cut, black jeans, an equally tight-to-his-scrawny-chest black button down, and a bright pink tie that matched a few pink streaks in his dark, spiked hair.

He still looked twelve. He eyed the omelet Ali was cooking, licking his lips like he was starving.

Ali flipped it onto a plate, pushed it to Zach, and then turned to the door as Luke let himself in.

"Hey," she said. "Yours is next."

Zach stuffed a big bite into his mouth as he eyed Luke. "You don't knock, you just walk in?"

Luke looked at Ali, letting her field this one.

Ali sighed, and she flipped the next omelet. "Luke's living here too, Zach."

"Your mom didn't mention that. She just said he'd given you a place to stay."

"It's not what you think," Ali said.

"No?" Zach asked. "Because what I think is that you're too kind for your own good, and *someone*"—he glanced at Luke so as to leave no doubt who the "someone" was—"could take advantage of you."

"First of all, I'm not all that kind," Ali corrected. "And second, *Luke* is the kind one, letting me stay."

Not feeling particularly kind, Luke strode across the kitchen. He'd intended to shower. Instead, he parked himself on a barstool, sprawling his long legs out, making himself at home in his own place.

Ali gave him a look that he wasn't quite sure how to interpret. Annoyance, definitely. Maybe even some affection too.

He could match her on both. But he found himself oddly out-of-sorts at the vibe between her and Zach—which made no fucking sense. They were obviously very fond of each other. And just as obviously, they were old friends with the same level of comfort that he and Jack and Ben had. He didn't read any sexual tension between them.

Not that it mattered. Because it didn't.

What *did* matter was Zach's ability to defend Ali, if it came to that. And Luke wasn't at all sure the kid—who, granted, seemed sharp and eager to get this right—could handle the case.

Zach was scrolling through the notes he'd made on his iPad the day before. "So is there anything else you can think of that I need to know?"

"Yes," Ali said. "I talked to Edward this morning. He gets up early because once a week he enjoys driving the seniors to the early morning buffet at a casino in Tacoma."

More like he enjoyed the early morning Texas hold 'em table, Luke thought.

"The ground-breaking ceremony for the new rec center is scheduled for next weekend," she said. "The mayor himself donated fifty grand to make up for the missing funds."

"Wow," Zach said with a low whistle, "I'd like to run the mayor's financials to see where that money came from."

"It came out of his retirement account and is supposedly legit," Ali said. "Edward had some other interesting news too. He said that Mr. Wykowski was also in Teddy's office the night of the auction. Mr. Wykowski didn't say anything, because he was hiding from Lucille and her posse, who were chasing him. Mr. Wykowski says that it's rough being eighty-two and single, because the women that go to the center outnumber the men two to one."

Zach snorted orange juice out his nose. "*Dammit.*"

"And Mr. Lyons was in the hallway too, using that bathroom," Ali said. "Because the main bathroom…um, smelled like something died in there." She flipped Luke's omelet. "And then later, Mrs. Burland ended up in the office too. Says she got lost trying to find the coat room. She needs cataract surgery, but hasn't saved up the eight grand yet, which takes her off the suspect list because she can't see past her own nose. Plus she threw out her back last week trying to keep up with Lucille and can't even carry a purse. So it's unlikely she stole anything, except possibly someone's coat that she mistook for hers."

"None of that came out in the police report," Luke said.

Ali shrugged. "Probably no one thought to ask your grandpa."

"I spent summers here," Luke said with a shake of his head. "And I'm still blown away at how he knows everyone else's business."

"Oh, he knows yours too," Ali said.

This gave him pause. "What did he say about me?"

"That I shouldn't trust the man who once blew up all the Town Hall toilets."

"Hey, I was just a kid," Luke said, in his defense, over Zach's choked laugh. "And anyway, that was all Jack and Ben's doing. Mostly Ben's to be honest. He was good at blowing shit up."

Ali smiled. "He said you'd say that."

Luke shook his head. "What else?" he asked, as she transferred the omelet from pan to plate and handed it to him. He dug in, and flavor exploded in his mouth in a harmony of deliciousness. He hadn't realized how starved he was, and he closed his eyes to enjoy it. When he opened them again, Ali was looking at him.

"You know something else?" she asked.

"No." He stuffed another big bite in his mouth rather than tell her that, yes, he knew something else—her ex was a serious dick.

"If you know something that will help," Zach said, "you need to tell us."

Luke set down his fork and gave Zach a look that had the lawyer pulling back just a little bit. Brave but not stupid. Good to know. "The only thing I've got is what we all already know—there are more women in Marshall's life. I think whoever else was in his office the night of the auction is the key to this whole thing."

"We'll find her," Zach said, sounding far more sure of himself than Luke would have thought possible, considering the guy looked like he'd walked off an '80s punk rock poster. "Ali, did you see anything interesting in his office the next day?"

"No. I was only there for a minute both times. The first visit, I just grabbed the pencil pot. The second time, I..." She broke off and nibbled on her lower lip.

"What?" Zach pressed.

"I guess I was still pissed about what I'd heard the night before and—"

"Tell me again," Zach said, "what you heard."

She shuddered. "Teddy in the throes."

Zach grimaced. "Other than that."

Luke took in Ali's expression. She wasn't sad, she was pissed, and he was glad. Marshall didn't deserve a piece of her heart.

Neither do you...

"Anyway," Ali said. "I set his things on his desk."

"I read the police report, Ali, that's not all you did," Zach said.

She winced. "So I left him a sticky note telling him what he could do with his text breakup, where to stick it, how to stick it…that sort of thing. Big deal."

Luke already knew this, but he felt the pride fill his chest again. "Nicely done, by the way."

She shifted, looking embarrassed. "I threatened him. The police frown on that."

"You could plead temporary insanity," Luke said, wanting to lighten the mood.

Ali rolled her eyes, but looked far less vulnerable, and Luke nearly smiled because damn, she didn't need her ceramic lion or the owl. She had guts and brains in spades.

It'd been a long time since he'd ached to be with a woman for more than what they could give each other in bed. This was the problem with Ali, she made him ache. There was just something about her that drew him in, leaving him defenseless against her.

Not good.

"How bad is that note?" Ali asked Zach. "Bad? Or *bad* bad?"

"Bad isn't the right word," Zach said. "Let's go with…a little difficult."

She just looked at him. "You don't want me to freak out about writing that I was going to do something to him, and then something happened."

"I don't want you to worry," Zach said, and once again Luke felt his reluctant respect for the guy increase.

Zach glanced at the time and rose. "Gotta get to work." He turned to Luke. "If you learn anything else…" He pushed his business card toward him. "I'm all ears." He gave Ali a kiss on the cheek and sent Luke a long, unmistakable look that said *I'm watching you* as he moved to the door. "Stay in touch, Al."

Luke walked him outside.

At the end of the driveway, Zach faced him, eyes cool, smile gone. "Not that I have to defend myself to you, but I can handle whatever happens here."

"You sure?" Luke asked. "Because you need to be fucking *sure*. She trusts you."

"She *should* trust me. I've known her since grade school. And you've known her for what, five minutes?"

Luke had to give the puppy props. He had sharp teeth.

"Are you sleeping with her?" Zach asked.

"None of your business."

"She's my friend and my client. She's very much my business. And she's watching us right now, so try to look like you don't necessarily plan on kicking my ass."

Luke turned and glanced at the window, indeed finding Ali watching them. He lifted a hand in greeting.

She narrowed her eyes.

Zach smiled and waved at her, then turned his back to the house to slide Luke a measuring look. "Don't even think about climbing into her bed," he said. "She's way too vulnerable for the likes of you right now."

Having been told the same thing by Jack, Edward, and his own conscience, Luke felt himself getting pissed off. "I'll worry about me. You worry about the case."

"Fine. But I'll be watching you," Zach said.

"Yeah? Right back at ya."

Chapter 13

♥

Luke waited until Zach drove off before turning to the house.

Ali was gone from the window.

The place stood as it always had, a little bit quirky, a lot worn, but steady as his grandma had been.

His home away from home for just about all his life.

His grandma had worked hard for many years, but in that last year, she'd finally retired. Her hobby had been painting, and she'd used the garage as a studio. Luke had loved it there, the scents of the oil paint and his grandma's candles, the huge beanbag chair that had been his to crawl into and watch her work. The cookies she'd always had out…

Shaking his head at the memories, he punched in the code for the garage door and watched it open, blinking in surprise.

Because there was Ali, paintbrush in hand.

Clearly seeing something in his expression, she put

down the brush. There was a table between them, a work table. She made no move to go around it, leaving him to assume she needed the barrier.

He got that. He needed a barrier from her too. He just didn't know what the hell kind of barrier could possibly stand between her and his damn heart, since she was making dust of the walls he'd had in place by just breathing. It was her sweet courage, and the capacity she had for caring about everyone and everything. It was the way she kissed him, as if she was desperately clinging to the fleeting pleasure before it vanished. It was the fierceness with which she protected his privacy. It was her smile.

It was everything about her.

"It's going to be okay, you know," she said.

"Your life, you mean?" he asked.

"And yours."

For months, he'd been operating deep in negativity and bad shit. There'd been no light at the end of the tunnel. His glass was half empty. No silver lining...

Not Ali. Her world had fallen apart too, and yet she looked at things completely differently. It wasn't that she wore rose-colored glasses. No one who'd grown up as tough and fast as she had *could* wear rose-colored glasses. She simply chose *not* to live in the dark.

He admired and respected the hell out of that. He looked at the table and saw that she'd been painting a small ceramic bowl shaped like a canoe.

"I hope you don't mind," she said, gesturing to the table and her work. "We need a new key bowl." Since she'd chucked the other one at his head...He smiled at the memory.

"My grandma painted in here too." He looked to the

other side of the garage, where Fay's shelves still stood. He could almost see her, standing in front of her easel, the sun slanting in the window, casting her in a glow as she created magic out of a blank canvas. "I used to sit at her feet and watch." He pointed to the sheet-covered beanbag chair. "I even gave it a shot myself when she bugged me about it."

"Were you any good?"

"Not even a little bit." He lifted a shoulder, surprised to feel warm at the memories, not regretful.

She came around the table. "So you lived here with her?"

"During the summers," he said. "All my life, until she died."

Her smile faded. "I'm sorry."

"Yeah, me too." He stared at the garage wall. "She shouldn't have died like she did."

She touched his arm. "What happened?"

He blew out a breath and ran a hand over the back of his neck. "Mornings weren't her thing. We all knew it. Sara used to joke that in order to wake her up, we ought to just stand in the doorway and throw a two-by-four at her and then run like hell."

She smiled. "My mom's like that."

"I learned young to leave her alone until she'd had her caffeine. Then the summer of my sophomore year in college, I was here working for a lumber company, and one day I got her up too early. Jesus, she lit into me and we got into a big, old fight." He felt that familiar clutch of guilt. "I knew she needed me to move some boxes and furniture around for her, but I was a total dick about it. I left early for work and didn't come home for my lunch break like we'd planned. After work, I went out on the water, and after that, hit a bar with the guys. I didn't come back here until late." He paused. "I found her on the bathroom floor. Stroke."

"Oh, no," Ali said softly, voice thick with pain for him. "Oh, Luke, how awful."

He'd never forget the horror and gut-wrenching fear that had taken over his body at the sight of her. He'd dropped to his knees and tried to find a pulse, but she'd been cold and long gone. "It'd happened hours before. She probably lay there wondering where the hell I was and why I didn't help her."

She touched him, ran a hand down his back, saying nothing for a long moment. "How long until you were able to come back to the house?" she asked.

"Ten years."

She went still, clearly doing the math. "This is your first time back?"

"Yeah." He wished like hell that he could see his grandma standing there painting, smiling, full of life, just one more time. She'd always been so forgiving. So willing to love him, no matter what. And there'd been plenty to forgive, most notably the incident two years prior to her death, when he'd screwed up in a different way.

By failing Sara.

He'd failed them both, and Luke would give just about anything to be able to tell his grandma how sorry he was, that he never should have left her like he had. That he'd regretted it every single day since. That she was the reason he tried so damn hard these days to make sure he had nothing else to regret. "It was a long time ago," he said.

"You and I both know that doesn't matter," she said quietly.

He stared down into her face, which was creased into an expression of honest concern. In the here and now, she had plenty to be worried about. Instead, she was worried about him and something he'd gone through ten years ago. "Yeah. I'm okay."

"You're probably ready to get back to San Francisco by now," she said softly.

"Actually," he said, "I love it here. I always have. But I need to get back. My commander's been calling."

She nodded, accepting, which wasn't the same thing as being indifferent to his imminent departure, because she was the least indifferent person he'd ever met. She felt things to the bone. In fact, she had a capacity to feel things that he'd never had.

Or maybe it'd been so long he'd just forgotten how.

She could change that. At the thought, his chest tightened and burned with a need that wasn't just physical, though there was that too. He wanted to let her warmth wash over him, wanted to feel things like she did.

Just for a moment, a single moment.

Or maybe two...

Hitting the touch pad on the wall to shut the garage door, he stepped close to her, sliding his hands up her bare arms to cup her face.

She met him halfway, winding her arms around his neck, her sweet kiss stealing the very air from his lungs. When her tongue touched his, it sent a bolt of hunger through him so strong he wasn't sure he'd survive it. Pulling her up against himself, he enjoyed the feel of her, including the way her heart pounded hard into his.

When they broke apart, she stared up at him, breathing unsteadily. He touched her jaw, and she took his hand, wordlessly turning, tugging him with her. Into the house. Through the kitchen. Into her bedroom.

The walls were sky blue with sheer white drapes blowing gently in the breeze, beyond which lay a view of the water.

Home…

But by far, the more heart-stopping view was right in front of him. "Ali," he said, his voice low and gruff. He wanted this. Christ, he wanted this. But…

She shut the bedroom door, leaning back against it to smile at him. "You look like you're facing some sort of forbidden fruit."

Truer than she could have imagined. He knew damn well that being with a man meant something to her. Lots of things meant something to her. He admired that about her—greatly—especially since he wasn't feeling much for anyone or anything these days.

She could change that, a small voice inside him said, *if you let her*. He opened his mouth with no idea what he was going to say, but she pushed off the door and came close, pressing a finger against his lips. "Shh a minute," she whispered. "I just want to see something…"

And then she went up on tiptoes and kissed him again.

He heard himself groan, and then his arms tightened around her as he opened his mouth wider on hers, willing to let her lead, to let her take this wherever she wanted to go.

She kissed him back, deeper, and his heart started to pound because he knew *exactly* where she wanted this to go.

Same place he did. Still, he shouldn't let it happen. He shouldn't...

And yet he couldn't bring himself to pull away. Just one more taste, he thought. One more touch. His hands skimmed up her back, bared by her halter dress, and she arched into him seeking more.

God. God, she was so sweet, her lips clinging to his, her fingers digging into his arms like he was her anchor. And when she moaned and rubbed up against him, he knew.

He was in trouble. Deep trouble.

He'd been fantasizing about her, just like this, melting in his arms, taking everything he gave her and wanting more still. The reality of it was even better than the fantasy. She was warm and soft and eager. *His*. A ridiculous thought that didn't stop him from taking, from slanting his mouth over hers more fully and cupping her breasts, sliding his thumbs over her pebbled nipples. He wanted her in his mouth, every part of her, and was tugging on the tie at the back of her neck toward that very goal when someone rang the doorbell.

They broke apart and stared at each other.

"Wait here," he said, and gently nudged her aside to open the bedroom door.

He took his time walking through the house so as to not open the door with a full-blown hard-on. But looking through the peephole took care of that.

Ted Marshall stood on his doorstep.

Chapter 14

Ali followed Luke through the house and then went still when he opened the front door.

Teddy stood there in a business suit that, unlike Zach's, fit him perfectly.

"What are you still doing here?" he asked her, looking just as shocked as Ali.

What was *she* doing here? "Oh no. *You* first," she said, going for polite, but not quite making it.

"I'm looking for my backup cell phone," Teddy said. "I was going to ask the new tenant if he'd found it."

"You sure you don't want to accuse me of stealing it?" Ali asked, not even in the realm of polite now.

"Did you?"

Luke slid a hand to the nape of her neck.

Right. She had no idea if Zach could defend premeditated murder. "You might want to close your eyes," she said to Luke, "so that you don't have to testify against me."

He smiled.

"Oh for crissake," Teddy grumbled. "For the last time, *you* were the only one in my office who had a motive." He pulled off his expensive reflector aviator sunglasses, the ones she'd used to think made him look so hot, and stared at her. "So what's going on here anyway? And what's wrong with you? You're all...flushed."

Extremely aware of her kiss-swollen lips and just-made-out hair, Ali stormed off to the kitchen, opened the junk drawer, and—shock—found Teddy's spare phone. Grabbing it, she slammed the drawer and brought it to the front door. "I didn't steal it, and for the millionth time, I didn't steal that money either."

"Then who did?"

"I don't know!" She tried to take a calming breath. It didn't help. "And I don't even know why you thought it would have been me."

He sighed. "You need the money. You always need money."

Low blow. It took her a minute to catch her breath. "There are more important things than money," she said. "And have you thought that maybe one of your other girl-friends might have done it?"

Guilt flashed for a single beat on his face. "Look," he said, "whatever Melissa and Aubrey have told you is—"

"Aubrey?" Ali stared at him. "You had both Melissa and Aubrey on the side? Seriously?"

Ted's face had closed up. "All I'm saying is that you've been misinformed—"

"Stop," she said, lifting a hand. "You're just reinforc-ing your ass-ness."

"Fine. I don't have to explain myself to you anyway."

His gaze flicked to Luke. "And what's going on between you two? You found a way to stay here, huh?"

This time Luke tensed, and Ali grabbed *his* hand. "Don't bother," she murmured.

Luke didn't take his eyes off Teddy, but he kept his thoughts to himself, looking *extremely* dangerous to Teddy's well-being. "You've got your phone," he said quietly. "Leave now."

"I'm going, but I want to talk to you first," he said to Ali. "Alone."

He was very brave, or very oblivious. Either way, Luke didn't budge, and Ali was choking on all the testosterone. "Oh for God's sake." She turned to Luke. "It's okay."

When he still didn't budge, she stepped outside and shut the front door. "You have two seconds," she said to Teddy.

Teddy eyed the front door warily. "My attorney advised me to stay away," he said. "But you really embarrassed me, Ali. At work. In town. I thought we were okay, that we had a good run and then it was over, no hard feelings. So I have to know—why did you do it? You had to know you wouldn't get away with it."

"I *didn't* do it—"

"I'm trying to work my way up to council and then to mayor," he said, "and you made everyone doubt and mistrust my judgment."

"*Me?* You were sleeping with half the town! You made yourself look bad."

"Ali, you broke into my office and stole back a stupid ceramic pot that you'd given me. That's just ridiculously stupid. Stupid and childish."

"I didn't break in." But she flushed because he was

right, on all accounts, and she hated that. "Yes, okay, it was stupid and childish. But I was hurt. You'd walked away without so much as a look back. You didn't deserve the pencil pot."

"Forget the fucking pot!" he yelled, and then made a visible effort to relax. He even poured on a little Teddy charm. "Look, I was just trying to be nice, okay? You were cute and fun, and when you had to get out of your apartment, I wanted to help you out. So I offered to share a place."

This stunned her. "I thought we were a thing."

"Okay, yes, we had a thing. But you weren't *my* thing."

She stared at him. "You could have told me," she finally managed.

"You're right, I should have told you. I should have said that I'd made a mistake. That you weren't my type."

"And what is *that* supposed to mean?"

He sighed. "Forget it."

"Tell me."

"Fine," he said. "We're…different."

"You mean you're a cheating bastard and I'm not?"

He sighed again, the put-upon ex-boyfriend, suffering through the breakup talk. "That's not what I meant."

No, actually, she knew what he meant, she knew exactly. He'd come from money and she'd come from nothing.

"I want that money back, Ali. I mean it." And with that, he strode off the steps like he owned the world.

She'd have given just about anything to be holding the new key pot she was making so she could wing it at the back of his thick skull. In fact, she whirled around looking for something, anything, to bean him with.

"Later," Luke said, joining her on the porch after clearly having listened to the whole exchange. "I'll hold him down for you."

"When?" she demanded.

"When you don't have witnesses."

She followed his gaze to Mrs. Gibson, who lived on the other side of Luke's grandfather's house. Fifty-something, she was a local teacher, soaking up the spectacle from her doorstep.

Luke waved at her.

Mrs. Gibson returned the wave and went inside.

"We'll make Facebook before the hour's up," he muttered.

Luke could feel Ali vibrating with emotions.

"I really want to hit him," she said.

"Bloodthirsty," he murmured, taking her hand, running his thumb over the pulse racing at her wrist. "I like it."

She didn't look at him, and he realized she was shaking. "Hey," he said softly, pulling her inside, turning her to face him.

She looked down, so he bent his knees to put them nose to nose. "What are you doing, letting him get in your head like that?" he asked.

"I—" She pushed him. "I don't know."

But he knew that she did know. She hated that someone believed she might have stolen that money, hated knowing that anyone thought she was a thief, even if that someone was the cheating bastard Ted Marshall.

"Forget him, Ali."

She covered her face. When she shuddered, his heart stopped.

"I'm not crying," she said through her fingers.

"Thank Christ." But his relief was cut off by the solo tear that tracked down her cheek. Drawing in a deep breath, he pulled her in close. "Ali," he murmured helplessly.

"Don't," she said, muffled against his chest.

"Forget it. I'm going to be nice to you for at least a second. You'll have to just stand there and bear it."

"No, I mean I'm all sweaty now. I think it's the fury."

Her body was overheated, her skin damp. He didn't care. He lifted her chin and looked her over.

"I'm a wreck," she said, trying to turn away. "A complete wreck. And a fraud."

"Why, did you take the money?"

"No!" She took in the teasing in his expression and squeezed her eyes shut. "I wanted to be someone different here," she said, and broke his heart. "Not an invisible no-body florist's assistant from White Center."

"Do not listen to him," he said, maybe a little harshly, but he wanted her to hear him. Really hear him. "You're not a nobody. And you *are* a florist, a great one. You also teach ceramics. Hell, Ali, half of your students are in love with you. You care enough to be nice to nosy, old men. You helped a stranger avoid the rest of the world, even when he was a total ass. You'd give that stranger the last of your paycheck simply because you thought it was the right thing to do."

"It *was* the right thing to do," she said. "And you weren't a *total* ass."

"You'd probably give away your heart and soul if it was needed," he said. "But that would be a shame, because you're one-hundred-percent heart and soul. You're the real deal, Ali, the way the rest of us have forgotten how to be."

"I have…faults."

"Yeah," he agreed, "but they're not the ones Marshall said." He ticked them off on his fingers. "You wear your emotions on your sleeve, and you care. Hell, most people would say those are *good* things."

She snorted, and he smiled, relieved. "But one thing you're not, Ali, is invisible. You're standing right here, strong and beautiful—"

"No—"

"*Beautiful*," he repeated fiercely, stunned to find that he meant it from a very personal standpoint. He stared at her, impacted on a visceral, physical, and mental level by her. "So beautiful," he whispered, and then he kissed her.

Ali didn't think anyone had ever told her she was beautiful before. It should've felt like a cheesy line, but it didn't. Mostly because though she knew he meant it, she also knew he didn't *want* to find her beautiful.

In some twisted way, it was that reluctance that made her feel better. She didn't want to feel anything for him either. She didn't want to feel anything for anyone ever again, and yet she wasn't hardwired that way. "I'm all sweaty," she said again, even as her hands fisted in his hair.

"That's okay," he said silkily, his mouth brushing her temple. "We're going to get even more so."

The words made her shiver. So did the way he pressed her up against the wall right there in the foyer.

"I thought we were a bad idea," she said.

"We are." Her halter top slid down, revealing her bare

breasts. He'd been so smooth she'd not felt him undo it. Then his fingers caught in the hem of the sundress, and he slid it up to her waist.

He sure was quick when properly motivated. "So this is what?" she asked breathlessly, already so excited she was rubbing her thighs together. "A pity fuck?"

His smile was heated and wicked as he kissed her. "That's a two-part question," he said. "Yes to the pity part, but it's not for you, it's for Marshall."

If she'd had enough air in her lungs, she would have laughed.

"Now," he said, pressing closer so there was no mistaking his intent—as if she could mistake anything about his pinning her to the wall with his hard body. "As for the fuck part…" He kissed her again, until she nearly forgot herself.

"Are you sure?" she managed to ask, staring up into his gorgeous blues. "Because you weren't sure a few minutes ago."

He rocked into her, and she felt exactly how sure he was. It tugged a moan from her, and she let her head fall back. This gave him better access and he took it. Lowering his head, he kissed her throat, her jaw. The corner of her mouth.

"What changed?" she managed to ask.

He licked her pulse point. "Watching you turn all violent when you got pissed off."

Oh, God, his tongue. "That was sexy?"

"Yeah. Big time." A big, warm, callused hand slid into the back of her panties and palmed her bare bottom. "Everything you do is sexy."

His mouth and the placement of his talented hand were

driving her crazy. *He* was driving her crazy, and she struggled to get closer to his big, tough body. "Luke?"

He didn't answer, presumably because his lips were busy moving along the curve of her jaw, her throat, her breast, teasing her nipple, which had long ago tightened for him. But they had to talk first, or at least *she* had to talk. "*Luke?*"

"Hmm."

"I haven't been intimate with Teddy in weeks. You know that, right? You heard him mention it when they were searching the house."

He lifted his head and met her gaze.

"I just wanted to make sure you really knew," she said softly. "Once we moved in together, things got…weird. After only a few weeks, he started working late, and then he got allergies and snored. He slept in a different room than me, and…" *For the love of God, Ali, zip it and let him do you.*

Pushing her hair back from her eyes, he traced a line along her jaw. "It's been a long time for me too," he said quietly. "So long I can't remember the last time." He kissed her shoulder. "I have a condom." He gestured with his chin to his wallet, which lay on the small foyer table at her hip.

She started to reach for it, but he dipped his knees and ran his tongue around her nipple and then sucked the tight bud into his hot mouth.

She moaned, and her head fell back against the wall. She arched, trying to get him to take more, and felt him smile against her damp skin as he made his way to her other breast. His fingers trailed down her quivering stomach and then slipped between her thighs. "Mmm," he said. "Hot *and* wet."

And then he dropped to his knees.

"Luke…"

Not bothering to answer, he stroked the pad of his thumb over her panties, but apparently that wasn't nearly good enough, because then he caught his fingers in the sides. "Pretty," he said, "but they have to go." Slowly dragging them down, he kissed her just beneath her belly button. And then lower, letting his teeth graze over her, his rough jaw scraping her soft skin. His lips applied pressure, and his tongue brought to mind all the wicked things he might do to her. Her knees wobbled.

"I've got you," he murmured, a big, callused hand gliding up the inside of her legs. He kissed first one inner thigh, and then the other, and then…in between.

Her hips jerked.

"Easy," he murmured, and gripped her hips tightly, holding her to the wall while he gently, but thoroughly, began to take her apart with his tongue and teeth. It was the sweetest, most exquisite torture. Dying to have him inside her, she begged, "Please," her pulse racing, her heart pounding.

But he still teased.

"*Luke…*"

"I like the way you say my name," he said, his mouth against her wet flesh.

She had her fingers in his hair, holding on as he drove her out of her mind with slow, hot laving of his tongue, leaving her trembling and beside herself. And still he took his time, until finally, God finally, he took her to the edge and nudged her over.

When she finally caught her breath and her eyes fluttered open, Luke surged to his feet, one arm around her lower back, the other just underneath her butt as he hoisted her up.

"Wrap your legs around me," he said, voice low and rough with need.

She did, wrapping her arms around him too, drawing him tightly to her.

"The condom," he said, eyes as intense and heated as his voice.

With shaky fingers, she opened his wallet and dug out the condom. "Here?" she breathed. "Now?"

"Here. Now."

His words should have felt presumptuous, pushy. Aggressive. Instead, she was more aroused than she'd ever been, making needy little whimpers as she tore at his clothes to get skin to skin.

With calm, steady ease, he took over. He undressed them both, and then, pressing her into the wall to free up his hands, rolled on the condom.

She quivered just watching him. Then his hands were back on her, sliding along the underside of her thighs, angling her hips. And then, hot, fierce, eyes on hers, he slowly thrust into her in one sure stroke, pushing to the hilt and holding there, giving her nowhere to hide.

She didn't want to hide.

For once, just for this once, she wanted to let go and revel in the delicious sensations of being wanted, cherished, needed, and not worry about what came next. Rocking into him, she tried to match his rhythm, but she was pinned and unable to move. He could move though—and did—pulling out only to push back in, his body taking hers along for the ride.

She cried out, the sound of her pleasure echoing

through the house. Her last thought before her mind shut down completely was for the neighbors—specifically, Luke's grandfather.

Please, she thought, *please let Edward's windows be closed.*

Funny, Ali thought hazily some time later from flat on her back on the foyer floor, the moments that marked the most important things in a woman's life. For her, it'd been graduating high school, moving out of White Center, learning that she was strong no matter what happened, and...

Getting busy with Luke Hanover up against the wall.

Her body was still quivering, little aftershocks of sheer pleasure, and she was pretty sure she couldn't have moved to save her life.

Beside her, Luke stirred, then came up on an elbow and looked down at her, his eyes still dark with heat. "You good?"

"I moved beyond good a few minutes ago."

He was thinking about smiling, she could tell. "How far beyond?" he asked.

"The stratosphere."

She thought maybe that would tug a smile from him, but it didn't. In fact, he looked a little stern as he helped her up, holding her steady until she found her sea legs.

He moved away, presumably to deal with the condom, but he didn't come back. She found him a few minutes later standing at the kitchen sink, hands braced on the countertop, staring out the window at the ocean.

She took a moment to soak him in, because he could still steal her breath. Wearing only his board shorts and nothing else, he was all tanned, smooth skin and lean sinew.

Paddleboarding did a body good.

Though he didn't move as she walked into the room, the muscles of his back and shoulders were tense.

"Hey," she said, "having an orgasm is supposed to relax and rejuvenate you. You don't seem relaxed or re—"

"I'm leaving. You know that right? I'm going back to my job in San Francisco. I don't know when exactly, but soon. I have to."

She drew in a deep breath. She knew all too well, which was a bitch of a problem, considering she'd promised herself not to do this again, not to follow the same patterns as her mom and sister and fall for a guy who would leave her. "I know."

"I want you to get a restraining order against Marshall so he can't come back here and bug you again."

"I don't think he will," she said. "And besides, we both know he hasn't done anything to warrant an order. Plus I'll be getting an apartment. The search has been slowed down a little by the fact that no one wants to rent to a thief, so—"

"Stay here."

"What?"

He turned to face her, gaze unfathomable. "Keep the house. You can get a roommate if you want. I don't care. I just want you to stay here."

"Luke—"

"The house suits you. My grandma would like knowing there was someone here who loved it as she did."

How was it that she wanted to both comfort him and jump him again at the same time? "Luke." She moved to him, slipping her arms around his waist, laying her cheek against his chest. "It's okay that it was just sex. I knew that going in. You don't have to feel guilty."

"It's not guilt." His arms came around her, and he pressed his cheek to the top of her head. "I just...Christ." He squeezed her. "That wasn't just sex."

Her heart squeezed, but then he took one look at her face and blew out a breath. "I don't know what the fuck to do with this, Ali. I'm leaving."

"I know."

"This can't happen again."

"I know that too." She stared up at him, a little blown away by the intensity of his words and the fierceness of his expression. Not possessive, exactly, but definitely protective. Something inside her cracked open just a little bit and let him in, which was terrifying her because he was bound to disappoint her.

They always did.

Chapter 15

Ali was up at dawn the next morning and was off and running for work, not allowing herself to let her mind wander. She couldn't *afford* to let her mind wander, or she'd get mired down in the fact that the money still hadn't been found. That she was still the only viable suspect at this point.

That she'd slept with Luke.

Okay, so there hadn't been *any* sleeping involved. Which meant that every single minute of it was imprinted on her brain—the best collection of minutes in her entire life.

She hit the flower market in Seattle for her weekly supply run. While she was there, she took an extra few minutes to drop off a bag of donuts and coffee for her mom and sister, which given the decibel of happy squeals they let out, made their day. Then she hightailed it back to Lucky Harbor to unload the week's supplies for Russell's shop.

There was a low wind howling through the quiet rooms, echoing the unsettled feeling in her gut. It was still early when she opened for business and got to work on the preordered arrangements that were due that day. Russell didn't show up to help. She knew he wouldn't show up until well after noon. And when he did, he'd be out of sorts and unhappy, as he had been from the day Paul had moved to Vegas without him.

Ever since their breakup, Russell kept talking about the shop's lack of profit, and how he wanted to close up. But Ali still believed the place had something to offer Lucky Harbor. If Russell would only give her some of the reins that she'd been begging for, she'd show him how much.

But he'd taken the business over from his sister. It wasn't a life's passion for him, and he'd not put much, if anything, into developing the business. He had a base of fairly steady customers, but hadn't shown any particular interest in catering to them. Nor had he put any effort into attracting *new* customers or cultivating more business.

Ali had all sorts of ideas, but no power. She wanted to create a website where people could order online, from the convenience of their own home or work. But Russell wasn't interested. He didn't want to be bothered with computer work, no matter that Ali had offered to do all of it.

Stymied there, she'd toyed with some changes, incorporating live plants, ceramics, and other local artists' work too, but Russell had been frustratingly resistant. Determined to show him, she spent some time now clearing space to make some displays. She worked hard at it and was proud and breathless when Russell showed up.

But he went straight to his office without a word, not even noticing that Ali had rearranged the shop.

"Hey," she said, following him back, "you okay?"

"I talked to Paul last night," he said, turning to her with a light in his eyes that she hadn't seen in a while: excitement. "He said he was sorry for being such a crazy, possessive bitch, can you believe it? A man who can admit he was wrong."

"That's sweet," she said.

"I know. And he thinks we should make up." He plugged his cell phone into the wall. "My battery died, and I'd left my charger here. I want to see if he called or texted."

"I hope he did," Ali said. "Um, about the shop…I rearranged some of the front. I wanted to show you—"

"Be a doll and get me some coffee?" Russell asked, eyes on his phone.

"Sure."

"And see if Leah has any pastries? Get a dozen assorted shipped to Paul, but make sure there are palmiers. Paul loves palmiers."

"Okay," Ali said. "And speaking of Leah, I was thinking it might be cool to offer a same-day delivery special. Flowers and pastries. We could do themed baskets, like birthdays and—"

"O-M-*G!*" Russell squealed.

"You like it?" Ali asked, relieved. "I'm so glad because—"

"No, Paul texted! He bought me a ticket to Vegas for next weekend!"

"But…" Ali's mind whirled for a reason to not close

the shop again. "You'll miss the big ground-breaking ceremony for the new rec center."

"Let's see…" Russell held out both hands, miming weighing something between them. "Getting laid… watching a bunch of pretentious town council members slap themselves on the back and pretend to shovel some dirt around…" He grinned and rose to his feet and swept Ali off hers and kissed her soundly. "Long weekend alert ahead, Doll! *Woot!*"

Woot.

Later that afternoon, after a long day on her feet, Ali was sitting on the back-office work counter. Leah had come over with the leftover custard puffs for the day, and the two of them were inhaling them like they were going out of style. A daily tradition.

"Can't believe how busy we were today," Ali said. Their afternoon had been wonderfully successful for a change.

"It's you," Leah said, also on the counter, mouth full.

"Yeah?" she asked. "You think it's the way I rearranged the shop floor and displayed ceramics as well?"

"No. Well, yes. But you know the police are getting really close to an arrest, so I also think people are coming in to appease their curiosity. They want to see if you're looking guilty. Or wearing twenty-dollar bills."

Ali blew out a breath and eyed the last puff. After what Leah had said, reminding her how close she was to jail, she suddenly needed that last puff more than air.

"Go ahead, have it," Leah said. "Probably you need the strength to keep boinking Luke."

Ali, who'd just taken an unfortunately big sip of tea, choked.

Leah had to hop off the counter and pat her on the back. "You don't blink at the idea of wearing twenty-dollar bills," she said, "but you nearly asphyxiate yourself on the thought of boinking Luke?"

"Stop saying that!"

"Which part?" Leah asked innocently. "The wearing twenty-dollar bills, or the boinking Luke?"

"*You know what part!*"

Leah smiled. "The boinking then. Probably I should have mentioned that my custard puffs are aphrodisiacs. So really, it's not your fault."

Ali grimaced. "That's not what we did. *Boinking.*" She paused. "Not exactly."

Leah's auburn hair was piled on top of her head, tendrils slipping free to frame her face and her startling green eyes. She looked at Ali for a long moment before her smile slowly faded. "Uh-oh."

"No." Ali shook her head. "No uh-oh."

"Oh there's definitely an uh-oh," Leah said. "If you can't joke around about the boinking, then there's a *huge* uh-oh."

"And why is that?"

"Because that means it's not just boinking."

"Okay, you have *got* to stop using that word," Ali said.

"I mean who could blame you," Leah mused. "Luke's hot as hell. But…"

When Leah trailed off, Ali looked at her. "But what?"

"He's…"

Ali's stomach tightened uncomfortably. Most likely that was not panic, but the four custard puffs she'd just consumed. "Too good for me?"

"What? No." Leah leaned in and gripped her hand

hard. "*Hell*, no. If anything *you're* too good for every man on the planet. It's just that Luke's not exactly diamonds and heartstrings, you know? And you are."

"No, I'm not." Diamonds and heartstrings implied being a keeper, and she wasn't sure she was cut out for that. But Leah gave her a long look, and Ali sighed. "Okay, so I dream of that *eventually*, but—"

"No buts," Leah said firmly. "Look, Luke is tough and hard and badass, and everything else that makes up the fantasy, you know? But you need the reality, Ali. You deserve the reality."

On Monday, Ali was behind the counter putting together a happy birthday bouquet of roses for a customer when Aubrey walked into the flower shop wearing a perfect dress, perfect high-heeled sandals, and perfect, smooth, straight blonde hair.

Ali hadn't seen her since Teddy had dropped his little I'm-also-doing-Aubrey bomb, and frankly, she could have gone a lot longer without seeing her. Like, say, forever. Instead she tightened her grip on the roses and accidentally stuck herself with a thorn. "Ouch!" She put pressure on the wound with a napkin and glared at Aubrey.

"Don't look at me like that," Aubrey said. She held out a brown bag. "Here."

"What's that?"

Aubrey sighed. "Teddy told me he told you. So I guess it's an *I'm sorry* present."

Ali came around the counter and peered into the bag. It was a tube of hair anti-frizz.

"It's the stuff I use." Aubrey ran a hand over her hair.

"It costs nearly a million dollars, but I figured I owed you."

"Since you slept with Teddy, you mean."

Aubrey winced. "Okay, yes. Yes, I slept with him. But in all fairness, he really did tell me that you and he weren't a thing. I'd never have slept with him otherwise. I can promise you that."

"No?"

"Hell, no," Aubrey said, looking pissed off. "I actually thought I had a shot with him. With his heart, I mean." Disgusted, she leaned on the counter. "He was always so sweet and kind and warm and funny. And charming! I mean, I really thought…" She sighed and shook her head. "Look, for what it's worth, I asked about you. He said he was moving out. But then after the auction, everything came out about you, about Melissa, and I felt so stupid. I really thought I'd been his one and only. But I wasn't even his number *two* and only," she said tightly.

Ali set down the napkin and studied Aubrey more carefully. "So you didn't know about Melissa either?"

"No. When I found out, I dumped him. I even threw his phone at him. Broke it too." She winced. "Apparently I have a temper."

"Enough to steal the money?" Ali asked hopefully and already knowing the answer. Aubrey might be too pretty, but she wasn't a thief.

"No. I didn't steal the money." Aubrey's eyes narrowed. "*Hell* no."

"Just checking."

"And for what it's worth," Aubrey said, "I don't think you did either. Or Melissa."

"So who does that leave?"

Aubrey shrugged. "Half the town?"

Yeah. Great.

"So we're still…friends?" Aubrey asked.

"We weren't ever really friends," Ali admitted. "I'm too jealous of your hair."

Aubrey pointed to the anti-frizz. "No longer a problem."

After Aubrey left, Ali went into the bathroom and flipped on the light. *Eek.* She read the directions and squeezed out a dime-sized dollop, and like magic, the frizz vanished. It didn't end up quite as smooth and shiny as Aubrey's, but Ali stared, entranced by her own hair. *Nice.* "Best breakup ever," she announced to her reflection. "Lost a man. Gained a maybe friend." And the best hair product she'd ever had.

She locked up the shop and called Zach, filling him in about Aubrey.

"I just talked to Luke," he said. "He ran a financial search on everyone involved."

"Can he do that?"

"No," Zach said. "But you tell him that, because he's one bound and determined man to save your cute hide. Anyway, no one's made any suspicious deposits, including Aubrey."

"Wait." Ali shook her head. "You and Luke are working together?"

"Only for you, babe."

Ali drove to the beach house on autopilot. Hungry, she headed into the kitchen and went straight to the refrigerator.

"Stop," Luke said. "Seriously, you've got to stop."

At the low, authoritative voice, Ali automatically went still before realizing he not only wasn't in the kitchen, he also wasn't talking to her. She went to the window and found him on the deck with Edward.

"You can't bribe me with food," Luke said to his grandfather.

"Everyone can be bribed with food." Edward lifted the foil on the plate he held.

"Pastries," Luke said reverently.

Ali found herself wanting to smile. Luke had been busy, either holed up on his computer or working outside replacing the wood siding that had rotted out over the past few years. During these small renovation projects, Ali had found that she could stare at him in a tool belt for just about as long as she could stare at him in his swim trunks. She'd wondered if he was avoiding her to be alone or because he didn't want to be tempted by her.

She already missed him. Not that it mattered.

"Not just *any* pastries," Edward said, wafting the plate beneath Luke's nose. "*Leah's* cream puffs."

Luke inhaled deeply. "There's brushed sugar on top of the whipped-cream puffs."

"Uh-huh, and they're loaded with butter too. They'll corrode your arteries, but you'll die happy."

"Living's overrated," Luke said, and took one. "You know you haven't spoken directly to me in years."

"*You* haven't spoken to *me* in years."

"Two-way street," Luke said, mouth full, but still managing to sound unimpressed. "We going to talk about it?"

Edward popped a pastry into his mouth.

Luke nodded. "So we're going to keep ignoring it then. Sticking with something we're good at."

Ali thought about what it'd be like to go years without speaking to her mom or Harper and felt her chest tighten. It would hurt, badly. She imagined that's what she heard barely masked in Luke's voice now.

Hurt.

Wanting to help, she moved to the back door, if for no other reason than to alert them of her presence, but then Edward spoke again.

"Sara says you're doing good," Edward said.

Ali hesitated because they were almost actually talking, and if she butted in now, they'd stop.

"You didn't bring these pastries over here to tell me that you know I'm good," Luke said.

"Okay, fine. I brought them so that you'd think about continuing to help Ali."

Luke stared at him. "Let me give you some advice," he finally said, "stick to what you do best, which is butting out of the stuff that matters."

Ali sucked in a breath. *Walk away, Ali. Just leave them to this.* But she couldn't. She ached for them and wanted to somehow fix it. Again she reached for the door, but Luke sighed, his voice softer when he spoke again. "And I'm going to keep helping Ali. Jesus. You think I wouldn't? But I'm leaving soon, you know that."

"When?"

"If my commander had his way, I'd already be gone."

"Then you need to hurry up," Edward said. "Figure this shit out now. You getting anywhere?"

"Yes, but too slowly," Luke said, sounding frustrated. "This town, for all the rumors, likes its secrets."

"Positive thinking, boy-o," Edward said. "It's all about positive thinking."

"Yeah? Since when?"

"Things change," Edward said, so quietly that Ali almost missed it. "People change. It's never too late to get to the bottom of all the secrets."

"You sound like a fortune cookie," Luke said.

"This isn't a game, Luke. This is every bit as important as any of your big, fancy city cases."

"Hell, I know that. How could you think I don't know that?"

"Because you're taking your sweet-ass time getting to the bottom of it. You're the hotshot. Make it look like Mr. Fancy Town Clerk *gave* her that money."

There was a stunned beat of silence.

"She didn't steal the money," Luke finally said.

Ali didn't know which shocked her more, the fact that Edward thought she'd stolen the money…or that Edward would suggest that Luke frame Teddy.

"Okay," Edward said, "of course not." He paused. "But seriously, if you go with the angle that Marshall *gave* it to her—"

"How about the angle that she's *innocent*," Luke said.

"Well, sure, but that's going to be a challenge, isn't it? I mean she was caught red-handed with that money band in the pot."

"She was framed."

Ali couldn't breathe. She simply couldn't drag air into her chest. She brought her hand up and pressed it against her rib cage but it didn't help.

"You think she was framed," Edward said.

"Yes," Luke said.

"You think she's innocent."

"Yes."

Edward's voice filled with relief. "Good. Then you'll help her. Even after you leave, you won't be able to stop yourself. It's what you do."

"You haven't read the papers lately, I take it," Luke said dryly.

"It's what you do," Edward repeated firmly. "Stop reading your own press. And also, Eddie Kitzsky needs your help. He thinks his guys are stealing from the till at the bowling alley."

"So why doesn't he fire them?"

"Because they're his nephews, and his wife'll kick his ass. He wants you to catch them at it and then kick their asses for him so he can stay married."

Luke bit into yet another pastry and let out a heartfelt moan—a sound that did something unspeakable to Ali's good parts.

"So good," Luke said, licking sugar off his lower lip. "Pastries should always be for dinner."

"Might want to slow down a little," Edward said. "That's your fifth or sixth one."

"So?"

"I used to be able to eat like that," Edward said wistfully. "The night of the auction I ate a ton, and then sat on the pot whole next day because of it."

Luke went still. "You were at the auction?"

"Everyone was at the auction. I drove the seniors, who were like a bunch of drunken sailors on a four-day leave. I'm telling you, you get old and suddenly you can't hold your liquor anymore. Or your bladder."

"You were at the auction," Luke repeated.

"Just said so, didn't I?"

"There's been some problem with the surveillance

cameras on the building," Luke said. "Apparently they've been down for several weeks, but it's not in the budget to fix until next quarter. You see anyone come out with a big bag?"

"Like a purse?" Edward asked. "Only every woman in the place."

"No, this would've been bigger than a regular evening bag," Luke said. "Something the size of a large briefcase or duffle bag."

"I see where you're going with this," Edward said, "but I wasn't looking. I was playing Angry Birds on my cell phone while the crowd dispersed. What about the gas station across the street from Town Hall? Maybe their cameras caught some action."

"I'll check with Sawyer. Thanks."

"I gotta go take my pill." Edward started to walk away and then stopped. "As for you, get to it already. And by get to it, I don't mean *get to it*. Not with Ali. She's too sweet for you."

Luke frowned. "Why do people keep telling me that?"

"Because it's true." Edward walked away, around the side of the house and out of sight.

Ali had to hustle to look busy. Ears burning, she began making breakfast for dinner.

Don't get to it…

Too late, she could have told Edward. And anyway, sleeping with Luke—again—was the *last* thing on her mind.

Except it wasn't. Not even close. Right now, it was the *only* thing on her mind. He might have honed his instincts by being a detective on the hard, tough streets, but he knew how to apply them to making love. He could read her body and know what she needed before *she* knew. He loved to touch. He loved to kiss, loved to taste.

He was magic.

But that was beside the point. The point was her life was out of control.

And Luke's life? Also out of control.

Around her, the house was quiet. Too quiet. Had Luke left too? Gone out on the water on his paddle-board? Begun another renovation project? Gone around the front to come in and then gone to bed? If she'd eaten an entire plate of pastries for dinner, she'd need to go to sleep too.

She turned back to the stove. When the phone rang a minute later, she jumped, and then answered breathlessly.

"I'm looking for Luke Hanover," a cool female voice said.

Another reporter. "*How are you people getting this number?*"

"This is Angelina Montclair from the *Chronicle*. Tell him I'll give him a fair interview, facts only. Tell him—"

Ali hung up.

The phone immediately rang again, and she snatched it up, getting angry. "Stop calling here or I'll—"

"He *needs* to give this interview," the reporter said, tone firm. "If he doesn't, his career's going to be in the toilet. If he wants to save it, he needs to—"

Ali hung up again, and then on second thought, pulled the phone from the wall. And even though she'd been expecting Luke to walk in any minute, she still nearly leapt out of her skin when he came up behind her. He crowded her so that she could feel the heat of him at her back. Her eyes drifted shut to better savor the experience.

"Protecting my honor?" he asked, voice low enough that she couldn't gauge his mood.

"Yes," she said breathlessly. "And it's turning into a full-time job."

"Except for when you're eavesdropping," he said.

Well, crap. She turned to face him and winced. "Okay, yes, I was eavesdropping. Some people turn to alcohol or chocolate. I eavesdrop." Her face was heated. "It used to be the only way I could learn stuff from my mom, not that *that's* an excuse. I'm sorry."

"Don't be," he said quietly, something in his voice making her chest tighten. "You don't have to eavesdrop with me, Ali. I'll tell you whatever you want to know—always."

She searched his gaze for a clue to his thoughts, but got nothing. "I wanted to tell you I was there, but you two were talking, and I didn't want to interrupt. Are you going to help Mr. Kitzsky?"

"Yeah. His nephews are idiots, but not completely moronic. They know where their bread's buttered. I'll clunk their heads together, and that'll be it." He looked over her shoulder into the pan. "Smells great."

What smelled great was him. It was all she could do not to turn her head and bury her face in the crook of his neck and inhale him.

"I'm guessing that omelets are your specialty," he said, sounding a little amused. She hoped.

"Yep." She flipped the omelet, but then had to admit the truth. "Actually...omelets are the *only* thing I can cook."

He tipped back his head and laughed, and the sight was so innately sexy that he took her breath. "Do you really think the gas station might have footage of the thief walking out of Town Hall with the money?" she asked.

He stole a slice of cheese and popped it in his mouth. "So you did hear everything."

"Including the part where your grandpa thought I stole the money? Yeah." She tried to sound neutral, but was pretty sure she failed.

Luke let out a breath and reached around her to turn off the burners. "If you were listening, then you heard exactly how much he cares about you."

She didn't say anything to that. She couldn't. There'd been a lot of people in her life who'd claimed to care about her. It didn't always mean much. "He tried to bribe you with pastries to help me."

"I can't be bribed." He met her gaze. "You know I never do anything I don't want to do."

Her heart gave a little treacherous leap. He was in board shorts again, as sky blue as his eyes, with a drawstring that was loose. One little tug, she thought. His muscles were taut, his skin damp. He'd been paddleboarding.

She had no idea why the sight of him, a little wet and a lot hot, made her both of those things as well. "I don't either…" she whispered, "do things I don't want to do."

"Liar." He stroked a finger along her cheekbone and then tucked a wayward strand of hair behind her ear, lingering at the sensitive skin there.

She shivered, and his eyes heated. "You're a pleaser," he said.

"Was," she corrected. "*Was* a people pleaser. No more. I've turned over a new leaf. I only please myself now."

A very small smile curved his mouth, and he lowered

his head so that they shared their next breath. "There's an image," he murmured. "You pleasing yourself."

She let out a low, nervous laugh, and he bent to nip her lower lip.

"I'd want to watch," he said.

Oh, Lord. "I think we're getting off the subject here," she managed.

Eyes on hers, he slowly ran his hands up her arms and then back to grip her hips. Okay, the hell with getting off subject, she thought, as his mouth brushed hers with just the lightest pressure. She heard a moan, *hers*, and at the sound, Luke got more serious about the kiss, taking it deep and hot until she swayed toward him.

A long, delicious moment later, he pulled back a fraction and looked down at her. She realized her fingers were curled into his biceps and that she was actually trying to tug him closer. But he wrapped his fingers around her wrists and pulled her hands away, taking them down to her sides. "We said we weren't going to do this," he said.

Aroused from head to toe, she nodded. "Right." And then shook her head. "Why is that again? Is it because the first time was so awful, or because people keep telling you not to sleep with me?"

"If I can't be bribed, I sure as hell don't give a shit what people think." His voice was low and incredibly sexy, and he tightened his grip on her wrists, still restraining her from touching him.

Which was suddenly all she wanted to do.

"As for it being awful," he said, "we both know it was the polar opposite of awful."

"So…?"

"So we said we weren't going there," he repeated, and

she wasn't sure if it was disappointment or relief when he let her go and turned away.

"Actually," she said to his back. His bare back. Tanned. Sleek. Ripped with strength. "*You* said that we weren't going to go there. Because even though you're leaving and it was so awful, I still want to. Go there, that is."

With a half laugh, half groan, he faced her again. "Ali. We can't."

"I know." His board shorts were low, revealing gorgeous abs, cut obliques, and a most impressive erection. At the direction of her gaze, he let out another tortured-sounding laugh and then walked out of the kitchen, vanishing into the depths of the house.

A few seconds later, she heard a shower go on.

It was several minutes before she could breathe or swallow. Still shaky, she divided the omelet, leaving half on a plate for him.

She ate, listening to the water run, noting that he stayed in there a *long* time, during which she did her best not to imagine what he was doing.

Or how she'd rather be doing it for him.

Chapter 16

The next day on her lunch break at the flower shop, Ali called her mom to check in.

"I just set up your sister with a guy from the security office at the casino," Mimi said. "He wears a gun and everything."

Harper and a guy with a gun—seemed like a nightmare waiting to happen. "Mom, maybe she wants to meet her own guys."

"Honey, we all need a little help here and there. You still seeing that very good-looking Luke?"

"We're not seeing each other, not like that," Ali said.

"Well why not?"

Yeah, Ali, why not? "Because I don't need a boyfriend," Ali said.

"Well of course you do, Ali-gator. Every woman needs a man to make her smile, to make her feel pretty, to buy her clothes…Don't you like him?"

Ali sighed. "To tell you the truth, it's a little confusing just how much I do."

"Aw, love's not really all that confusing, not when you get right down to it," Mimi said. "You either feel it or you don't."

Said the woman who'd felt it more than most.

But Ali thought about that as she arranged and delivered flowers all afternoon. Did she feel it for Luke? *Could* she feel it for Luke? And given that love had never done a damn thing for her, why would she want to?

Lucille came in to buy some flowers for Mr. Wykowski. "He's under the weather with hemorrhoids," she said. "I wanted to cheer him up with my stripper-pole jazzercise moves, but I threw out my lower back in class last week, so dancing's out."

Ali did her best not to picture Lucille in a stripper-pole class.

"Looking for new Intel," Lucille said. "You didn't confess, did you?"

"No."

"Good. Make 'em sweat."

"I didn't steal the money," Ali said, beginning to feel like a broken record and getting a little pissed about it too.

"Of course you didn't, honey. You're far too sweet. Don't pay attention to anyone who says otherwise. Keep your chin up." Lucille patted her hand, paid her for the flowers, and left.

Just before closing, Zach called to check in. "How are you doing?" he asked.

"Holding my breath," Ali said. "I think I'm about to be arrested any second. I'm not crazy about wearing stripes, Zach."

"Actually," he said, "the jumpsuits are orange in your county."

Ali laughed and then covered her mouth. "It's not funny. Oh my God, Zach. This is so not funny."

"You won't get arrested," he said.

"Because there's not enough evidence?"

"No, because your sister said if I got you out of this mess without an arrest, she'd consider sleeping with me."

Ali choked out another laugh, this one with more real amusement, and hung up. She was closing up when Russell poked his head out of his office. "Hey, cookie, thinking about cutting out Thursday for Vegas."

Ali did her best not to show her dismay. *More* days off wasn't in the plan; she needed the money. "But Thursdays are good business days."

"I know, but Paul's making the big bucks doing the stars' makeup and hair. He bought us tickets to Celine."

"I don't think Celine's still playing."

"She's a drag queen. Great reviews."

Russell was absolutely glowing—though that might have been his spray-on tan, hard to tell. Ali didn't have the heart to tell him how badly she couldn't afford this. "How about I run the shop for you while you're gone?" she asked.

His smile froze a little; it was the expression of a man who didn't know how to tell his beloved little floral designer that though he was fond of her, he didn't trust her to run his shop.

"I can do it, Russell," she said earnestly. "I want to do it so badly, to stay here in Lucky Harbor and make something of this place. Let me show you."

He inhaled dramatically, then blew it out. "I don't know. You have an awful lot going on."

"Which is why I need this." She paused. "Unless…you don't trust me with your money—"

"It's not that," he said quickly. *Too* quickly. "It's just that I'm a control freak. You know that. I can't let anyone else run the show. It's all me."

"I understand." But she didn't, not really. Nursing the invisible wounds that only a pastry of some kind could cure, she headed next door to the bakery. The closed sign was up, but the door hadn't been locked yet. The bakery was empty except for the big guy leaning negligently against the glass display counter dressed head to toe in his firefighter gear.

Jack.

"Hey," she said, surprised to see him, "where's Leah?"

"Boxing up some goodies for the fire station."

Leah came out of the back holding a pink box, looking flushed and irritated. "Next time," she said to Jack, smacking the box up against his broad chest, "don't show up at the last minute. Not everyone is moved by your pretty face and the way that uniform somehow manages to show off your ass."

Jack grinned. "And that's not even my best part."

Leah rolled her eyes.

Jack leaned on the counter, all tough, male grace as he worked at charming Leah. "I'll be sure to tell all the fires to put themselves out so that we don't piss off the best pastry chef this side of the Continental Divide."

Leah blew a stray strand of hair from her face and narrowed her eyes. "Only on *this* side of the Continental Divide?"

"In all the land," he corrected.

"Hmmm," Leah said.

Jack studied her face. "You're still mad about the other day."

"You think?"

He laughed. "Hey, you're the one who left your computer signed into your Pinterest account. I merely pinned a pic of you from last Halloween wearing an eighties leotard and leg warmers."

"Yes, with the tagline that read '"Keep On Loving You" by REO Speedwagon is the theme of my life!'" she said.

Ali snorted, but swallowed it when Leah sent her a look.

"On second thought, give me those pastries back," Leah said to Jack. "You don't deserve them."

He held the box above her head and pulled out his wallet, presumably to pay, but Leah sighed, shook her head, and pushed him out the door. "Go. Get out before I do something regrettable to you with those pastries."

"Promises, promises," Jack said, playfully tugging on a strand of her hair as he left the shop.

Ali was grinning. Leah pointed at her. "Stop that. I don't want to talk about it. He thinks he's funny."

He was. Very funny. "It was nice of you," Ali said, "not charging him."

Leah sighed. "All the firefighters have been fighting that bush fire out in Desolation Flats, and he's coming off three long, hard, hot days. They need a pick-me-up."

"Or like you said, *pretty face in a hot uniform.*"

"We're just friends, have been forever. We went to high school together."

The door opened, and the bell jingled again. Both women turned to watch Luke walk in. He was in long cargo shorts, a surf shop T-shirt, and an opened button down, the very picture of a guy on vacay—except for his watchful, alert gaze. He smiled at Leah and then gave Ali the "come here" gesture.

Ali moved toward him, brushing against him as he held the door open for her. Outside, she blinked at the bright sun. "What are you doing here?"

"Looking for you."

She wanted to ask if this was a social or business visit, but his face gave her the answer even before he spoke.

"Talked to Sawyer," he said. "He's still working on getting the surveillance video from the gas station. Apparently the owner's been on vacation, and the son—who was supposed to run the place in his absence—closed the place down and went fishing for a few days."

Ali wasn't surprised. This was, after all, Lucky Harbor. Lucky Harbor had its own sense of time, and it rarely ticked along with the real world. "In the meantime," Luke said, "I've got something else." He pulled out his cell phone and brought up a photo. "You recognize this?"

It was a close-up of the Silver Pine pencil pot she'd taken from Ted's office. It'd been confiscated as evidence when the police had come to the house. "Yes," she said, "of course."

"Do you have a signature for your pottery, something that identifies it as yours?"

"I carve my initials into each piece."

"And then you add a star to the glaze?"

"A star? No," she said, confused. "Why? What's going on?"

"Sawyer let me take a look at the evidence. Professional courtesy." He zoomed in on the little pot. "See that?" he asked. "You've got a crack on the inside."

"Well, I made that pot months ago. It's been manhandled and—"

"I'm not questioning the quality of the pot, Ali. Look closer." He zoomed in even further. "See it?"

"Yeah, there's something in the crack…" She squinted. It was a sliver of something blue with a tiny white star on it. "Huh."

"Odd, right?"

"Yeah," she said. "Very. What's a nail tip doing stuck in the crack of my ceramic pot?"

Luke stared at her. "Nail tip?"

"Looks like the tip of an acrylic fingernail to me. But I don't have fake nails, and I never use fingernail polish because it chips so easily with the work I do."

Luke shook his head, and then shocked the hell out of her by leaning in and giving her a quick, hard kiss on the mouth. "Hot *and* smart."

She felt the glow from her toes to the roots of her hair, and in some very interesting spots in between. "You think whoever this nail tip belongs to was the one who put the bill wrapper in the jar?"

"I think it's possible."

"I don't know anyone with blue fingernails with white stars," she said.

"How many people live in this town?"

She shrugged. "We've grown to five thousand-ish, I think."

"And half of them are female…"

"There's only one beauty salon in town," Ali said.

"And it's just two buildings down." She went still. "Melissa runs it."

He nodded. "But her nails are green-and-white stripes right now."

She didn't want to know how he knew that. Okay, so she did. She totally wanted to know. In fact, her immediate reaction was nearly to blurt out, "How do you know this?" but her brain reminded her that they weren't "involved." Which meant she had no business in his business, even though he had just kissed her in public outside the bakery. And given that she'd thought she and Teddy had been a thing when they obviously hadn't been, she clearly wasn't all that up on the rules of Defining Relationships 101. "Can you text me this pic?" she finally asked. "I want to send it to Zach."

"I'll send it to him."

"Okay, but I still want it." She wanted to go see Melissa herself.

Evening was coming. Dusk at the base of the Olympic Mountains was fickle as hell. Though the day had been warm, with the drop of the sun came a drop in temperature, and Ali wrapped her arms around herself.

Luke pulled off his outer shirt and held it out for her. She gratefully slid her arms into the soft cotton and hugged it close to hold in his lingering body heat.

"I'll send you the pic," Luke said quietly, "but I don't want you showing it around." He met her gaze, his own very serious. "I want you to trust me to do it."

"But—"

"Look, I know that this is *your* life, and you like to handle things yourself. I get that. I respect that," he said. "But say that you're sleeping with a bunch of women who don't know about each other. And then one of those women discovers that you're also sticking it to half the town. What do you do?"

Ali stared at him. "Sneak into his office and take back a gift?" she joked weakly. But her humor faded fast. "Or…steal the cash in his possession to make him look really bad." She sighed shakily. "Damn. I really walked right into this."

"You got in the middle of someone's plan," Luke agreed. "And that someone has fifty big ones under their mattress and is feeling pretty damn safe right now—at least until you start stirring shit up, shifting the blame from you to them." He met her gaze, his own very serious. "I'm going to let Sawyer know that the star isn't your signature and the fingernail should be run through forensics with the other evidence. And you…"

"You want me to be careful," she said softly.

He leaned in and gave her a kiss, right there on the sidewalk. "*Very* careful."

She nodded and then smiled because she could see the fierce determination in his eyes. To get to the bottom of this mess. To protect her. And seeing it, she felt her own fierce determination too. Along with something new.

Hope.

Chapter 17

Normally, Luke's favorite time of day was the opposite of what his grandma's had been—dawn's first light. But not on the days after he stayed up until two in the morning to catch the two knuckleheads closing up their uncle's bowling alley and skimming from the top of the day's take.

Luke didn't have to knock their heads together. As it turned out, they ratted on each other, and Luke was confident he scared the shit out of them and that their skimming days were over.

He finally fell gratefully into bed, but was woken only a few hours later at the ass crack of dawn by the buzz on his phone as an email came in from his commander.

Time's up, Hanover. Be here by this weekend to prepare for Monday's review.

Well, hell. Today was Wednesday, and his gut clenched at the thought of leaving now. He hadn't finished painting the house. Or repairing the beach stairs. Okay, so he hadn't even started the stairs, but he'd planned on it. And he wanted to see Ben. Luke had hoped he'd be back by now. He didn't want to leave without seeing him. Nor did he want to go before Ali's case was resolved.

Hell, he didn't want to leave. Period.

Pushing out of bed, he slipped into swim trunks and got on the water before the sun came up. He'd get to that painting, and also fix the cranky plumbing so there'd be no problems after he left, but first this. He paddleboarded through the silent water, watching the sky burst into light. The wind was at his back, and beneath him the water was so clear and deep that he could see schools of fish speed through the current, racing him.

It was the closest thing to a religion he'd ever had. The church of the wind and surf.

He paddled until his arms were quaking with exhaustion and then headed back. At the dock, he pulled his board out of the water and came to a stop.

His grandfather was sitting on the dock, feet dangling as he smoked a cigar, watching Luke through a ring of smoke.

Luke leaned the paddleboard against the dock, glanced at the stairs up to the still-dark house. "Early for you, isn't it?"

Edward shrugged.

Fine. Not up to bashing his head up against the blank wall of his grandfather's stubbornness—hell, he still had a concussion from the last time—Luke started to pick up his board and go. But he stopped, blew out a breath, and turned back. "Thanks for making me think about the surveillance tapes."

"Guess you're not an island all unto yourself then, huh?"

Luke thought of the nice, hot shower he'd intended to take and the omelet he'd been hoping to talk his pretty tenant into fixing him. Instead he voiced what had been bothering him for ten years. "You still blame me?"

Edward took a long drag on the cigar and contemplated the orange glow of ash on the tip. "That was never the question."

"No?" Luke thought of his grandma Fay's funeral and the family gathering afterward, right here on the beach in fact. Fay had been widely beloved. Everyone had come, milling around, crying, telling stories, laughing…just wanting to be together to commiserate about the loss of a woman they'd all cared about.

Luke would never forget how Edward had stood on this very dock, his back to the crowd, staring out at the water.

Silent.

Luke could remember the heaviness in his gut looking at his grandfather's proud, stiff shoulders and the tightening in his own chest when he'd walked up to him, until they were standing side by side.

All of Luke's life, Edward had been a rock. A hard-ass, tough, rugged rock, with little to no softness. Even so, Luke had never so much as seen the man lose his temper. Not once. He'd certainly never seen him brought to his knees by grief. But that's what had happened, and on that day when Luke had lifted his own head, there'd been tears streaming down Edward's face.

The sorrow had nearly choked Luke, sorrow and regret and guilt, but he'd somehow managed to speak. "It was my fault." He could remember saying those four words clearly, quickly, like ripping off a Band-Aid. Just as he could remember Edward's response.

Or lack of.

Because Edward had said nothing at all, not a single word. He'd simply given one sharp shake of his head and walked off.

Away from the house.

Away from Luke.

He'd vanished for a few days, which wasn't unusual for Edward. He went off on trips all the time. Back then, he'd still been working as a fish and game warden, so his disappearance had been considered normal. Everyone knew he and Fay had been separated for decades. Just as everyone knew that it hadn't mattered. He'd still been head over heels in love with her, and clearly devastated by her death.

A week later, Edward had resurfaced, but by then Luke had gone back to San Francisco. Sara had still been in jail, and when Luke had gone for his weekly visit with her, he'd told her everything.

Sara, always the mediator, had tried to soothe Luke by telling him to stop with the guilt. In no way did anyone, *especially* their grandpa—a man who'd hurt Fay himself—blame Luke for Fay's death. Just like no one blamed him for Sara being in prison.

But Luke knew she was wrong. Because *he* blamed himself for both of those things.

Water continued to slap up against the pylons of the dock and the shore. The air was scented with pine, wet sand, and cigar and filled with the roar of the high tide hitting the rocky shore.

Edward took another long drag on his cigar.

"You know those things'll kill you," Luke said.

"They haven't yet."

Luke waited but Edward didn't say anything else, just sat there taking in the view. And yet Luke knew damn well he wasn't here for the view. He waited some more and got nothing, so he stretched out on the dock, leaned back on his elbows, and let the morning rays dry and warm him.

"You're finally claiming the house," Edward eventually said.

Ah. *There* it was. Luke threw an arm over his eyes to block the bright sun. "You're still pissed off she left me this place," he said.

"I was never pissed off that she left you this place."

"No?"

"No. Christ," Edward grumbled, "how can someone so smart be so stupid?"

Luke assumed that was a rhetorical question and kept his silence.

"I was pissed that you let her memory go to waste," Edward said. "That you left here without looking back. That you stayed away. That you don't give a shit about anything or anyone." He paused. "That you forgot about her. Us."

Luke sat back up, fury and grief fighting for space in his throat. "No. Hell no. You don't get to say that to me."

"Just did, boy-o."

"I've forgotten exactly *nothing*," Luke said. "I live in San Francisco. My job's there."

"And what, that job's kept you busy twenty-four seven for ten years? Is that what I'm supposed to believe?"

"Yeah, actually. The job's pretty demanding, which you damn-well know."

Edward nodded. He'd worked in law enforcement. He did know. "So you're here now because why? The going got rough?"

Luke stared at him. "You think that's what I do? I just walk away when the going gets rough?"

Edward shrugged. "If the shoe fits…"

Luke pressed the heels of his hands to his eyes, but nope, nothing was going to take care of the new headache brutally kicking in behind his lids. "Fuck it," he muttered, and pushed to his feet. "Fuck this." He grabbed the T-shirt he'd left on the railing, shoved it over his head, and was striding away when he heard his grandfather mutter, "Walking away again."

Luke whipped back, his emotions far too close to the surface now. But he'd started this, he'd damn well finish it. "I didn't walk away from her. She *died*."

Edward got to his feet, a slow painful movement that had Luke feeling yet a new stab of guilt. When had his grandfather gotten old?

"You walked away from *me*," Edward said. "From the town that loved you. You closed yourself off and never looked back. *That's* walking away. *That's* what you do."

"I'm here now, aren't I?"

"For how long? Until something bad happens?"

"No, until I have to go back to my life."

Edward just shrugged and turned away, dismissing him. Luke did the same, striding up the stairs to the deck and shoving the back door open.

Ali, standing at the stove, gave a startled squeak and whirled around, wielding a wooden spoon like a weapon.

When she saw him, she sagged, a hand to her heart. "Jesus, Luke."

He headed straight through the kitchen, intending to put a lot of space between the two of them so that he didn't scare her into next week with his bad attitude.

"Made you an omelet," she said.

He shook his head. "I'm good."

"I left out anything green."

Well, shit. The scent of her cooking was making his mouth water, and right on cue, his stomach rumbled. He turned back to face her and found her eating up the sight of him.

His body, already revved up on adrenaline, reacted predictably, but he didn't move toward her. Refused to touch her when he felt so out of control. "I can't do this right now, Ali."

"Do what?"

"Be civil."

"How about eating. Can you eat?" She pointed to a kitchen chair, and Luke had no idea why, but he sat.

Face creased into an expression of adorable concentration, she flipped the big, fluffy omelet onto a plate and pushed it his way. She poured him an orange juice and then repeated the whole thing for herself. As if realizing he needed some space, she hoisted herself up on the far side of the counter, her legs folded beneath her, eating with him in companionable silence.

"Thanks," he said when he'd finished.

She nodded, hopped off the counter, and went to pass by him. With no idea what he was doing, he snagged her wrist.

She turned to him, a question in her eyes. Then with a

soft smile, she stepped between his legs and cupped his jaw. "Maybe I can help make you feel a little better," she said quietly, and bent and gave a gentle kiss to one corner of his mouth.

He closed his eyes against the assault of emotions that battered him. "Ali."

She simply kissed the other corner of his mouth.

So sweet, he thought. So warm. "Ali, I can't—"

"Be civil. I know." She straddled him. "So don't. Be you, Luke. And let me be whatever you need."

He was staggered. "I won't use you."

"I wouldn't let you," she said simply, and pulled off her tank top, leaving her in a pink bra and gauzy skirt. She unhooked her bra and let it fall away.

He closed his eyes and took a deep breath, but it didn't matter. His body didn't need to see her, she was already imprinted on his brain. "I'm leaving in a couple of days," he said. "I have to be back in San Francisco this weekend."

"Okay."

Beautiful, satiny, smooth skin, sweet curves…His hands came up and cupped her breasts, his thumbs brushing over the tips.

She sighed in pleasure, and he figured it was a good thing he was sitting down, because she knocked the wind from him, every time he was with her. "Be sure, Ali."

Pulling back, she smiled into his gaze, eyes calm and direct. No sign of the nerves that suddenly lived in his gut.

"Don't worry." Her lips were close enough to brush over his with every word. "I know what this is."

Oh, thank Christ she knew. Because he sure as hell didn't.

Very gently, she pulled his shirt up and off, humming her approval as her hands slid over his chest. Her hips rocked, the core of her pressing down on his erection. He groaned and leaned in, pressing his face to her heart.

"I also know what this isn't," she murmured, her hands sliding into his hair to hold him at her breast.

When the words sank in, he started to pull back, but she tightened her grip. "I'm going to rock your world, Detective Lieutenant Luke Hanover, and you're going to rock mine."

He didn't know how she did it. She took him outside himself and made him feel nothing but in the moment, with her. Turning his head, he ran his tongue over her nipple, loving the way she sighed in pleasure, melting against him.

"And then," she said huskily, breathing heavy, "we're going to go back to being just friends."

They *were* friends, he realized with some surprise, though he had no real clue as to how or when that had actually happened. But it had, so her words disturbed him because they weren't *just* friends.

Not even close.

If they did this again, now that they'd become even more emotionally invested in each other, it'd be far more mind blowing than just rocking each other's world. He already knew that.

Did she?

She looked into his eyes, her own warm and full of emotion, so much emotion that his throat tightened. Yeah, she knew.

And yet she was once again putting him first, ahead of her own problems.

It was going to be hell to walk away from her while wanting more and knowing he couldn't have it.

Wouldn't have it.

But he didn't have the strength to go yet. He wanted this. For right now, he wanted nothing else. They could have this, he told himself, and they could keep it just what it was. Light. Easy.

But even he recognized the lie.

She kissed his jaw. "Looking pretty serious for a man who's got a sure thing in his lap, half naked," she murmured.

She was right. He slid his hands up her slim back, urging her to lean into him so that they were chest to chest. He kissed her shoulder and then nipped the spot.

Teasing.

She was already panting a little, rocking her hips, stroking his ego—among other things. He nipped her again, a little harder, and then made a move for her nipple again, sucking her into his mouth. The hungry sound she made egged him on, and so did the way she tightened her fingers in his hair with every little tug of his mouth.

"Luke. *Please, Luke.*"

Oh yeah, he was going to please. He pushed the hem of her skirt up to her waist. "Hold this."

She reached for it reflexively, freeing up his hands. Running the pad of his finger over her tiny, sky blue cotton panties, he caught the material and scraped them aside, giving him a view that made him groan out her name. She was wet and glistening. For him.

She rocked against him again, and he tore open his board shorts, giving himself some desperately needed room.

"Oh," she whispered, all breathy, staring down at him with flattering raptness.

He reached for her, then stilled, letting out a long string of oaths. "No condom," he managed.

"I'm on the pill."

Her trust meant more to him than he could have possibly imagined. But how the hell was he supposed to keep this light when everything about it felt more like…everything?

She was still holding her skirt up like he'd asked, and it was the sexiest thing he'd ever seen. Pulling her in, he wrapped his arms around her, kissing her deeply, wondering why he even bothered to keep his distance. There was no distance with her. None.

She returned his kisses with wild abandon. "It's crazy…" she whispered against his mouth, "what you do to me."

"Tell me," he said. "Tell me what I do to you."

"You look at me like I'm the best thing you've seen all day. You make me feel…I don't know. Pretty. Sexy. And important to you. You make me *feel*, Luke."

She was all those things to him. And she made him feel too. She made him feel so fucking much that his heart was going to burst through his ribs. "Ali," he breathed, and then slanted his mouth across hers. He'd meant to just make a quick connection, but she moved with him, taking the kiss hotter, deeper, pressing her body to his.

It turned him inside out and upside down and sideways. She was all he'd thought about, dreamed about since he'd returned home, her hot, curvy bod, warm, soft skin, her wild hair flowing over his shoulders and arms. She murmured his name like he was the best thing that had happened to her all day, and he gave himself up to her, sucking on her lower lip, sliding his tongue to hers, ravishing her until they were both trembling. "Raise up," he said, voice hoarse.

She eagerly scrambled up, giving him the room he needed to slide into her. The sensation of filling her rocked his world. Hers too, if her wild breathing meant anything. Holding still, giving her a moment to adjust, was the hardest thing he'd ever done.

"I love that too," she whispered.

He kissed the frantically beating pulse at the base of her neck. "What?"

"The feel of you." She arched against him wordlessly, demanding more. "Your mouth on me."

He made his way along her jaw to just beneath her ear. "What else?"

With a shiver, she tightened her grip on his hair. He didn't care if she made him bald, as long as she didn't let go. "That you know my sweet spots."

"You're one big, sweet spot."

She bit his lower lip, and when he sucked in a breath, she laughed at him softly.

He laughed too. Laughed, while so close to her that he could feel her heart beating. It was the most amazing thing he'd ever experienced. Cupping her sweet ass in his palms, he thrust into her.

She stopped laughing and moaned his name again as her own movements brought her closer to the edge.

"God, Ali," he said, voice low and thick. He couldn't help it, watching her take her pleasure on him was turning him on so much he could hardly draw a breath. "You're so beautiful. Every time I see you, I just want to drag you down and have my way with you." Her hips were driving him insane, and he tightened his grip, trying to slow her down so he didn't lose it in a spectacularly embarrassing fashion.

But she obviously thought his control was of the superhuman variety, because she cupped his face and leaned in, letting her breasts lightly brush his chest again. She smiled at him, the hot little minx.

He smiled back.

And then they were kissing, devouring each other, lost in the moment. He knew she was close, straining for it. Wanting to watch her, wanting to push her over the edge, he stroked a thumb over the sweetest of all her sweet spots.

She tore her mouth free to pant for air, gripping his wrist to hold him there.

Stroking her both inside and out, he watched as she began to tremble.

"*Luke.*"

"I know."

"Don't stop."

"I won't."

She came, flying over the edge with his name on her lips. He tried to hold on, tried to hold back, but it was too late. He was lost. Lost, and yet somehow found. It was as simple and terrifying as that.

Chapter 18

Luke concentrated on dragging air back into his lungs. He was still in the kitchen chair, with Ali's dead weight on his chest. Maybe one day they'd actually make it to his bed.

Except they weren't going to have a "one day."

Ali hadn't moved at all. Luke stroked a hand down her back, relieved to feel her breathing. "I didn't kill you then."

"Death by orgasm," she murmured, still not moving. "Not a bad way to go." But after another long moment, she sighed, rose, and began to put herself back together, covering up that amazing body.

A damn shame.

Luke managed to find his legs and took their plates to the sink. When he turned back, he caught her staring at his ass.

She blushed. "You have some dirt on it, that's all."

"I was sitting on the dock."

"Talking to your grandfather."

"Eavesdropping again?" he asked.

"No, since I couldn't hear the words." She paused. "But the body language said plenty. Are you close to him? It's hard to tell."

"Used to be." He paused. "I thought he blamed me for my grandma's death."

"Oh Luke," she murmured. "No."

He shrugged. The truth was the truth.

"And now?" she asked.

"He says he was mad at me for leaving Lucky Harbor."

She came close, invading his space, running her hands up his chest to cup his face. He wasn't buried deep inside her body, but the gesture was just as powerful. "Her death wasn't your fault," she said.

"And the leaving?"

"Were you supposed to stay here just to make him happy?" she asked.

"There was no making him happy."

Ali's fingers massaged his skull, melting his bones. He'd just had her, and he wanted her again.

"You seem pretty fond of blaming yourself for everyone and everything," Ali said. "Wonder why that is? You don't want to be happy?"

"Happy?" Unsure how they'd gone from post-orgasmic glow to this, he shook his head. "There's not much to be happy about, and I'd have thought that you'd know that better than anyone."

Ali cocked her head and studied him with what he was certain was more than a dash of pity. "You think I should be unhappy?" she asked.

Even as he sensed a trap, he opened his big, fat, stupid mouth. "Aren't you?"

She went still a beat and then pulled back. "Why? Because someone I thought I could trust walked out on me with nothing more than a text? Because I think my boss is going to close the flower shop and I'll lose my job? Because I've been falsely accused of a crime that people in town actually believe I committed?" She gave him a little push that actually wasn't so little. "I'm not defined by someone I thought I was dating, Luke, or what I do for a living. I'm not defined by what people think of me. My happiness comes from within, and I—"

Oh shit. Her voice broke.

She shook her head and pointed at him. "And here's the thing."

Oh, good. Thank God. There was a thing. He listened, desperate to get past this without her tears.

"I know I might *look* like a ball of fluff," she said, "but I'm not. Not even close. And the fact that I get up each morning and put a damn smile on my face is the same as…Batman putting on his cape."

"I—"

"I'm not done. It's…protection. It's my shield. It's me waving my middle finger to the world, because I *choose* to be happy. The bottom line, Luke, is that I know what matters and what doesn't." She gave him a look that would have wilted the plant on the kitchen island if she hadn't been taking such good care of it. "And I'd think that *you* would know that better than anyone."

With his own words thrown back at him, mocking him, she turned and headed for the door.

He sighed. "Ali…"

But she was gone.

* * *

Luke was woken the next morning by a call from Sawyer. "The video is in," he said. "We found nothing, but it's all yours if you want it."

Luke *did* want it. He rolled out of bed, and twenty minutes later he was on his way. He made a pit stop at the beauty salon. A brunette in her early twenties was opening the shop. "Melissa's first appointment isn't until noon," she said when he asked. "I don't expect her for a few hours."

"I'll come back," Luke said. "But out of curiosity, have any of you done a blue manicure with white stars lately?"

"Actually," she said. "Melissa—"

"Is right here…"

Luke turned to find Melissa standing there.

"You're looking for a manicure," Melissa said with a broad smile. "A blue one at that. Wow. I so did not see that one coming. I mean I've heard San Francisco can turn a man, but you, Lieutenant Sexy? You've got so much testosterone that you *ooze* pheromones. Please come back to the straight team. We need you."

He blinked. "What? No." *Jesus.* "The manicure isn't for me."

"Well, that's a relief."

"So?" Luke asked both women. "A blue manicure?"

"Didn't you have a blue manicure last month?" the brunette asked. "We were experimenting with the new spray brush, remember?"

"Didn't keep them blue for more than a few minutes," Melissa said casually, and sipped from the coffee in her hands. "Now if you'll excuse me, I've got a last-minute emergency appointment." She started to walk into the studio, then turned back to Luke. "I'm the only game in town, but it's not far to other salons," she said. "In fact, there's one not too far down the road in Ocean Shores, and they specialize in original nail designs. You might check with them. But just out of curiosity, why are you asking?"

"Nothing important," he said.

"Uh-huh." She gave him a long, speculative look, then vanished inside.

Thoughtful, Luke walked back to his truck and found Jack in the passenger seat, slurping coffee like his life depended on it. There was a look on Jack's face that had Luke's gut clenching. "Ben?"

Jack's expression immediately lightened. "No, man. He's fine, as far as I know. I haven't heard from him, but last time he emailed, he was pretty sure he'd be home soon." He jutted his chin toward the salon. "You get yourself a nice cut and color?"

"Yeah, real nice. What are you doing here?"

"Leah's dating some new guy. I ran him," Jack said, "and he's got a record."

"You ran him? Since when does a firefighter run people?"

"Hey, I have friends in high places, okay? And it was for the common good."

Luke shook his head. "What's his record?"

"He's got a library debt."

Luke stared at him. "Well, hell, Jack. We should string him up for that."

"Hey, if he can't keep a library book safe, he sure as hell can't take care of one little pastry chef."

"So you're waiting here to tell her that?"

"No, I'm going to tell *him* that. I'm waiting for him to

get out of there. He's currently sucking up to Leah, looking for date number two."

Luke laughed. Jack and Leah had been friends since their school days. The kind of friends who moved each other's parked cars to different streets, or set them up on bad blind dates for the sheer entertainment value. But this curiosity about who Leah was dating was new. Very new. Jack wasn't a possessive guy about anything. He'd lost his dad early in a tragic fire. Since then Jack hadn't taken much of anything too seriously—except his job. "You're crazy."

"Says the guy who just came out of a beauty salon," Jack said.

Luke stared at Jack, trying to figure out the odd tone in his voice. "I thought you and Leah were just friends."

"Yeah, and friends don't let friends date potential felons," Jack said. "And aren't you supposed to be back in San Francisco?"

"Aren't you supposed to be putting out fires?"

"I'm just coming off four twenty-fours and going straight to bed."

"Not yet you're not." Luke turned over his engine and pulled out into the street.

"Hey," Jack said.

"I need your help," Luke said.

At the sheriff's station, they were directed to Sawyer's office. He took them to the one and only spare room—the interrogation room. There they had a computer and the gas station's surveillance tapes from the night of the auction.

"We've been over them," Sawyer said, "there's nothing."

"Well, if there's nothing…" Jack said on a yawn.

"So where does that leave you?" Luke asked Sawyer.

Sawyer shook his head. "We've run Ted's and Ali's financials. Nothing sticks out. We've gotten forensics back on the office prints. Everyone and their mother was in that office. The only real evidence we have is the bill band found in Ali's possession."

"And the toe ring and the blue acrylic nail tip."

"With nothing to connect either of them to the crime," Sawyer said.

"Melissa says there's a salon in Ocean Shores that specializes in original nail designs. Whatever that means."

Sawyer shoved a hand through his hair. "Okay, that definitely did not come out when I talked to her. I'll check on that."

"And how about Melissa's financials? She might be feeling spurned…"

"We're still looking at her, yes. But…"

"But what?"

"Ali stole the damn ceramic pot," Sawyer said. "That looks bad. None of the other players had anything, including motive."

Luke's gut churned. "An arrest on circumstantial evidence? *Weak.*"

Sawyer sighed. "Small town mentality here, man. Give me a break."

"She's innocent. If you didn't find anything on the video, that tells us either the money wasn't taken out that night at all, or the thief didn't leave by the front door because they had access to the back door."

"Like an employee," Sawyer said. "I know. Working on that. Also, we've put out word that there's a reward. Five grand. That might help."

Luke hit a key on the computer so that it booted up.

Jack groaned. "Let me guess. We're going to watch all of the video."

Luke turned up the volume. Jack sighed and took a seat. "Yeah. We're going to watch all of the video."

Two hours later, they'd watched people come and go from the building and it'd yielded nothing but a gut ache from all the soda and chips they'd consumed from the vending machine down the hall.

"Can I go to sleep now?" Jack asked, yawning wide.

Luke's phone rang. His commander. *Shit.*

Jack looked at him. "Problem?"

Luke answered. "Hanover."

"Tell me you're here in San Francisco," the commander's voice boomed, loud enough for Jack to wince.

"Not yet," Luke said.

The commander's response was a string of oaths. "What the hell are you doing there?"

"I'm still on vacay," Luke said. "Resting."

"If only," Jack muttered.

"Resting," his commander repeated.

"I'll be back in town for the internal review on Monday," Luke said.

"See that you are or don't bother coming back at all."

Luke opened his mouth, but the line was dead. He thought about what would happen if he left town now. He'd get to keep his job—a job that, until recently, had defined him. *Still* defined him, even if he felt he'd let everyone in San Francisco down.

But if he left now, Ali was possibly going to be arrested for a crime she didn't commit.

"If you get yourself fired," Jack said, "you could—"

"No," Luke said.

"You don't even know what I was going to say."

"I don't care. I'm not going to get fired."

Jack sipped his soda and thumbed one-handed through his phone for a minute.

From inside Luke's pocket, his own phone vibrated. He pulled it out, saw the incoming text from Jack, and slid him a look. "Really? You texted me?"

Jack opened a package of peanut M&M's. He tossed one up in the air and caught it in his mouth.

Luke shook his head and read the text out loud. "Take a job here in Lucky Harbor." He looked at Jack. *What?*"

Jack shrugged. "You know you want to stay close to Ali."

"I can't."

"Why?"

Luke sighed and scrubbed a hand over his face. "I'm not right for her."

Jack coughed and said "bullshit" at the same time.

"Look," Luke said, "I'm on a roll right now with screwing things up. I'll disappoint her. In fact, I already have. She deserves better."

"She deserves to be allowed to make up her own mind," Jack said. Then he shrugged again. "Or you can just keep things all fucked up, retire, and then paddle-board for the rest of your life. You know, if real life is too hard for you."

After her ceramic class at the junior college, Ali drove through town toward the beach house. It was a dark night, a jet-black sky littered with stars that twinkled like diamonds. She headed up the hill, getting more and more tense until she pulled into Luke's driveway. At the sight of his truck there, she let out the breath she hadn't realized that she'd been holding.

He was still here.

Not for long, she reminded herself, and got out. She waved at Edward, who was getting out of the Dial-A-Ride van.

"You hanging in there?" Edward asked.

"Always."

He smiled at her clearly standard response, but his surprisingly sharp eyes said he wasn't fooled. "You're a sweet girl," he said, "sticking around to watch out for him."

She let out a low, mirthless laugh. "You have that backward, don't you? You know that Luke watches out for himself."

Edward nodded. "He does. He also watches out for everyone else, always."

She knew this to be true. She'd managed to hold onto some good resentment when it came to Luke thanks to their last conversation, but she found herself softening now.

"But I'm really talking about his heart," Edward said. "You're watching out for his heart. No one does that. He doesn't usually allow it. But he's allowed it with you. Either you pushed him into it, as his grandmother always did with her nosiness, or he cares about you. A lot."

Ali slowly shook her head. "I think you've misunderstood—"

"You care for him, too."

"Well, of course," she said. *Way too much.* "But—"

"No use backtracking now. It's all over your face."

She sighed. "Anyone ever tell you that you're a little nosy too?"

He smiled. "You'll do, Ali. You'll do. Here's some advice—he thinks he's so big and bad, thinks that nothing can get to him. But we both know otherwise. He's been hurt and disappointed by people who've claimed to care about him. You won't do that. You love him. You're good for him."

She stared at him. "I don't—" She closed her mouth, her heart picking up speed. She couldn't find her words. "We're not…" She shook her head and spoke the one truth she knew for a fact. "He's leaving."

"You're good for him," Edward repeated with utter steel. "We all see it."

She was almost afraid to ask. "Who's all?"

"I take it you don't go to Facebook very much." He smiled again. "Probably for the best."

Shaken, Ali went inside. The house was empty, but Luke had painted the living room. She walked through the kitchen, where her attention was caught by a movement outside the window. She grabbed a flashlight and headed out to the dock, finding Luke sitting there in the dark, feet dangling in the water, head tipped up, staring at the stars as if they held the secrets of the universe.

There was a bottle of Scotch at his side. "What are you doing?" she asked.

"Drinking."

Hmmm. She sat next to him and eyed the bottle. One-third gone. She eyed Luke. Probably also one-third gone. He'd been on the water, she guessed, given that he was in his board shorts, which were so low tonight as to be almost indecent. His long-sleeved T-shirt was thin and fit to his leanly muscled torso, his mouth turned up in a trouble-filled smile as he studied her right back.

He looked like sex walking, and at just the thought, her body quivered. "I'm mad at you."

"You might have to get in line," he said. He hesitated. "I'm sorry I was a dick."

She sighed. "You weren't. I care about you, Luke."

Tilting his head up, he met her gaze, his own fathomless. "Ali—"

"I care," she repeated. "But I'm not going to let what I feel for you—no matter how it turns out—define my happiness. No one but me can do that."

He looked at her for a long moment, then the corners of his mouth quirked. "You're the strongest person I know, did you know that?"

She stared at him, stunned. "No."

"You are." He tipped the bottle back and took a long swallow. When he was done, she held out her hand for the bottle.

With an amused glint in his eye, he handed it over.

It took less than a second for the liquor to burn a hole clear to her belly, and she coughed.

He patted her on the back and took the bottle back, and also another shot. She looked at his profile, barely outlined by the night sky, and felt her heart clench. Either she was having a heart attack or everyone else was right—she really was falling for him hard and fast. "Do you believe in love?" she asked.

It was his turn to choke, and he lowered the bottle, swiping his mouth with his arm as he stared at her.

"I'm just asking," she said quickly. "Not declaring or anything."

"Okay, but *why* are you asking?"

Fair enough question, but she'd sort of hoped he'd let it go. "People keep suggesting that maybe I'm falling for you."

He stared at her. "I don't think I'm authorized to have this conversation."

"Hey, I'm not saying it's true or anything," she said defensively. *Sheesh.* "But I guess now I know how you feel about it."

He caught her when she would have made her escape, moving faster than a man with a third of a bottle of Scotch in him should be able to move. He held her next to him on the dock in the dark, with the crickets singing and the water slapping up against the pylons below them.

So peaceful. So devastatingly peaceful.

"I enjoy your company," he finally said.

She turned her head and gave him a glare—wasted on him because he was staring out at the water as if transfixed.

"I even crave it," he said, sounding insultingly surprised. "More than I'd thought possible."

"Well gee," she said, "thanks."

He looked at her then. "But much as I do, you know that this isn't leading to a walk down the aisle, a tricycle in the yard, or us getting old and sharing dentures."

"Do people actually do that? Share dentures?" The alcohol had made its way through her system now so that she felt nice and…buzzed. "Because that's kind of ick…"

"Ali."

"Yeah." She blew out a breath and nodded. "I guess I knew all that already, since we're supposedly not going to have more sex, even though we already blew that." She paused. "But tell me again why we're supposedly not going to have more sex?"

He paused, like he was having trouble remembering himself. "Because someone's going to get hurt."

"Ah." She nodded and was relieved to find that Scotch was good for more than just a buzz. It worked as a numbing agent as well. "Something we can agree on then, because that does happen to me. Sex, then hurt. Every time so far, actually."

He turned his head, his eyes reflecting regret and sorrow. "Ali—"

Not wanting sympathy, she grabbed the Scotch and toasted him. "To…" She broke off and considered. "Not having any more mind-blowing sex." She took another sip. This one didn't burn nearly as badly. In fact, it went down smoothly, and a delicious warmth began to spread within her.

Luke let out a low laugh and took the bottle back from her.

"You think I'm funny?" she asked.

"No. I think you're dangerous as hell. And sexy as hell. And smart as hell, smarter than me." He toasted her now. "To you, Ali."

"For what? Driving you crazy?"

"Well, you are *very* good at it," he said.

Now she laughed, and tried to reach for the bottle again, but she missed. *Huh.* And that's when she noticed that her vision was blurry. She blinked, but it didn't help, so she used both hands to try to make a double-fisted grab for the bottle and *still* missed.

He grinned. "You're wrecked."

"Am not." Little bit… "So what's the pity party about?"

"Not a pity party." The alcohol hadn't seemed to affect him all that greatly, though the way he was easily slouched back on the dock was evidence he was feeling pretty damn relaxed.

"All alone on the dock with a bottle of booze feels like a pity party," she said. "What's the matter?"

He looked at her for a minute and then shook his head. "What the hell, you're not going to remember this anyway."

"I'm not *that* drunk."

"Yeah you are. You're a lightweight."

She'd have attempted to dispute that, but her tongue wasn't cooperating. "Tell me."

"It's Thursday."

"All day," she agreed with a nod. In truth, she couldn't remember *what* day it was.

"I have to go to San Francisco by this weekend," Luke said.

"To visit?"

"No. I'm visiting here. I'm going back to stay."

Her smile faded. "Oh," she said softly, "right." She'd almost forgotten there for a minute.

He tossed back another shot.

She grabbed the bottle and did the same, and then went to set it down—or at least that's what she meant to do, but she missed the dock and it fell into the water below.

She stared down at the black, choppy water swirling beneath them. "Whoops."

He stared at the water too. "I wasn't done with that."

"I'm so sorry!" She turned to fully face him, surprised to find her world spinning good now. Apparently she *was* a lightweight. "Want to go in after it?"

"Hell no. That water is damn cold tonight."

She looked up into his face, taking in the square, scruffy jaw, the mouth that could be both firm and soft, the eyes that missed nothing, and felt her breath catch.

He was leaving.

And her mom and Edward were right. She *was* in love with him. "Luke?"

"Yeah?"

"You're so pretty."

He smiled. It was an uninhibited smile. A wolf smile. And it made her nipples get very perky. "I think I'm indicated."

"Intoxicated?"

"Yeah, that."

His smile widened.

Oh my, she thought, heart fluttering at the sight. Trying to be cool, she leaned back and ended up going the same way as the Scotch—ass over kettle backward into the waves.

Luke was right, she thought with a gasp that filled her mouth with water. The ocean was damn cold tonight.

Chapter 19

♥

"Shit," Luke said, rising to his feet as Ali surfaced, sputtered, and went back under. "Shit," he said again, and dove into the water after her.

The shock of the cold water sucked the air from his lungs as he hauled Ali into his arms, treading water for the both of them.

She was shivering, but not hurt or scared—or so he assumed by the way she laughed with abandon and wrapped her arms around his neck.

"You didn't have to come in," she said. "I can swim."

Except she wasn't. Still laughing, she was holding onto him, making no attempt to keep herself afloat. Her sundress clung to her skin, and her hair lay in dark tendrils on her shoulders.

And his.

"You weren't kidding about the water," she said. Clueless to the fact that he was the only thing holding her up, she wrapped herself around him like Saran Wrap. "Are you okay?" she asked.

"I'll let you know when my balls defrost."

This set her off laughing again, and she dropped her head to his chest.

Shaking his head and smiling in spite of himself, he gathered her in close and got them both to the shore. When he dragged her out of the water, she dropped to her knees.

"That was fun," she said. "Let's do it again."

He took in her grinning face. Her eyes were shining as bright as the stars, and just looking at her was a kick in the gut.

He was leaving.

How was he going to leave her?

And why did it matter so much? They'd known each other for a blink in time. But already she was a tie, binding him here to this place he loved so much. He felt his mouth curve in genuine amusement when she stared at him. "Whoa," she said, "you're making my world spin."

"Pretty sure that's the Scotch," he said, but he dropped to his knees next to her.

She leaned into him, letting out a soft, dreamy sigh. "I'm pretty sure it's you," she said softly. Then she cupped his face, pulled it to hers, and kissed him, long and hot and wet.

He let himself get lost in her for a deliciously long moment, then pulled free. "You're toasted."

"Mmm…toast," she purred. "I really like peanut butter toast. When I first moved out on my own, I used to eat peanut butter for dinner 'cuz it was cheap. I'd stick a spoon in the jar and lick it slowly, like a lollipop, to make it last."

He felt his heart clench again, hard. And utterly unable to help himself, he tugged her back in and kissed her again. She tasted of Scotch and warm, sweet Ali. And something else.

She tasted like his.

"You know," she said very seriously, "you're all wet."

He laughed.

She grinned up at him, clearly pleased at the sound. She spread her arms and lay back, eyeing the sky. "You don't see this many stars in White Center, you know. Too many lights. Plus going outside at night was a huge, big, no-no. My cousin Lacey went outside at night once, to get her schoolbooks out of her mom's car, and never came back."

"Jesus," he said, all amusement fading. "What happened?"

With a sigh, she closed her eyes. "They found her body two days later in the river."

He leaned over her, stroking the wet hair from her face. He wanted to erase all the bad in her world and leave only the good, but as he was a part of the bad, he had no idea how to do that. "Tell me they caught the guy," he said.

"It was her boyfriend. Turned out, he'd won a big pile of cash at the slots that day, and she'd stolen it from him." She sighed again, maybe thinking about the money she was accused of stealing. "Can I have another shot?"

"It's gone." He stroked the wet hair from her face. "And besides, that's not what you need."

"No?"

"No," he said, and picked her up into his arms.

"Oh," she said, clutching at him. "Are you taking me in, Officer?"

"Yes."

"Are you gonna interrogate me?"

"No, you're going to exercise your right to be silent." He carried her into the house, set her down by her bed and stared at her sundress, which was clinging to her like a second skin.

A *sheer* skin, and there were no buttons or zipper on the front.

"I don't do silent so well," she said.

No shit.

"Maybe you should get out your cuffs," she said kinda hopefully.

His body went from zero to sixty at the image of her cuffed to his bed, begging him to take her however he wanted.

And he wanted. He wanted her in every possible way. With a hand to her hips, he turned her away from him and finally located a zipper. He slid it down and gulped.

No bra.

Thong panties.

Close your eyes, asshole, he told himself as he peeled the drenched and clinging dress down her curvy bod.

But he didn't close his eyes.

Biting back the groan at the perfection in front of him, he reached past her, pulled the blankets down, and poured her into the bed.

"Can't go to bed with wet hair," she said, rolling to her back, exposing her breasts. "It'll get crazy."

He wasn't sure how she could tell the difference, but he loved her crazy hair. "It's good," he said, stroking it from her face.

"Really?"

"Really." Her nipples were hard, two perfect gum-drops, and his mouth watered. He yanked the covers up to her chin. *There*. He was sweating, and feeling like he should be awarded a medal for being a saint.

Ali made a soft, disagreeable sound and kicked the blankets off, revealing her glorious body again. And then, before he could stop her, she grabbed his hand and tugged until he fell on top of her.

Well, okay, so he *could* have stopped her, but he didn't, and he didn't really want to think about that, because then she wrapped her arms and legs around him, holding him there.

"Mmm," she said dreamily.

He let out a low laugh against her temple and tried to extricate himself, but every time he freed a limb, she tightened another. She was silent through this, eyes closed. Then suddenly she opened them and looked right into his. "You haven't left yet."

Sucker punched right in the gut because he knew she didn't mean right this moment. She meant that the men in her life left her. All of them. "It's my house," he teased, not in any shape to have this conversation.

But she didn't laugh, and that took him aback. He stopped trying to free himself. "Ali," he said, low. Desperate. "I'm trying to do the right thing here."

"Well, don't." She rocked up into him and moaned.

The sound gave him a rush. "You're going to sleep," he said firmly.

"Who will keep my feet warm?"

"I'll get you an extra blanket."

"A stick in the mud," she muttered. "Who'd have

thought that the hot, sexy Luke Hanover's nothing but a stick in the mud?"

"You'll thank me in the morning." Again he pulled the blanket up to her chin, firmly tucking her in so that he wasn't tempted to do anything stupid.

"My panties are wet."

He dropped his forehead to hers.

"And my shoes are still on."

He sat back on his heels. Again she kicked the covers off and lifted her foot for him to remove her sandal.

He pressed her foot to his chest and went to work on the buckle over her ankle, doing his damnedest not to notice that her panties were as sheer as her dress had been.

A white lace thong that barely covered her mound.

She smiled up at him, her eyes soft and dreamy and glazed over. He felt the helpless smile curve his mouth in return. "You're trouble," he said. "You know that?"

"I've been told."

An innocent response, but it reminded him of exactly how often she'd been disappointed and hurt. He was *not* going to be one of those men.

Ever.

"I also tend to drive people crazy," she said. "Especially men. I drove all my mom's men right off. She'd say 'Oh, Ali-gator, there goes another one.' I'm pretty good at doing it to my own men too, driving them off." She sat up and tried to pile her hair on top of her head using the hair band she'd had around her wrist, but she was having some coordination issues. And then the thing got stuck in her hair, so there she sat, in her barely there panties, arms up over her head, hands entangled in her hair, looking like a walking/talking wet dream.

"Luke?"

Deciding it was safest to leave her hands restrained, he ignored her, the same way he was trying to ignore the unintentionally gut-wrenching tales of her life, as he fought her sandal off.

"Hey," she said, tugging on her hair.

"Hey, yourself." When he finally got her sandals off, he leaned in carefully to take over the hair fiasco. He managed some sort of bun, though it was lopsided.

She smiled at him in gratitude, all flushed, a little damp, and looking hotter than anything he could possibly imagine. "Kiss me, Luke."

A demanding drunk, he thought, amused, and gave her a short, sweet smackeroo.

But he'd greatly underestimated her determination.

"Mmm," she said, wrapping him up tight in her arms, deepening the kiss, drawing him into her nefarious plans like a moth to the flame. He let her have her way—hell, who was he kidding, he probably wanted it even more than she did—but when she slid her hands beneath his shirt and then paused, he sucked in a breath. A few moments ago he'd been trying to extract himself but now all he could think was: *Up or down, Ali?*

She chose up first, brushing his nipples, tugging a low groan from him. Then down, over his abs and farther, her fingers playing with the tie on his board shorts.

When she tugged, he caught her hands and pinned them above her head. He had no idea where the hell he found the strength, but he couldn't let her do this. He kept trying not to get sucked in by her.

And kept failing. But she had the singular ability to both break his heart and make him yearn and burn.

He'd told Sara she was work, but she wasn't work at all. Nor was she a vacation diversion. She was...real. The first real thing in his life in far too long.

Ali fought a hand free and touched his face. "You're a good man, Luke, you know that?"

With a groan, he tried to concentrate on anything besides the sexy, warm woman beneath him. Her curves were pressed up against him, chest to chest, hips to hips, thighs to thighs.

But that's not what was grabbing him by the throat and holding on. As always, it was her eyes. And all the things he could see there, which was everything, every single thing, including the fact that she cared about him.

Far more than he deserved.

He dropped his head to the pillow beside hers, thinking here she was, all sweet and sleepy, snuggling up to him. And here *he* was, wanting to fuck her until she screamed his name.

Some good guy.

"Ali." She didn't answer.

He lifted his head to kiss her goodnight because he *was* leaving.

Right now.

But caressing her hair from her face, he had to laugh softly. Her eyes were closed, her mouth slightly open, her limbs loose and relaxed.

She was fast asleep.

And he hurt just looking at her. Pressing his lips to her temple, he breathed her in. "You're perfect," he whispered, "just the way you are."

Chapter 20

♥

Lucky Harbor was a town of hearty souls, and they rose early, whether for work or play. Ali had always been one of those early risers too, but this morning, she tried to get up and could only groan in misery.

"Yeah. Thought you might be having trouble."

Along with Luke's dry tone came the scent of coffee. Ali whimpered in gratitude and cracked open an eye. "Why is the world spinning?"

"Because alcohol is a finicky bitch." Luke set a cup of coffee on the nightstand. "You going to live?"

Not at all certain, she sat up, clutching the covers to herself as it all came back. Last night. The Scotch. Falling into the water…She took a peek beneath the covers. Just a thong. "Oh God, I'm naked."

"Not quite," Luke said. "And not for lack of trying either."

She stared up at him, remembering everything but completely unable to get a read on his mood. He was dressed for paddleboarding, looking like a Greek god. "You didn't want me."

"Wrong. I just prefer my women conscious."

His board shorts were lifeguard red today, down to his knees and frayed at the hem. "You were a lifeguard?" she asked.

"Yeah, with Jack and Ben. But only because we got to sit on the beach and look at girls in bikinis all day. It was a no-brainer."

He could still fit into a bathing suit from ten years ago, which was a good reason to hate him. That, and the fact that he didn't appear to be the slightest bit hungover. Where was the justice in that? "Who got the most girls?"

"Ben. He had his dad's truck and a black Lab pup named Ketchup. Both Ketchup and the truck were babe magnets."

"You should have gotten a dog."

He smiled sexily, as if the memories were that good. "I did okay."

She bet.

"I have news," he said.

Uh-oh. "Good or bad?"

"I wanted to tell you last night, but you fell asleep on me," he said without answering her question. "There's nothing on the surveillance tapes."

She absorbed the hit of it and shook her head. "I'm not going to get lucky today in bed or out of it, is that what you're saying?"

At the look of regret on his face, she blew out her breath. "Forget it. I know, you're leaving and you don't want anyone to get hurt, blah, blah, blah. And anyway,

I might be getting arrested today, so it doesn't matter. I hope Zach isn't in L.A." Not wanting to face him, or the fact that her heart had tightened painfully, she plopped to her back and covered her head.

"Ali, we're going to figure this out."

She felt her heart squeeze at the "we." She knew he believed that, but she wasn't sure she did.

"Ali."

She closed her eyes. "I'd like to be alone," she said softly. She needed to get used to that.

"Ali—"

"Please, Luke." And whether it was the threat of tears in her voice or something else, she heard him go. She rolled over and fell back into a fitful sleep, and this time when she woke up, the sun was a little higher and she felt a little more human.

She was also alone. She staggered out of bed, and as she got ready for work, there was only one call from a reporter. Progress.

She drove to the flower shop. It was locked up and dark, which was odd since it'd been Russell's one morning a week to open.

But Russell was still sitting in his car, sipping from a to-go coffee mug, staring pensively at the shop. Ali slid into his passenger seat, making him jerk in startled surprise and spill his coffee.

"*Crap*," he said, looking down at the stain spreading over his trousers.

"Go ahead." She handed him a napkin. "Just tell me."

"Tell you what?"

"That you're closing the shop."

Russell let out a long breath. "I'm sorry, Sweetkins. I

should have told you, I know. But God, the thought of dis-appointing you…"

He'd done exactly that by keeping it from her, but she didn't add to his burden by saying so. "Are you sure about this?" she asked softly. "Really, really sure?"

He nodded solemnly, but his eyes were lit with excite-ment. "I leave in a few days. Paul's ecstatic, said he can't wait. He needs me."

And Russell needed out of Lucky Harbor. She under-stood. She really did. But she stared with longing at the building, which was exuding quirky charm and ambiance despite the dark windows that broke her heart. She'd give just about anything to be in a position to take over the flower shop.

"Heard there's probably going to be an arrest soon," Russell said quietly.

"Yeah."

"Want to talk about it?"

There was something in his voice, and she turned her head to his, a funny feeling in her stomach. "I didn't do it."

"Of course not, Kitten."

She swallowed the hurt, because that's what she did. When she fell down, she picked herself up without wait-ing for a helping hand. And though she now had the new panic of being unemployed burning a hole in her esopha-gus, she eyed the notebook on the dash.

The. Notebook.

Russell was a complete technophobe. He had his en-tire client base in that notebook, not to mention his bookkeeping records handwritten in purple ink in his bold scrawl.

And it was all right there… "Russell, I have a question."

He tensed a little. "Okay."

He looked worried, like maybe she was going to ask him to help her hide the damn money. She bit back the frustration and the urge to spill his coffee again. "What if I wanted to buy the flower shop?"

"I don't own the actual store, you know that. I lease the spot. And I got out of the lease last night. I talked to the owner; Mr. Lyons was a hard-ass about it, but…"

Ali stared at him. "Mr. Lyons owns the building? *My* Mr. Lyons, from the senior center?"

"Honey, he owns half this street. He's also Aubrey's great uncle. You didn't know?"

"No…" Ali's mind started racing. "And I didn't mean I wanted to buy the physical space…" Though if she could, she'd love to lease it. "I meant your book."

He sucked in a breath and put a hand to his chest as if she'd shot him. "My book?"

"Well, that and the rest of your records. The business. If I took it over…"

"Sweetkins, the shop is done. There's just no money in it."

She didn't want to hurt his feelings, so she picked her words carefully. "I think I could make a go of it."

Russell studied her for a long moment, then smiled. "You know what? I think you're right."

"So how much?"

"I'll have to think about it. I need start-up money for the new salon Paul and I want to run in Vegas."

Ali tried not to think too much on her way home. But it really started to hit her. She was thoroughly unemployed.

"But you haven't been arrested," she told herself in the rearview mirror. Her reflection didn't smile. It wasn't funny. In fact, panic gnawed at her gut, but it was beaten back by the sight of a man in Luke's driveway. He was aiming his phone at her as she parked, clearly trying to take a picture.

"Hey!" she yelled at him. "Stop that."

He didn't stop. He clicked a series of shots. "I'm looking for Luke Hanover," he said as he kept snapping pictures. "I'd like to get him as well."

"You're trespassing," she told him, fresh out of patience, calm, or anything nice. "Go away."

He didn't, so Ali put the truck in neutral and revved her engine, intending to intimidate. But her engine coughed like a weenie, and her gas gauge jerked toward empty. Dammit. Understanding the phrase "going postal," she put the truck into gear, and this time the guy lowered his phone and took off running.

Satisfied, Ali shoved the truck into park, but before she could open her door, Luke was right there, offering her a hand, mouth curved into a barely there smile. "Nice job, Tex."

"He was looking for you," she said. "He wanted a picture. Not going to happen on my watch."

He cocked his head, his gaze running over her features, which she carefully schooled into a blank expression. "Yeah, I'm getting that," he said slowly. "You okay?"

"One hundred percent."

"Were you really going to run him over?"

"I was going to flatten him like a pancake."

He nodded. "You're fierce as hell, you know that? Remind me to never get on your bad side."

"Not that that's a real worry, since you're leaving. Right?"

He looked at her for another long beat. "Ali—"

"Nope." She shook her head and started inside the house. "Sorry, I've gotta—"

He caught her hand and pulled her back around.

"Look," she said, "you're the lone wolf. I get it. And also, I'm sorry if I hit on you last night." She grimaced. "*And* all the time. I know how awkward it must be to have to constantly fight me off."

His sharp, blue eyes never wavered from her face. "Not what I was going to say."

"No?"

"No. And I'm not fighting you off. What I'm fighting off is my urge to toss you down to the grass right here and show you who wants who."

Her girlie parts perked right up. *Stupid girlie parts.*

Tightening his grip on her, he reeled her in. "Now tell me what's wrong."

She let out a shaky breath. "Russell closed the shop. I'm unemployed."

"Aw, hell." He gathered her in against him. She resisted for about two seconds, and then caved like a cheap suitcase, because there was nothing better than a Luke Hanover full-body hug.

"I'm sorry," he said, kissing her forehead.

Closing her eyes, she just breathed him in, unable to respond. As big a blow as the closing of the shop was, not to mention Russell's moving away, having Luke exit her life was going to be the biggest loss of all.

Luke walked Ali inside, wishing like hell he knew how to make this better for her. He'd always been careful to go into any given situation knowing the rules; in his job, his dating life, everything.

But from the moment Ali had come into his life, he hadn't understood a damn thing. Feeling helpless, he stood there in the center of the kitchen. "You hungry?"

She gave him a small smile. "You don't cook."

"No, but I'm an expert at take-out—"

A horn honked out front at the same time that Luke's phone rang. He pulled it from his pocket: Jack.

"Get your ass out here," Jack said. "Your grandpa's on his way to the ER. Chest pains. I'll drive."

Luke looked around for his keys but gave up. He grabbed Ali's hand and pulled her with him out the front door. "Come on."

"What's wrong?"

He was moving fast, forcing her to run to keep up. "It's Edward—"

They both stopped short at the sight of the Lucky Harbor Dial-A-Ride white van in the driveway. Jack rolled down the window and waved for them to hurry. The side door was open.

"What the—" Luke stared at the other passengers: Mr. Lyons, Mr. Elroy, and Mr. Wykowski.

"Everyone wanted to go," Jack said. "You coming today or tomorrow?"

Luke shook his head and gestured Ali in. He'd barely snapped his seatbelt when Jack hit the gas. "How bad?" he asked.

"He was conscious and responsive when he was loaded at the senior center," Jack said.

"He'd just driven us back from bingo," Mr. Lyons said. "We were talking about the new rec center, and the ground-breaking ceremony tomorrow, and how nice it was to build new things. He was talking about Fay, and his son—your dad, of course—and also you kids. You and Sara. He said something about how old things need to be respected too. Old things like family ties. And then he clutched at his damn heart…" Mr. Lyons's voice broke. Tightening his lips, he turned his head and stared resolutely out the window.

Luke glanced at Ali, who stared back at him, her eyes shimmering with unshed tears as she reached out and clasped his hand. He stared down at their entangled fingers and thought *if that old fart dies before I get there, I'll kill him…* "I've got to call Sara," he said.

"Done," Jack said.

"You called her first?"

"I like her better." Jack met Luke's eyes in the rearview mirror. "And I came for you in person. That has to count for something."

"You called her first," Luke repeated in disbelief.

Jack blew out a sigh. "Okay, yeah. I called her first. A couple of years ago, she made me promise that if anything ever happened to him, I'd call her immediately."

"Before me."

"*You* didn't make me promise," Jack pointed out. "And anyway, everyone knows chicks are better at this shit, man. She's getting on a flight. We need her here. *You* need her."

They made it to the ER and sat in the waiting room, waiting on news. Several hours later, Sara ran in.

Tall, athletically lean, with her blue eyes filled with worry, she walked right into Luke's arms.

"Nothing yet," he told her. "We're waiting on tests. They haven't let us see him."

Sara nodded and sniffed, wiping her nose on his shirt. He let that one go and introduced her to Ali.

"Sorry," Sara said, swiping beneath her eyes. "I see Luke, and I always cry. It's a silly reaction, but I just always know that when he's in charge, it's all going to be okay, you know?"

"It *is* going to be okay," Luke said.

Sara gave Ali a soggy smile. "See?"

A few minutes later, the doctor came out. "Intestinal distress," Dr. Josh Scott said.

They all just stared at him.

"I'm sorry," Luke said. "What?"

"He didn't have a heart attack," he said. "He ate two pastrami on rye sandwiches, three large dill pickles, and an entire bag of spicy Cheetos. He had indigestion."

Sara grinned broadly. "Sounds like grandpa."

Dr. Scott shook his head. "He has dangerously high cholesterol, and we're setting him up with a dietician. But otherwise he's as healthy as an ox."

Luke was the first to go in to see him. Edward was propped up on his hospital bed eating Jell-O.

"You've got to be kidding me," Luke said.

Edward frowned. "Don't take that tone with me. I could have died today."

"You had gas."

Edward pointed the spoon at him. "But you didn't know that. Were you worried?"

"No."

Edward gave him a small, knowing smile. "Liar."

Since Luke's legs were suddenly wobbling from relief, he sank to the side of his grandpa's bed and scrubbed his hands over his face. "You scared the shit out of me."

"Why, because you nearly let me die without fulfilling your promise to Sara?"

Luke dropped his hands from his face. "What promise?"

"To give me a hug."

"You want a *hug*," Luke said with disbelief.

"You deaf, boy?"

Luke stared at him. "If I hug you, do you promise not to die on me?"

Edward's smirk faded, and he set the Jell-O down. "I promise not to die today. How's that?"

"Good enough," Luke said, and hugged him tight.

Chapter 21

♥

That night Sara stayed in Lucky Harbor at Luke's house. Ali made omelets while watching brother and sister, fascinated by their relationship.

Sara was at the table, flipping through one of Fay's old photo albums. "Jeez," she said to Luke, "here's one of you up in a pine tree on the bluffs. What were you, Luke, ten? Grandma had just told you not to climb any, remember? So of course, Ben dared you, and you climbed a damn tree. You got up about forty feet and then froze. We had to call the fire department, and Jack's dad had to come with his ladder truck and save you. You were such an idiot."

"Thanks," Luke said.

He'd been quiet, very quiet, and Ali knew that the worry about his grandfather had left him exhausted.

"Here's another one," Sara said, pointing to the next page. "You tried to windglide from the roof straight into the water, you freakazoid. Look, remember that? You broke an arm and a leg. You're lucky you didn't crack your skull." She paused. "Probably because your head's too thick to break."

Luke gave a small, distracted shake of his "thick" head but didn't say anything.

Sara gave him a worried glance before flipping through the pages some more, and Ali realized Luke's sister wasn't trying to bait him for the hell of it, she was trying to coax him out of his mood. Her heart melting for both of them, Ali brought over two plates with omelets. She stroked a hand over Luke's shoulders and felt the tight knot of taut muscles, so she stopped to rub his neck.

With a grateful sigh, he dropped his head forward to give her room to work, eyes closed, silent.

Sara stood up. "Be right back." Two minutes later, she came back in with two stacks of files—one large, one small—and plopped them down onto the table.

"What's this?" Luke asked.

"I didn't want to tell you, but I stopped in to see Craig."

Luke narrowed his eyes. "You stopped in on my commander?"

"No, I stopped in on my ex-boyfriend," Sara said. "I knew him first, if you'll remember, and he wasn't your commander back then. I borrowed these from him." She pointed to the first stack of files, which was a foot thicker than the other stack. "Know what those are?"

"Your criminal records?"

"Funny, har-har," Sara said. "They're the cases you've closed. The cases you solved. The cases filled with scores and scores of people whose lives you changed for the better."

She pointed to the much, *much* smaller stack. "Those you can pout about. Those are your supposed failures. Without that stack, without you being good at your job, this stack—" She tapped the big one, "—these people's lives would be destroyed. So take a good, hard look, Luke, and tell me that you don't always do your absolute best. That you didn't give each and every one of your cases a little piece of your heart and soul."

She paused, and when she spoke further, her voice was softer and very, very gentle. "You didn't fail grandma. You certainly have never failed me. And you didn't kill Isabel Reyes. Say it. Say that you know you're a good man, the best man I know. That there's still enough heart and soul left inside you to go on. Because if you've given up, Luke, I don't know what I'll do. I'll..." Her voice broke.

Looking pained, Luke reached for her.

She curled into him. "*Tell me*, Luke."

"I'm okay," he said gruffly.

Sara lifted her head and searched his gaze. "Really?"

"Really."

"Okay." She nodded and sniffed. Then she stood up and gathered the files quickly, but Luke caught her before she could run off. "The files," he said. "They're not from Craig. He'd never have given them to you."

"Of course not," she said.

He shook his head. "What did you fill them with?"

She bit her lower lip. "An empty ream of paper from your printer."

"You're a nut," he said.

And then they ate omelets.

*   *   *

The next day at the ground-breaking ceremony, Luke watched the crowd, wondering if the thief was also watching. Just about everyone in Lucky Harbor was at the building site, where the early afternoon sun beat down on the empty lot and the masses, who were held back by a wide, yellow ribbon.

Ali was next to him, and they were off to one side, trying to lie low. On the other side of the ribbon, up on a makeshift platform of plywood, stood Tony and Bree Medina. The mayor and his wife were both holding shovels and smiling into the cameras. Near them were Ted Marshall and a handful of town council members. Bree was telling one of the council members about a show she'd recently seen, and Ali suddenly tensed.

"What?" Luke asked.

She sneezed. "That show," she whispered. "The one Bree's talking about? I found two ticket stubs to it in the key pot the night Teddy moved out." She sneezed again. "Sorry, it's her perfume. It gets me every"—sneeze—"time."

He squeezed her in close, pressing her face to his chest. She breathed in deeply and let out a soft, little "mmm," which shouldn't have done anything to him, but completely did. She was always trying to inhale him, as if the scent of him was the best thing she'd ever smelled. He felt the same about her. "You okay?"

She set her head on his shoulder. "I was going to ask you the same thing."

"I'm fine." She'd been incredibly gentle with him since yesterday, when they'd rushed to the hospital for his grandfather. Quiet, warm…a solid presence in his life.

But now the clock was ticking down.

He knew he'd been quiet and withdrawn. Knew, too, that Ali thought it was because of his grandfather. And it was.

Some of it.

The rest was because he was trying to wrap his brain around the fact that he was leaving...and didn't want to be.

He scanned the crowd and then eyed the platform again, watching Marshall wave at the crowd, charming everyone in his path. Tony and Bree moved across the stage, both of them soaking up the crowd's attention. And suddenly his eyes locked in on a most interesting thing.

Unable to believe it, he turned to Ali, who tore her gaze off Bree and met his gaze, her own wide.

She'd seen it too.

Bree was beautiful and always very carefully made-up, complete with designer clothes and torture devices on her feet masquerading as high-heeled sandals. Her toes were easily visible, as was the very clear tan line across her second right one. She'd worn a ring there, recently, and long enough for it to leave a definite impression.

"Oh my God," Ali whispered. "It's her!"

"It's as circumstantial as the bill band being in your possession," he warned her.

She was smiling. "Yes, but..."

He smiled back. "Yeah. *But.*" It was good. Really good. Bree was blonde. Bree would have had access to the back door the night of the auction. She would have parked in the back, in employee parking, and not gone out the front door. And the coup de grace—she had clearly been wearing a toe ring and wasn't now.

They escaped through the crowd and went back to the

house. Luke went straight to his computer and his magic search programs.

Ali leaned over his shoulder, her hand resting on his bicep. He resisted the urge to flex like a caveman and toss her over his shoulder and drag her to his bedroom. Instead he typed in Bree Medina and then stared at the screen. "Well, hello."

"What?"

"She filed divorce papers two months ago."

"Divorce?"

"Yeah, and then..." He scrolled down. "She withdrew it. She withdrew the papers on..." He let out a slow whistle.

Ali leaned in closer. A strand of her hair caught on his jaw. She smelled great.

"Wow," she said. "She withdrew the divorce two days after the money went missing." Turning her head, she stared at him. "What does that mean?"

"Something made her want to leave the mayor," he said, "and then something changed her mind. Maybe she thought she'd found someone better."

"Better than the mayor?"

"Tony Medina's a good guy," Luke said, "but look at Bree. She keeps herself up. She's forty-five and looks twenty-five. Tony's a balding, paunchy, fifty-year-old who works twenty-four seven." He met Ali's gaze. "Maybe Bree got lonely or bored. And then maybe she also got distracted by a younger man, a walk on the wild side, someone who gave her something Tony's money couldn't—the feeling of being young and alive."

Like you do for me...

"You're thinking she was also fooled by Teddy."

"You said Aubrey thought *she* was Marshall's one and only," he said. "But what if Bree thought so too? What if Bree thought it was the real deal? So she files for divorce, and then she discovers Marshall's screwing other women and gets ticked."

"And then tries to frame him for taking the money."

"It's a lot of maybes," Luke warned. "And I'm just thinking out loud here, but I bet I'm in the ballpark."

Ali was looking revved up and ready to kick some ass. Loving that fight in her, he tugged her into his lap and nuzzled the sweet spot on her neck, the one that made her purr like a kitten.

"Mmm," she said in a soft, sexy moan, tilting her head to give him better access. Which he took, sucking on the soft skin just beneath her ear before working his way south. He *loved* the southlands…

Breathing heavily, she slid her fingers into his hair and arched into him. "We weren't going to do this again…"

"I know." Damn, he really did know. It'd been his idea. Stupidest idea he'd ever had. "Ali…"

She squirmed off his lap, and he felt the disappointment in every inch of his body. Some inches more than others.

But then Ali dropped to her knees between his sprawled legs and sent a slow smile up at him, stopping his heart. "Sometimes," she murmured, opening his jeans and reaching inside, "rules are made to be broken."

Much later, Ali lay on the kitchen table, a little sweaty and a whole lot delirious from pleasure. It took her five full minutes to catch her breath and roll onto her side to eyeball Luke.

He was still flat on his back on the table, too, eyes closed. He wore only his jeans, still opened, indecently low on his hips. He was sprawled out like a decadent dessert, the kind that was totally fattening, but was so good that you couldn't regret the calories. She ran a finger down the center of his chest to his abs, which contracted at her touch.

Eyes still closed, he groaned. "Okay, but you've got to feed me first. I'm a growing boy."

She stared at his erection. "I can see that…"

Snorting, he moved unexpectedly, and quick as lightning, he rolled onto her, pinning her to the table.

She pushed at his chest. "Hold on a second."

Pushing up to his elbow, he took his weight off of her and gave her a "what's up?" gaze from heavy-lidded eyes—his bedroom eyes.

"I've been thinking," she said. "I bet Bree hid the money at Teddy's place."

"You've been thinking? When? When could you have been thinking?"

"Earlier. But it makes sense, don't you think?" she pressed. "If her goal was to frame him, she'd want to—"

"Earlier? You mean earlier when I was buried so deep inside you that I could feel your tonsils as you screamed my name and—"

She covered his mouth and laughed. "I did not scream. Exactly. And what? Is my mind supposed to turn off?"

Looking a little bit out of sorts, he rolled off of her, and it made her laugh again.

"Sorry," she said, "women's brains are different."

"No shit."

They sat up, and she began pulling her clothes back on.

"At this point, all we have is circumstantial. I heard that tomorrow Teddy and some of the town council members are going off for a team-bonding fishing overnighter. I'm going to wait until after I get back from my mom's birthday party and then go check out his place for the money."

"No," Luke said. "Hell, no. It's too dangerous. If you find the money there, everyone's going to think you planted it."

She warmed at his concern, but reminded herself not to get used to it. He hadn't said word one about seeing her after he left, and hell if she'd beg for crumbs. "I have nothing to lose. Everyone already thinks I stole the money. And I'll be careful, trust me." She shoved her feet into her sandals.

"Where are you going?" he asked.

"I want to talk to Aubrey."

"Wait for me." He pulled up his jeans and looked around, probably for his keys, which seemed to elude him daily, even though they were right there on the counter in the new key bowl she'd made.

"Can't wait," she said. "I'm on a tight schedule to stay out of jail."

He choked out a laugh. "You weren't on a tight schedule a few minutes ago."

"Well that was different. I got distracted by an orgasm."

He let out a very male smile of satisfaction. "*Three* orgasms. Pretty good for someone who was 'thinking.'" Leaning in, he kissed her. "You want to do this alone."

She needed to get used to alone. She met his gaze, wondering if he was going to even discuss it. His leaving. What might happen between them after he did.

But he said nothing.

"Yes," she said, "I need to do this. Alone."

"You don't have to."

"You're leaving, remember?"

His jaw tightened. "I'm not likely to forget."

She let out a breath. *Stay strong.* "Aubrey'll be far more likely to talk to me if I'm by myself."

Looking like he got it but didn't necessarily like it, he nodded. "Call Zach. Tell him about Bree. I'll call Sawyer."

"I will," she said, "since jail doesn't work in my plans very well. Hard to be a self-sufficient, well-rounded, contributing member of society from behind bars. Plus I don't think I could learn how to paddleboard there either." She was doing her best to sound positive and upbeat. This was the trick to denial. Sound positive and upbeat and maybe you'll buy it.

"Paddleboard?" he asked.

"Yeah. I've been watching you, and I've decided it's on my bucket list."

"A bucket list is for someone who's dying."

"Well," she said as lightly as she could, turning away from him on the pretense of checking her reflection in the small mirror above the foyer table. "I don't see myself living through a prison sentence," she quipped.

Two hands gripped her by the shoulders and turned her back around. He stared into her eyes, and she could tell by the grim set of his jaw that he could see her fears. "You're not going to jail."

She nodded, but she must not have looked convinced, because he dipped down a little to look into her eyes, his own fierce. "You're *not*."

Someone knocked on the kitchen door, and Ali jumped. She turned and peeked out the window over the sink and saw the broad-shouldered Jack standing there. "Oh my God," she whispered. "If he'd shown up five minutes ago, he'd have heard us!"

"Us?" Luke inquired, amused, giving her a look that had her blushing to her roots.

Right. *She* was the noisy one. She couldn't help it, not with him.

At her embarrassment, his eyes softened, filling with affection. "I love the noises you make," he said huskily. "Sexy as hell." He pulled open the door.

"Hey," Jack said, "I'm not interrupting, am I?" And before they could answer, he pushed his way in. "Need to borrow a paddleboard."

"It's in the shed, not the house," Luke said.

"Need a wetsuit too."

"It's June," Luke said. "Only pussies need wetsuits in June."

"I've got a date later. Can't risk shrinkage."

Luke started to shove him out, but Jack planted his feet. "Not going anywhere until you give me your wetsuit. I can stand here all day. You know I can."

Luke muttered an oath and turned to the door himself. "There's one in the garage somewhere. Hold on."

When he was gone, Jack turned to Ali and flashed her a smile. "You can feel the love between me and him, right?"

Ali laughed. He was absurdly handsome and even more absurdly charming. "I can absolutely feel it."

"Luke's the son of two doctors," Jack said, "so it's probably not his fault that he's such an ass. Or that he thinks he's always right."

"Is he? Always right?"

"Yeah, but don't tell him that. It'll go straight to his head. He's got that classic hero complex thing going. It's why shit hits him so hard. He likes to blame himself."

"Thanks, Dr. Phil," Luke said dryly, coming back into the room, tossing a wetsuit at him. "You can leave now."

"Sure. Oh," Jack said, turning back, "I'm supposed to tell you, Joe Wykowski wants you to figure out who's stealing the reclaimed lumber he has stacked on the side of his house. It's worth a fortune. He suspects it's his ex-wife's boyfriend's son, who's a carpenter, if that helps."

"If he knows who it is…" Luke started.

"The guy carries his nail gun on his hip like he's Dirty Harry," Jack said. "They need you and your badass attitude. And *real* gun."

Luke stared at him. "So I'm what, the new geriatric private detective of Lucky Harbor?"

"Hey, I'm not the one who found Mr. Schmidt's GTO," Jack said. "On shift last night, I had to rescue Mrs. Myers's cat out of a tree, and she was telling her entire bridge club about you. Apparently they all have various problems that they need the *local investigator stud muffin* to solve—*their* words, by the way. Not that you're not a total stud muffin; you're just not my type."

Ali laughed.

Luke manhandled Jack out the front door and then turned to Ali. At his expression, her heart squeezed. She'd watched him pretend not to care about anything, even as the opposite was true. He'd helped his sister get on her feet and stay there. In his job, he did whatever was needed. He'd fixed up the house he'd neglected.

And then there was her. He'd given her a place to stay, a friendship…and more.

They'd grown up so differently. His parents had expected a lot out of him, looking to him to pretty much raise himself and his sister too. As a result, Luke stood up for himself and others too weak to do so.

Ali admired that, so much.

"About earlier…" Luke said.

She took in his expression. "It's okay, Luke," she said softly. "You don't have to give me the speech."

"The speech?"

"The one where you rationalize how we got naked again, and how it's the *last* time, yadda, yadda."

A ghost of a smile curved his lips. "I thought it was blah, blah, blah."

"Look, you're right to hold back with me," she said. "Historically I've made some bad decisions, and—"

He snagged her and hauled her in close. "There's *nothing* wrong with you," he said with quiet steel. "Not one thing. You're perfect."

"Well—"

"Say it," he said.

She softened and cupped his face. "Luke, I—"

"Say it, Ali. Say you're fucking perfect."

She stared up at the fierce look of protectiveness in his features and felt her heart clutch. She needed to lighten this mood of his and fast, or she wasn't going to be responsible for jumping him. "I'm fucking perfect," she said.

It worked. He flashed a smile. "I really like it when you say 'fuck.'"

Chapter 22

♥

Ali found Aubrey at her desk in Town Hall, typing away on her computer, her brow furrowed.

"Does everyone always work on the weekends?" Ali asked.

"Just the lucky ones." Aubrey looked up and took in Ali's hair with assessing eyes. "You're supposed to use that anti-frizz every day."

Ali ran a hand down her hair and grimaced. "I forgot today. Listen, I have a question."

"No, I'm not still doing my boss."

"I actually wasn't going to ask that. Although I'm kinda wondering why you still work for him."

It was Aubrey's turn to grimace. "It's a good job," she said. "And I can resist him." Though she didn't really look one hundred percent sure. "Listen, I'm pretty busy, so…"

"Is there anyone else?"

"Excuse me?"

Ali moved closer and leaned in. "I'm wondering if there's anyone else that Teddy's seeing. Other than you and Melissa."

Aubrey looked at her for a long time. "You have someone particular in mind?"

"Maybe."

Aubrey arched a perfectly waxed brow and looked like she might have something to say, but Gus walked by with a mop.

Aubrey and Ali remained quiet until the hallway was empty again.

"We can't talk here," Aubrey said.

"I know. Just tell me you know something."

"Not concrete."

"Would you be willing to call me if that changes?"

"You mean if the couch gets put into use again, something like that?" Aubrey asked.

"Yeah."

Aubrey went pensive, then sighed. "Damn, I really liked this job."

Luke drove into town and found Sawyer at his desk, head down on his arms. "Bad day?"

"Some high school punks drove all the way up to Mt. Hood—three hours each way—loaded up fifteen truckloads of snow, drove it all the way back into town, and packed in all the doors to the school last night. Not yesterday afternoon. Not after dinner. At three a.m. Summer school detention had to be cancelled today."

"Could be worse," Luke said.

Sawyer lifted his head and blinked bleary-eyed at Luke. "I'm afraid to ask."

"I think Bree Medina stole the fifty grand."

Sawyer stared at him and then silently handed Luke his empty coffee mug.

Luke took it, walked down the hall to the service table, filled it with straight, hair-raising black, and brought it back to Sawyer's office.

Sawyer drank, winced, and then drank some more. Eyes far more sharp now, he looked at Luke. "What the fuck?"

Luke opened his mouth, but Sawyer stood up. "No, wait. Not here."

They headed out in Sawyer's utility vehicle while Luke gave him the rundown.

"Jesus," Sawyer said and called the mayor. "Hey, Tony. Yeah, we did get a great turnout at the ground-breaking ceremony earlier. Listen, what's Bree up to? She busy?" he paused, listening. "I just wanted to talk to her about redecorating my office...I understand. Tell her I hope her mom's feeling better real soon." He slid his phone away. "Bree's gone to her mom's place in Ocean Shores for a few days."

"Ocean Shores," Luke repeated. "Her mom lives in Ocean Shores. Where the next closest nail salon is. We should..."

Sawyer pulled over and used his smartphone to find the number and make the call. When he hung up, he looked at Luke. "Bree is a client there, and they said she has gotten blue, starred nail tips before." He pulled back onto the street, made a few turns, and stopped about half-way down a street, pointing to a duplex on the corner. "Marshall's new place."

There was no activity.

Sawyer turned off his vehicle. "Marshall cancelled a meeting with me, said he wasn't feeling good. Think that's a coincidence?"

"I don't believe in coincidences," Luke said.

"Me either."

"So what are we doing?" Luke asked.

"You forget what a stakeout looks like?"

"No." Luke slouched in his seat. "But a heads up would've been nice. We don't have any food."

Sawyer leaned forward and opened his glove box. Inside was a treasure trove of candy bars and other crap food.

"Nice," Luke said, helping himself.

Half an hour later, the mail carrier worked her way down the street. Two minutes after that, Marshall's front door opened. Teddy appeared in boxers and an opened bathrobe.

"He's dressed like he's sick," Sawyer said.

Or like someone who'd just gotten laid. "Only pussies wear bathrobes."

"I have a bathrobe. The wife bought it for me."

Luke looked at him. "Chloe bought you a bathrobe?"

"It's from her day spa."

"You ever wear it?"

"Hell no."

"I stand by my point."

Teddy stepped outside. Before he got anywhere, a man's necktie came around his neck from behind.

In Sawyer's vehicle, both he and Luke tensed for action, but then the shadowy figure behind Ted materialized into the shape of a woman. She wore a black leather bustier, matching thong, and thigh-high, stiletto boots.

Bree Medina, the mayor's wife, the one supposedly visiting her sick mom. She slapped Teddy's ass and then pulled him back inside by the tie.

The door slammed shut.

"Jesus," Sawyer said, rubbing a hand over his eyes. "I don't think I can unsee that…"

That evening, Ali stood at the work table in the garage, completely lost in the cool, wet clay. In the zone, she worked and shaped, using her sensory skills instead of her brain so she could just be.

She heard the truck pull into the driveway, so when someone came up behind her, she knew it was Luke. He didn't touch her, but she doubted a piece of paper could fit between them. "You want to play *Ghost*?" she murmured.

He stepped into her, brushing up against her so that she could feel his erection. "Do I feel like a ghost to you?" he softly asked.

She faced him and felt her heart tug at the sight of him soaking up the sight of her. "I need a shower," she said, gesturing to the front of her, which was a mess.

"Funny, so do I."

Don't get sidetracked by his hunkiness, she told herself. He was hiding it pretty well, but he was pissed at something. Her gut tightened a little bit, and maybe her heart too. He let her see the real man, something she knew he shared with few others. "You okay?"

"I was with Sawyer. We saw Bree at Marshall's new place."

She could tell that there was a whole lot more to this story. "And?"

"And it was a…compromising situation."

"Compromising how?" she asked.

"*Compromising.*"

She looked up into his face. "Just tell me, Luke. Were they naked, rolling around on fifty thousand dollars in cash?"

"Not quite naked, and no cash. But Bree was…taking charge. I'm pretty sure Marshall is tied up with his own necktie about now."

Her jaw dropped. "Seriously?"

He lifted a hand, like *Boy Scout's honor*. Except there was no way Luke Hanover had ever been a Boy Scout.

She drew a breath. "So we've linked the mayor's wife and the town clerk to an illicit—and what might or might not be a BDSM—affair." She shuddered. "It has a high ick factor, but it's not necessarily illegal."

"True," he agreed. "We've got to smoke out the money."

"How?"

"If she's got it," Luke said, "she's hiding it somewhere. Not in a bank account, but somewhere accessible. Holding it over Marshall's head." He stepped close, crowding her. "All we have to do is catch her with it."

"Oh, well, if that's all."

He gently pulled her in.

"Careful," she warned, "I'm covered in clay."

"Ali, the police are going to announce there's an arrest imminent."

She went still even as her heart began to pound. "They've already done that," she said.

"Yes, except this time they're going to leak that it *isn't* you."

She let out a breath. "Okay. I like the sound of that. Keep going."

"Bree's under surveillance," he said.

"You think she's going to move the money."

"I know it," he said. "It's what I would do if I'd just gone from scot-free and in the clear to guilty as hell. I'd get rid of the evidence." He stroked the hair back from her eyes, letting his fingers linger on her.

Yesterday, she would have been touched by the sweet gesture. But right now, sad and aching for him, it just hurt—hurt and pissed her off. He'd stood by her, believed in her when others hadn't, let her stay when all he wanted was to be alone—and yet he was leaving tomorrow. And as attentive and wonderful as he'd been, he hadn't said one word about seeing her again. In sudden overload, she poked his chest with a clay-covered finger.

"Hey," he said.

She did it again, getting clay on his white T-shirt.

"Stop that."

She didn't.

"Ali." He caught her wrist when she went to poke him a third time. "*Stop.*"

"Right. I'll just stop. Stop caring about you…" *Stop wanting you, stop loving you.* Except she couldn't seem to manage any of that. Once again, she was going down with the sinking ship that was her heart.

But she wasn't going down quietly. Nope, not this time. With her free hand, she scooped up a fingerful of the soft clay on the table and streaked it across his chest.

He stared at her, easily catching her other hand as well. "What the hell's gotten into you?"

"You said you like to keep things real, but you don't,"

she said. "You wear your cynicism better than you do your badge. I get that you do it to keep your heart protected from whatever's going on, but what's going on is that we're falling for each other."

She couldn't blame him for staring at her like she'd just announced she had two heads. She hadn't meant to let that slip, but it was out there now and she couldn't, wouldn't, take it back.

"Ali," he said quietly. "I told you—"

"Yeah, yeah, you told me." She was tired of his calm steadiness. Did he ever lose it? Why wasn't he losing it like she was? He was still holding her, and instead of trying to pull away, she stepped into him. Her sole intent was to cover him with more clay until she felt better, a plan that utterly backfired because it put her up against him.

Which she liked *way* too much, and which of course was the problem. "Yes," she said, "you told me. You told me plenty. I guess I don't listen very well. It's a Winters trait, you know. Denial. And I'm damn good at it."

"I don't want to ever hurt you, Ali."

"You're hurting me now."

He let out a long breath, released her hands, and then made the mistake of closing his eyes.

Ali slapped some more clay on his chest, with both hands this time, and turned back for more clay.

"What the hell are you doing?"

"Fighting dirty—unlike you. You won't fight at all. You play clean and safe."

"You think I play clean and safe?" he asked, his voice deadly calm. Not his eyes, though. His eyes were fired up as he grabbed two fistfuls of clay.

Gulp.

"You know what?" she asked quickly, raising her hands. "*Uncle*."

"Too late." He stalked her slowly, surely, on legs far more steady than hers, and then hooked her leg so fast she never saw it coming. She fell right onto his grandma's sheet-covered beanbag chair.

Before she could scramble free, he was on her, pinning her down, running his hands from her throat to her ankles, spreading clay all over her body.

"I can't believe you did that!"

He rose in one fluid motion, satisfaction unmistakable on his face. He took a step back, slipped in a puddle of water she'd spilled earlier while softening the clay, and went down on his ass.

She scrambled to her knees and crawled to him. "God. God, Luke. Are you okay?"

"No. I think I broke my ego."

Relief making her giddy, she dropped her head to his chest and laughed.

His hands came up and possessively gripped her butt. "I'm not playing clean or safe, Ali. Not with you. And that's the problem. I'm feeling things I shouldn't be feeling." And then he rolled them, tucking her beneath him.

"There's something else you're feeling," she said.

"No kidding." He rocked into her, eyes intense and glittering with heat, a forearm on either side of her head. The overhead light caressed the tough, sinewy lines of his body, emphasizing the flexed muscles of his shoulders and biceps.

Around them the air felt charged. There was a soft vibration just beneath her skin, the hum of anticipation that spread warmth through her, settling into her good spots. She let her eyes drift over his face, let the hunger for him show. And her need...

Whispering her name, he lowered his head, brushing his mouth along her jaw to her ear. "You kill me. You know that, right?"

Wrapping her legs around him so that he was settled between her thighs, she arched up. This was it, she realized. Their last night... "It's a good way to go," she murmured.

Choking out a low laugh, he cradled her head in his hands, his fingers entangling in her hair. "Not on the floor." He rose, and pulled her up.

"Okay," she said, and looked pointedly at the workbench. She was assessing it for sturdiness when he choked out a low laugh and pressed up against her back. "Still killing me," he said, pulling her back around so that now the smooth steel of the table hit her at the lowest curve of her butt. "Like this. I want to watch you come." He hoisted her up so she was seated on the table. His hands ran up her legs, settling on her inner thighs before slowly pressing them open so he could step between.

Lowering his head, he concentrated on removing her apron, swearing when he had trouble with the knot. "This wasn't my intent tonight," he said, and giving up on the string, he tore it with his hands, giving her a little thrill deep in her belly.

"It's not your fault," she murmured. "Clay is sexy."

He laughed low and rough. "I'm pretty sure it's you, Ali."

She took in a deep, slow breath, smelling the wet clay

and the scent of clean, heated male, and experienced a wave of desire that had her quivering.

When Luke finally freed her of the apron, he tossed it over his shoulder. Her sundress followed shortly, and then her bra. "Christ, you're beautiful." He snagged her bikini panties and slid them down her legs, leaving her in nothing but mud boots.

And a lot of clay.

A ragged groan rumbled from his chest. "My favorite look on you," he said, taking her in from his prime position between her dangling legs, which were spread and held open by his lean hips. "It's like a feast." He bent over her, a hand on either side of her hips. "And I am starving." He kissed first one breast and then the other, lingering to nuzzle.

His jeans were rubbing against her inner thighs and between, and she shivered. There was something incredibly erotic and completely sinful about being naked and sprawled out for him while he was still fully dressed. Even more so when he dropped to his knees on the garage floor and used his tongue. She might have come right off the table, but Luke caught her hips in his big hands, holding her in place so he could devastate her with slow, purposeful care. It took an embarrassingly little amount of time for her to completely fly apart. Even less the second time.

And then he was inside her. Wrapping his arms around her, he lifted her so that they were chest to chest, and began a slow, delicious glide in and out of her body.

"How?" she managed, breathless. "How is this better every single time? Is it because we don't want it to be?"

Latching his lips onto her throat, he shook his head.

The gentle tugs of his mouth sent shock waves straight through her, and she cried out and clutched at him, tightening around him.

"Oh fuck, Ali…" he growled, tightening his grip. "Not going to last if you keep that up."

She did it again. In retaliation, he nipped at her shoulder, her collarbone, the swell of her breast, wrenching a moan from her as heat and pleasure spiraled. Somehow she managed to open her eyes and watch the intensity on his face as he moved inside her, which proved to be her undoing.

He came with her this time, hard, shuddering as he buried his face in the crook of her neck. She trembled, little aftershocks of pure pleasure, and Luke tightened his grip in a soothing, protective embrace. His heat seeped through her, consuming her until she felt like she might burst again as he breathed her in, nuzzling, kissing, nibbling her throat and jaw and ear.

Loving her.

Not that he'd admit it. Unable to help herself, she clung for a few minutes, trying to remember everything about this moment. Everything.

He let her cling for long moments, as if he felt the same. Finally he raised his head and met her gaze. She knew he was checking to see if she was okay, so she reached up, brought his face back to hers, and kissed him.

Because she wasn't okay.

He was leaving.

Chapter 23

♥

The next morning, Ali woke up entangled with a big, warm, hard body.

Luke.

After their garage foray, they'd eaten, and then he'd taken her to bed.

His.

He was still deeply asleep on his back, one arm bent with his hand beneath his head, the other gripping her butt like he owned it.

She took a good, long last look at him, ignored the ache in her heart, and she slid out of the bed.

He mumbled something and rolled over, burying his head beneath his pillow. The rest of him was bared to the world, that strong back, those mile-long legs, and the best ass she'd ever had the pleasure of viewing. With a sigh, she slipped out of his bedroom.

He was leaving today, and her sadness had nothing to do with the distance between San Francisco and Lucky

Harbor. It was that there'd been no mention of continuing this. Whatever this was. So really, the distance was irrelevant.

But she refused to watch him go.

She drove to Eat Me and had the now-famous Grace's chocolate chip pancakes. Lucille was there with her blue-haired posse. She came over to Ali and gave her a hug. "Heard Detective Lieutenant Stud Muffin is leaving," she said. "Thought you could use some TLC."

"I'm fine."

"Good. Because men don't make the world go around. Although," she said, eying Mr. Wykowski as he entered the café, "they do make it more interesting."

To say the least.

"Been meaning to ask you about your ceramics," Lucille said. "A little birdie told me that Russell isn't interested in selling your stuff in his shop."

"A little birdie?"

Lucille grinned. "Okay, Leah. And the truth is, I covet your ceramics. I thought you might be interested in having a show at my gallery. If we price things right, you might even be able to pay that fancy attorney of yours."

"You'd do that?" Ali asked.

"Of course. You're good."

Ali smiled. "And if I wasn't?"

"Well, then, this conversation would have stopped at Detective Lieutenant Stud Muffin."

Ali's phone rang. Russell wanted to see her, so she headed to the flower shop. It wasn't open. It wouldn't ever be open again, at least in this version. Russell had boxed everything up and was standing at the front counter. He didn't look as sad as she felt. He didn't look sad at all. He was happy.

And she was very happy for him. And devastated for herself.

Russell smiled and pulled her in for a hug. Then he handed her...the book.

She stared down at it. The thing was ancient and frayed at the edges, with notes and pieces of paper sticking out everywhere. "Your business?"

"Yep. Lucky Harbor Flowers is yours, what there is of it. All you need is a place."

"But I don't have money to pay you," she said.

"Consider it severance."

She hugged the book, then thrust it back. "I can't take it, Russell. It wouldn't be right."

He didn't take the book. "Then pay me when you get the shop open and in the black."

She lifted her gaze to his. "How do you know I'll get to open a shop?"

"I know," he said, confident. "Of course, you'd have to stay in Lucky Harbor for that book to have any value..."

Ali looked down the street. It was very early. The strings of white lights were still on, twinkling like Christmas in June on the pine trees lining the walk. Until the theft of the money, she'd loved it here. Loved the people, the way it felt like home. And her three S's were here: stability, security, and safety.

So hell if she'd let herself run off with her tail between her legs when she'd done nothing wrong. "Yes," she said quietly. "I'm staying."

Russell smiled and hugged her again. "Keep in touch."

She would. And someday soon, although she had no

idea how, she would open the flower shop. *Her* flower shop. It was what she wanted, with all her heart.

There were other things she wanted too. She wanted the money mystery solved. She wanted people to know she wasn't a thief. She wanted her mom and sister to be safe and happy.

She wanted…

Luke.

She drove home.

Home.

She parked and stared at the big, old, beautiful house. Granted, she was a sucker for a place with character but…home?

This wasn't her home. It was Luke's.

Yet there was no denying that she'd fallen for the place and the man, despite knowing better. Luke didn't want her to feel this way, except that particular message wasn't exactly sticking to her brain. The thing was, actions spoke far more loudly than words, and Luke's actions were telling her a very different story than his words.

His truck was still here.

She walked through the house toward the kitchen, needing something for her suddenly dry throat. Scotch was her first choice, but she'd proven incapable of handling that. She poured herself a glass of iced tea, and with her gut saying that Luke would be on the water, she stepped out onto the back deck. Hearing voices, she moved so that she could see the dock below. Edward was sitting there with his usual cigar, though she was hoping it was unlit, since she knew his doctor had told him to quit.

Luke had just pulled himself and his board out of the

ocean. Water sluiced off the body she knew she'd never get tired of looking at.

It'd only been a couple of weeks, but he'd gotten a hold of her heart. Maybe some things took no time at all, but the fact was, he'd proven that he was a man she could believe in. A man unlike any other man in her entire life.

She was still thinking about that when the men's words floated up the stairs to reach her.

"Don't be an asshole," Edward said. "Not to her. You're living with her, falling for her, letting her think it's okay to fall for you." He jabbed his cigar at Luke. "You telling me when you leave here today that you're not going to ever look back?"

Luke set his board against the dock and ignored his grandfather.

"You telling me you can just walk away *again*? Because let me tell you, boy-o, being alone? *Not* all it's cracked up to be. Now that I've looked death right in the face—"

Luke snorted. "You had gas—"

Edward jabbed with the cigar again. "Say it one more time and I swear I'll stroke out on you right here, right now, just to spite you."

It was a distance but Ali was pretty sure Luke rolled his eyes as he leaned back on the railing, arms crossed over his chest.

"All I want," Edward said, "is for you to learn from other people's mistakes. *My* mistakes."

"I'm not you," Luke said quietly. "Ali and I both know what's going on here, and what isn't."

Edward stared at him. "You want me to believe you're just helping her, that she's just a job to you?"

Ali held her breath for the answer, and when the quiet "yes" came, the blood roared in her ears. The first time he'd referred to her as a job had been to his sister, and he'd had a handy excuse for it then. This time the quiet conviction in his voice overrode any excuse.

Looking disgusted, Edward shook his head.

Ali tried to absorb the terrible, wrenchingly painful truth of it all, telling herself that this was not new information. But it still knocked her back a step. And then another.

And then she'd whirled and escaped into the house. She grabbed her purse and shoved a few things inside.

She had to go.

Still, she slowed long enough to leave a note hastily scrawled on a napkin, because leaving without a word was rude. Mimi had taught her better than that. Taping it to the fridge, she took one last look around, at the kitchen, out the window at the two men on the dock, one who'd been like a surrogate grandfather to her, the other who'd been...

Everything.

Her eyes were too blurry to see clearly, but she snatched the keys out of the ceramic bowl by the door and then stopped and eyed the bowl.

She thought of what had happened to the pencil pot she'd left Teddy, how it'd been shoved in a drawer. She couldn't leave this one to that fate, so she snatched it as well. She'd have to come back for her other things, of course, but later. Much later.

Like after Luke was gone.

She opened the front door and then faltered for a beat, but she didn't stop. Because for the first time in her life, she was going to leave first.

* * *

Luke turned from his grandfather and entered the house. He'd woken up alone. After paddleboarding and the run-in with his grandfather, he was hoping Ali was back. He needed to get on the road, but he wanted to…

Hell. He didn't *want* to say goodbye.

But it was Sunday. He'd pushed his luck as far as he could with his job. The review was in the morning. He needed to go or face the consequences.

Edward had come in behind him. "Feels quiet in here."

Yeah, it did. And Luke's gaze snagged on the napkin taped to the fridge.

Dear Luke,

Thank you for letting me stay when you wanted to be alone. For helping me when you were on a break from doing just that.

For saving me.

Ali.

Luke stared at Ali's words, dread spreading through him like wildfire. He hadn't saved her.

She'd saved him.

Why would she leave a note like this? What had happened that would make her write it? His mind raced in reverse, back to a few minutes ago, to what he and his grandpa had been discussing on the dock. Shit. It wasn't what chased her off, but who. *He* was why she'd run.

And his grandfather was right—without her, the house *was* quiet. He finally got what he'd wanted, to be alone. Except that wasn't what he wanted at all. Whipping around, he went in immediate search of his keys. Naturally, he hadn't left them on the counter. Or anywhere that he could see.

"What the hell are you looking for?" Edward asked.

"Keys," Luke grated out, moving into the living room to look there.

"She's got that key bowl, you know. You should try using it sometime. She made me one. It works like a charm."

The key bowl. He'd put his keys in the key bowl. He strode back into the kitchen, but the thing wasn't on the counter. Where the hell was it?

"Now what?" Edward asked.

Luke shook his head. "I have no idea where the stupid bowl is, but I have to go after her. I...fucked up."

"Well then why are you still standing here?"

"Because I still can't find my keys."

Edward shook his head. "Your grandma, she used to smack me upside the head whenever I'd lose my keys. Always worked too. I'd always find my keys right after she did it. Come closer, let's try it."

"You were married for like twenty minutes," Luke said. "When did you have time to lose your keys?"

Edward leaned in and smacked him on the back of the head.

"Ow. Jesus!"

"Two *years*," Edward said. "We were married for two years. And it'd have been a helluva lot longer if I'd gotten my shit together sooner." He fished deep in his own pocket and came up with a set of keys. "Connect the dots, you idiot. Be smarter than me."

Luke stared at the keys. "Tell me those aren't for the Dial-A-Ride."

"What, you have a problem with it? 'Cuz you can always just walk. Maybe you'll even catch Ali too. Sometime next year."

Luke sighed and took the keys.

Ali didn't let herself cry on the road to her mom's house. No, that'd be dangerous and stupid, and she tried really hard not to do anything dangerous and stupid.

So she did the responsible thing—she pulled over to the side of the road to sob her heart out. Right in the middle of it, Zach called her.

"What's wrong?" he asked immediately, obviously hearing the emotion in her voice.

"Nothing—oh my God. You're calling because I crossed the county lines without even thinking about it, right? They called you."

"Who?" he asked.

This stumped her. "The crossing-the-county-lines police?"

Zach laughed. "Relax, no one's going to arrest you for visiting your mom. I got your message about Bree. Are you sure?"

"Yes, but they haven't found the money."

"Luke'll sniff it out. He's not the type to let something he cares about go."

And yet he let *her* go…

She and Zach hung up, and Ali went on to what she was exceptionally good at—picking herself up and telling herself things would be okay. She blew her nose, slid on her dark aviator Oakley knockoffs, and got back on the road.

She arrived in time to sit at her mom's table and chop veggies.

"No one ever eats the veggies," Mimi said, sitting on the counter with a mirror in one hand and her eyeliner in the other. "But it seems classy to have them out, you know? *You get the beer?*" she yelled to Harper in the back of the old, tiny, narrow house.

"*Mama, this is a damn surprise party*," Harper yelled back. "*Stop asking questions about it and practice your surprised look!*"

Mimi grinned and practiced in the mirror. "How about this, honey?" she asked Ali. "Do I look surprised?"

"Yes," Ali said without looking. She munched on a piece of celery and wondered if Luke would eat celery. It was green, which probably put it on his taboo list.

"Did I tell you I'm learning how to do taxes?" Mimi asked. "It's going to change everything, honey. You'll see."

She was eternally optimistic in spite of the fact that life had never handed Mimi Winters a single thing, including a break.

But the thing was, Mimi believed wholeheartedly that everything could change, and up until recently, so had Ali. All along she'd thought all she had to do was leave White Center and that would *change everything*. All she had to do was become the best damn florist in Lucky Harbor and that would *change everything*. All she had to do was love Luke and that would *change everything*.

But if wishes and dreams were sure things, the world would be a whole different ball game. And deep down, she'd always known that. And, she had a feeling, so did Mimi. But that had never once stopped her mom from trying to impart hope into both of her daughters' hearts. Ali's chest tightened a little bit. "I love you, Mom."

Mimi looked up, surprised, then smiled softly. "Aw, baby. I love you too. What time's Luke coming?"

"He isn't."

Her mother set down the mirror, her expression of surprise a real one this time. "Why not?"

"Because we're not together. I've been telling you that. Besides, he'd be on his way back to San Francisco by now." Ali closed her eyes and dropped her head to the table. "And I messed things up."

"Oh, Ali-gator." Mimi hopped down from the counter and sat next to Ali, hugging her close. "It happens. Listen, we'll go to the Victoria's Secret outlet store. We'll get you something pretty, and you can make it up to him—"

"No." But that did squeeze a laugh out of her. "It's not like that. I messed up by falling for him."

"Well how's that messing up?"

"Because he didn't fall back."

"Oh honey. What man wouldn't fall for you? You're strong and smart, and so pretty. Although you should smile more. You've got those nice white teeth—"

Ali pushed to her feet. "I'm going to go see if Harper needs any help outside decorating. You keep working on your surprise expression, okay?"

Two hours later, the party was in full swing. Ali had been sent to the store—twice—and was back in the tiny, cramped, hot kitchen, her mom's cake in one hand, a knife in the other. She'd come inside to put the cake away, but now she was thinking she needed a third piece.

Problem was, a third piece would put her at about a million calories for the day, so she cut off a bite-sized portion. She ate right off the knife, because everyone knew that the calories eaten right off the knife didn't count.

She was leaning over the cake stuffing her face, when she heard footsteps behind her. She turned, then nearly fell over in surprise at the man standing in the doorway.

"Luke?"

His shoulders nearly brushed the jamb on either side of him, making him look far too big for the place. He was wearing a T-shirt, faded Levi's, and battered athletic shoes. The casual wear should have had him fitting right in, but he didn't really. Maybe he had the hard-edge and see-all eyes it took to survive in this neighborhood, but his badassness came from being a cop, not from worrying about having a job and putting food on the table or whether it was safe to walk to his car.

"What are you doing here?" she asked, surreptitiously swiping her face, hoping she didn't have chocolate all over it. "Why aren't you gone?"

"I wanted to see you before I left."

White Center wasn't exactly en route to San Francisco. He'd gone pretty far out of his way to talk, but she needed to protect herself. And get over him. Getting over him would be supremely helpful. "I'm pretty busy here, Luke."

He slid a glance at the cake in her hands. "Yeah, I can see that. Should I give you two a moment alone?"

"No. *Yes.*" She noted that she sounded peeved, which was good. It hid the hurt. And she *was* hurt. So damn hurt, with no one to blame but herself.

He came forward and took the knife out of her hands, setting it far out of her reach. Then he very gently took the cake as well.

"How did you find me?" she asked. "And why are you even here?"

Mimi stepped into the kitchen and said in a horrified voice, "*Ali Anne Louise Winters*, how is that a way to talk to your man?" She put a hand on Luke's arm and smiled up at him. "You made really good time from Lucky Harbor, honey."

"I did," he said, and dipped down to kiss her on the cheek. "Happy birthday."

Mimi fawned over that. "Oh my, aren't you the charmer." She smiled at Ali. "Isn't he, Ali?"

"Yes," Ali agreed tightly. "He's quite the charmer. But he's not my man, Mom. We've discussed this."

Mimi sighed, and Ali braced herself for the lecture. *A man is everything, Ali. Don't disappointment him, ever. Be what he needs you to be...*

But Mimi said none of that. She simply stepped around Luke, cupped her daughter's face, and smiled gently. "Just talk to him, baby."

"Mom—"

"I know you've been let down. And I also know that's more my fault than any man's."

Ali sighed and brought her hands up to her mom's wrists. "Oh, Mom. That's not true."

Mimi smiled sadly. "You always were the sweet one. My miracle," she said to Luke. "So willing to see only the best in me." She turned back to Ali. "But honey, maybe you could try to see the best in him too." Then she kissed both of Ali's cheeks, patted them gently, and left the two of them alone.

Chapter 24

♥

Luke didn't touch Ali. God knew he wanted to. She was standing there, arms wrapped around herself, the don't-touch vibes coming off of her like lightning bolts.

He'd caused that. Instead of keeping his mouth shut and saying goodbye to her, he'd ruined what they'd shared during their short time together. Worse, he'd hurt her. "I called you," he said quietly. She hadn't picked up. He'd called her again, and Mimi had answered, saying that Ali had gone to the store and left her phone. Mimi had invited him to her party.

Luke had been on his way regardless, but the invite had been nice.

"My mom's dying of curiosity about you," Ali said.

"She's protective of you."

That brought her gaze to his. In all this time, she'd been an open book. But she'd closed herself off now, shuttering everything from him.

His own doing. "She wanted me to know you were upset," he said.

Ali made a sound and closed her eyes, and he stepped closer. "I told her it was my fault," he said, "and that I wanted to come see you."

"Well, you're seeing me now."

"Ah…" he said helplessly, "we need to talk."

"Not here." And with that, she walked outside.

He drew a deep breath and followed.

They didn't go around to the back, where the party was ramping up, if the raucous laughter and loud music meant anything. Instead, she started walking down the street.

Luke went with her. "Ali—"

"Not here either."

He decided to shut it and let her lead.

But she stopped so short at the sight of the white Lucky Harbor Dial-A-Ride van, he nearly plowed her over.

She swiveled her head and looked at him in disbelief.

He shrugged.

"You drove the Dial-A-Ride here?"

"Someone took the key bowl," he said, "with my keys in it."

She stared up at him. "Oh my God. That was me. I took the bowl." She smacked herself on the forehead. "I've *got* to stop doing that."

He smiled, and they walked in silence a few blocks.

Weeds poked through the cracks in the beat-up asphalt in front of the houses that had seen better days decades ago. Some had bars in the windows, and others had flowers in pots on their porches.

"We lived on that corner once," Ali said, pointing to a

place on the right, where there was a skeleton of a Chevy up on blocks. "We also lived across the street."

"Where does that loan shark asshole live?" he asked. "The one who threatened to sell you?"

She took a look at his face. "You want to beat the shit out of some guy who scared me fifteen years ago?"

"Badly," he said.

She shook her head again, but there was the very smallest of smiles on her face.

"Ali."

"I still don't want to talk."

Fine. He'd give her a few more minutes, but that was it because then he *was* going to talk.

And she would listen.

Hopefully. Because, actually, he hadn't had a whole lot of luck in getting Ali to do anything that she didn't want to do.

They walked another few streets, and then she pointed to a house just like all the others, this one pale yellow and nearly falling off its axis. "That one," she said. "That's where we lived with The Pincher."

His chest squeezed hard, like maybe his heart was swelling and bumping up against his ribs. "I'd like a moment with him too," he said grimly.

A minute later, they came to a deserted elementary school. Ali slipped in between a small gap in the linked fence, like she'd done it a hundred times.

Luke eyed the gap. Not nearly wide enough for his shoulders, even if he squeezed in sideways. With a sigh, he climbed the fence.

Ali had claimed a swing and was watching him. There was something new in her face now. She was more than just closed off to him. She was closed off *period*, disassociated from their surroundings. He'd seen this all too often on the job, so he knew exactly what it meant. It meant that being here had brought her memories that were hard—if not impossible—for her to deal with. "Talk to me, Ali."

"Well…" Her gaze tipped upward to the corner of the structure supporting her swing. "There's that web right there, and I'm wondering where the owner of it is."

"Long gone," Luke promised.

"And then there's the fossilized dog poo just behind you. Don't step in it."

"Ali."

"I love getting to see my mom," she said quietly. "And my sister." She shook her head and kicked off gently to swing. "I just hate being here."

He moved behind her and gave her a big push.

She sighed as she flew through the air, leaning back into the motion of the swing as if to savor the motion and the sun on her face.

"You went to school here," he said, staying behind her, continuing to push her.

"I went to school here, yes. I also used to run away here. And hid away here too, when it was necessary."

He'd stayed in back of her so that she wouldn't have to look at him when she talked, sensing that she needed that. But now he was glad that she couldn't see his face, because although he was good at hiding his feelings, he couldn't seem to do it with her.

"I left here," she said. "I wanted to go somewhere new and be smart and independent. I wanted people to like me. I wanted a new life. I wanted to be happy."

He stopped her motion, and from behind her, pressed his cheek to the top of her head. "You are all of those things," he said, "and more. Smart and sweet and caring." He twisted the swing so that she faced him. Squatting before her, he took the steel chains in his hands, caging her in between his arms. "I'm going to talk now," he said.

She opened her mouth, but he leaned in and kissed her to shut her up. "What you heard me say to Edward," he said, moving back just enough to speak, "I shouldn't have said."

"I shouldn't have stood there as long as I did," she said. "When I heard you two talking, I should've gone back inside."

"Lots of should haves. But you overheard me talking out my ass, Ali. You're not a job to me. Not even close."

She leveled him with those big, hazel eyes. "Then why did you say it? *Twice?*"

He blew out a breath and tried to put it into words. "I guess I was just coming to grips with what's going on between us and I wasn't ready to discuss it." He let out a low, pained laugh. "Hell, Ali, I'm not good at talking about this stuff, even when I *am* ready."

"And you're not," she said, eyes on his. "Ready?"

It was a question, not a statement. And a fair one. "I didn't think so," he admitted. "And the thought of being yet another man who's disappointed you or let you down—"

She pulled back a little more at that. "I'm not your responsibility, Luke. I *won't* be your responsibility."

"I know that. But I care about you."

She nodded, and yet her face was still closed off. Luke knew she felt off balance. Their location wasn't helping much, but that wasn't the number-one problem. The number-one problem was him. Him and the stupid, idiotic words that he'd thrown out there to get his grandpa off his back. "You're not just someone who needed help," he said to her, leaning in so that her knees touched his chest. "I don't think of you like that."

She was looking at him but through him, and worse, she was tensed for flight. He was already losing her. He could feel it. He was losing her before he'd even realized the miracle that he'd had.

Because like Mimi had said—*she* was a miracle.

His miracle.

She'd brought him back to life. He wasn't sure how, or what he was going to do about it, but he knew that he had to figure his shit out fast before it was too late.

"I don't *need* help," she said.

"I know. *I'm* the one who needs it."

This brought him a very small smile. It would seem she agreed that yes, he needed help. "I love your determination," he said. "You're tough and resilient, Ali. And amazing." And he wanted her. More than he'd wanted anyone before. That alone was enough to terrify him, but he was willing to put the terror aside to make this right between them.

"You've got to go," she said. "It's late. And your job's on the line. You're going to have to drive all night to make it for your review."

He didn't move, and she closed her eyes. "Please don't look at me like that," she whispered.

"Like what?"

"Like you love me."

His heart stopped. Just stopped. "I think I do," he said.

He instantly knew his mistake. It was one of those big, life-altering bonehead moments that he couldn't take back.

"You *think* you do," Ali repeated softly. She sucked in some air, then shook her head with a low laugh. "You think…No. No, Luke, I'm here to tell you that you don't. Because if you did love me, we'd have discussed like rational adults what would happen after you go back to San Francisco. Instead, we're here, with you about to toss your cookies because you think it *might* be true that you feel something for me. God, the horror."

"Ali—"

"Oh, no. I'm not done." She poked him in the chest. "The fact is, Luke, you don't do love. You don't because that would mean *feeling*, and you don't like to do that either. I get it though. I really do. You think you let other people down, and now you've got it all mixed up in your head somehow, and you think you're unworthy of love. And that's just bullshit."

He scrubbed a hand over his face. "Ali—"

"You've closed yourself off to receiving love, which sucks, especially because that means you can't give it either. I get that too. You're a detective because you're good at it and because it allows you to stand back and observe. And the biggie—you get to stay distant. Which, by the way? You're freaking fantastic at."

He wished like hell he wasn't holding onto the chains of the swing so he could touch her. But if he let go, she'd spin.

And then she would walk.

He'd faced bullets and bad guys in his work, and yet he was still a coward. Ali Winters, floral designer and pottery artist, was the brave one. She was so brave that she was going to walk right out of his life because she knew she deserved better.

And indeed, she rose to her feet, bumped him back, and walked away.

Chapter 25

♥

Ali was still in White Center with her mom and sister at ten that night when she got a phone call from Aubrey.

"She's gone off the deep end," Aubrey said.

"Who?" Ali asked.

"You Know Who," Aubrey said cryptically. Like it was *She Who Shall Not Be Named*. "I was working late, and she tried to sneak into Ted's office. We scared the crap out of each other. She got irritated at me and left. I don't know why I'm calling you with this."

"Because even though you have perfect hair—which is annoying—you're a good person." Ali chewed on her lower lip, trying to imagine what Bree had wanted to do in Teddy's office. Except she didn't have to imagine. She *knew*.

Bree was going to put the money back. "Did she say where she was going next?" she asked Aubrey.

"No."

"Is Teddy still at his team-building fishing trip?"

"Yes. You think I should call him?"

"What would you say?"

There was a pause. "Good point," Aubrey said. "I'm going home now. I put in my resignation today. I realize it's a Sunday night, but the powers that be will get it in the morning."

"Wait— what?"

"Yeah. I'm switching gears. I don't know what gear yet, but I'll get there."

"Wow," Ali said. "Well, thanks for the call."

"Yeah, and by the way, we're even now."

"Oh, not hardly," Ali said.

"Really? How's your hair?"

Ali looked in the mirror over her mom's faux antique table. Smooth. Shiny. "Good," she admitted.

"We're *completely* even," Aubrey said, and hung up.

Ali kissed her mom and sister goodbye and headed back to Lucky Harbor.

Bree was on the move with the money.

Ali was going on the move too, to catch her.

The highway was narrow and windy and took a lot of concentration to drive at night. This was good because it gave her no time to think about Luke. Or that he'd come to see her.

Or dropped the L-bomb.

Except he hadn't.

She had. She wanted to thunk her head onto the steering wheel, but the road was badly rutted, and she was upset, not suicidal.

So she occupied herself by replaying the conversation with Aubrey in her head. She'd have liked to call Luke, but he was long gone by now. And because that gave her a quick stab to the chest, she called Leah.

"Hey," Leah said, sounding worried. "It's late, you okay?"

"To be determined later."

"Uh-oh," Leah said.

"Yeah. Listen, are you up for a little..." Ali grimaced. "B and E?"

"Always." Leah laughed, then she got serious. "Wait. I thought you were kidding, but...are you? Kidding?"

"No." Ali filled her in on Aubrey's call and how she intended to go search Teddy's place for the money.

"Aren't you dating a certain hot detective?" Leah asked.

"No."

"No?"

"Long story," Ali said. "You in or not?"

Leah blew out a breath. "What the hell. There's nothing on TV. You don't think Bree will go back to the office now that Aubrey left?"

"No, I don't think she'll risk it again. I think she's going to go to Teddy's to dump the money. It's just a feeling."

They arranged to meet at eleven thirty. Ali turned her phone over so she didn't have to look at the lit-up screen that revealed no missed texts or phone calls.

Her own doing, of course. But though she'd managed to get her heart broken, she refused to have her spirit broken too. Hell no. She was on a mission to fix her crazy life.

She'd worry about her heart later.

She parked, turning to look as Leah slipped into her truck and handed her a brown bag.

Ali peeked in the bag. "What are these?"

"B and E clothes. All black."

Ali pulled out black jeans and a long-sleeved black T-shirt and then eyed the taller, leaner Leah doubtfully. "I hope these are your fat jeans."

"Just strip. I've got an hour before I have to get back to give grandma her meds."

Ali pulled off her clothes and shimmied into the ones Leah had brought, which wasn't so easy behind the steering wheel.

"Cute undies," Leah said.

"Stop looking."

"Hard to miss the neon-pink boy shorts and demi bra. Victoria's Secret?"

"Fifty-percent-off sale."

"Nice," Leah said. "The bra makes your boobs look perky."

Yeah, well, that was a complete waste given how her day had gone.

Or how her love life was going.

"So what's the plan here?" Leah asked.

"We wait for Bree," Ali said. "I think she's going to come here to his house." And hopefully not in black leather. "It'll feel safer to her than risking the office again."

Leah eyed Teddy's dark house. "Maybe she's already been, or she's there right now. We should call her, except I don't know her number."

Ali had an "aha" moment and tore through her purse for the book from Russell.

"You're going to read?" Leah asked. "Now?"

"No, I think I have her number." *Come on, Russell,*

come through for me... Ali flipped through the pages, hoping and praying.

As an interior designer, Bree had ordered lots of flowers from Lucky Harbor Flowers, and indeed, she had her own page with preferences and contact information. Ali pulled out her cell phone and punched in Bree's cell number.

"What are you going to do if she answers?" Leah asked.

Ali wasn't quite sure until indeed, Bree answered.

"Hello? Who's this?"

"Ali Winters. I was just calling to see if you really wanted this delivery at midnight."

"What the hell are you talking about?"

"Well, Russell left me directions to make a delivery for you." At the lie, Ali looked at Leah.

Leah covered her mouth with her hand to hold back her horrified laughter.

"I don't have a delivery on order right now," Bree said, sounding like she was on the move.

Ali strained her ear to the phone. Had that been a horn she'd heard? "Are you sure?" she asked. "Where are you right now, because I can bring it by and—"

"It's late," Bree said.

Definitely in a car, Ali thought. There was a radio playing softly and an engine running. "Oh. Right," she said. "Well, okay, then. So...how about a drink? Or a late-night brownie at Eat Me?"

Click.

Ali winced and slid her phone away. "She didn't want to talk. Nor did she mention where she was. But I'd bet my last dollar she was in her car."

"Maybe she's on her way."

"Or she's on her way back to the office," Ali said. "Hey…" she peered out the window, looking down the street to the Lexus parked in front of Teddy's place. "That's Teddy's car. He must have gotten a ride with the other guys to their fishing thing." She turned to Leah. "Let's peek inside."

"You have his keys?"

"I know his code." They got out into the dark night in their black B&E gear and sneaked up on the car. Ali punched in the code. "I'm getting into the back," she said, eyeing the gym bag on the seat. She opened the back passenger door and quickly turned off the dome light to avoid highlighting her activities to any neighbors who might still be up.

Leah got into the front seat and shut her door. Ali didn't shut hers, because she wanted to be able to hear someone coming up on them. "I've got his gym bag," she said. "I bet my iPod's in here. He stole it."

"Seriously?"

"I had better music, and he was always borrowing it for workouts. I want it back."

Leah flicked on a penlight and twisted to shine it so that Ali could see.

"Nice," Ali said.

"I like to be prepared."

"You have any candy in there? You know, in the name of preparation?"

Leah handed her a lollipop.

"I love you," Ali said. She popped the lollipop in her mouth and unzipped the gym bag. In unison, they both wrinkled their noses and jerked back from the odor of stinky guy emitting from the bag.

"Ew," Leah said. "Guys are disgusting."

Ali pulled the lollipop out of her mouth and stared into the bag. How badly did she want her iPod? Enough to move the stinky clothes around?

"Just do it," Leah said.

"You sound like a Nike commercial. I need more light."

Leah leaned closer with the light. "Hey," she said.

"What?" Ali instinctively checked out the windows to see if anyone was coming. "What's wrong?"

"You tell me. You've been crying."

Ali sighed. "Forget it."

"Oh, crap," Leah said. "What did he do?"

"Who?"

"Luke."

That Leah assumed Luke had blown it brought a warm fuzzy to Ali's heart, even as she laughed without much mirth. "It was me," she admitted. "He's got this way of making me feel like the prettiest, smartest, most wonderful woman on earth," she said.

"That bastard."

"No, you don't understand." Ali hesitated. "I fell for him. And it'd never work between us."

"Why not?"

"Why not?" Ali stared at her. "Have you seen him? He's totally out of my league."

"Bullshit," Leah said.

"And he's law enforcement."

"So, hot guy with a gun." Leah shrugged. "Still not seeing the problem here."

"My people don't go out with law enforcement," Ali said, "it just isn't done."

Leah laughed. "Your people? You mean women? Because, honey, women in general melt over guys like Luke Hanover."

"Yes," Ali said, diving into the unpleasant task at hand to search Teddy's bag. "But you can't make him melt back, now can you?"

Leah paused. "He doesn't feel the same as you?" she asked, sounding quite up in arms over this possibility.

"Actually, I'm pretty sure he does," Ali said, "but he told me right up front, he wasn't going to get involved. I wasn't going to get involved either, so there's no one to blame here but my inability to follow my own decree."

"Men suck."

"I am in complete agreement. And look." Ali pulled her iPod from a side pocket of Teddy's gym bag.

"Wow. He's perfect for politics. He's got that lying, cheating, stealing thing down."

"Are you keeping a lookout?"

"Yeah— oh shit."

This was immediately followed by the back door opening, and a big body sliding in next to Ali. "Yeah, oh shit," said a low male voice. A low, unbearably familiar voice, and both Ali and Leah squeaked.

"*Luke*," Ali breathed, a hand to her chest.

"I need the both of you to go back to your vehicles and drive away," he said in his cop voice.

Ali blinked. "What's going on?"

Luke slid a look at Leah. "Give us a second?"

"No," Leah said.

"Excuse me?" he asked, voice still low and authoritative but with a hint of disbelief.

Women probably didn't tell him "no" very often.

"No," Leah said again, "I'm not deserting Ali."

He softened slightly. "You aren't deserting her," he said. "You wouldn't. But I need a moment with her, alone."

Leah looked at Ali questioningly. Ali nodded, and Leah started to get out of the Lexus, but then whirled back and put a finger right in Luke's face. "I'm watching you," she said.

Luke didn't laugh. He didn't get pissed off. Instead he nodded seriously and touched the tip of his finger to Leah's. "I'm watching me too. It's okay, Leah. It's going to be okay."

Leah stared at him for another moment, then nodded. "See that it is."

Ali had no idea what to make of that exchange, but apparently Leah didn't have the same problem. She flashed Luke a small, but much warmer, smile and then vanished into the night.

In the dark interior of the car, Ali closed her eyes. "You didn't go. Why didn't you go?"

"I couldn't leave you."

Oh. Oh damn, that was good. "Luke—"

"What are *you* doing here?"

"Aubrey called. Bree's gone off the deep end. I think she'll come here."

"I told you she was under surveillance."

He *had* told her that. Why hadn't she remembered that?

"Listen to me, Ali," he said, all cop again. "Teddy's car, house, and office are under surveillance too. Half the police department is staking out Town Hall. Bree's already been there. Aubrey finally left work for the night, and Sawyer's covering all the bases. We've got someone in place in Teddy's backyard. No one's home that we can see."

"So…you want me to go."

"I want you out of here, yes. I want you safe. Bree's moving the money tonight. We're sure of it. She needs to get rid of it since the word is out about an arrest first thing in the morning."

Ali nodded. She understood all that, but she didn't move. She couldn't take her gaze off his face. "I really thought you were gone," she said softly. "Oh, Luke. Your job. Your review—"

"It'll have to wait." He paused. "Or not. Ali," he said very seriously, "I know that the men in your life have fucked you over. I promised myself that I wouldn't do that to you. I didn't want to get involved."

She tried not to react to that blow. "I know."

"But things change."

She tried to see his expression, but with little to no ambient light in the backseat, she couldn't see it clearly. "Your job, your *life*, is in San Francisco."

"As it turns out, only the job," he said. "And it also turns out that I'm not just the job."

She wasn't sure what that meant, whether to accept the odd surge of hope that suddenly blocked her throat or go with the panic licking at her gut. She worked at getting herself calm and wasn't entirely there yet when she said, "I'm sorry I said you're distant and that you don't feel. I shouldn't have. I picked a fight because I was hurt."

"I know. But you did mean it, and that's okay. It's true. And I want you to say what you mean, always. I can take it." He paused. "*We* can take it. We're tougher than words, the two of us."

Ali's heart stopped and then started again in staccato beat. "Luke—"

The front passenger door jerked open. Cool night air rushed in and so did a figure.

A female figure, but not Leah.

Luke squeezed Ali's thigh, but she didn't need the warning to be quiet.

There was a fiddling in the front seat and a very small beam of light. The woman had a flashlight.

Bree.

"Shit," she muttered when she couldn't get the glove compartment open. "Shit, shit, shit..." Then the thing suddenly opened and some stuff fell out.

"God, he is such a slob," she said, dumping everything in the glove box to the floorboards. Then she began to stuff something back in there from the duffel bag in her lap.

Money.

Chapter 26

♥

Ali couldn't believe it. Bree was working on getting money—and lots of it—into the glove compartment. But then she couldn't get it closed, no matter how much she pushed and shoved and swore. Bills were sticking out, and Bree swore at them too. Finally, she used the heel of her very wicked-looking boot to kick it closed.

Luke was doing something with his phone. Ali was working really hard on holding her breath, because Bree's perfume was getting to her. She was running out of air…

And then it escaped, a very loud, unladylike sneeze.

With a startled shriek, Bree whirled around, penlight in her mouth.

And a gun in her hand.

"Oh for God's sake," she muttered when she saw who it was. "Could this get any worse? Hands up," she ordered, swinging the gun back and forth between Ali and Luke like a pendulum.

Ali raised her hands, but Luke was slow to respond.

"*Now*," Bree warned him.

"You need to put the gun down, Bree," he said calmly.

She didn't. "What the hell are you two doing here?" she asked. "Especially *you*," she said to Ali.

"Me? What about *you*?"

"I'm having a fucked-up day, obviously!" Bree yelled. She blew a strand of hair out of her face, which was damp. In fact, she was uncharacteristically ruffled from head to badass-boot-covered toe.

"Put the gun down, Bree," Luke said again.

"Well, I can't now!" She glanced at Ali. "You screwed everything up. *Everything*," she said. "You and your stupid, sweet, easy-going, artsy-fartsy ways. This is all your fault, you know that? Teddy was *mine*. And then you fell for him, and he couldn't resist you, another sweet little thing who thought he walked on water. He was mine first, dammit!"

"But"—Ali stopped to sneeze again, twice in a row—"you're married to the mayor."

"Yeah. And he's also a financial planner, don't forget. I can't, because he's always working. He's a workaholic whose lover is his job. And the great thing for him is his lover doesn't care that he stopped working out and snores."

Ali just stared at her. "So you started sleeping with the town clerk?"

"Teddy fell in love with *me*," Bree said, jabbing the gun near Ali's face. "Said he needed a *seasoned* woman, one who knew what to do with a man. He said that no one else could keep up with him. Well *I* managed to keep up with him just fine. I gave him whatever he wanted."

Ali didn't want to think about what that meant. She sneezed again.

"Stop that!" Bree yelled.

"It's your perfume. And you're making me nervous. Why do you even have a gun?"

"We live in Washington. Everyone has a gun." Her eyes were dialed to straight-up, bat-shit crazy. She was flushed, and her hair was sticking to her face. "Is it hot in here? It feels hot in here. Fucking hot flashes. It's the twenty-first century, and we can't cure hot flashes."

"I wasn't the only one Teddy was with," Ali said. "You know that, right? He was cheating on *all* of us, Bree, not just you."

"He told me you two were just roommates," Bree said. "And I didn't know about Melissa until the night of the auction, that skinny, young, taut-skinned bitch. I wanted to kill him, but he told me that it didn't mean anything, that I was still his one and only."

"So you forgave him by stealing the money?" Luke asked.

"Hey, sometimes a woman snaps, okay?" She swiped her forehead with her free hand. "My God. Someone open a fucking window!"

"Put down the gun, and I'll open all the windows," Luke said.

She jabbed the gun at him again. "Listen, smartass, you might be sexy as hell, but I'll shoot you if I have to. Dammit!" She fanned her face. "This is out of control. All I wanted was to *be in a position* to frame Teddy so he'd straighten up. But *you*!" She whipped the gun back to Ali. "You went into his office and blew it."

"Hey, half the town was in his office that night."

"But *you* took the pot, the one I'd put the bill wrapper into," Bree said. "To frame *him*, not you."

"Yeah," Ali muttered, "I've really got to stop doing that."

"Marshall's not worth this, Bree," Luke said. "It's not too late to stop. Give me the gun."

Bree's face crumbled a bit, but she kept the gun level at his face. "The heart wants what it wants," she said. "And I wanted Teddy. Only he turned out to be as big an ass as the rest of them. Hell, look at his life. He's sleeping with half the women in town, and no one even knows. I tried to frame him, and he walks. Shit just doesn't stick to him. And the bastard never breaks a sweat. He's like the Energizer Bunny; he can keep going and going. A girl can't do that. We get bladder infections." Bree swiped her forehead again. "Tonight was the night that his luck was going to change. I put the money in here, and I was going to call the police."

Luke had been slowly lowering his hands. Ali was going to trust that he knew what the hell he was doing, because she could scarcely draw air into her lungs. It was the gun. Every few seconds, it swung from Luke to her, back and forth. It was one thing to see it happen on TV, it was another entirely to be faced with the reality of it.

"Stop moving," Bree screeched, and Ali went still. Except then she realized Bree was talking to Luke. "I told you, hands up."

Luke ignored her directive, leaving one hand half raised, the other dropping to scratch his chest. "You never said—how did you get the money in the first place?"

"After we did it on his couch, I found a red silk bra behind a cushion. Melissa's, of course, as I learned later.

So when he left the office to get rid of the condom—he thought he was being clever by doing that in the hallway bathroom so that no one would ever find out about us—I took the money from his bottom drawer and dumped it into my briefcase. I left one of the money wrappers in his stupid pencil holder so he'd have evidence on him."

"And he didn't notice any of this when he got back from the bathroom?" Luke asked.

"No. He suggested I leave first so that we weren't seen together, which worked for me. I wanted him to be the last in the office—not realizing, of course, that Miss Perfect over here was going to fuck that all up. *Twice.*"

Ali blinked. "You think I'm perfect?"

Luke hadn't taken his eyes off of Bree. "You're losing it, Bree."

"You *think*?" She jabbed the gun in his direction. "And for the last time, I said *hands up*. I mean it." The gun shifted back to Ali. "I'll shoot her, Luke. And I really don't want to do that."

Luke pressed his knee into Ali's. For comfort, she thought, and glanced down. His phone in his pocket was glowing.

He'd gotten it on somehow. He'd been a busy guy, because he'd also tugged up his pant leg, revealing an ankle holster and the gun he had there.

Oh, God. Did he really expect her to grab it? She glanced at him and found his eyes on hers, steady and sure.

Yes. He did. Because he believed in her.

I've got you.

His words, he'd said them to her several times now. She hadn't been in a place to fully believe him before, but by now, she absolutely believed him.

He nudged her again.

Right. The gun. She didn't have to fake the next sneeze, but she added a dramatic head toss to go with it, bending forward with the momentum. She was wrapping her fingers around Luke's gun when Bree yelled "*Hey!*"

Luke, apparently tiring of waiting for Ali to get the gun, made his move without her. Lunging forward, he reached over the back of the seat to grab Bree's wrists and shoved upward.

Bree's gun went off, blowing a hole in the car's roof.

"Ali," Luke said, "get out of the car, take cover. Can you do that?"

Ears ringing from the close-range gunshot, Ali stared at him still strong-arming Bree's hands above their heads with the back of the seat between them. "Y-yes."

"Excellent," he said calmly. "Do it now, Ali."

Oh, God, she couldn't leave him. Wouldn't leave him. He was in an awkward position trying to control Bree from the backseat. And then she realized he was holding back, waiting for her to get to safety so that a stray bullet couldn't hit her.

Reaching behind her, she opened the car door and stumbled out, still holding Luke's gun. She couldn't use it. She had no idea how, plus she couldn't see in the dark to aim. She crouched behind the back rear tire, her fingers shaking so badly it took three tries to pull out her phone.

She knew Leah would have called the police by now, and surely the cops in Teddy's backyard would be coming any second, but she still hit 9-1-1.

From the inside of the Lexus, the gun went off.

Oh, God…

"9-1-1 emergency dispatch," a disembodied voice said in her ear. "What is your emergency?

"Sh-shots fired," Ali said through chattering teeth. "Off-duty officer and a crazy woman with a gun."

"Location?"

Ali gave the street name and the Lexus's license plate. "*Hurry*," she said, and peeked around the back of the car.

No one had emerged.

She crawled to the open back door, using the light from her phone to see with one hand, pointing the gun with the other.

Luke was still sitting in the backseat, sprawled out now with Bree's gun in his right hand pointed at her.

The streetlight shined into the interior of the car, highlighting Bree in bold relief. She was still in the front seat on her knees facing Luke, hands raised. Her hair was crazy, her makeup smeared, her eyes shiny with unshed tears.

No gunshot holes.

The streetlight didn't light up the backseat, so Ali couldn't see Luke's face at all, but there was a stillness to him that terrified her. "Luke?"

"It's okay," he said evenly, holding Bree's gun. "Bree's done now. Right, Bree?"

Bree bobbed her head. A sob escaped her, and she covered her mouth with one hand, leaving the other in the air.

Ali didn't want to blind Luke, so she very carefully lifted her phone just high enough to see his body. And her heart stopped, just stopped dead in her chest. "You were hit."

"I didn't mean to," Bree whispered. "I just wanted to put the money in here. I just wanted Teddy to get what he has coming to him. That's all."

Ali shoved the gun into the back of her waistband to

free up her hands. She had no idea why, but she'd seen it done in the movies. Then she crawled into the backseat, leaned over Luke, and tore open his shirt.

"I love it when you get rough," he said.

"Shut up a minute." The bullet had gone into the meaty part of his shoulder but it looked terrifyingly close to his chest. She could hear the sirens now and sagged in relief. She peeled Luke's shirt down his arm and pulled him forward just enough to see that the bullet had also exited his body. She pulled off her own shirt and pressed it to his front to try to staunch the bleeding.

He grimaced in pain. "Ali."

She leaned over him. "Right here."

"Take the gun."

She took Bree's gun from his fingers. This put her in the possession of two guns. *I Love Lucy* does *Criminal Minds*.

"Keep an eye on her," Luke said.

Since Bree had collapsed on the front seat and was quietly crying into her hands, this wasn't difficult. Ali twisted to keep her in sight. "Done."

"Good," Luke said. "I'm going to pass out now. Nice bra though…isn't this how we met, with you in your underwear?"

And then his eyes closed.

Raw fear nearly choked her. Still holding the gun on Bree, she sank to his side. "Go ahead," she told him, her tears falling onto his face. "I've got you."

The street had come alive with police. The first ones to the car were two cops, both with guns pointed right at her.

That's when she realized she was still holding a gun on Bree. "No," she said, shaking her head as it occurred to her that they probably thought *she* was the one she'd called 9-1-1 about, the crazy woman with a gun. "Oh, no. It's not what you think—"

"Ma'am, put the gun down."

"Okay, dropping the gun now." She dropped it at her feet and then was unceremoniously yanked out of the car and away from Luke.

That's when the other gun fell out of her pants and hit the ground. "Okay," she said. "I know this looks bad, but—"

But nothing. She was quickly and perfunctorily searched for more weapons and pulled clear of the scene. She craned her neck trying to see Luke around the officer dragging her away, but all she could see was a sea of uniforms. There were voices yelling out medical jargon with a sense of urgency that shriveled her soul. She couldn't hear over the rush of the blood roaring in her ears. She couldn't see. "I need to—"

"You need to relax, ma'am."

"Those weren't my guns."

"They were in your possession."

"Yes, because I was holding them for Luke. That's Bree Medina in there, the mayor's wife. She stole the money from town. The fifty thousand? We caught her trying to put it in Teddy's car to frame him. You'll see it in the glove box." He wasn't listening to her rant, she could tell. "Please," she said, "I just want to make sure Luke gets to the hospital."

"He's on his way."

And indeed, just then the ambulance pulled out, heading down the street, lights and siren going.

And then Ali was once again taken to the police station.

Chapter 27

♥

The slow, annoying beeping broke into Luke's consciousness first. And then an antiseptic smell. Ah, *shit*.

A hospital.

He drew in a breath, and pain shot straight through his shoulder and chest, clogging the air in his lungs. Getting shot hurt like a bitch, but oddly enough, he felt a heavy pressure on his *good* side. He opened his eyes and blinked the room into focus.

The pressure was Ali, asleep in the chair at his bedside, her head pillowed on his good arm, wearing…a firefighter shirt.

On the other side of his bed sat Jack. He was leaning back, booted feet up on the bed, hands casually linked on his belly, all relaxed, as if he were watching a ball game. He wore his firefighter uniform—minus the shirt.

"Morning, Sleeping Beauty," Jack said.

"What the fuck?"

Jack smiled grimly. "You caught Bree with the stolen

dough, got her confession recorded on your phone, got shot, had surgery—you're one lucky son of a bitch, by the way—and you're about to get the girl."

Luke looked at Ali. Her hair was wild and crazy and in her face. Her mouth was open a little, and she was drooling on his forearm. He'd never seen her look more beautiful.

"Don't wake her," Jack said. "She had a rough night."

Luke's heart kicked, and one of his monitors beeped a warning.

Jack leaned forward. "Relax, man, she's fine. It's just that when the cavalry showed up, she was holding a gun. The call had gone out about a crazy lady with a gun so…"

"Jesus." Luke wished she wasn't on his good arm so that he could touch her. "Did they—"

"Drag her off you kicking and screaming? Yes. And took Ali downtown." Jack lifted a hand. "She's okay. Your phone made a great witness, and Bree herself confessed everything. I came here first, saw you into surgery, then went down to the station to see what I could do, but Ali was already being released. I brought her here, where we've been ever since."

"So it's over?"

"The hard way, but yeah. You saved the day, man."

"Ali did," Luke said.

Jack shook his head. "I'm pretty sure it was you—"

"No, she saved me," Luke said. "She…" He couldn't tear his gaze off her. "I've been pushing her away since the beginning."

"Tried, you mean."

Luke let out a low laugh, then sucked in a breath of

pain. "Oh, Christ, don't make me laugh." He inhaled very carefully, then let it back out again. "I did try. And she let me think I was getting away with it too."

"She loves you."

Luke's gaze touched over Ali again. "Yeah." *His own miracle.* "Go figure."

"With all that bad 'tude and surly grumpiness," Jack said, "what's not to love?" He paused. "You love her back?"

"More than my own life."

"Which became pretty clear when you put your body between mine and a bullet," Ali said groggily, lifting her head. Her eyes locked on Luke's, searching.

He could see the worry, the strain, the fear in every line of her face. "I'm okay," he said, and then turned to Jack. "Right?"

"Well, your MLB pitching career is over, and PT is going to be a bitch," Jack said, "but your arm and shoulder will eventually be okay. As for your psyche, that's a whole different ball game. Oh and some other good news—Ben's coming back. Unlike you, he's all in one piece, no bullet holes." He rose, stretched, and then bumped his fist very gently to Luke's hand sticking out of the bandages. Walking around the bed, he kissed Ali on the top of her head before walking out of the room.

Ali never took her eyes off of Luke. The night had been the longest of her entire life—being held at the station while Luke had been here, then sitting in that OR waiting room with Jack, pacing through the hours.

If Luke had gone to San Francisco when he'd planned on going, this wouldn't have happened. But he'd stayed to help straighten out her life, and it had nearly cost him his.

"Stop," he said, voice gravelly. Tired. His eyes were knowing. "Stop blaming yourself."

Her throat burned so much that she couldn't speak. "You took a damn bullet for me, Luke."

He lifted his good hand and cupped her face. "I'd do anything for you, Ali."

That was becoming quite clear, and she leaned over him, very, very serious. "Anything?"

"*Anything*."

"Then love me," she whispered.

He slid his fingers into her hair, stroking it from her face. "Done," he said softly.

She was quite certain her heart couldn't swell any more without bursting a rib. "I want one more thing."

He let out a small smile. "You mean other than my life and also my heart and soul?"

She didn't return the smile, couldn't. "Let me love you back."

His smile faded. "Ali—"

"I don't care that you'll be in San Francisco. I don't. Hell, I'd move there if you wanted me too. I love you, Luke. I have from that very first moment you looked at me like I was a crazy, naked woman in your house."

"You *were* a crazy, naked woman in my house." He stroked a finger over her temple, down her jaw. "You need to think about this, Ali. Loving me isn't a day in the park. I'm stubborn and like to be right. I rarely make my bed. I can never find my fucking keys. And last but not least, I love you so hard it hurts. I might die of it, actually, which makes me a short-term bet at best."

With her heart in her throat, she had to both laugh and cry as she dropped her hand to his good shoulder. "I already know you're stubborn as a mule. And I can let you be right—half the time."

She felt his smile and lifted her head. "And an unmade bed works for me," she said softly, "because then we can just get back into it whenever we want without worrying about messing it up."

She felt his hand fist on the back of her shirt, holding her close. "You're the best thing that's ever happened to me," he said fiercely. "The very best." Then he nudged her in closer for a kiss—

"Ahem."

Ali broke away from Luke and turned. In the open doorway, peeking around the curtain, was Sawyer and the mayor.

"Luke," Sawyer said, nodding. "Ali."

The mayor, somber, greeted them as well.

Ali had seen both men briefly in the station last night, though neither had spoken to her. Sawyer had had his hands full with the night's activities. Tony—no doubt called when Bree had been brought in, still sobbing about how she'd been framed by her "own stupid life"—had looked exhausted and solemn.

Which was how they both looked now.

"Wanted to make sure you were still kicking," Sawyer said to Luke.

A very small smile curved Luke's lips. "Been through worse."

"I imagine you have. Couldn't have figured this one out so fast without you."

"It was Ali," Luke said.

Sawyer nodded. "I know. I also know you missed your review. I called Commander O'Neil. They're proceeding without you, but your job's safe and intact." He met Ali's gaze then. "You're a social media sensation this morning."

Oh boy. "You mean like *Hapless Florist Nearly Screws Up Investigation*?"

He smiled. "I believe they said something about Calamity Jane meets Annie Oakley…"

Ali groaned. Luke tried to laugh but choked it off with a sound of pain that had Ali whipping back to him.

"We'll make this short," the mayor said. "Obviously, I'm horrified at the part Bree played in this."

He was careful not to claim her as his *wife*, Ali couldn't help but notice. Probably Bree's days with that title were severely numbered.

Tony looked at Ali. "I wanted to do this right away." He pulled out his phone and accessed a video.

It was the senior center, the room Ali used as a classroom. All the seniors were there, crowded close to the screen, a sea of wrinkled, anxious faces.

"We never should have doubted you, Ali," Mr. Wykowski said.

"And we love and admire you," Lucille said.

"Stay," Mr. Elroy said.

"Please," Mr. Lyons said.

Mrs. Burland was sitting there tight lipped. Lucille smacked her in the arm. Mrs. Burland glared at her, and then into the camera she said, "I know you're smarter than to let a bunch of nosy-bodies chase you away, Ali Winters."

Edward's face appeared. "You're special," he said. "Special and amazing."

"So special and amazing that I'm gifting you the first and last month's lease money for the shop Russell vacated," Mr. Lyons said. "And now for the reward money…"

The video pulled back to get all of them in the same shot. They held a huge mock-up of a check in the amount of five thousand dollars, written to…her.

Ali gaped.

Tony slid his phone away and pulled out a piece of paper.

Her check.

"The reward money," Tony said.

"*Oh*," she breathed, stunned. She looked up at the mayor. "But I can't accept this. Luke—"

"It's all yours," Luke said.

Ali stared down at the check in shock. "It's so pretty," she whispered reverently.

Sawyer laughed, and both he and the mayor left.

"Wow," Ali said with a shake of her head. "I feel like I won the lottery."

"That's not all you won," Luke said.

She leaned in and kissed him. "A trip to Disneyland?" she teased.

"If you want," he said seriously, "but not what I was thinking."

"Some lease money for my flower shop?" she asked, waving the check.

"Most definitely, but still not quite it. Keep going, Ali. You're getting warmer."

"Luke—"

"Need a hint?"

"*Please*," she said.

He tightened his grip on her. "Me. Us." He kissed her. "*This.*"

She couldn't breathe again, but this time it was because hope and love and affection were tangled in her throat, vying for space. "We're an us?"

"Yes," he said, "which is a much better deal for me than you, so be sure—"

She put a finger against his lips. "I'm sure. In fact, I've never been so sure of anything in my life."

Epilogue

Two weeks later, Ali picked up a tray of tea and coffee with hands that weren't quite steady. "I'm so nervous."

Luke, still wearing a sling but getting more and more movement back every day, leaned in and kissed her. "You'll nail this."

"Like she did you," Leah quipped. She picked up the second tray, filled with the pastry goodies she'd made for the grand opening of the new flower shop.

Ali's Blooms.

She'd signed the lease and was officially in the space next to the bakery again.

It was all she'd ever wanted.

Half the town was here for the opening party, and the other half was on their way.

"She can nail me any time," Luke said, and snatched a custard puff from Leah's tray and stuffed it in his mouth. He gave Ali one more quick kiss, tasting like vanilla.

She hummed her pleasure. Just looking up in his warm, blue eyes quelled her nerves. He was her rock.

And she was his, she marveled. He believed in her, trusted her, needed her. Wanted her.

He'd gone to San Francisco for the Reyes review, but he was still on medical leave, so he'd come right back to Lucky Harbor. Sawyer had offered him a job, and he was going to take it. Ali was over the moon that he was staying here in Lucky Harbor.

Catching her looking at him, he gestured for her to set the tray down, then nudged her closer with his good arm. Lowering his head, he pressed his mouth to her ear. "I'm never going to get tired of finding you looking at me that way. Like you have to have me right now."

She laughed, then looked around to make sure Leah wasn't too close. "I just had you," she whispered. Right before they arrived here, in fact. "And I wasn't looking at you like that. If you must know, I was thinking I can't believe you're mine."

"Believe it." He pulled back to look into her eyes. "I belong to you, heart and soul and…" He pressed up against her, making her laugh when she felt him, hard at her belly so that the "and" was clear.

"Tired of me already?" he asked with a smile in his voice.

"Not quite yet. You?"

His eyes darkened, and he kissed her again. "Never."

Her heart skipped a beat. "Never is a long time," she said.

His voice was low, fierce. And very sure. "That's what I'm counting on."

Always on My Mind

To all the real-life firefighters out there, you are true heroes.

And to the people in the field who gave me so much help on the research (and shared some amazing stories!), I'm forever grateful:

Mississippi Commissioner of Insurance and State Fire Marshal Mike Chaney
The Mississippi State Fire Marshal's Office
Chief Deputy Fire Marshal Ricky Davis
Deputy James "Jimmy" Jackson, Fire Marshal Supervisor
State Deputy Fire Coordinator Brad Smith

Chapter 1

Saying that she went to the annual Firefighter's Charity Breakfast for pancakes was like saying she watched baseball for the game—when everyone knew that you watched baseball for the guys in tight uniform pants.

But this time Leah Sullivan really did want pancakes. She also wanted her grandma to live forever, world peace, and hey, while she was making wishes, she wouldn't object to being sweet-talked out of her clothes sometime this year.

But those were all issues for another day. Mid-August was hinting at an Indian summer for the Pacific Northwest. The morning was warm and heading toward hot as she walked to the already crowded pier. The people of Lucky Harbor loved a get-together, and if there was food involved—and cute firefighters to boot—well, that was just a bonus.

Leah accepted a short stack of pancakes from Tim Denison, a firefighter from Station #24. He was a rookie, fresh from the academy and at least five years younger than her, but that didn't stop him from sending her a wink. She took in his beachy, I-belong-on-a-Gap-ad-campaign appearance and waited for her good parts to flutter.

They didn't.

For reasons unknown, her good parts were on vacation and had been for months.

Okay, so not for reasons unknown. But not wanting to go there, not today, she blew out a breath and continued down the length of the pier.

Picnic tables had been set up, most of them full of other Lucky Harbor locals supporting the firefighters' annual breakfast. Leah's friend Ali Winters was halfway through a huge stack of pancakes, eyeing the food line as if considering getting more.

Leah plopped down beside her. "You eating for two already?"

"Bite your tongue." Ali aimed her fork at her along with a pointed *don't mess with me* look. "I've only been with Luke for two months. Pregnancy isn't anywhere on the to-do list yet. I'm just doing my part to support the community."

"By eating two hundred pancakes?"

"Hey, the money goes to the senior center."

There was a salty breeze making a mess of Leah's and Ali's hair, but it didn't dare disturb the woman sitting on the other side of Ali. Nothing much disturbed the cool-as-a-cucumber Aubrey.

"I bet sex is on your to-do list," Aubrey said, joining their conversation.

Ali gave a secret smile.

Aubrey narrowed her eyes. "I could really hate you for that smile."

"You *should* hate me for this smile."

"Luke's that good, huh?"

Ali sighed dreamily. "He's *magic*."

"Magic's just an illusion." Aubrey licked the syrup off her fork while managing to somehow look both beautifully sophisticated and graceful.

Back in their school days, Aubrey had been untouchable, tough as nails, and Leah hadn't been anywhere in the vicinity of her league. Nothing much had changed there. She looked down at herself and sucked in her stomach.

"There's no illusion when it comes to Luke," Ali told Aubrey. "He's one-hundred-percent real. And all mine."

"Well, now you're just being mean," Aubrey said. "And that's my area. Leah, what's with the expensive shoes and cheap haircut?"

Leah put a hand to her choppy auburn layers, and Aubrey smiled at Ali, like *See? That's how you do mean...*

Most of Leah's money went toward her school loans and helping to keep her grandma afloat, but she did have one vice. Okay, two, but being addicted to Pinterest wasn't technically a vice. Her love of shoes most definitely was. She'd gotten today's strappy leather wedges from Paris, and they'd been totally worth having to eat apples and peanut butter for a week. "They were on sale," she said, clicking them together as if she were Dorothy in Oz. "They're knockoffs," she admitted.

Aubrey sighed. "You're not supposed to say that last part. It's not as fun to be mean when you're nice."

"But I am nice," Leah said.

"I know," Aubrey said. "And I'm trying to like you anyway."

The three of them were an extremely unlikely trio, connected by a cute, quirky Victorian building in downtown Lucky Harbor. The building was older than God, currently owned by Aubrey's great-uncle, and divided into three shops. There was Ali's floral shop, Leah's grandma's bakery, and a neglected bookstore that Aubrey had been making noises about taking over since her job at Town Hall had gone south a few weeks back.

Neither Ali nor Leah was sure yet if having Aubrey in the building every day would be fun or a nightmare. But regardless, Aubrey knew her path. So did Ali.

Leah admired the hell out of that. Especially since she'd never known her path. She'd known one thing, the need to get out of Lucky Harbor—and she had. At age seventeen, she'd gone and had rarely looked back.

But she was back now, putting her pastry chef skills to good use helping her grandma while she recovered from knee surgery. The problem was, Leah had gotten out of the habit of settling in one place.

Not quite true, said a little voice inside her. If not for a string of spectacularly bad decisions, she'd have finished French culinary school. And not embarrassed herself on the reality TV show *Sweet Wars*. And…

Don't go there.

Instead, she scooped up a big bite of fluffy pancakes and concentrated on their delicious goodness rather than her own screwups. Obsessing over her bad decisions was something she saved for the deep dark of night.

"Jack's at the griddle," Ali noted.

Leah twisted around to look at the cooking setup. Lieutenant Jack Harper was indeed manning the griddle. He was tall and broad shouldered and looked like a guy who could take on anything that came his way. This was a good thing, since he ran station #24.

Fire Station #24 was one of four that serviced the county, and thanks to the Olympic Mountain range at their back, with its million acres of forest, all four stations were perpetually busy.

Jack thrived on busy. He could be as intimidating as hell when he chose to be, which wasn't right now since he was head-bopping to some beat only he could hear in his headphones. Knowing him, it was some good, old-fashioned, ear-splitting hard rock.

Not too far from him, leashed to a bench off to the side, sat Kevin, a huge Great Dane. He was white with black markings that made him look like a Dalmatian wannabe. Kevin had been given to a neighboring fire station where he'd remained until he'd eaten one too many expensive hoses, torn up one too many beds, and chewed dead one too many pairs of boots. The rambunctious one-year-old had then been put up for adoption.

The only problem was that no one had wanted what was by then a hundred-and-fifty-pound nuisance. Kevin had been headed for the Humane Society when Jack, always the protector, always the savior, had stepped in a few weeks back and saved the day.

Just like he'd done for Leah more times than she could count.

It'd become a great source of entertainment for the entire town that Jack Harper II, once the town terror himself—at least to mothers of teenage daughters everywhere—was now in charge of the *latest* town terror.

Another firefighter stepped up to the griddle to relieve Jack, who loaded a plate for himself and stepped over to Kevin. He flipped the dog a sausage, which Kevin caught in midair with one snap of his huge jaws. The sausage instantly vanished, and Kevin licked his lips, staring intently at Jack's plate as if he could make more sausage fly into his mouth by wish alone.

Jack laughed and crouched down to talk to the dog, a movement that had his shirt riding up, revealing low-riding BDUs—his uniform pants—a strip of taut, tantalizing male skin, and just the hint of a perfect ass.

On either side of Leah, both Ali and Aubrey gave lusty sighs. Leah completely understood. She could feel her own lusty sigh catching in her throat, but she squelched it. They were in the F-zone, she and Jack. *Friends*. Friends didn't do lust, or if they did, they also did the smart, logical thing and ignored it. Still, she felt a smile escape her at the contagious sound of Jack's laughter. Truth was, he'd been making her smile since the sixth grade, when she'd first moved to Lucky Harbor.

As if sensing her appraisal, Jack lifted his head. His dark, mirrored sunglasses hid his eyes, but she knew he was looking right at her because he arched a dark brow.

And on either side of her, Ali and Aubrey sighed again.

"Really?" Leah asked them.

"Well, look at him," Aubrey said unapologetically. "He's hot, he's got rhythm—and not just the fake white-boy kind either. He's also funny as hell. And for a bonus, he's gainfully employed. It's just too bad I'm off men forever."

"Forever's a long time," Ali said, and Leah's gut cramped at the thought of the beautiful, blond Aubrey going after Jack.

But Jack was still looking at Leah. Those glasses were still in the way, but she knew his dark eyes were framed by thick, black lashes and the straight, dark lines of his eyebrows. And the right brow was sliced through by a thin scar, which he'd gotten at age fourteen when he and his cousin Ben had stolen his mom's car and driven it into a fence.

"Forever," Aubrey repeated emphatically. "I'm off men *forever*." Leah felt herself relax a little.

Which was silly. Jack could date whomever he wanted, and did. Often.

"And anyway," Aubrey went on, "that's what batteries are for."

Ali laughed along with Aubrey as they all continued to watch Jack, who'd gone back to the griddle. He was moving to his music again while flipping pancakes, much to the utter delight of the crowd.

"Woo-hoo!" Aubrey yelled at him, both she and Ali toasting him with their plastic cups filled with orange juice.

Jack grinned and took a bow.

"Hey," Ali said, nudging Leah. "Go tip him."

"Is that what the kids are calling it nowadays?" Aubrey asked.

Leah rolled her eyes and stood up. "You're both ridiculous. He's dating some EMT flight nurse."

Or at least he had been as of last week. She couldn't keep up with Jack's dating life. Okay, so she *chose* not to keep up. "We're just...buddies." They always had been, she and Jack, through thick and thin, and there'd been a lot of thin. "When you go to middle school with someone, you learn too much about him," she went on, knowing damn well that she needed to just stop talking, something she couldn't seem to do. "I mean, I couldn't go out with the guy who stole all the condoms on Sex Education Day and then used them as water balloons to blast the track girls as we ran the four hundred."

"I could," Aubrey said.

Leah rolled her eyes, mostly to hide the fact that she'd left off the real reason she couldn't date Jack.

"Where you going?" Ali asked when Leah stood up. "We haven't gotten to talk about the latest episode of *Sweet Wars*. Now that you're halfway through the season and down to the single eliminations, the whole town's talking about it nonstop. Did you know that there's a big crowd at the Love Shack on episode night?"

Yes, she'd known. At first she'd been pressured to go, but she couldn't do it. She couldn't watch herself if anyone else was in the room.

"You were awesome," Ali said.

Maybe, but that had been the adrenaline high from being filmed. Leah had pulled it off by pretending she was Julia Child. Easy enough, since she'd been pretending that since she'd been a kid. After the first terrifying episode, she'd learned something about herself. Even as a kid who'd grown up with little to no self-esteem, there was something about being in front of a camera. It was pretend, so she'd been able to break out of her shell.

The shocking truth was, she'd loved it.

"And also, you looked great on TV," Aubrey said. "Bitch. I know you were judged on originality, presentation, and taste, but you really should get brownie points for not looking fat. Do you look as good for the last three episodes?"

This subject was no better than the last one. "Gotta go," Leah said, grabbing her plate and pointing to the cooking area. "There's sausage now."

"Ah." Aubrey nodded sagely. "So you *do* want Jack's sausage."

Ali burst out laughing, and Aubrey high-fived her.

Ignoring them both, Leah headed toward the grill.

Jack flipped a row of pancakes, rotated a line of sausage links, and checked the flame. He was in a waiting pattern.

The status of his life.

Behind him, two fellow firefighters were talking about how one had bought his girlfriend an expensive purse as an apology for forgetting the anniversary of their first date. The guy thought the present would help ease him out of the doghouse.

Jack knew better. The purse was a nice touch, but in his experience, a man's mistakes were never really forgotten, only meticulously cataloged in a woman's frontal lobe to be pulled out later at her discretion.

A guy needed to either avoid mistakes entirely or get out of the relationship before any anniversaries came up.

"Woof."

This from Kevin, trying to get his attention.

"No more sausage," Jack called to him. "You know what happens when you eat too much. You stink me out of the bedroom."

Kevin had a big black spot over his left eye, giving him the look of a mischievous pirate as he gazed longingly at the row of sausages. When Jack didn't give in, the dog heaved a long sigh and lay down, setting his head on his paws.

"Heads up," Tim called.

Jack caught the gallon-sized container of pancake batter with one hand while continuing to flip pancakes with his other.

"Pretty fancy handiwork," a woman said.

Leah.

Jack turned and found her standing next to Kevin, holding a plate.

Jack gave Kevin the *stay* gesture just as the dog would have made his move. Great Danes had a lot of great qualities, like loyalty and affection, but politeness was not one of them. Kevin lived to press his nose into ladies' crotches, climb on people's laps as if he were a six-pound Pomeranian, and eat...well, everything. And Kevin had his eyes on the prize—Leah's plate.

Jack gestured Leah closer with a crook of his finger. She'd shown up in Lucky Harbor with shadows beneath her forest-green eyes and lots of secrets in them, but she was starting to look a little more like herself. Her white gauzy top and black leggings emphasized a willowy body made lean by hard work or tough times—knowing Leah, it was probably both. Her silky hair was loose and blowing around her face. He'd have called it her just-out-of-bed look, except she wasn't sleeping with anyone at the moment.

He knew this because one, Lucky Harbor didn't keep secrets, and two, he worked at the firehouse, aka Gossip Central. He knew Leah was in a holding pattern too. And something was bothering her.

Not your problem...

But though he told himself that, repeatedly in fact, old habits were hard to break. His friendship with her was as long as it was complicated, but she'd been there for him whenever he'd needed her, no questions asked. In the past week alone she'd driven his mom to her doctor's appointment twice, fed and walked Kevin when Jack had been called out of the county, and left a plate of cream cheese croissants in his fridge—his favorite. There was a lot of water beneath their bridge, but she mattered to him, even when he wanted to wrap his fingers around her neck and squeeze.

"You have any sausage ready?" she asked.

At the word *sausage*, Kevin practically levitated. Ears quirking, nose wriggling, the dog sat up, his sharp eyes following as Jack forked a piece of meat and set it on Leah's plate. When Jack didn't share with Kevin as well, he let out a pitiful whine.

Falling for it hook, line, and sinker, Leah melted. "Aw," she said. "Can I give him one?"

"Only if you want to sleep with him tonight," Jack said.

"I wouldn't mind."

"Trust me, you would."

Coming up beside Jack to help man the grill, Tim waggled a brow at Leah. "I'll sleep with you tonight. No matter how many sausages you eat."

Leah laughed. "You say that to all the women in line."

Tim flashed a grin, a hint of dimple showing. "But with you, I mean it. So...yes?"

"No," Leah said, still smiling. "Not tonight."

"Tomorrow night?"

Jack spoke mildly. "You have a death wish?"

"Huh?"

"Rookies who come on to Leah vanish mysteriously," Jack told him. "Never to be seen again."

Tim narrowed his eyes. "Yeah? Who?"

"The last rookie. His name was Tim too," Jack deadpanned.

Leah laughed, and Tim rolled his eyes. At work, he reported directly to Jack, not that he looked worried.

"I'll risk it," he said cockily to Leah.

Jack wondered if he'd still be looking so sure of himself later when he'd be scrubbing down fire trucks by himself. All of them.

Leah yawned and rubbed a hand over her eyes, and Jack forgot about Tim. "Maybe you should switch to Wheaties," Jack said. "You look like you need the boost."

She met his gaze. "Tim thought I looked all right."

"You know it, babe," Tim said, still shamelessly eavesdropping. "Change your mind about tonight, and I'll make sure you know *exactly* how good you look."

Jack revised his plan about Tim cleaning the engines. The rookie would be too busy at the senior center giving a hands-on fire extinguisher demonstration, which every firefighter worth his salt dreaded because the seniors were feisty, didn't listen, and in the case of the female seniors, liked their "hands-on" *anything* training.

Oblivious to his fate, Tim continued to work the grill. Jack kept his attention on Leah. He wanted her to do whatever floated her boat, but he didn't want her dating a player like Tim. But saying so would be pretty much like waving a red flag in front of a bull, no matter how pretty that bull might be. She'd give a stranger the very shirt off her back, but Jack had long ago learned to not even attempt to tell her what to do or she'd do the opposite just because.

She had a long habit of doing just that.

He blamed her asshole father, but in this case it didn't matter because Leah didn't seem all that interested in Tim's flirting anyway.

Or in anything actually.

Which was what was really bothering Jack. Leah loved the challenge of life, the adventure of it. She'd been chasing that challenge and adventure as long as he'd known her. It was contagious—her spirit, her enthusiasm, her ability to be as unpredictable as the whim of fate.

And unlike anyone else in his world, she alone could lighten a bad mood and make him laugh. But her smile wasn't meeting her eyes. Nudging her aside, out of Tim's earshot, he waited until she looked at him. "Hey," he said.

"Aren't you worried you'll vanish mysteriously, never to be seen again?"

"I'm not a rookie."

She smiled, but again it didn't meet her eyes.

"You okay?" he asked.

"Always." And then she popped a sausage into her mouth.

Jack got the message loud and clear. She didn't want to talk. He could appreciate that. Hell, he was at his happiest not talking. But she'd had a rough year, first with the French culinary school disaster, where she'd quit three weeks before graduation for some mysterious reason, and then *Sweet Wars*.

Rumor had it that she'd gone pretty far on the show, outshining the best of the best. He knew she was under contractual obligations to keep quiet about the results, but he'd thought she'd talk to *him*.

She hadn't.

Jack had watched each episode, cheering her on. Last night she'd created puff pastries on the clock for a panel of celebrity chefs who'd yelled—a lot. Most of Leah's competition had been completely rattled by their bullying ways, but Leah had had a lifetime of dealing with someone just like that. She'd won the challenge, hands down. And even if Jack hadn't known her as well as he did, he'd have pegged her as the winner of the whole thing.

But she wasn't acting like a winner.

Had she quit that too?

Because the truth was that she tended to run from her demons. She always had, and some things never changed.

She met his gaze. "What?"

"You tell me. Tell me what's wrong."

She shook her head, her pretty eyes surprisingly hooded from him. "I've learned to fight my own battles, Jack."

Maybe. But it wasn't her battles he wanted to fight, he realized, so much as he wanted to see her smile again and mean it.

Chapter 2

The next morning, Leah walked to the bakery. From her grandma's house, downtown was only a mile or so, and she liked the exercise, even at four in the morning.

Maybe especially at four in the morning.

Lucky Harbor sat nestled in a rocky cove between the Olympic Mountains and the coast, the architecture an eclectic mix of old and new. She'd been to a lot of places since she'd left here, but there'd been nowhere like this small, cozy, homey town.

The main drag of Lucky Harbor was lined with Victorian buildings painted in bright colors, housing everything from the post office to an art gallery. At the end of the street was the turnoff to the harbor, where a long pier jutted out into the water with its café, arcade, ice cream shop, and Ferris wheel.

Right now, everything was closed. Leah was the only one out on the street. She loved the look of Lucky Harbor on sleepy mornings like this, with the long column of fog floating in from the ocean, the twinkle of the white lights strung along the storefronts and in the trees that lined the sidewalks.

Like a postcard.

And all of it, right down to the salty ocean air, evoked a myriad of memories. So did the bakery as she unlocked it and let herself in. It was warm already, and for now, quiet. Later, Riley would show up. Riley was a Lucky Harbor transplant who'd made her way to town as a runaway teen and then had been taken under the wing of Amy, a friend of Leah's. Riley had grown up a lot in the past few years and was now a part-time college student who worked a few hours a week at both the local café and the bakery. At the moment, though, Leah was alone. She flipped on the lights, and as always, the electricity hummed and then dimmed, fighting for enough power before settling. The cranky old building needed a renovation in the worst way, but Mr. Lyons was so tight with his money he squeaked when he walked.

So tight that he had the building in escrow. No word yet on what the new owner might be like, though he'd promised everyone that he'd honor their leases. This left them safe for the rest of the year at least.

Leah turned on the ovens. They were just as temperamental as the old building. She had to kick the broiler plate twice before hearing the *whoomp* of the gas as it caught. One more day, she thought with some satisfaction. The bakery was going to hold together for at least one more day.

Her grandma Elsie had been baking for fifty-plus years, but she hadn't experimented much in the past few decades. Leah had pretty much taken over, updating the offerings, tossing out the old-fashioned notion of frozen cookie dough, taking great joy in creating all new, all fresh every morning.

It was a lot of work, but she welcomed it because there was something about baking that allowed her to lose herself. Several hours later, she might have had to kick the ovens no less than twelve more times, but the day's offerings were looking damn good. Bread, croissants, and donuts…not exactly the fancy fare she'd gotten used to creating at school or on *Sweet Wars*, but she loved it anyway. And she'd done it all in spite of the equipment.

After that, she shelved her freshly made pastries in the glass display out front and dreamed about finishing culinary school someday. She stopped daydreaming when the bell over the door chimed for the first time that morning. Forest Ranger Matt Bowers strode in mid-yawn.

Leah automatically poured him a Dr. Pepper on tap and bagged up two cheese danishes—his morning special.

"Enjoyed *Sweet Wars* the other night," he said. "You're the best one."

If you can't be the best, Leah, don't bother being anything at all.

Her father's favorite sentence. His second-favorite sentence had been *Christ, Leah Marie, don't you ever get tired of screwing up?* And then there'd been her personal favorite. *You're going to amount to nothing.*

She knew there were people who'd had it far rougher than she had growing up, but his words had always sliced deeply, and her mother's halfhearted attempts to soften the blows with "he means well" or "he loves you" hadn't helped. Instead, they'd left her confused, hurt, and feeling like she could never please.

As a result, she wasn't very good with praise. It made her uncomfortable, like there was a standard that she couldn't possibly live up to.

"Tell me the truth," Matt said. "You won the whole enchilada, right?"

She handed him his breakfast. "I can't say," she told him. "Contractual promises."

Matt took a big bite of the first danish and sighed in pleasure. "Oh yeah. You totally won."

When he was gone, Leah sampled her danish and had to admit he was right about one thing at least. The danish was good.

The bakery door opened again, this time to one of the finest-looking cops in all the land—Sawyer Thompson.

"You're pretty good on that show," he said while she bagged up his favorite, a chocolate chip roll. "You win?"

"Not allowed to say," she said, starting to feel grateful for the contract she'd signed, the one that said keep her mouth shut or else. She handed him his bag.

He took a big bite of the roll and sighed. "You so won."

In spite of herself, Leah flushed with pleasure as he smiled at her, paid, and left.

"Seriously," Ali said from behind Leah, having come in the back door, undoubtedly for her midmorning donut. "You get all the hot guys. It's so unfair."

"You sell flowers," Leah told her. "I sell sugar. Do the math." She gave Ali a bag of donut holes to go and put it on her tab.

And so went the morning. People coming in, buying her stuff—which was good—and asking about *Sweet Wars*—which was bad.

If you can't be the best, Leah, don't bother being anything at all.

"Get out of my head," she said and went back to work. By noon she was ready for a nap, and she still had two more hours to go before Riley would show up. Leah still had to take her grandma for her physical therapy appointment, then grocery shopping for dinner, and then, if Leah was very lucky, she'd catch some sleep. She was going to be thirty this year, and she was already fantasizing about naps. Maybe she should try to get into the senior center…

But she knew it wasn't the hours making her tired. She was used to hard work. Nor was it being displaced, living on a futon in her grandma Elsie's tiny house for the duration of her rehabilitation. Leah was good at the wanderlust, nomadic lifestyle. She should be. She'd hit four colleges in four years, trying out premed, poli-sci, even journalism before going back to her first love.

Baking.

But coming back to Lucky Harbor had thrown her a bit. Elsie's knee surgery had been unexpected. Leah was grateful for how well her grandma was getting around, but the meds made it hard for Elsie to get up early in the morning and handle the baking. So Leah had come to help out for a week or so.

Except she'd passed the one-month mark and she was still here.

The door chimed again, and Dee Harper entered the shop, smiling at the man holding the door open for her.

Her son, Jack Harper.

Kevin was outside, his leash hooked around the wrought-iron bench beneath the picture window. Nose to the glass, the dog was eyeing the display cases like he hadn't eaten in a week.

Jack pointed at him. Kevin licked his chops but sat on his haunches, and then Jack's broad shoulders filled the doorway as he gently nudged his mom to the front counter.

"Hey," he said with a smile at Leah as he sniffed appreciatively. "Smells amazing in here."

"Thanks." She drank in the sight of him. His hair had been cut short again. More for the ease of care than style, she knew. He'd always been way too good-looking for his own good, and that hadn't changed. If anything, time and hard-won experience had only made him more drop-dead gorgeous.

Which wasn't really fair.

But more than his physical prowess was his incredible charisma and easy charm. The joke was that he could coax a nun out of her undies. But that natural magnetism was missing today.

"Anything, Mom," he said to Dee, gesturing to the wide display of choices spread out before them. "Everything. Whatever you want."

"Honey, I told you. I'm not all that hungry."

Jack's eyes were shadowed, his jaw rough with at least a day's growth. "The doctor said to eat, remember? He said if you want to walk through the castles of Scotland like you told him, then you have to build up your strength. And you love Leah's pastries."

Dee smiled at Leah.

Leah smiled back, working hard at not letting her sympathy or worry show. Dee Harper was fighting breast cancer. The chemo was the worst of it, and it was kicking her ass. Leah held out the plate of pastry samples she had on the counter. "Here, try one of my fruit tarts. They're something new I've been working on, but I'm still not sure I got them right. What do you think?"

Dee's expression said that she knew Leah was full of it. They both knew Leah never put out anything that wasn't as perfect as possible. Her father's legacy again—be perfect or be nothing at all. Mostly it was easier for Leah to be nothing at all, but baking was one of those things that she had to do. Like…breathing.

Dee took a bite of a tart. Her clothes were a little loose, and she wore a handkerchief to hide her hair loss. Leah saw the bandage around her forearm and knew they'd just come from the doctor. Jack pulled out a chair for his mom and waited until she sat before he limped very slightly back to the counter. Jaw set, he eyed the selection. "One of everything."

"Go sit," Leah said. "I'll bring it to you."

He didn't sit. He stood there at the counter, shoulders tense, his mirrored sunglasses shoved up on top of his head, saying nothing as he stared into the display.

Heart aching for him and for Dee, Leah poured two glasses of sun tea and brought them to the table. Dee had pulled a ball of yarn and two knitting needles from her bag and appeared to be working on a scarf. She made beautiful blankets too and sold her wares at various local art and craft fairs as her health allowed. When it didn't, friends sold them for her, as Leah had done last weekend.

Leah went back behind the counter and put together a tray of assorted goodies, bringing that to the table as well. Dee stopped knitting to squeeze her hand in thanks and made a token effort to eat some more of the tart.

Leah made her way back to Jack, still standing there at the counter. He shifted, the motion stirring the air with the scent of male skin and laundry soap.

"You okay?" she asked quietly.

"She needs food, and she won't eat. I thought your stuff would be irresistible."

"I meant your knee." Leah wiped her hands on her apron and took a step back to eye his long legs. He'd been a Hotshot for years, one of the rural firefighters who jumped out of planes to fight fires in the mountains and on the plains, until a knee injury five years ago had side-lined him. He'd taken a job working for the Lucky Harbor Fire Department. Not nearly as exciting, she knew. "What happened?"

He shrugged dismissively. Guy code for "nothing."

"Did you go see a doctor?" she asked.

He gave another shrug and turned to face her. "I need you to get her to eat."

His voice was low and a little raw. But that's not what got her. He'd asked her for something, for help, and he never asked lightly. Though it made Leah want to comfort him with a hug, she did an about-face and went back to the table. Sitting next to Dee, she nudged the plate of goodies closer to her as Jack's phone rang.

"I've got to take this," he said and strode out of the bakery.

The minute he did, Kevin leaped on him, tall enough on his hind legs that man and dog were nearly nose to nose. Jack ruffled Kevin's big head and gave him a push.

Kevin slid to the ground and rolled over on his back, exposing his belly. Obliging him, Jack squatted low, stroking the dog into ecstasy as he spoke into his phone.

Leah did her best not to look at his ass through the window, but it was hopeless. He had a great one.

Beside her, Dee set down the tart. "It's like old times, the two of you."

Not quite, but Leah knew what she meant. Back then, as the new girl, she hadn't fit in, and Jack had been the only one to tolerate her. He'd allowed her to tag along after him and his friends, though he'd always sent her home well before they'd gotten themselves into trouble.

And oh, how she'd resented that. She'd loved trouble. She'd loved *him*, the way he had of making her forget her miserable home life, or how he'd make her laugh. He'd been far more than an escape from a rough childhood for her. He might have been two years ahead of her in age and light-years ahead of her in experience, but he'd been her best friend.

They'd kept in touch over the years with texts and emails. They'd talked when she'd needed a familiar shoulder to cry on. Jack had always been far more stoic though, but he'd done his own fair share of calling her just to "make sure she hadn't fallen off the deep end." Leah had usually interpreted this to mean he needed to vent, and she'd drag out of him whatever was on his mind. She'd treasured those calls the most, being needed by him. They'd come all too rarely because Jack didn't like to need anyone.

"It's nice," Dee said.

Leah reached out and squeezed Dee's hand. "It's nice to be back."

"You're concerned about me. Don't be. I'm going to be okay."

"I know," Leah said, and hoped to God that it was true.

Outside, Jack rose, one hand holding the phone to his ear, the other resting on Kevin's head, which came up to his hip.

"I really didn't want anything to eat," Dee said. "But he wanted me to so badly."

"He's worried about you."

"Well that makes us even, because I'm worried about him too. Did he tell you? He needs another knee surgery, just like what your grandma had, but he's too stubborn to get it done."

"No," Leah said, her gaze roaming back to Jack's broad shoulders. "He didn't mention that."

"He pushes himself too hard."

"You know why," Leah said softly.

"Yes," Dee said. "I know why."

Everyone knew. Jack's dad had been a firefighter. He'd lived and breathed the job. And then he'd died on that job, becoming a local hero. What else was the boy of that hero supposed to do except become a firefighter as well and do his best to live up to the legend?

"I ruined him," Dee said.

"What? No," Leah said emphatically. "*No*. Dee, you raised him well. You—"

"I fell apart when his daddy died." She nodded at Leah. "Don't you pretend otherwise. I fell apart, and Jack watched me. And now he doesn't do relationships."

"Dee," Leah said, managing to find a laugh. "Your son has had more relationships than I have shoes. And we all know how many pairs of shoes I have. Too many to count."

Jack had always been irresistible to the opposite sex. Maybe because he'd always been tall and built with that protective, chivalrous air. Or maybe it was that spark in his rich caramel eyes, the one that said *I'm trouble and worth every minute of it.*

In any case, Jack had had a way of getting himself into, and then smoothly out of, any so-called relationship with a girl without it ever getting ugly. He was what Leah jokingly labeled "a picker." There was always some reason that he couldn't take his relationships to the next level. Too clingy. Too ostentatious. Too crazy. She'd long ago decided not to obsess over what excuse he'd use to dump her, knowing there were too many to worry about.

Dee was shaking her head. "I'm talking about a *real* relationship, Leah. One that lasts long enough for him to bring her home to meet me. He avoids doing that." She paused. "Well, except for you, honey."

Leah's stomach tightened. She and Jack hadn't ever really gone there.

Except that once. That *almost* once.

"He'll find the right woman," she said quietly. "It only takes one."

"But when?"

"Maybe he's working on it."

"He's not." Dee's brow was creased in worry, and her voice wobbled. "He's not working on it at all. And he's going to end up alone, as I have. And who could blame him? Ever since his dad died, it's all I've shown him."

"Dee—"

"It is my fault, Leah. He won't get too attached. I taught him that. I have to undo it before it's too late."

Her words grabbed Leah by the throat and held on. She wanted to say something, *anything*, like "it's not too late" or "there's lots of time," but looking into Dee's eyes, she knew that might not be true. Leah had a lot of faults, big, fat faults like running tail when the going got tough, pretending everything was okay when it wasn't, and sometimes, late at night when no one was looking, she even ate store-bought cookies.

But she didn't lie.

"I want to make this right for him," Dee said quietly. Desperately. "I need to make this one thing right at least."

Jack was a black-and-white kind of guy and not all that complicated when it came right down to it. He hated closed spaces—an endless source of amusement to his co-workers. He hated snakes. He hated green toenail polish.

And yet Leah could bank on the fact that he'd date anything blond and stacked, even if that stacked blonde lived in a small closet filled with snakes and wore green toenail polish.

She also knew he was the most stubborn man on the planet. He'd argue the sky wasn't blue, and it took an Act of Congress for him to admit when he was wrong about anything. But above all else, he was extremely careful not to share his heart. Which meant that Dee *couldn't* make this right. And yet there she sat, looking so worried and so heartbreakingly ill.

From the other side of the window, still on the phone, stood Jack, his posture giving away nothing.

But Leah knew he was worried sick too.

Kevin, now sitting on Jack's big boot, was also looking worried. Worried that there wasn't any food in his near future.

But Jack…

Damn. "He's okay," she said, hoping like hell that was really true.

"But how do you *know*?" Dee asked.

"Because…" And that's when it happened, when Leah's brain disconnected from her mouth. "We're together."

Dee went still.

So did Leah, still with shock at her own words.

"Wait," Dee said slowly. "You and Jack…*really*?" she asked, as if she didn't trust her own hearing.

"Uh—"

"Oh my goodness, honey." Dee was looking like she'd just found out it was Christmas morning and Santa had come. "Oh my goodness!"

For someone who didn't lie, this was a hell of a way to jump into the pool. Not a lie, Leah corrected.

A fib.

A fib told in order to give Dee the one thing Leah had to offer—a little peace of mind. Jack wouldn't care. Probably.

Okay, he was going to care.

Unless…unless he never found out. Was that too much to hope for?

"You and Jack," Dee repeated, a slow, warm smile creasing her face. A *real* smile, one that seemed to light her up from within. "I've hoped," she said, "oh how I've hoped. But he's always got some silly woman in his sights, and you're never here, and plus you're both so damn stubborn—"

The bakery door opened, the bell dinged, and Dee whirled around to face her son. "Oh, Jack! Oh, sweetheart, I'm *so* happy."

This clearly surprised the hell out of Jack. He stood there taking in his mom's expression, obviously trying to figure out what had happened in the span of the five minutes he'd been outside that could have changed her mood so drastically.

And also her appearance, Leah realized. Because Dee was...glowing.

"You should have told me," Dee said, practically vibrating. "Did you think I wouldn't have been thrilled to hear that you and Leah are together?"

Jack's gaze locked on Leah, brow raised.

Okay, so maybe he was going to find out.

Chapter 3

♥

You and Leah are together… Jack's mom's words bounced around in his head like a Ping-Pong ball as he stared at Leah for an explanation.

She had a hell of an explanation if her blush was any indication. "It just sort of came up," she said, nibbling on her lower lip.

He recognized the tell. She nibbled on her lip whenever she stepped in the proverbial pile of shit. "It just sort of came up," he repeated, nodding like this made perfect sense to him. But then he shook his head because it made absolutely no sense at all. He knew he was off his game big-time, crazy with worry over his mom, but this was not computing. "What exactly *sort of* came up?"

"Why, you and Leah, silly," his mom said with a delighted laugh.

A laugh.

Jack hadn't seen her so much as crack a smile in weeks.

Maybe months.

And here she was, laughing. Had it been only a day ago that she'd been lying on her couch in her Sunday best, arm poised dramatically over her eyes, as she told him that she was just going to die quietly and try not to make a mess "so don't mind me."

"Me and Leah," he said slowly, aware that he was starting to sound like a parrot. "What?"

"Honestly, Jack." His mom was still smiling easily, like she had in the old days. The *very* old days, before his dad had died. "I'm the shaky one today," she said. "Turn on your brain." She was beaming with joy.

And Jack got his first real sense of doom. It started deep in his gut and ended up dead center between his eyes as a tension headache.

Back in the spring, when they'd first gotten his mom's diagnosis, his summer goal had been simple—get his mom through it. The goal was now in sight, the light at the end of the tunnel visible. It was August and she was beating the cancer, though granted the treatment was now the one endangering her.

But he should have known nothing was ever as simple as it looked.

"It's so wonderful," his mom said, hands clasped together. "I was just telling Leah that I'd always secretly hoped, but you two seemed so set on ignoring all the chemistry between the two of you. Remember back when Leah graduated high school, sweetheart? You were home from college for the summer, just before she left town. Remember how much she loved you back then?"

Leah made a sound of embarrassment and started to turn away, but Dee smiled at her. "It's true, honey, you know it is. You used to do his homework for him, remember? He was perfectly capable of doing it himself, except that he hated English and history. He needed to keep his GPA up for that scholarship and you…well, you remember."

Yes, it was clear by the look on Leah's face that she remembered exactly. Two grades behind him, she'd managed to save his ass *and* keep up with her own school load—and since her father had required straight A's of her, not to mention the hours of filing and other administrative work she'd had to put in every day at his dental practice as well—this had been quite the feat.

"And then when Jack Senior died," Dee said, "and he fell apart, you were there for him."

Jack opened his mouth but closed it again. What was he going to do, remind his mother in public that she had been the one to fall apart? That it'd been all he and his cousin Ben could do to keep the house and their lives together? The doctors had eventually been able to treat her depression, but her bouts of anxiety had never abated.

"No one else could console him," Dee said to Leah. "Not Ben. Not me. No one." She paused. "Only you, Leah."

Admittedly, Jack had grieved and grieved hard. He'd been a teenager who'd lost his father unexpectedly, and then he'd grown up in the shadow of his dad's legend.

But there were worse things.

And yet his mom was right about one thing. Leah had been there, no matter what she faced in her own home life. She'd found time to make them meals, do his homework, cover his ass however it had needed covering.

She'd done that for him. She'd been his rock.

"I really thought the two of you would go for it back then," Dee said, and Leah sucked in a breath.

Jack did his best not to react because he wasn't willing to admit that he'd thought the same. That he'd thought it up until the day Leah had walked away.

Always running.

"You're right, Dee," Leah said, her gaze on Jack. "The chemistry finally got us."

"Did it?" Jack asked her softly.

"Yes." There was a long, indefinable beat when something seemed to shimmer between them, and then suddenly Leah was a study of movement, hustling to put some space between them. "I was about to tell your mom that it's not a big deal," she said, very busy wiping down the other tables, way too busy to meet his gaze. "And that we'd like to keep things under wraps."

"Under wraps?" Dee asked.

"Yes," Leah said. "Because as you know, Lucky Harbor doesn't keep its secrets very well. We'd rather no one knew yet."

His mom looked so disappointed. "So this is…new?" she wanted to know. "This relationship between you?"

Leah did glance at Jack then, two spots of color on her cheeks as, unbelievably, she deferred the question to him. He crossed his arms and blessed her with his you've-got-to-be-kidding-me expression.

"Um," she said, blanching a little bit. "Sort of new, yeah. A little bit."

Dee processed this. "I bet it happened at the music festival on the pier, right? I saw you two dancing that night. So romantic, so sweet."

The festival had been a month ago. Jack remembered that he and Leah had shared one quick dance and then he'd been called into work. And if he'd enjoyed it a little too much, the way Leah's skirt had twirled around her thighs, how she'd felt against him, he'd told himself he'd gotten caught up in the moment.

"Yes," Leah said. "It happened at the music festival. We had late-night brownies at the café afterward, and that was that."

"But Jack was called to work that night on a suspicious fire," Dee said. "I remember because he called me from the station at midnight to make sure I got home okay."

"Late, *late*-night brownies," Leah corrected.

"Don't you make your own brownies?" Dee asked.

"Once in a while I cheat," Leah said, sounding a little strained.

No wonder. Lying was damn hard work.

Jack moved around the counter to face her. She was wearing jeans and a long halter top that had some flour on it.

He was six feet two, but they were still nearly nose to nose thanks to a pair of strappy, high-heeled sandals. How she worked in her seemingly endless supply of shoes he had no idea, but they were sexy as hell.

This was confusing too. When had she become sexy as hell? And why? They were friends. Nothing more. She'd made that evident a long time ago. "Why do you wear shoes like that to work?" he asked. "You're going to break an ankle."

"Aw," Dee said, delighted.

He looked at her. "What?"

"You noticed her shoes! Jack, do you know what that means?"

That he'd gone over the deep edge? He put a hand to his head. Was the world spinning? He felt a little dizzy.

"Listen," Leah said. "Forget my shoes. About the other thing. About…us." She swallowed. "Your mom was worried about you." Her eyes were desperately trying to communicate something to him.

Probably that she was crazy.

Which he already knew.

Jack turned to his mom. "Mom, we've talked about this. I don't want you wasting your energy worrying about me. You need to be focusing on yourself right now."

Oh, Christ. Suddenly this was all making sense, the chain of events that had led to Leah's proclamation that they were a "thing."

Not that it mattered, because this wasn't going to happen. They were not going to lie to his mom.

"It haunts me at night, Jack," Dee said.

Ah, damn. He loved his mom, more than anything. But if she gave the "I've had a good life and all I want is for you to meet a great girl so I can die happy" speech he was going to burst a blood vessel. "Mom—"

"It's all my fault, Jack. Don't you see? After your dad died—"

"No," he said firmly. "*Nothing* about that was your fault."

It really hadn't been anyone's fault, which of course had made it all the harder to accept. Jack knew he wouldn't have made it through that time without Ben or Leah—something he'd never told her but should have.

Which meant that he couldn't kill her for this latest stunt.

"I never showed you it was okay to move on from grief," Dee said. "That's why you never have any meaningful relationships with women."

Jack opened his mouth to say he didn't have the lifestyle for that right now anyway, just as the power blinked out and then back on. Then something sizzled, and this time, when the lights flickered and went out, they stayed out.

"Crap!" Leah said. "My soufflé." And she vanished into the kitchen.

"You okay?" Jack asked his mom.

"I'm great, actually."

She was still smiling. *Jesus.* "Wait here," he said and followed Leah into the kitchen.

She stood in front of one of the ovens, staring gloomily into the small window.

"Don't start with me," she said. "Do you have any idea how long it takes to make a great soufflé? And now it's all going to be ruined. Dammit! I knew better. The power's been going on and off for days. Mr. Lyons looked at it and replaced the fuses. They should've lasted longer than this."

Jack frowned. "This has been going on for days?"

"Weeks, actually. Maybe longer. At first, I thought maybe Grandma had forgotten to pay the bill, but I made sure it got paid on time this past month."

Jack strode out the kitchen door to the back alley, moving along the wall to the electrical panel. Just as he opened it, the flower shop's back door opened too, and out came a harried-looking Ali.

"Jack," she said in surprise, a pair of clippers in one hand, a rose in the other. "Did you turn off the power?"

"No." He looked inside the electrical panel and swore. The wiring was a mess, crisscrossed and frayed. The building was so old that they still had fuses behind the wiring, and he could see two right off the bat that were blown.

The entire downtown commercial row of Lucky Harbor was quaint and historical, but not necessarily practical, since most of the buildings were a hundred-plus years old. This building, one of the oldest, was in serious need of a big renovation, but the historical society—currently run by Max Fitzgerald—had a pretty restrictive rein on the county building department and the permits, all in the name of protecting history.

But what they were *really* doing was unintentionally preserving Jack's—and all the other firefighters'—jobs because this was a disaster waiting to happen.

Leah had followed him out. She stuck her hand into her pocket and came out with a palm full of fuses.

"Look at you with all the preparedness today," he said dryly.

She winced. "The fuses keep blowing," she said quickly, clearly choosing to ignore their situation, and they did have a situation. "I have to be prepared," she said, "or I ruin whatever I'm cooking."

Their gazes met. Aware of Ali standing within hearing range, Jack said none of what he wanted to say. Which was along the lines of: *What the fuck, Leah?* Instead he said, "We need to find out what's wrong with the wiring and why the fuses are blowing."

"Oh, we know why," Ali offered. "The place is falling apart."

"What about the new guy?" Jack asked. "The one who bought this place?"

"He's got the money," Leah said. "But the inspection didn't go well, and he's been making a stink about the hidden problems and condition of the place. He wants the price reduced. But Mr. Lyons says he sold the place as is and he doesn't give a rat's ass about the problems and that Mr. Rinaldi can cry him a river. So the sale might fall through."

"Why is Lyons selling in the first place?"

"He wants to retire and get a 'chickie.' And I'm pretty sure he doesn't mean a chicken," she said with a shudder.

Jack took the fuses from her and began to change them out. "We have something else to discuss," he said.

Leah glanced at Ali, then back to Jack. She bit her lip again. "Later."

Oh, there was going to be a later.

"There you kids are," Dee said, coming out with the plate of pastries that Leah had made for her. Jack ground his teeth and kept working on the fuses as Dee offered the plate to Ali, who happily partook.

"Oh my God," the florist said with a moan as she took her first bite of a pastry. "So good. Did you know that her grandma swears that Leah somehow makes these with restorative powers? You'll feel like a million bucks after you eat her stuff, Dee."

Dee smiled. "I already feel like a million bucks, but it's not the food. It's thanks to Jack finally getting his head on straight and being with Leah."

Ali stilled, and then, eyes wide, turned to Leah.

But Leah was now choking on a scone, and probably, Jack thought with grim satisfaction, a good amount of guilt as well. She pointed to her throat, indicating she couldn't talk.

Ali pivoted and looked at Jack.

Jack peered deeply into the electrical panel, wishing it would ignite. Where was a fire when he needed one?

"Big news, right?" Dee asked Ali happily.

"Leah dating my boyfriend's BFF? Yep," Ali said. "That's big news all right. The biggest."

"They didn't want anyone to know," Dee said, completely oblivious to the fact that Leah was behind her back making a knife-across-her-throat gesture at Ali.

"Silly kids," Dee said. "As if you can keep a secret in this town."

"Silly kids," Ali agreed, smiling widely at the still-motioning Leah. "They should know better."

"Yeah, well, I have to go," Leah said. "Stuff." She gestured vaguely to the bakery. "In the oven." And with one last glare at Ali, she vanished back inside the bakery.

Dee beamed at Jack and then followed after her.

Jack got the last fuse back in. The power came back on. He turned and nearly plowed into Ali, who was still grinning. "What?" he said.

"Nothing." But she laughed.

He gave her a steely-eyed stare, which didn't appear to intimidate her in the least. In fact, she laughed again, obviously delighted. "It's just that you spent most of last month watching me squirm as Luke and I fell in love," she reminded him.

"Yeah?" he said. "So?"

"So," she said, and poked him in the chest, "it's going to be fun watching you squirm for a change."

"It's not what you think."

"No, Jack," she said, heading back into her shop. "It's not what *you* think."

He stared at the door as she shut it gently in his face. "What the hell does that mean?" he asked.

But the door didn't answer him.

Chapter 4

♥

When Jack returned to the bakery, Leah was in the kitchen, furiously whipping something in a bowl, her cell phone pinched between her ear and her shoulder.

"We have to talk," he said.

Leah gestured that she needed a minute.

Jack leaned against a counter and crossed his arms, prepared to wait her out.

She gave him a few side glances as she whipped the hell out of whatever was in the bowl. "Uh-huh," she said into her phone. "Uh-huh. Uh-huh."

Something in her voice clued him in, and he pushed away from the counter, heading toward her.

With a squeak, she stopped whipping. "Uh-huh," she said, faster now, and in a higher octave. She held up a finger, indicating she wanted him to wait a minute.

But oh hell no was he going to wait another damn second. Instead, he reached for her phone.

"Hey," she hissed. "I'm on a very important call—"

He pulled it from her fingers and looked at the screen. It was black.

He narrowed his eyes at her.

She winced and then jumped when the phone rang for real, flashing "Grandma Elsie."

"I have to answer that," Leah said.

He held it above his head.

"Jack."

"Not until you explain your little stunt in there." In case she wasn't clear on which "little stunt," he jabbed a finger to the front of the bakery, where through the small window between the kitchen and front room, he could see his mom once again at the table waiting for him. She was talking to Riley, who'd just showed up for work.

Probably telling Riley all about him and Leah being a thing. *Jesus.*

Leah used his momentary distraction to push him back to the counter and tried to crawl up his body for her still-ringing phone. With those heels, she was plastered to him, chest to chest, hips to hips, thighs to thighs, all their parts lining up neatly—and damn if he didn't forget about her phone.

Which is how she snatched it from him with ease. "Hi, Grandma," she said breathlessly, shooting Jack a reproachful look before turning her back to him. "You okay?"

"No," Jack said, checking out her ass.

Behind her back, Leah waved her hand at him. "Shh!"

Still recovering from their full-body contact, he had to let out a long breath as he realized that once again he'd been the only one to feel anything.

And why the hell was he feeling anything at all?

Frustrated, he strode out to the front room and found his mom happily consuming a raspberry tart. "What the hell does it mean if I notice a woman's shoes?" he asked her.

She smiled sweetly.

"What's that? What does that smile mean?" he asked.

She refused to answer.

Leah spent the rest of the day baking like mad, an ear cocked to the door for Jack. She was torn between the terrible hope that he got a call from work—not a serious call, mind you, maybe just a cat up in a tree—and getting the inevitable awkward conversation between them over with. The problem was that she couldn't envision the conversation. No doubt he'd start with a *what the hell, Leah*, and she'd say...what? What could she possibly say? *I'm sorry I let my stupid, pathetic crush out of the bag*? No. Hell no. Maybe she could say *well, I thought pretend was better than nothing*. No, that was even more revealing.

Okay, so the real problem was that she had no excuse. None.

Yes, she'd wanted to ease Dee's mind, but they both knew there were far better ways.

Thankfully, Riley worked the front of the shop for her, serving their customers and allowing Leah to avoid having to face anyone. But eventually Riley had to leave to make the day's deliveries.

The moment she did, of course, was the moment the bell chimed. Leah came out from the kitchen just as Ben McDaniel walked in.

Ben was Jack's cousin, and when he wasn't in a third-

world country designing and building water systems for
war-torn lands with the U.S. Army Corps of Engineers,
he and Jack shared a duplex a few blocks down, near the
fire station.

Leah smiled at him, and knowing he wasn't one for
small talk, she turned to pour him a coffee, black, and
bagged up a bear claw.

His standard fare.

He paid, and then instead of leaving as he usually did,
he leaned against the counter and drank his coffee, watching her over the lid. Deceptively chill and laid-back, he
gave off an almost surfer-guy vibe, but in truth he was
about as badass as they came.

"What?" she finally asked.

"You tell me what."

She lifted a shoulder. Look at her being all cool and
casual. One had to be with Ben; he could spot a weakness
a mile away. "I can't tell you if I won *Sweet Wars*."

He shook his head. Not that.

"I'm not talking about this morning," she said. At
least not until she talked to Jack. Which she hoped to
do…never.

Ben dug into his bear claw, looking as if he had all the
time in the world, and for all she knew, he did. He'd just
come back from being on loan to the Department of Defense for the past eight months in Iraq. Before that, it had
been Haiti and the earthquake aftermath, and before that,
Japan's tsunami, and so on.

But before any of those adventures, once upon a time,
he'd actually worked in Seattle at a normal nine-to-five
job—until his wife had died.

He finished his bear claw, balled up the paper, and

made a three-pointer in the trash can across the bakery with no visible effort. "Thanks," he said, and was gone.

Leah blew out a breath. Another bullet dodged, she thought and went back to work.

Since she'd been handling daily baking, she'd also taken on some responsibilities that were new to the bakery, such as a little catering. She created wedding cakes and baked for showers and reunions or whatever event came her way. The equipment—hello, ovens, looking at you—was killing her slowly, but she was still managing to enjoy it immensely. Two days ago, she'd created a dozen cream puffs for the B&B. The job had been incredibly stressful because the B&B was owned by three sisters, one of whom was a chef—a really great one.

Leah had angsted over those twelve stupid cream puffs like they were for the royal palace, spending hours making sure every fraction of an inch of each one was perfect. She had no idea if she'd succeeded until a few hours ago.

Tara had called from the B&B and said the cream puffs were so amazing she needed three dozen more for a baby shower, and could Leah rush the order for this afternoon?

Leah was currently rushing toward a heart attack.

Bent over the tray, she was obsessing over each little puff with one eye on the clock when Aubrey strode in.

The beautiful, cool blonde struck a pose in the center of the bakery as if she were mugging for the paparazzi, one leg out in front of the other so the slit on her skirt opened and flashed a trim thigh. She waited expectantly.

Leah looked up from her task. "Well hi there, Angelina Jolie."

"Not the leg," Aubrey said, annoyed. She wriggled her

foot, drawing Leah's gaze to the gorgeous leather boots. "I finally have better shoes than you. I won't be eating all month, but they're totally worth it. I need you to be jealous."

Leah laughed but bent back over her cream puffs. "I don't have time to be jealous. I don't have time to talk."

"Why?" Aubrey asked, giving up her pose. "You always have time to talk."

Leah swiped her brow, spreading a dab of frosting over her temple. "I've only got thirty minutes before I have to have these delivered. And if I keep talking, I'll mess them up."

"What are you smoking? They're perfect," Aubrey said, and actually reached out to take one.

Leah smacked her hand away. "Oh my God, don't touch!"

"Well, jeez. I just wanted one," Aubrey said, rubbing her hand. "And I take back what I said. You're not nice at all."

Leah sighed. "You can't have a cream puff. They're for a fancy gig at the B&B."

Aubrey rolled her eyes. "You do realize you're not on TV, right? This is Lucky Harbor, not Paris. Drop some dough in a vat of grease and slap them on a tray, and people will be happy."

"That's not true," Leah said. "And it does matter. Each order matters. They have to be perfect, or why would I bother at all?" Leah went still, then set her pastry bag aside and staggered back a step. "Oh my God."

"What?"

She stared at Aubrey in horror. "I've turned into my father. Quick. Shoot me."

"I would," Aubrey said, "but I'm not all that keen on prison. Maybe I should just call the people with the white straight-jackets to come get you."

"This isn't funny," Leah said. "I need sympathy."

"I don't do sympathy. Call Ali for that." Aubrey strode closer to the displays. "But while I'm here, I'll take two cannoli. They have lots of calories, right?"

"Yes."

"Good. They're for my sister. I like it when she's fatter than I am. And they're free today since you snapped at the customer and that's not allowed."

Leah bagged the cannoli and shoved her out the door just to get rid of her.

By the end of the day, Leah was frazzled and on edge. She'd finished her orders, but Jack hadn't called. His silence felt weighted and suspicious. She opened her back door and peeked out. No one. She stepped out and nearly jumped out of her skin when Ali came out of her door at the same time. "You scared the crap out of me."

"Did I?" Ali asked. "Who did you think I was?"

A big, built, pissed-off firefighter. "No one. Gotta go. Night—"

"Hold it right there," Ali said. Clearly she wasn't done working for the day because she was holding a vase and a sprig of baby's breath. "Explain about earlier."

"Well, the fuses blew, so—"

"You and Jack," Ali said. "Explain you and Jack."

"Listen, it's been a long day, and—"

"Oh no. You're not going anywhere. Not until you answer my question." She pointed the sprig at Leah. "You and Jack. Yes or no."

Leah sighed. "Yes. Okay? Yes." *Dammit.* "Sort of."

"Sort of," Ali repeated. "You take up with the hottest guy in Lucky Harbor and you don't tell me?"

"I thought Luke was the hottest guy in Lucky Harbor."

"The hottest guy's best friend then," Ali corrected. "And don't change the subject, missy."

Leah sighed again. "It's just pretend, Ali. I made it up."

Ali gaped at her, then let out a low laugh. "You made it up? You just decided you suddenly had to have him—which, hello, any woman with an ounce of warm blood in her body would understand—and then you figured you'd just say it out loud and it would be so? How does that even work? Because I'd like to have a million dollars—"

"This isn't a joke, Ali. I'm in big trouble here."

"No shit," Ali said on another laugh. "Jack's pretty laid-back but he's not a guy you can push around. He's not going to like being played with."

"I'm not trying to play with him. I'm just trying to make his mom happy."

"Oh. *Oh...*" Ali breathed. "I get it." Then she shook her head. "Except I don't."

Leah sighed. "You've seen Dee. The chemo and radiation are making her sick, really sick. She was feeling down, and I just wanted to..." She shrugged helplessly. "I don't know, make her feel better. She's so worried about Jack. She feels bad about some of the choices she's made over the years, choices that she thinks led to Jack not being big on relationships. She was *down*," she said again, guilt swamping her.

"Dee's been feeling down for a very long time," Ali said gently. "You know that."

This Leah already knew. She'd been there in those

years right after Jack's dad's death. She'd seen Dee slowly fall apart, and she'd watched Jack and Ben—teenagers at the time—have to hold it all together for her; the house, the bills, the memories, everything. Leah had done whatever she could but had still felt so helpless. "Maybe me and Jack being a thing will help."

Ali shook her head. "Jack would be the first one to do whatever he needed to do to make his mom happy. But pretending to be in a relationship? That doesn't sound like him at all."

Leah grimaced. "Yeah, well, that's because it wasn't his idea."

The amusement came back into Ali's gaze. "You sprung it on him?" She let the smile come. "Would've loved to see that."

"This isn't funny, Ali."

"Yeah, it is. You got Jack to actually agree to this *pretend* relationship?"

"Not exactly."

Ali stared at her and then laughed. She laughed so hard she nearly dropped her vase. Finally, she straightened and swiped at a few tears of mirth. "Oh God, this is good. Jack in a *pretend* relationship."

"A *secret*, pretend relationship," Leah reminded her.

"A *secret*, pretend relationship," Ali repeated. "The single women in town are going to go into mourning." She was still grinning. "Luke's going to love this."

"You can't tell him!" Leah said. "Everyone has to think it's real."

"Aren't you cute." Ali patted her on the arm as if she were a three-year-old. "Leah, it *is* real."

Leah gaped at her. "What? No. No, no, no. It's…not."

Mostly because she'd already had her chance and blown it.

Big-time.

Which actually put Jack on her ever-growing list of regrets.

Twice.

Ali just smiled and turned, heading back inside her shop.

"It's not," Leah called after her. "It's all for Dee."

Ali lifted her hand, waved, and shut the door.

"It is!"

"Whatever helps you sleep at night," Ali yelled back through the wood.

"Well, dammit." Leah whirled in the other direction and headed to her car. "It *is* pretend," she told her rearview mirror. "Completely."

Chapter 5

Leah picked up her grandma for physical therapy, already mentally calculating the rest of the hours left in the day. She had to work on bookkeeping—her grandma had been extremely lax about that—and then there was the stack of payables about two feet taller than their receivables. But Leah was working hard on all of it and trying to increase business while she was at it, and it was starting to work.

"You're so sweet to do all this for me," Elsie said. "But honey, I could have taken the Senior Dial-A-Ride."

"I don't mind," Leah said as they parked at PT. "And I didn't want you to get stuck waiting."

"I have my lover," Elsie said and waved her ebook reader. "I can wait forever with my Kindle fully charged and ready to please me."

"A lover who can never leave you," Leah said with a laugh, turning off the engine. "Smart."

Her grandma's smile faded some. "Is that what you think of men? That they'll leave you?"

Since that was far too serious a conversation for the moment—and absolutely one she didn't want to have—Leah shook her head and reached over to hug her grandma. "You smell like roses."

Elsie huffed out a low laugh. "That's code for 'mind your own business, Grandma.'" Pulling back, she gently patted Leah's cheeks. "I'm happy to have you back, Leah. So happy."

"I'm happy to be back."

Her grandma's blue eyes held Leah's for a long beat. "It's been good for you, right?" she said. "Being here? Being happy here?"

And there it was. The elephant in the room.

Yes, Leah's childhood had not been happy here in Lucky Harbor. But her parents had retired to Palm Springs, thirteen hundred miles south. And after her dad's death, her mom had stayed down there. The distance worked for them both, more than it should. "Yes," she said. "I'm happy here."

"Your mom says you called the other day," Elsie said.

Leah made an obligatory call every other week, during which she and her mom had a shallow conversation. Yes, she was fine. Yes, she was still baking. No, she hadn't found a man to marry her... "I did," she said to her grandma. "She sounds happy."

Elsie's smile was just a little sad and a whole lot knowing. "I'm proud of you, honey."

"Yeah, well, you might want to change your mind about that when you find out that I ordered not one but *two* new ovens today."

"Leah!"

"I'm paying for them," she said quickly. They'd filled up her entire shiny new credit card, but she'd wanted to do it. "Grandma, it had to be done. You can't continue with the business you have without new ovens; you just can't. We're putting out too much product now. We needed to do this."

Elsie sighed. "But I don't want you to pay for them."

Leah ignored this to help Elsie out of the car, but Elsie grabbed her hand and squeezed it gently, waiting until Leah met her gaze. "I'm so very proud of you," she said fiercely. "You've been a godsend. A perfect godsend."

"Perfect?" Leah laughed softly. "I have faults, Grandma. Lots of them."

"Of course you do. Your biggest fault is that you care too much. And you work too hard. But the good news is that I really am starting to feel so much better. I'll pick up the slack again soon."

Leah nodded. That was a good thing. A *great* thing. She'd come home to help, and she'd done that. But it was time to move on soon. She needed to be gone before *Sweet Wars* got to the finals in three weeks.

Long gone.

"You're really doing better?" she asked Elsie. She couldn't—wouldn't—leave until she was sure.

"Oh yes. And you have your own life to get back to," Elsie said, then added with a sly hopefulness, "I'm guessing you have your own bakery to open?"

Everyone knew grand prize for *Sweet Wars* was $100,000 to open a pastry shop. "You know I can't tell you—"

"Phooey," Elsie said. "I hate contracts and rules."

Leah smiled, knowing damn well she'd inherited that trait. "I want you to just concentrate on enjoying your break," she said. "Are you? Are you okay with the way I'm running your bakery?"

"*Our* bakery, honey. And are you kidding? You've doubled business. I'll sure miss you."

Leah thought about staying and what that would cost her. Elsie, catching her hesitation, patted her hand. "No worries. I know there's more out there for you than being back here in Lucky Harbor. You were on the cover of *Martha*, for God's sake."

The nurse came out and called Elsie just as Leah's phone started vibrating. She pulled it out of her purse and looked at the screen.

Jack.

Her wits deserted her, and with a wince, she dropped the phone back in her purse, where it vibrated for another minute before finally falling into an irritated silence.

Jack wouldn't let her ignore him for long. She was thinking about that, and how she might explain herself to him, when Mr. Lyons came through the front door leaning on his cane.

"Hey, cutie," he said, signing in for his appointment. "Saw you on—"

"*Sweet Wars*," she finished for him. "I know. I can't tell you what happens, sorry." Three more shows. She had three weeks to figure her shit out. "Contractual obligations and all—"

"No, I mean I saw you on Facebook. You're dating Jack Harper. Good man, that Jack."

Leah stared at him. "What?"

"Yeah. Now, as far *Sweet Wars* goes, you're killing the

competition. I've got a twenty on you taking it, but I'd go up as high as fifty if you'd give me a little clue…"

"Don't you even think about giving him a clue," Elsie said, coming out from the back. "He'll use it to win against the other, less fortunate seniors."

"Ah, now that hurts." Mr. Lyons slapped a hand to his heart and dramatically staggered back a step. "The prettiest babe in town doubts me."

"Poker night, last week," she said. "You coaxed everyone into making it strip poker. Then you counted cards and won the pot, which was three hundred bucks."

"Okay, true." He winked at her. "Which you know firsthand since you were there."

"Grandma?" Leah asked, shocked.

Elsie waved her off and continued to glare at Mr. Lyons.

He simply flashed blinding white dentures. "How about I use some of my ill-gotten gain to wine and dine you? The diner's having a two-for-one special. My treat."

"I have plans."

"With that chain-smoking, stuffy, old, stick-up-his-ass Maxwell Fitzgerald?" Mr. Lyons asked.

"Why…" Elsie glanced at Leah. "Of course not. Don't be ridiculous." She wrapped her arm around Leah. "Good day."

"Elsie?"

Elsie turned back to Mr. Lyons.

"You know I'm just having fun, right? At our age, it's all we've got. Well, that and pumpkin pie night at the senior center. My offer of dinner stands," he added more seriously. "Even after the special's over."

Elsie looked surprised as Leah led her out the door.

They went home, and Leah made dinner. When Elsie had gone to bed, Leah took a long shower until she ran out of hot water. Afterward, she had a text from her self-proclaimed boyfriend.

Squinting her eyes to read it—because that always made things easier to take—she opened the text.

You can run, but you can't hide.

Chapter 6

♥

Jack's earliest memory was being four years old and proudly wearing his dad's firefighter hat to the dinner table. It'd been far too heavy for him, and he'd barely been able to see because it kept falling over his eyes, but his dad had laughed.

And Jack had loved the sound.

There'd never been a question of what he would grow up to be. He'd become a firefighter, like his dad.

Period.

His schedule at station #24 was busy but he didn't mind the odd hours, or the job, really. No, it wasn't jumping out of helicopters into massive wildlife fires—which he'd loved—but the work meant something.

And yet there was no denying he was restless as hell.

It was true that city firefighting could be exciting, but Lucky Harbor wasn't exactly "city." And if there wasn't enough of that excitement to suit his adrenaline-junkie soul, he told himself that at the ripe old age of thirty-two, he'd learn to deal with it.

He was still waiting for his brain to do just that.

He and Kevin ran to work, and he had to admit his knee was slowing him down some. He really thought he'd just rehab it himself, but after months of working on it, he wasn't so sure. And yet he'd been the surgery route before and knew what that would mean—an enforced down period. Since that didn't work for him, his immediate plan was to ignore it until he couldn't.

In the meantime, he did his best to fill his time with things that interested him. He'd become the county's hazmat specialist and had gotten additional certificates in fire management and arson investigation. His off-shift hours were filled with whichever adrenaline rushes he could find. Paddle boarding with Luke. Mountain climbing with Ben. Women.

He'd had a good run there too, he could admit. In fact, he was right smack in the middle of a good run. Or had been—until Leah's little bombshell.

It'd gotten out overnight that they were "dating," and he'd already fielded an unhappy call from Kayla, a waitress he'd had plans to see later in the week, telling him not to bother to call her back.

There'd been nothing but radio silence from Danica, a local flight nurse he'd casually seen a few times. It wasn't anything serious, nor would it be, but he hoped that meant she was on shift and not reading Facebook.

Facebook, the evil incarnate. Or maybe that was Lucille herself. Lucille was older than dirt, shorter than a yardstick, and Gossip Central. She'd posted the "news" of his and Leah's relationship and then pictures of them together throughout the years. This included one of Leah's middle school graduation, where his mom had made him wear a suit. Another of them at the pier with Leah clutching a life-sized teddy bear he'd won, with him posturing like a complete idiot.

Jack had been fielding calls and texts all damn day long—except from the one person he wanted to hear from, of course.

Leah, who was still avoiding him like the plague. She'd always been good at lying low when she wanted, and clearly that was her modus operandi at the moment. Unfortunately for him, she was going to get away with it now that he was on rotation for three straight days.

He and Kevin entered the station at seven in the morning to the sound of applause, which startled Kevin into barking like a maniac.

Jack set his hand on the dog's head and gave his shift crew a long look. "Never mind the assholes, Kevin."

Kevin quieted and sat, glaring at the crew for startling him.

No one looked apologetic. There was senior firefighter Ian O'Mallery, and Sam and Emily—both five-year veterans—one of whom was always partnered with their rookie Tim, also present. And then there were two paramedics, Cindy and Hunter.

All still grinning at Jack.

"Lieutenant's gotta girlfriend," Cindy sang. She'd made breakfast and was dishing out egg sandwiches.

Jack snatched one and scowled. "Don't believe everything you see on Facebook."

"How about everything we see with our own eyes?" Tim asked. "'Cause I saw you two at the pancake breakfast."

"Yeah?" Ian said, curious as a sixteen-year-old girl. "What did you see? Anything good?"

Tim shook his head. "I saw that I've got more game than our LT. *And* I'm pretty sure I have a shot at his girl too. She smiled at me. She's got a really hot smile."

"Which reminds me," Jack said. "You're heading to the senior center in fifteen minutes for their fire extinguisher training."

Everyone laughed but Tim, who scowled. "Hey, I'm tired of being the dickhead who gets all the grunt work."

"Then don't be the dickhead," Emily suggested and handed him her empty plate.

"Oh hell no," he said. "I'm not doing dishes again. Hey!" Tim called after her as she walked away.

"New guy always does dishes," she called back.

Their day started with a woman who'd run her car into her own mailbox and gotten trapped, and ended with rescuing a stoned-off-his-ass guy from up a tree—not that they ever figured out what he was doing in the tree.

The next morning, they were woken by a two-alarm fire, and everyone hit the trucks.

At the scene, Tim fought to the front to jump down first, but Ian grabbed him by the back of his shirt. "Remember this time, you're still on probation. Stay back. Observe."

"Come on," Tim said. "You all take turns being point. Let me do it for once."

"No."

The convenience store attached to the gas station was on fire. The building, as old as the rest of town, ignited.

Ian and Emily—with Tim allowed to shadow and assist—rescued two smoke-dazed victims from the store before it was fully engulfed—the clerk and a customer. But when everyone looked around, only Ian and Tim had come out. No Emily. Then they all heard the alarm bell on her gear going off. Her breathing apparatus was running out of air. She'd gone to a window to try to get out, but her air pack was stuck on the window seal. Jack got to her, yanking her out from the outside.

"Close call," Emily said when the flames were out, giving Jack a big thank-you hug from her perch on the back on the ambulance, where she was being treated for a few second-degree burns on her knees.

Too close. He was still sweating.

During the pickup, Jack made his usual walk around the site and found a vagrant in the back of the building, huddled between a smoking shrub and a concrete pillar, suffering from a minor head injury. They treated him at the scene, and then he was transported to the hospital.

Deputy Chief and Fire Marshal Ronald McVane was about a decade past retiring, but still sharp. He was on site taking pictures and making a post-incident analysis.

"Got a few cigarette butts in the lot," Jack told him. "Not surprising given that it's a convenience store. There's other material there, and what looks like it might have been a bucket of rags. Point of origin was there. The contents of the Dumpster went up like timber, catching the siding on the building."

"The vagrant?"

"Maybe," Jack said. "But he says he didn't start a fire. But he also swore that he saw Santa Claus smoking crack on the roof before the fire ignited." Jack shook his head. "Something about this whole setup seems too neat and smart."

"And the vagrant isn't either of those things," Ronald said and sighed. "Hell."

"This fire was set on purpose," Jack said.

"Hell," Ronald said again.

Back at the station, everyone was on decon duty, decontaminating their masks and regulators and refilling the air tanks. Most of them also used the opportunity to wash their gear, though some guys like Tim liked to leave it dirty to show how tough they were.

Tim was prowling the living room. "That fucking dog!"

The dog in question was sitting on the couch like he owned it, the tatters of a leather wallet scattered around him. There was a good reason he hadn't made it as a station dog the first time around. He didn't listen, he was the Destroyer of All Things Expensive, and he was smarter than all of them put together.

Tim snatched up the biggest piece of leather and thrust it under his nose. "You ate the cash and left the leather? You're killing me."

"Aw," Cindy said. "Don't yell at him."

"Did he eat *your* money?" Tim demanded.

"I don't have any," Cindy said. "Chill, dude."

"If you keep yelling at him," Jack said, "he's going to shit in your shoes later."

"He already did that!" Tim glared at Kevin. "Bad dog!"

Kevin's ears lowered, and he blinked as slow as an owl, looking a little confused.

Jack patted him on the head. "He has some separation anxiety that we're working on. We left him behind."

"Because it was a day call and too hot to keep him in the truck."

"Yeah," Jack said. "But he doesn't understand that."

"Then he should have eaten *your* wallet." Tim blew out a breath, calming down. "He has an eating disorder. He eats everything."

"It's called being a Great Dane."

Tim threw his hands in the air and plopped on the couch. "Just do something about him."

Jack turned to Kevin, who straightened hopefully, like maybe there was another wallet in his near future.

"Hear that, Kev?" Jack asked him. "I need to do something about you."

Sensing he wasn't going to be getting a doggie biscuit anytime soon, Kevin sighed, strode to his bed—right next to the couch—where he turned around three times and plopped down with a heavy "oomph."

Tim pointed at his own eyes and then at the dog. "Watching you," he said.

Kevin closed his eyes, set his head on his paws, and farted.

Jack went into his office. Writing up his report on the convenience store fire, he came upon something interesting. The building was in escrow. This always changed things. It was shocking how often a property owner became an arsonist, and he made a note for Ronald and their investigation.

Before bed, he checked his phone. Not a word from his pretend girlfriend. He fell asleep wondering if that was a good or bad thing.

The next day, the entire platoon once again ran ragged from start to finish. The first call came early. A drunk twenty-year-old idiot had set a fire at his parents' home, lighting a cigarette on the kitchen stovetop and leaving the flame on before falling asleep. The house had been built in the 1930s and had a balloon-frame construction, in which there was a gap between the inside and outside wall. They tried using a thermal imaging camera to find the hot spots, but that proved ineffective, forcing them to use a hook to pull out whole chunks of heavy plaster walls to check for flames.

The guy's elderly parents were pulled safely from the structure, but "Baby Al" was out cold. Until they tried to move him, and then he started yelling and pitching a fit. Jack and Ian went in and dragged the screaming guy out. Still drunk, he fought them tooth and nail, making it a real struggle to save the jackass's life. Jack took a punch to his left eye that pissed him off and ached like a bitch.

From there, they had a few medicals, a few regulars— people who called for attention—and a report of smoke at a house on the south side of town. The smoke was central- ized in a bedroom that could have been on that TV show *Hoarders*. When they shoveled the furniture and debris clear, they found a myriad of wires: phone, clock, com- puter, and so on, all crisscrossed and frayed.

And also a giant vibrator. Like eighteen inches giant.

The entire platoon managed to remain professional un- til they were on the engine, and then as a collective whole they completely lost it, laughing all the way back to the station.

When the next episode of *Sweet Wars* aired, Leah hadn't planned on watching, but her grandma insisted, which was how she ended up staring at herself as she created a three-tiered lemon meringue tart as if her life were a DVD. She tried to remain distant from it, but though she was good at the distance thing with others, she'd never really mastered it for herself. So she took in her relaxed, smiling self whipping a meringue under the pressure of cameras, the other contestants, and the exceedingly tough, hard-assed celebrity judges.

Go her.

"I don't like the panel. They yell too much. But that host, he's a cutie."

Rafe Vogel was also the producer of *Sweet Wars*, and while he was most definitely "a cutie" on the outside, he more resembled a snake on the inside.

"And look at you," Grandma marveled. "I can't get over you," she said, as on screen Leah moved quickly and efficiently in spite of Rafe walking around stirring up angst and tension as he barked out the clock's countdown. "You're the doll of the season."

"No."

Elsie scoffed and reached over, picking up the current issue of *TV Guide*. Spread across the front of it was the entire cast, with Leah front and center.

Leah pointed to the woman next to her. "Suzie's good too," she said.

"Not as good as you." Elsie set the *TV Guide* down on the coffee table and clapped her hands in glee. "You won it. I know you did. So when do you leave? The prize was one hundred grand and your own bakery, right? In the place of your choosing? You going to give me a hint?"

"You know I can't tell you who won," Leah said automatically, thinking how in the hell was she going to do this? How was she going to get out of Lucky Harbor before everyone saw the finals? How could she just leave the bakery, Elsie, Ali...Jack.

"I'm just so proud of you, honey. I'll admit, you had me scared for a few years there. Switching colleges and career paths like other women switch hair color. I know your daddy didn't help, making you doubt yourself all the time. He wasn't a good man, Leah. Watching you suffer…" She shook her head. "I should have done more for you."

"No, Grandma," Leah said gently, putting her hand over Elsie's. "You did everything you could. You were always there for me."

"Always will be." She turned her hand over in Leah's and squeezed her fingers. "You've made something of yourself."

If only that were true…

Chapter 7

Jack followed up his seventy-two hours on shift with a day of sleep for recovery. Then he and Kevin hit the park for Jack's weekly baseball game.

Kevin was an old hat at baseball. He had a routine. Tied to the dugout bench in the shade, he usually dozed through the first few innings, and then by the bottom of the fifth he'd be nosing through the guys' bags for snacks. If he played his cards correctly and gave the right player the puppy dog eyes, he might find a good lap to cuddle in.

No one had ever told him that he wasn't a lap dog.

Today when Jack arrived, Luke and Ben were already on the bench lacing up their cleats. The three of them went way back. Luke had spent summers in Lucky Harbor at his grandmother's house. Ben had lived with Jack and his mom when his family had detonated early on. After Jack Senior's death, Dee had raised both boys—and also Luke—as if they were brothers.

And they were brothers, in all the ways that counted,

which meant that they were a perpetual pain in each other's ass.

Ben looked up as Jack and Kevin walked toward them. He took in Jack's obviously careful gait—his knee was hurting like a sonofabitch—but didn't say a word.

Luke was much more blunt. "You look like shit," he said and held out a fist to Kevin.

Kevin lifted a paw and bumped Luke's hand. It was his one and only trick.

"I'm not the one with the flu," Jack said. "Sam's out, which leaves us without a backup pitcher."

"And…," Luke said.

"And what?"

"And you have something else to tell us," Luke said.

Jack looked at Ben, then back to Luke. "What else would there be?"

"I don't know, maybe the fact that you and Leah are getting hitched."

Jack, who'd just taken an unfortunate sip from his water bottle, choked.

Ben patted him on the back. Actually, it was more like a pounding that sent Jack forward a few steps.

"So, when's the big day?" Luke asked.

Jack swore, swiping a forearm over his chin to mop up the water he'd just spit out. "Ali tell you?"

Luke grinned. "You mean it's true?"

"No, it's not true. Jesus."

"There's a whole Pinterest thing on you two," Ben said, sitting on the bench. Kevin immediately leaped into Ben's lap. For years, Ben had been closed off, not wanting to be close to anyone. He was gone for months at a time, and when he came back, he rarely talked about the things he'd seen and done. Jack and Luke had long ago given up revealing their worry to Ben; it just pissed him off.

And no one wanted Ben pissed off.

But they did worry. A lot.

But Ben, who rarely let anyone touch him, simply wrapped his arms around the huge dog and kept talking. "Lucille's been pinning ideas for your wedding and inviting others to do the same."

Jack stared at him. "What the hell is Pinterest?" he demanded.

"Hell, I've been on the other side of the planet in a country without running water and even I know what Pinterest is," Ben said. "What the hell's going on with you and Leah?"

Jack blew out a breath. "Leah told my mom we were a thing."

"Ah." Ben nodded like this made perfect sense. Which was good. It should make perfect sense to someone.

"I'm fucked," Jack said.

"Yes," Ben said. "If you're very, very lucky."

Jack gave him a level-eyed gaze.

Ben shrugged. "She's smart, funny, and wears really hot shoes that make her legs look a mile long. You should've done her a long time ago."

"It's *Leah*," Jack said. What the hell was wrong with everyone? Ben had been there growing up. He knew what Leah had gone through; he'd heard the yelling every night. He knew Leah had sought comfort—platonic comfort—from Jack all through his high school years. He knew that they were just friends.

Of course, what he didn't know, *couldn't* know, was

how on so many of those nights that Leah had sobbed all over Jack, he'd done his best to give her what her parents wouldn't. "Love you, Leah," he'd whisper.

She'd clutch at him tighter. "Forever?"

"Forever," he'd promised, always. But that had been a damn long time ago. Before she'd walked away and not looked back. "It's not a real thing," he said now.

"Only because you're stupid," Ben said.

Luke started laughing and couldn't stop, so Jack shoved him and then sat down to exchange his running shoes for cleats. Since Luke was still cackling like a hen, he tugged his hat down lower over his eyes and stalked off toward the field.

He was first baseman, and since no one else could be bothered, he was also team captain.

And their best player. Usually.

But not today.

As he discovered the hard way, a bad mood apparently made his game shit. First he missed an easy fly ball and then a line drive. And then, to make his humiliation complete, he struck out.

Lucky Harbor enjoyed its baseball as much as he did, and the stands were full. He could see Danica on the top row. They'd talked about having drinks at her place sometime this week. He wondered if it was possible they were still on.

She waved at him.

He started to wave back, but then he saw his mom two rows below Danica. Sitting with...

Leah and her grandma.

His mom was beaming.

Jack couldn't be sure from this distance, but he thought

maybe Leah was squirming. She had good reason to squirm, since he was going to kill her later.

To make sure she knew, he pointed at her.

She slunk down a little and pretended not to see him.

From the dugout, Kevin whined. He loved Jack's mom, and he loved Leah. Basically Kevin loved the ladies, period. But not a single woman had ever enjoyed Kevin's way of greeting, which was a nose to the crotch.

Which is why he was tied up in the dugout.

At the top of the third inning, Luke, their catcher, called a time-out and jogged out to Jack. Ben strolled over from the pitcher's mound.

"What?" Jack said.

"You tell us what," Ben said.

"I suck today. So what? You two were both pussies last week. Maybe it's just my turn."

"You're not usually a pussy," Ben said. "You're usually more like your dad."

Solid. Steady as a rock. Never faltering, never taking a misstep.

Well, except for the one that had killed him.

"Get the hell off my plate," Jack said.

"Touchy," Luke noted.

"Needs a Midol," Ben said.

They played the rest of the game with a minimum of errors, but it was too late.

They got their ass handed to them.

Afterward, they hit the Love Shack, the local bar and grill. They were halfway through a pitcher of beer and sliders when Lucille walked by and snapped a picture of Jack.

"Hey," he said.

Lucille might be meddlesome, but she also sometimes kept Jack's mom company when she was in treatment and he was working. "What are you up to?"

"Who, me?" She smiled and slid her dentures around some. "Nothing at all. I just needed a picture for—"

"If you say Facebook…," he warned.

She smiled a little broader. "Ah, don't get all alpha on me. I just wanted to put up a pic of you and Leah side by side. Unfortunately, Leah's not nearly as accommodating as you." She thumbed through her photo album on her phone and then showed him a picture.

Leah, flipping off the camera.

In spite of himself, Jack laughed. But he wasn't laughing a half an hour later when he went to the bar for another pitcher for his table.

Danica was there, and he gestured for another drink for her, but she shook her head, her pretty blond hair flying.

"Hell no, I'm not having a drink with you," she snapped with surprising venom.

Huh. Not nearly as friendly as she'd been in the stands earlier at the game. Which meant… "You heard," he said flatly.

Her eyes were daggers. "That you're nearly engaged? Yeah, I heard, and B-T-dub? You're an asshole for humiliating me like this. Consider date number three off the table." She stood up. "Your loss, by the way, because I give *great* date number three." She started to walk away, but he caught her, a little surprised by her venom since things had been so casual between them. Still, he wanted to explain so there were no hurt feelings.

"It's not what you think, Danica," he started. "I—"

She tossed her drink in his face.

It was a fruity white wine.

Jack hated fruity white wine. He was still wiping it from his eyes when Danica snatched her purse and sashayed her very fine body right out of the bar.

Jack turned to the table where Luke and Ben were watching with great amusement. Ben offered him a silent toast with his beer.

Luke just grinned. "Man," he said to Jack, "she just went all cage-fighter on your ass."

At that, Ben actually let out a rare laugh.

And happy as Jack was to hear it, he could only shake his head.

That night, unable to sleep, Leah was in her grandma's kitchen working on her cream puff recipe, determined to figure out a way to produce them faster. She had the ingredients spread out before her when her grandma appeared in the doorway looking pleasantly round and comfortable in a big, fluffy robe that nearly swallowed her up.

"Oh," Elsie said, sounding surprised to find Leah up. "My goodness, honey. You're not still obsessing over making perfect cream puffs?"

"Just a little. I need to figure out how to make a larger batch and have them look as good as those from a smaller one. I can't seem to do it."

"But you're not on TV now. It's what's on the *inside*, not the outside, that matters."

"Are we still talking about cream puffs?"

Elsie smiled. "It's a lovely night. Why aren't you out?"

Leah laughed. "It's Lucky Harbor. Where would I go?"

"I don't know...the arcade, the Ferris wheel. Have a bonfire on the beach. Live a little!"

"I'm not sixteen, so the arcade is out," Leah said wryly. "And bonfires are illegal. It's high fire season right now."

"It's a sad state of affairs when a woman your age can't find fun."

"Baking _is_ fun."

"Hmm."

From the depths of Elsie's purse on the table came the sound of her cell phone ringing. "I'll get it," Elsie said, and dove on it like a woman four decades younger, snatching the phone before Leah could get a look at the caller ID screen.

"_Hola_," Elsie sang sweetly, and then let out a big smile. "Why yes," she said, sounding very happy. "Yes, it's me." She glanced at Leah and lowered her voice. "Call me back in five? Great." She hung up with a sort of dreamy smile and then looked at Leah again. "You really should turn in, honey. It's late."

"I'm not tired yet."

"Oh, okay. Well, then _I'm_ going to turn in."

"Who was that?" Leah asked.

"Hmm?"

"On the phone. Who was that?"

Elsie shook her head and pointed to her hearing aid. "Damn thing needs to be looked at, it's not working right." She turned away. "Night."

When she was gone, Leah just stared at the empty doorway for a long beat. Her grandma was keeping secrets.

But then again, so was Leah. She understood the need for privacy, more than most. And until she'd left Lucky Harbor, she'd never had any privacy at all, unless she'd been here, with Elsie. Difficult as it was, Leah would give her grandma the same consideration.

The night was quiet, and she moved about the house, cleaning up from dinner, straightening out some of her grandma's bills, switching money around to rob Peter and pay Paul, and checking email.

She had one from Rafe, offering her a "job opportunity that you can't possibly turn down for when you're done playing house in Mayberry." He went on to outline what they wanted from her, which was to have her host her own reality show, following a group of fledgling pastry chefs in their final semester of school.

Anxiety knotted in Leah's chest. Hadn't she needed exactly this, a reason to leave town soon, for when her grandma was all better?

She hit REPLY and typed up her requirements. She wanted producing credit, and she wanted out of Lucky Harbor *before* the finale of *Sweet Wars* aired.

She stared at the email for a long time before hitting SEND. Soon as she did, her phone beeped an incoming text from Aubrey.

Holy smokes, Batgirl. Tonight's bar incident is spreading faster than Lucille can work her phone. You do realize that you so owe Jack now, right? Like big owe. I expect details.

Leah blinked at her phone and then texted back. *WTH happened to Jack at the bar?* She stared at her phone, impatient for a reply that didn't come. Giving up on waiting, she searched for Aubrey's contact info and hit CALL. "What happened to Jack?" she asked when Aubrey answered.

Aubrey chuckled and then there came a low, male

voice in the background, murmuring something she couldn't quite catch.

"Who's that?" Leah asked.

"I'm just leaving the bar and apparently I need an escort," she said with careful disdain, sounding tipsy. "Even though it's just Lucky Harbor."

The low murmur came again, and Aubrey laughed, a little coldly. "I'm fine," she said, presumably to her escort. "Look, I have a stun gun, and I know how to use it. Fair warning, buddy."

"Aubrey, who is that with you?" Leah asked. "And you're not driving, right?"

"Nope. I'm going to call for a ride—"

"*I'm* driving you," the mystery male voice said, speaking low but perfectly clear, and Leah recognized it with relief.

Ben.

She relaxed, knowing Ben would take care of Aubrey whether she liked it or not. "What happened?"

"I had a real shit day," Aubrey said. "Do you have any idea the hoops you have to jump through to start up a business? The paperwork, the permits, the fees…I needed a drink bad. Okay, two. I needed *two* drinks, and I might have forgotten to eat dinner. And now Mr. Tall, Dark, and Mercenary here says I'm going to let him make sure I get home okay or else." She lowered her voice. "And I gotta be honest, that 'or else' is sort of making me curious—"

"I mean Jack," Leah said. "What happened to Jack?"

"Oh. Right. Well— Hey! You keep your hands to yourself, Mr. Mercenary, jeez!"

"You nearly broke your ankle," Leah heard Ben grate out. "Stop walking and talking at the same time."

"Fine," Aubrey said, and then came back to Leah. "Danica tossed her drink in Jack's face."

Leah gasped. "What? *Why?*"

"Apparently they were supposed to have date number three tonight, and according to Danica—who yelled this at Jack, by the way—everyone knows what happens on date number three. She said she wouldn't go on a date number three with a guy who was nearly, almost, maybe engaged. And that's when she threw the drink in his face."

"Oh my God. *No.*"

"Oh yes," Aubrey said, sounding greatly amused. There was also a male snort, as if Ben too found this very funny.

Leah did not. "Who told Danica that we were…nearly, almost engaged?"

"I don't know." There was a sort of murmured conversation, during which Leah assumed Aubrey was conferring with Ben. Then Aubrey was back. "Mr. Mercenary says maybe you should check the mirror."

"I didn't do it!" Leah said. "I didn't tell anyone." Except Dee, which she *still* felt like shit about. And Ali. And her grandma… Oh good God. "Okay, so maybe it was me, but I never said *engaged!* I said we were *dating.*"

"Yes, but this is Lucky Harbor," Aubrey pointed out. "It's like playing telephone. I once thought I was dating the town clerk, and it turned out he didn't consider it 'dating' at all."

"That was not your fault," Leah said.

"But this might be your fault," Aubrey said.

Yeah. "This is bad. Very, very bad."

"No kidding, because now you've gotten Jack cut off of sex from every female within gossip distance," Aubrey said.

Leah thunked her forehead to the wall.

"Leah?" Grandma Elsie's voice came from the bedroom down the hall. "Is someone at the door, dear?"

"No, it's just me. Sorry to disturb you." She took a deep breath. "This isn't happening," she whispered. "Was he mad?"

"I think he was more shocked. I'm pretty sure he doesn't get rejected a lot."

"No," Leah agreed. Jack was usually the one doing the rejecting.

"So now you owe him."

Leah quivered at the thought but brushed that aside. "I'm not going to sleep with Jack. I was just trying to do him a damn favor."

"Oh, I doubt there will be sleeping involved," Aubrey said. "Danica was quite clear. She said she gives great date three. My guess is that it's at least oral. Maybe even the biggee."

"The biggee?"

"*Butt stuff,*" Aubrey said in a dramatic stage whisper.

"Okay, that's it. Give Ben the phone."

There was a brief pause, then Ben came on. He didn't say a word, but she could sense his amusement.

"You'd better take good care of her," she warned him.

"Don't you think you should worry about your own problems?"

"I'm not kidding. You're driving her home, right? Just shove her inside her place, okay? Don't let her talk you inside. She's on a man embargo, but it's been a few months, and she's drunk..." Not to mention Leah had no idea how long it had been for Ben, and he was still trying to adjust to civilian life. He and Aubrey alone together was a disaster of massive proportions just waiting to happen. "She might temporarily forget about the man embargo and try to seduce you," Leah told him, "and then she'll hate you in the morning."

"So is it her virtue or mine you're worried about?" he asked.

"You're not taking me seriously."

"On the contrary, I'm taking you very seriously. But I'm a big boy, Leah."

She replayed back in her mind what she'd just said to him and realized that in man-speak, she'd just pretty much told him to go sleep with Aubrey. "Okay, you know what? Forget everything I just said."

He laughed softly. "You're cute when you backpedal. Haven't seen you do that in a while."

"Dammit! I'm coming down there right now. Wait for me. I'll take her home myself."

"I've got this, Leah."

"Ben—"

"Worry about yourself," he said and disconnected.

She agonized for a minute and then decided she couldn't live with herself if she didn't at least check on Aubrey, even if it meant seeing Jack. She drove to the bar, but though the place was still kicking, there was no sign of Aubrey or Ben.

But Aubrey's car was still in the lot.

Leah pulled out her phone and texted her.

You'd better be snoring and not having inappropriate rebound sex with Ben, who'd better not be having inappropriate stateside-again sex with you.

There was no response. *Crap.* But since she didn't have the moral high ground here, she tilted her head back and stared up at the moon. It was a gorgeous night. Warm. Quiet.

She didn't want to go back to her grandma's. She wasn't sure what to say to Jack, so going to him was out too. Plus there was that little matter in the back of her mind.

You owe him…

Rifling around in the back of her car, she came up with a bathing suit. Then, hiding beneath a towel, she changed.

A long, moonlight swim had always cleared her thoughts; hopefully tonight would be no different.

She bypassed the pier. It was illegal to jump off. Not that she had any problem with breaking a rule now and again, but it was low tide. She was restless, not suicidal.

She walked to the water, which was calm. A half moon cast a lovely, peaceful blue glow as she tried to swim off her regrets. Telling Dee that she and Jack were together. That it had gotten out to everyone in town. What had happened at the bar with Danica.

Leah had known Jack had been dating a couple of other women, and that hadn't stopped her. In fact, she hadn't even thought of them when she'd spouted off to Dee.

What did that say about her?

And now, thanks to Aubrey, she was also worried about owing him. At the thought of all that might entail, she got a full-body shiver. Deciding to attribute that to a chill, she kept swimming.

You're just a screwup, Leah. You'll never amount to shit.

She told her inner voice to shut up but couldn't help but wonder if, for the first time, Jack would turn his picker skills on her. Would he find a way to dump her as a friend, citing her inability to finish anything? No, that was nothing new. Her lack of morals, given the lie she'd told his mom? No, Jack lied too. His entire career was based on the lie that he'd wanted to be a firefighter like his dad, when she knew damn well he'd only done it out of obligation. Sure, he'd loved being a Hotshot, but she sensed his restlessness. He wasn't loving his job.

Damn. They were both so screwed up. She slowed a moment and glanced back to the shore, catching sight of a big, built, attitude-ridden shadow that changed the rhythm of her heart rate even more than swimming. She blew out a breath and kicked it into gear, going hard and fast so she'd be too winded to talk, much less think.

Maybe he'd get tired of waiting.

But Jack had the patience of Job, so it was far more likely she'd drown.

Unfortunately, he'd save her before that happened. He was good at saving her. Dammit. Trembling with exhaustion, she turned back, knowing she couldn't outwait him. She'd never been able to.

Chapter 8

♥

It wasn't all that difficult to find Leah, once Jack set his mind to it. Since the beginning of time, when she'd been troubled, she'd been drawn to two things.

Him.

And the ocean.

She hadn't come to him. That was new. There'd been a time when she'd have come to him no matter what was troubling her.

Except, of course, at the moment *he* was the source of her trouble, even though it was of her own making. The last time that had been the case, she'd left Lucky Harbor.

But he knew she couldn't leave now. She was here for her grandma, and though Leah had plenty of faults, her grandma meant too much to her. Unlike himself... He tried not to resent that, but there was no getting around the fact—he did resent it. He was pissed off that she had no idea what she'd meant to him back then.

Or now.

"Woof?"

The soft, snuffling question came from a sleepy Kevin in the shotgun position at his side. Reaching over, Jack ruffled Kevin's fur reassuringly, getting licked from chin to forehead for his efforts. Kevin wandered a little bit away and started sniffing. Knowing the signs, Jack grabbed a baggie from his truck and waited.

Kevin continued to sniff around each and every rock within a twenty-foot radius, and then repeated his efforts. Twice. Finally, he sat and yawned.

"Just do it already," Jack said, waving the bag. "Before the pretty girl comes out of the water."

Kevin tipped up his head and stargazed.

"Fine." Jack shoved the bag in his pocket, his eyes following the form swimming out past the waves. She'd always been a hell of a swimmer. He could see flashes of pale skin as she moved quickly and efficiently at a full-out pace.

Clearly, she was trying to outswim her demons.

His heart squeezed a little, making room for a few other emotions besides his temper. Empathy. Maybe even reluctant affection. He could've gotten into the water with her, but it was after midnight and Christ, he was tired.

Nothing good ever happens after midnight.

His mom had always said so, and in this case, he was willing to bet it was true. So he sat on the sand, positioned halfway between her car and the water, giving her no easy escape. And waited.

And brooded.

When Leah had first moved to Lucky Harbor, right next door to his childhood home, his life had been long summer days of riding bikes and body surfing, and longer summer nights lying in his bed listening to her father yell at her through the open windows.

You never finish a damn thing, Leah. Not one damn thing. And you never will… You're going to amount to nothing.

Jack had been missing his own father at the time, and his gut would coil into a knot as she'd been spoken to so cruelly and thoughtlessly. "What the hell is wrong with you?" her dad would yell at her. "Didn't you hear me? Are you deaf? Are you stupid? Maybe that's it, you're stupid. Is that it, Leah Marie? You're fucking stupid?"

Jack could still remember being flat on his back staring up at the ceiling, his hands fisted into tight balls, thinking that the wrong dad had died. It'd been the unforgiving, thoughtless wish of a grieving kid, but he'd never forgotten the fury coursing through him at what Leah endured.

Or how sick he felt for her every time she'd crawl out of her window and into his. She'd stand there bathed by the moon's glow, eyes filled with hurt, and he'd want to slay her dragons. He'd scoot over and make room for her, and she'd curl up on his bed, letting him hug her while she cried. And sometimes, much later, in the deep dark of the night after she'd finally fallen asleep, he'd cry too.

He shook all that off now. He didn't want to think of Leah as the skinny, mistreated, spitfire waif she'd once been. Nor did he want to think of her as his girlfriend, pretend or otherwise. He didn't want to think of her at all. He wanted to be in bed with Danica, losing himself in the softness of her lush body.

Instead he was here. Danicaless. And in spite of a very long shower, he still smelled like wine.

The wind kicked up, and the temperature dropped. Not long now, he thought. Leah was tough as hell when it came right down to it, but she'd never liked to be cold.

At his side, Kevin stirred, sniffing the air, glancing restlessly at Jack.

"Yeah, she'll come out soon," Jack assured him. And then they'd deal with this mess she'd made. He wasn't sure what he wanted more. To wrap his fingers around Leah's pretty neck, or…

And actually, it was the "or" troubling him now. Because he was having lots of odd and unexpected urges as it pertained to Leah, and he didn't know what to do about them. Once upon a time, she'd been the only highlight in his day, the only one to make him smile. She was still that person, but there was something new between them, and he wasn't sure if it was good. In fact, he was pretty sure he should be running like hell.

Finally she swam in, and then she was standing up in the water, and he nearly swallowed his tongue. It'd been a damn long time since he'd seen her in a bathing suit. Maybe since high school, when she'd been a head taller than all the other girls and skinny as hell.

She was still tall but she'd filled out in all the right places and then some. She wore a black bikini, nothing but a few straps low on her hips and two triangles over her breasts, and as a wave knocked her around a little, everything jiggled enticingly.

And suddenly he went from slightly chilled to very overheated. Good Christ, she was…beautiful. It should've assuaged his simmering temper just looking at her, but instead it stoked it, making him tense as hell.

Leah, on the other hand, was looking pretty carefree as she lifted her arms and shoved back her hair.

At the sight, his brain utterly clicked off.

She saw him then. He could tell because, from one blink of an eye to the next, she froze every single muscle. It'd have been fascinating to watch, except for the fact that she was freezing up over *him*. She'd never reacted this way before. He didn't like it. And besides, *he* was the wronged party here. *He* was the one who got to be pissy.

"You're still here," she said flatly.

Kevin, who clearly hadn't received the temper memo, bounded over to her, his paws going straight to her shoulders as he gave her the universal Kevin greeting—a lick from chin to forehead.

"You big oaf," she said, and then hugged him before pushing him off her.

Kevin sat happily at her feet, panting, looking up at her adoringly.

"Nice," she said. "But I don't have any doggie treats on me."

With a sigh, Kevin flopped all the way down.

Leah met Jack's gaze. "You scared me."

"You need to be more aware of your surroundings."

Dripping water everywhere, she crossed her arms over herself. "It's Lucky Harbor."

He rose to his feet. "Bad shit can happen anywhere."

She met his gaze for one brief beat and then looked away. "What are you doing here, Jack?"

"I figured as your 'almost fiancé,' I should see how you're doing."

She winced but didn't respond.

"What the hell is this all about, Leah?"

"You *know* what it's about," she said, hugging herself a little tighter.

She always got defensive when she screwed up, and since she'd screwed up a lot, she had a lot of practice.

"My mom has enough going on," he said. "She doesn't need to be lied to."

"Maybe not. But she does need to be happy to heal. And this made her happy. All week she's been glowing."

He knew it was true, and a stab of guilt hit him that he hadn't been able to make her happy without help.

Leah didn't say anything more, but she didn't have to. Yeah, she'd gotten them into this mess, but he knew damn well it'd been out of the goodness of her heart. Jack knew that she thought she owed him for all those years ago, when he'd done his best to protect her, the chivalry having been deeply ingrained by his dad.

But they were even.

In the dark, Leah shivered, and that chivalry made him feel torn between enjoying the sight of her cold and wanting to wrap her up in his arms. "Where's your towel?"

"In the car."

He pulled off his sweatshirt and tugged it over her head.

"I'll get it wet," she said.

"It'll dry."

"I'm—"

"Just wear the damn sweatshirt, Leah."

There was an awkward silence while they stared at each other as behind her the water pounded the shore.

"I realize that this is really hard for you," she finally said, pulling on his sweatshirt. "Having everyone think you like me *that* way. You'll just have to pretend."

He narrowed his eyes. Had that been sarcasm? Or...
Hurt?

"There was a time when I wouldn't have had to pretend anything," he said. "But you flaked out, remember?
You pretended, and then you left."

She grimaced, swallowed hard, and looked away. "We
were just kids."

Was that how it played in her head? Seriously? "Does
it make you feel better?" he asked quietly. "To downplay
what we were to each other?"

She closed her eyes. "We were friends, Jack. Friends
who'd made a quick, knee-jerk, stupid decision to become naked friends and sleep together."

"Yeah. And then one of the friends didn't show," he
said, much more mildly than he felt.

"It was a bad idea. I was leaving."

"Which you forgot to mention."

She dropped her head back and stared up at the sky. "I
couldn't stay, Jack."

He took in her expression, filled with memories, and
nodded. "I know. But you should have told me you were
going."

"You had another girl in your bed by the following
weekend."

Had he? Hell, probably. But she wouldn't have meant
anything to him. Not like Leah had. His chest tightened
at the memory of the hole she'd left in his life. He didn't
want to go through that again. "I missed you."

She said nothing, and he shook his head. Fuck it. He
started to walk away, and then she spoke.

"Brandi Metcalf."

He stopped. "What?"

"Brandi Metcalf was the one in your bed by the next weekend." She turned her head and glared at him. "Pretty, blond Brandi with the perfect boobs." She emphasized this by cupping her hands out in front of her own breasts. "So don't even try to tell me you missed me."

He shook his head. Apparently he wasn't the only pissed-off one tonight. "How about the women I'm dating now?" he asked. "What am I supposed to tell them?"

She hunched her shoulders a little bit, clearly getting irritated on top of defensive. "You're the one who taught me how to dump someone, back in high school. You said"—she affected a lower voice, presumably imitating him—"just look him in the eyes, Leah, with your own gaze all carefully dialed in to sad and regretful. And then you say, 'I'm sorry, I just really need to work on myself right now.'" She went back to her own voice and gave him an eye roll. "You said that no one could argue with that."

Had he said that? Jesus. "I was an asshole, Leah."

She gave him a look that said he was *still* an asshole. So he proved it. "And who says I'm dumping anyone?"

She faltered for the first time, taking a minute to choose her words. "I guess I thought that for the sake of your mom, you'd do yourself in the shower like all the rest of us sex-deprived people." At that, she started to stride past him, but he caught her arm.

"Okay," he said. "Let's have it."

"Let's have what?"

"Well, I know why I'm pissed. Why the hell are you pissed?"

"It's not like it's going to be a walk in the park for me either," she said, giving him a little shot to the chest. "Pretending to like you."

"Me?" he asked, flabbergasted. "What the hell is there not to like about me?"

The sound she made assured him that she had volumes on the subject. "Don't get me started."

"I want to know," he said.

"Fine. You watch that stupid ice fishing show like it's a religion, you're a horrible backseat driver, you drink out of the milk carton—and FYI, so does Ben—you don't put the cap on your toothpaste, or put the lid down on the toilet, and you shush me when you're watching sports."

He stared at her. "That's quite a list of shortcomings," he eventually said. "Is that all?"

"No." She shoved her wet hair from her face, though she managed to keep her regal stance, nose firmly in the air at nose-bleed height. "I held back because I didn't want to be overly rude."

He laughed softly. "Don't hold back, Leah. Let's hear all of it."

"Well, your truck has more sporting goods than a store, you never say you're sorry, and your girlfriends look like supermodels. I mean, what is that? There's nothing wrong with real boobs, you know!"

He took it all in and had to admit that he couldn't say she was wrong, about any of it. "And yet you call *me* The Picker."

She ignored this. "*And* your mom told me that you need knee surgery again. You're just too stubborn to get it done. So you can add ornery to the list."

He blew out a slow breath. "It's not ice fishing," he said. "It's crabbing. And sometimes I *lose* the cap on the toothpaste, or Kevin eats it. And I don't need knee surgery; I'm fine."

Leah snorted. "You're always fine. Your knee could be falling off and you'd say you were *fine*."

"I fail to see the problem."

She snorted again, and he was starting to feel greatly insulted. "You're not exactly a walk in the park, Leah."

"No?"

"No. You're flighty, you live for your every whim, you downplay any real emotion you feel."

She hugged herself tight. "Good thing this is all pretend then, isn't it," she said softly.

"Yeah."

She was freezing. And hauntingly gorgeous, so damn gorgeous standing there wet and silvery by the moon's glow, like a goddess. It's *Leah*, he had to keep reminding himself. Leah, who'd once beaten him in a marshmallow-eating contest, only to puke all over him. Leah, whose dark-green eyes had a way of telling the world to bite her. Leah, who'd run off on him and left him heartbroken. He took a step into her—for what exactly, he had no idea—and she poked a finger into his chest.

"God," she said. "You're so..." Words apparently failed her, but she let out a sound that managed to perfectly convey how annoying he was.

"Ditto," he said, and then grabbed the finger drilling a hole between his pecs and tugged her hard enough that she lost her balance and fell against him.

He wrapped an arm around her waist, entangling a hand in her wet hair.

She went still as stone and stared into his eyes. And then lowered her gaze to his mouth.

Yeah, they were in sync there. Suddenly he couldn't breathe. Hers caught audibly in her throat, a good sign, he decided. Maybe she wouldn't knee him in the balls. Testing the waters, he grazed her jawline with his teeth.

She shivered.

Then he slid his mouth to the very corner of hers and was rewarded by the clutch of her hands on his shirt. Having her hold on to him like this, like he was her only anchor, sent a bolt of lust straight through him. "Leah," he murmured, hearing the surprise in his own voice, feeling the heat course through him as he finally—God, finally—covered her mouth with his.

Her lips parted for him eagerly, and he groaned, drowning in the erotic collision of her hot tongue and chilled, wet body.

Serious trouble. He was in serious trouble.

Because he had a taste of her now, a damn good taste, and it was better than he could have imagined, making him want the rest of her. With his fingers still in her hair, he pulled her in tighter, slanting his mouth across hers for more. She moved with him, into him, making the connection all the sweeter.

No. Sweet wasn't the right word.

Hot. She was so hot she was turning him inside out. And then she made another of those soft, surrendering sighs deep in her throat, the sound slaying him. She still had a death grip on his shirt and had managed to catch a few chest hairs while she was at it. He didn't care. Sliding a hand beneath his sweatshirt, he cupped her ass over her wet bikini bottoms, rocking into her.

She had to feel what this was doing to him. And given that she was breathing like she was running out of air, and still holding onto him tightly enough to bruise, she also had to know where this was going.

Kevin "woofed" softly, an I'm-tired-of-being-ignored woof. Jack waved at him to shut it and then kissed Leah some more, sinking deeper into her taste, her softness, her scent, all while wondering how the hell she could drive him crazy and make him ache at the same time. It was a feat that totally wrecked his equilibrium. Maybe it was just the kiss. Because holy shit, the kiss. He still had a handful of her sweet ass and he squeezed, wanting more. But they were outside and the night's temp was quickly dropping. She was wet, trembling with the chill, and there was absolutely nowhere to go with this. Not here, not now. He'd had no business kissing her like he had an endgame, and knowing it, he regretfully pulled back.

She blinked as if waking up from a dream. "What—" She cleared her throat. "What was that?"

"Insanity. It's going around."

She rolled her eyes but staggered a step as if her equilibrium was off too, giving him some grim satisfaction.

Kevin whined again, and Jack gave him the evil eye. Kevin sighed and sat.

Leah touched her lips as if to hold in the taste of him. "I'm sorry," she finally said.

"For?"

"Putting you in the position of having to pretend to like me."

Ah, hell. He drew a deep breath. Pretending wasn't his strong suit, and he could have said so. He could have also said that he liked her for real. But he wasn't going to. He'd been there, done that, bought the T-shirt, and he wasn't interested in a repeat performance. In fact, if he was going to pretend anything, it was going to be about *not* liking her. "Leah—" He broke off when Kevin nudged him in the gut and whined again. "What?" Jack asked him. "What's the matter?"

Kevin hunched and unloaded a mountain of poop. "Oh, for—" Before Jack could finish that sentence, Kevin shifted over a few feet and hunched again.

"Holy cow." Leah covered her nose. "What the hell are you feeding him?"

"Everything." Jack went to his truck for a shovel. He'd just tossed the bag into one of the trash receptacles when Kevin hunched again.

"Are you kidding me?" Jack demanded.

Kevin panted happily. Clearly feeling fifty pounds lighter, the dog pawed at the sand with his back legs, head proudly lifted as he then pranced toward the truck as if he were king.

Leah was still standing there looking shell-shocked.

"I know," Jack said. "It's bad. Breathe through your mouth. It helps."

She did just that, pulling his sweatshirt up over her mouth so all he could see was her eyes. It didn't matter. He had the taste of her on his tongue, the feel of her body still in his palms. He wanted to drag her up against him and plunder. Talk about bad ideas. "It's late," he said.

"Is that what you would have told your date tonight when she invited you in at the end of the night? That it was late?"

No. He'd have had her naked before midnight.

Naked and happy.

But this was Leah…and he tried really hard to not think about Leah naked.

Or naked and happy…

Except lately, he seemed to be doing nothing but.

Ever since she'd sprung this whole relationship thing on him, he'd thought of little else, and it was slowly driving him over the edge.

But he could get over that.

Or at least he could try.

Except now there was also this, *her*, in a little, itty-bitty, black bikini and his sweatshirt coming down to her mid-thighs, looking like his greatest fantasy come to life, and he didn't think he could handle any pretense at all. "Leah—"

"No," she said, shaking her head, backing away. "You know what? Let's not discuss this like rational human beings. Clearly we can't do that."

And in his sweatshirt and an air of righteousness, she headed to her car.

Chapter 9

♥

Leah yanked open her driver's door, but before she could slide in, Jack caught up with her, caging her in with one hand on the roof and one on the opened door. "Hold up," he said.

She turned to face him. "Move, Jack."

"I don't think so." His voice was calm as always, but there was an undercurrent now, the slightest tension. Which, coming from Jack, was tantamount to being wildly upset.

She didn't care.

All she knew was that he'd just kissed her, *really* kissed her. And it'd been so amazing that she'd lost herself in him, in a big way. He'd taken her in his strong, warm arms, and in that moment nothing else had existed. Not her fears, her screwups, her uncertainty, nothing.

How did he do that? Take her so far out of herself?

Even more shocking was watching him take care of his mom, Kevin, everyone around him, including her. The thought temporarily had all her bones melting and her good parts waking up and doing a boogie dance of happiness because she'd actually—gasp—*felt* something.

But Jack didn't want to feel anything for her. He didn't even want to pretend.

Her gut clenched because this was her fault. She'd wanted things to be different this time. The people here in Lucky Harbor, unlike her stupid school and show, mattered. Her grandma mattered. Her friends mattered. *Jack* mattered.

Picturing failing any of them, her chest tightened into a ball of anxiety and blocked her air passage.

"Leah." Still holding on to her, Jack pulled the hood of the sweatshirt up over her wet hair, then dipped down to look into her eyes. "It's not a rejection."

She braced herself to hold his gaze, but her throat was tight because it sure as hell felt like one. Which was only fitting, since she'd done the same to him. It'd been a long time, but sometimes it felt like yesterday.

It'd been her high school graduation, and there'd been alcohol involved. The party had turned a little crazy, and she'd gotten herself in over her head.

Jack had been her white knight, taking her home, sneaking her into bed before her dad could catch sight of her.

Leah had jokingly pulled Jack down over the top of her and said he should give her what she'd been looking for. He'd looked into her eyes, and with all his nineteen-year-old cockiness, told her if she'd been sober he'd be happy to show her exactly what she'd been looking for, and that he would ruin her for all other men while he was at it.

In the way of stupidly intoxicated seventeen-year-old

girls, she'd brazenly told him that she'd be sober tomorrow, and she expected him to make good on that promise.

The next night had come, but she'd been too afraid to go through with it because what if she blew it? What if she didn't have enough experience to interest him? What if she didn't turn him on?

But most important, he'd dumped every girl he'd ever been with. Did she want to be that girl, the one who lost him over one night?

So she'd choked. Panicked.

Run.

He'd never given her any indication of minding either way, so she'd figured no harm, no foul. She'd done the right thing because their friendship had been the most valuable thing in her life.

And she hadn't been willing to risk it.

Even as young and foolish as she'd been, she'd known that much. She'd much rather be in his life as his friend than in his past as an ex.

Now she'd risked all that with her lie to Dee.

"It's not a rejection," he repeated. "It's a time-out. We're just going to our own corners to think." He paused. "Do you understand?"

"Yes, I understand. I understand I'm such a bad idea that you need to think."

"No. We're a bad idea."

In her mind there was no difference, and she tried to slip into her car, but again he held on, pressing her into the door, cupping her face, and tilting it to his. At his touch, her body softened. Ached. She had to close her eyes against the unexpected onslaught of emotions.

"Leah. Look at me. Please."

It was the "please" that did it, softly but authoritatively uttered. Incapable of not responding, she did as he asked and met his gaze.

He ran a hand over his face and rolled his shoulders in an apparent attempt to assuage his weariness. It was such an unconsciously sexy move that it was hard to concentrate on the matter at hand. Which was that she was mad. And maybe hurt.

"You're one of the most important people in my life," he said. "I can't pretend things with you. I tried that already."

And she'd hurt him. She honestly hadn't realized that she even could, and she still wasn't quite sure that she believed it now. Jack Harper wasn't one to pine over anyone. "I'm sorry I got you into this," she said with real regret. "So sorry. But I think now we should try to see it through." She couldn't have said why she needed to so badly. "For your mom, Jack."

He was looking at her, into her, but she was good at building walls of self-preservation. Good at not letting people in. In the old days, she'd never been able to pull that off with him, had never wanted to, but in the years since, she'd learned new skills.

"We need rules for this," he said.

It took a moment for the words to sink in, and then the relief made her weak. "So we're going to do it?"

"With rules."

This didn't surprise her. The big, built alpha loved his control, and he loved rules. Hell, his entire world was run by rules. Not for him, of course, but for everyone else. "Let me guess," she said with a hint of amusement. "You don't want me to wear green toenail polish?"

He shuddered. "Hell no. But we have things to work out, Leah."

"Like?"

"Like the fact that this isn't real."

She absorbed the unexpected pang of the words. "Of course not."

"So no hurt feelings."

"No hurt feelings," she said softly. "How do you want to do this in public?"

"There's only public," he said. "Otherwise we're just… us."

"Okay," she managed, wondering why she was feeling raked over the coals. "So…in public. PDA. Are we going to agree on a level? Minimal? Moderate?"

He scowled. "PDA?"

"Public display of affection."

"I know what it is. I just don't know why we have to figure that out right now."

"Moderate," she decided. "Maybe hold hands, greet each other with a kiss, that sort of thing?"

He let out a barely there sigh, like this was paining him, and she started to get a little insulted. "How about the Fireman's Picnic?" she asked. "Do I get to be your date for that or do you already have a blond bimbo planned?"

"The picnic's not for another month," he said with the horror of men everywhere when faced with a decision more than five minutes out. "Just how long do you plan to play at this?"

"It's for your mom," she reminded him.

"How long, Leah?"

She stared up into his dark-caramel eyes. "I don't know."

He held her against her car, making her lose her train of thought. "You really think we can pull this off?"

She wouldn't have to pull off anything, not that she'd admit that. "Hey, I once took method acting for an entire semester. Piece of cake. And it's not like you're hard on the eyes. Dating the hottest firefighter isn't going to be a hardship."

He stared at her for a long beat, giving very little away. "You think I'm hot."

"You have a mirror, right?" She paused, giving him a chance to say that maybe she wasn't hard on the eyes either, but he didn't, and she decided to get out while she was ahead. Squeezing from between him and her car, she slid behind the wheel. She had to give him a little push to shut the door so she could drive off. Glancing back in her rearview mirror, she found him watching her go, a pensive expression on his face. He was confused.

She touched her still-swollen lips and thought, join my club.

She was two blocks away when her cell phone rang.

Jack.

"Hello?" she answered, breathless.

"I think you're hot too," he said. "Actually, you're a knockout, Leah."

She had to pull over and draw in some air. "I'm sorry," she said. "Can you repeat that?"

"You're a fucking knockout."

"Thanks," she whispered, but he'd already disconnected.

Jack pocketed his phone and looked at Kevin. "So a show of paws. Am I the biggest idiot on the planet, or the smartest?"

Kevin yawned.

"Yeah, you're right. Idiot." His only excuse was that she'd made him dizzy as hell, kicking him a little off balance and a lot off his toes.

He loaded Kevin into the truck and slid behind the wheel. Kevin climbed into the back, but halfway home he claimed the front passenger seat again, leaning in to lick Jack's jaw.

"Why do you smell like beef jerky?" Jack craned his neck and looked in the back. Yep, Kevin had gotten into and eaten his way through the emergency kit.

Again.

But at least Jack wasn't thinking about kissing Leah. Much.

He pulled into the duplex that he and Ben had bought together five years ago now. It was a two-story Victorian and freshly painted thanks to Ben's recent handiwork.

Ben's side of the house was dark, so Jack let himself and Kevin inside, not bothering with any lights since his immediate plan involved some serious shut-eye. He went for just that, but instead he ended up with hot, restless, erotic dreams involving Leah, both in and out of her black bikini.

Leah let herself into her grandma's dark house and ran right into a soft body.

"Oh," Elsie said, startled. "You're still up?"

Leah turned on the light. "Are you okay? Why aren't you sleeping?"

"Oh, you know." Elsie let out a little laugh. "My old bones creak and wake me up." But Elsie didn't look old. She looked...guilty. "Okay, so I was out. I...had a meeting."

"At midnight?"

"Is it that late?" Elsie asked. "Huh."

"Who did you meet?"

"Max Fitzgerald."

Elsie was on the Historical Society board with Max. She'd complained about him for years and years, calling him a liver-spotted, tight-lipped, tighter-assed renovation nazi.

The name fit. "Why did you have such a late meeting? You forget to pay your dues or something?"

Elsie grimaced and pulled her coat tighter around herself, but it didn't miss Leah's attention that Elsie was wearing her good "going out" shoes. Leah, once the master sneaker, felt her eyes narrow. "Grandma, what's going on?"

"Okay, but just remember, this all started out with me trying to surprise you," Elsie said.

"Me?"

"Yes. You've been working so hard and without a single word of complaint."

"Grandma," Leah said, both touched and irritated, "I love being here with you. I have nothing to complain about."

"But you've taken over so beautifully, and the place is such a mess. I know it is, Leah; don't even try to deny it. I just wanted to see what kind of renovations we could make. Cheaply, of course. Something to help you."

"I'm good with how things are," Leah said. "Other than wanting new ovens." She meant this, one hundred percent. In fact, the truth was that she actually loved the bakery's slightly antiquated setup. It made her work hard, made her think, made her concentrate. She liked having little brain power left over for anything else.

Like what the hell she was going to do in two weeks when the *Sweet Wars* finals aired and the gig was up? Or why she was happier here, back in the place that had once upon a time been the bane of her existence, than she'd been anywhere else.

Although she suspected this was because of a certain big, bad, gorgeous firefighter who, thanks to her own doing, was now her pretend boyfriend.

And a hell of a kisser.

"Well, you're a doll for putting up with everything," Elsie said. "Anyway, I wanted to see what I could do and ran the thought by Max first."

"Oh, Grandma," Leah said softly. "You give him way too much power."

"And he said I was absolutely welcome to make any renovations."

"Yes, because you have every right to," Leah pointed out. "Grandma—"

"And so I was just having a drink to thank him, and he…invited me to the firefighter's ball next month," she ended in a rush.

Leah opened her mouth again, but Elsie cut in before she could speak. "No. Don't say whatever it is that you're going to say. I was wrong about him. Okay, yes, he can be a fuddy-duddy, but he's also very conscientious about our town's history and takes his job seriously. And actually, he's a very nice man. I'm sorry if I let you think otherwise, especially because I know you don't think all that highly of the male race in general. And maybe that's my fault too, for not correcting your notion that they're all temperamental horse's patoots. That was just your daddy, honey."

"Well, I know that."

Elsie smiled a little sadly. "Do you? Because you're quick to judge a man, and even quicker to cut one out of your life."

This threw Leah off her game a little. "Of course I know it," she said. "I like men, Grandma." She'd been on her own a long time. Twelve years, actually, since the day she'd driven out of town at age eighteen and not looked back. She'd had relationships. Granted, nothing that had lasted, but as she'd told Dee, it only took one…

But did she really believe that? "I've had boyfriends."

"Had? Past tense?" Her grandma's eyes were sharp. "Don't you have a boyfriend right now?"

Well, she'd walked right into that one, hadn't she? "You mean Jack."

"Do you have more than one?" Elsie asked with a laugh.

Jack woke up before his alarm thanks to a sensation of being crushed. Sitting up, he turned on the light.

At some point in the night, Kevin had climbed onto the bed with him. The dog lay on his back, all four legs straight up in the air as if he were roadkill, snoring loudly enough to rattle the windows.

He had nearly the entire bed.

"Hey," Jack said and nudged him.

Kevin stopped snoring but didn't move a single muscle.

"I know you're awake."

Kevin slit open one eye.

Jack pointed to the floor.

With a sigh, Kevin heaved himself up and stepped off

the bed. He sent Jack one soulful look over his shoulder before heading out of the room. Two seconds later Jack could hear the sound of Kevin slurping water out of his bowl, and no doubt drooling everywhere while he was at it.

Jack rolled out of bed as well, showered, and then hit the road. He'd hired a day nurse for his mom, both to keep her company and to make sure she was getting everything she needed, especially when Jack was on shift and couldn't help her himself.

But when he stopped by his childhood home on the way to the station, Dee was already up and dressed and sitting at her kitchen table.

Kevin bounded into the room and would've taken a flying leap at her, but Jack grabbed his collar just in time.

"Gak," Kevin said, eyes bulging, tongue hanging out.

Ben stood behind the stove cooking a big spread of bacon, eggs, and french toast. "I thought you were home, still in bed," Jack said.

"You thought wrong."

Kevin, desperate to get at Dee, whined.

"Sit," Jack told him.

Kevin barked. His bark was loud enough to pierce eardrums, and everyone in the room winced.

"Not bark," Jack said. "*Sit.*"

Kevin offered a paw.

Jesus. "Kevin. *Sit.*"

Kevin turned in three circles and plopped down to the floor, which shook like an earthquake under the one-hundred-and-fifty-plus pounds.

Dee laughed. "Such a sweet boy."

Kevin smiled at her.

"Sweet, my ass," Jack muttered.

Ben began loading a mountain of food onto a plate, which he then brought to Dee.

Dee, who always ate less than a bird whenever Jack had tried to feed her, beamed at Ben. "Thanks, sweetheart." She gestured to Kevin, who all but scrambled his circuits trying to get up at the speed of light. Like a cat on linoleum, his paws fought for purchase as he raced to her side.

"Now you be a very good boy," Dee said to him, patting him on the head, which was level with hers. "Be a very good boy and sit for me. Can you do that, Kevin? Can you sit for me?"

Kevin sent her an adoring smile and sat.

Jack shook his head. "Fucker."

"Such a good boy," Dee cooed. "So much better than my potty-mouthed son."

"He's not a good boy," Jack told her. "He's a menace to society."

Kevin sent Jack a glare of reproach.

"What are you doing here?" Jack asked Ben.

"It was your turn to stock the fridge."

By "fridge," Ben meant Jack's fridge, as Ben didn't use his own. "Yeah? So?"

"So you bought beer, cookie dough, and peanut butter and jelly."

"Oh, Jack," Dee admonished.

"Hey," he said in his defense, "I got the basic necessities."

Ben shook his head. "No wonder you're single," he said in the tone that they both knew would rile Dee up, which in turn would effectively get Jack in trouble. Ben's favorite thing to do.

"He's not single," Dee corrected. "He's got Leah."

"Right," Ben said dryly. "Almost forgot."

Jack gave him a look. This didn't appear to bother Ben in the slightest. "So where's Carrie?"

"I don't need a nurse this week," Dee said. "I didn't want to waste your money, so she took on another patient."

"Mom, forget the money. I want you taken care of when I'm working."

Dee pointed at Ben.

Ben saluted her with his spatula.

Jack slid a look to Ben. He knew his cousin felt he owed Dee his life—multiple times over—for taking him in and keeping him on the straight and narrow.

Not that she'd always managed to keep Ben on the straight and narrow, but he'd turned out okay. If you counted being a little off your rocker okay...

"I'm fine," Dee said again. "Or I would be if I wasn't worried about you."

"Me?" Jack asked. "What about me? I'm fine too."

Ben, flipping a piece of french toast, gave a snort that made Jack feel twelve again and defensive as hell. "What?"

"Nothing. It's just that you're awfully cranky for someone who's fine," Ben said lightly.

"I'm not cranky."

Ben shrugged.

Dee's smile faded a little bit. "Are you cranky?" she asked Jack. "Why would you be cranky? I saw Leah yesterday afternoon, and she said things were great. You didn't mess things up with her since then, did you?"

Of course he had, thank you very much. Jack sighed and looked to Ben.

Ben just raised a brow, the asshole. "It's six in the morning," Jack said as evenly as he could. "How much could I have messed anything up?"

Concern filled Dee's gaze. "Oh, Jack," she murmured. "Was it your phone?"

"What?"

"You know," she said, waving a hand. "Your phone. I read in *Cosmo* that if a woman looks in her man's phone and he has anyone in his contacts with only a first initial, that means it's a…" She lowered her voice to a whisper. "Booty call. Grounds for a breakup. As is having eight contacts with the name Brandy, because chances are that they're exotic dancers you've met on business trips."

Ben pointed at a stunned Jack with a spatula. "No matter how much your girl presses you about your Brandys, deny everything until death."

Dee waved an irritated hand in Ben's direction. "You're not taking me seriously."

"Mom, I didn't mess anything up."

"Then where is she?"

"Leah?"

"No, the Tooth Fairy," Dee said, making Ben grin again. "Where is Leah, Jack?"

Probably concocting some new way to make his life a living hell, he thought darkly. Oh wait, *she'd already done that*. Ever since the kiss on the beach—kisses plural, as in many, many amazing kisses—he'd done nothing but think of her plastered up against him, or better yet, beneath him, soft and wet, sighing his name in pleasure…

And yet there was his mom, looking at him with those eagle eyes of hers, the ones that could always tell when he'd messed something up, so he ruthlessly clamped

down on the fantasy and shrugged. "It's six a.m.," he repeated.

"So she's baking?"

Right. She'd be baking. He nodded.

Dee relaxed and went back to eating. She had color in
her cheeks and looked happy. Jack would like to say that
he'd put that happy look on her face, but he hadn't. Ben
had, with his food.

And Leah, with her lie.

Ben was making another plate, loading it full for himself, and Jack snatched it.

Ben muttered "fucker" beneath his breath, which Dee
either didn't catch or ignored. "You going to be around
today?" he asked Ben.

"I don't need a babysitter, Jack," Dee said.

Jack didn't take his eyes off Ben.

Ben nodded.

"She's got an appointment day after tomorrow at ten,"
Jack said.

"I can drive myself," Dee said.

Ben nodded again affably. "But you'll let me take
you."

"I'm fine—"

"Of course you are," Ben said smoothly. "But this isn't
for you. It's for your idiot son. We don't want him worrying like a little girl while he's on the job."

Dee relaxed. "Of course not. But you have a life too,
Benjamin."

Ben lifted a shoulder. "I'm…in flux."

Ben didn't talk much about his job. Being a civil en-
gineer sounded innocuous but it wasn't the way Ben
did it. His last job, where he'd gone into Iraq for the

DOJ to design and build water systems for some of the war-torn towns, had obviously gotten to him, big time. Usually when he was in Lucky Harbor he went back to his woodworking, and actually he was a hell of a furniture maker when he wanted to be. But he hadn't picked up so much as a single tool since he'd been back.

So yeah, he was in flux. He *lived* in flux.

Luckily, he never spent much of his income so he had some flexibility. Others in Lucky Harbor hadn't been so lucky. The economic downturn had been hard on many of the businesses, and there were a lot of properties in trouble and on the market.

But things were starting to turn around. A few new businesses were coming in, and some of the properties were being built up and renovated, when the historical society loosened their bulldog grip on the regulations and permits.

There'd been some noise from the biggest developer sniffing around, a Mr. Rinaldi out of L.A., who was snatching up as many of the available properties as possible. He had three or four in escrow at the moment, including Elsie's bakery. He'd promised the current residents that nothing would change, but the rumor was that he planned on getting a whole strip of buildings on commercial row and running the town.

There were mixed feelings about this. Any commerce was good. It brought in money and kept people employed. But Lucky Harbor residents were used to being a tight-knit community, and there were fears that this was going to change.

Jack didn't care about that, but he did care about the bakery, so he hoped Mr. Rinaldi's word was good.

"What's that, honey?" Dee asked.

"I didn't say anything," Jack said.

"Yeah, you did," Ben said. "You mumbled something about the bakery."

Dee smiled. "He's got his girlfriend on his mind."

Jack put his empty plate in the sink, kissed his mom, and left, ignoring Ben's knowing smirk.

Chapter 10

♥

Leah's breath caught as Jack's body pressed into hers. His hands stroked up her sides and then his thumbs were brushing over her nipples. Moaning, she arched closer as he kissed her long and deep, grinding his lower body into hers. He was hard, so deliciously hard, and she ached for him. Tangling her hands in his hair, she kissed him deeper until he groaned her name.

Oh, how she liked the sound of her name on his lips.

Then his clever fingers found their way into her panties, and he let out another groan before breaking the kiss and nipping at her ear. "Jesus, Leah. You've got to remove your hand."

What?

She opened her eyes and realized that Jack was standing over her, where she'd fallen asleep at her grandma's desk. He was fully dressed and breathing heavily, making her realize that her right hand was cupping the bulge behind his zipper. She snatched it away as if she'd been burned, and he stepped back, leaning against the file cabinet.

It took her a shockingly long moment to catch her breath, but even then, she could still feel the bulge of him in her palm. The *big* bulge of him... "What are you doing?" she demanded.

"You were moaning and flushed and sweaty. I came close to check on you, and you molested me."

She groaned in embarrassment and covered her face while he laughed softly. In spite of the tension in every line of his body, he flashed a smile. "Busy, huh?"

There was a lull at the bakery every day around ten in the morning. Since Leah was usually up by 4:00 a.m. to bake and then serving customers by 6:00, that lull came with the urge to nap.

Usually she combated this with copious amounts of caffeine and something from her day's wares that had lots of sugar, but today she'd been stuck in the teeny-tiny office facing a stack of her grandma's bills. A little overwhelmed, she'd set her head down and clearly fallen asleep. "Yes," she said. "I am very busy." She bit her lip. "And sorry, about—" She gestured to his crotch. "Though it's your fault for not knocking. Why are you here?"

"Donuts."

"Donuts." She huffed to her feet, pushed past him, and headed out front. "You interrupted the best sex I've had all year for donuts."

"That's sad."

"Exactly why I needed the end of that dream!"

In tune to his soft laugh, she loaded him up a box of donuts and shoved him out the door.

* * *

From the bakery, Jack headed to work. His amusement had shifted into a solid, churning need centered right at his groin, which hadn't yet gotten the message that he wasn't getting any, despite how Leah's fingers had felt cupping him. Thinking about how she'd looked in the throes of her sex dream made him hard all over again. He'd told her she'd been moaning and hot and sweaty. What he hadn't told her was that she'd whispered a name.

His.

He blew out a breath and forced that from his mind—as well as the image of taking her on that desk, her long, gorgeous legs wrapped around him—so he didn't walk into the station with a boner.

Station #24 sat at the end of commercial row, between the pier and downtown. Once upon a time, the two-story brick building had housed the town's saloon and theater, but it'd long ago been converted to a firehouse.

There were three large garage doors out front, opened to reveal a fire engine, a ladder truck, an ambulance, and the county OES Hazardous Materials response vehicle. Beyond the garage, there was a utility-sized kitchen and a big open living room. Upstairs was a large sleeping area that looked like a frat dorm meets Three Little Bears, except it was the Six Little Bears with rows of twin beds.

Over the years, they'd added a pool table, an X-Box, a flat-screen TV, and some huge, comfy couches. Home away from home or, as they all spent more time here together than they did with their various loved ones, just *home*.

Half the staff were great cooks, and the other half knew how to order in with equally great skill. Eat Me, the local café, served the station on command, as did the Love Shack, the bar and grill down the street.

The station was staffed on a full-time basis with a rotating staff. They shared the site with Washington State Fire—where, by no coincidence, Jack had gotten his start in the first place as a rural firefighter, aka a Hotshot.

As head of shift, Jack usually arrived before anyone else, but today Tim was already there, head buried in a laptop. "Hey," the rookie said, barely looking up. "The B rotation caught a fire yesterday at the auto-parts store. Lucky bastards."

Jack had already heard from Ronald since the fire was of suspicious origin, but he looked over Tim's shoulder at the pictures of the scene on the laptop.

"Burned hot," Tim said. "Real hot. Bad luck for Lenny Shapiro."

Shapiro owned the auto shop. "Maybe it wasn't luck at all."

"You think it was arson?" Tim asked, surprised. "Nah, man, those rags shoved in that bucket…stupid place for them. Real stupid. Lenny should have known better." He shut his laptop. "You watch, on our rotation we'll get all medical calls. Or a false alarm. We never get the fun ones."

Jack went to his office and brought up the fire pictures on his computer. As Tim had noted, there'd been oily rags left in a bucket near a stack of boxes, and they'd ignited. But this was now the second fire in two weeks where oily rags were discovered in a bucket.

Jack went over everything he had on the fire and moved on to the paperwork required of him as the LT, while his unit worked their daily chores, pulling the equipment out onto the long driveway to be washed, stocked, and inventoried.

Jack had deposited the proceeds from the Firemen's Breakfast the week before, but he still had to make the statements for the beneficiaries. The breakfast itself had been made possible through the generous donations from the local businesses such as the B&B, the café, the art gallery, and many more, and they each would get a statement and an individual thank you. The FD had set a new record this year for number of meals served, and the profit would guarantee that the seniors would be getting three square meals for the rest of the year without cutting into the town's general budget.

He was just finishing up when they got their first call of the day from the library. As Tim had groused, it was a medical call, but then again, at least fifty percent of their calls were. A teenager—there with his entire class—had found the staff ladder irresistible. He'd climbed up twelve feet before his belt had gotten caught on the shelving unit, leaving him hanging upside down over the rest of his delighted class.

Jack was going to guess that it would be college before the kid lived it down.

After that, in quick succession they were called to a traffic collision and then a near drowning in the harbor. Later, they took the engine and truck to the elementary school for their annual Firefighters at School Day. By the end of that visit, every single kid between the ages of five and ten wanted to be a firefighter when they grew up.

Jack had once been one of those kids. He could still remember the day his dad had brought an engine to school. Jack had already known every inch of the truck and

gear—hell, he'd been playing with it all since before
he could walk—but he'd still been as enthralled as his
friends. He'd remained enthralled until the day his dad
died on the job. But by then, Jack's fate had been sealed.
Because how did the son of a devoted legend do anything
other than follow in his father's footsteps?

After the kids had gone back to class, Jack began
reloading all the supplies and gear. He heard the *click-
click-clicking* of a pair of heels, and his pulse jumped
once as he thought *Leah*, but it wasn't her. It was one of
the teachers, coming around the back of his truck, seeking him out.

Rachel Moore was a pretty brunette he'd met at the
gym. They'd been flirting back and forth for a few weeks
now, and the last time they'd run into each other during
a workout, she'd suggested maybe having a drink sometime.

"Heard about what happened at the Love Shack," she
said, carefully neutral.

Since this statement could cover a lot of ground, and
he wasn't sure if she was on a fishing expedition or simply making conversation, he made a noncommittal sound.

"People are saying you're…engaged."

Yep. Fishing expedition.

"Is it true?" she asked.

Jack looked into Rachel's pretty green eyes and sup-
pressed a sigh. A deal was a deal, and though Rachel
wasn't—as Leah had so delicately put it—a blond bimbo,
Jack had agreed to the insanity. Sort of. "I'm not engaged," he said. "But—"

"No, stop. I understand." Her smile was a little forced
now. "But you should have told me, Jack. When we were

at the gym, we flirted. Or so I thought." She shook her head. "I didn't realize it was just flirting. My mistake." With that, she turned on her heel and took her very hot self back inside the school.

Jack blew out a breath and headed around to the front of the truck, where Tim was waiting with a wide grin. "Hey, at least she didn't toss her drink in your face."

Jack narrowed his eyes, and Tim sighed. "Let me guess. The senior center again, right?"

Back at the station, they were in the middle of carrying hoses up and down the five flights of stairs on the training tower in the yard when the alarm went off.

They were sent to the senior center with reports of smoke pouring out of the kitchen. Knowing the seniors of Lucky Harbor, this could mean anything. Last year, Mrs. Burland had been making soup for herself when she'd had a heart attack. No one had known she was down until her soup had evaporated and the pan had caught fire. Mrs. Burland had lived. The kitchen, not so much.

Tim was in his seat, leaning forward, as excited as if he'd hit the lottery. "Please be a fire," he said. "Please oh please be a fire."

Ian slid him an annoyed look. "Remember, Rookie, follow our lead."

"Let me take point this time," Tim said. "Please?"

"No point," Ian said. "LT's point."

But this time when they got there, the only person in the kitchen was Lucille, wearing a neon-green velour track suit and bright-white athletic shoes.

"Jesus," Tim muttered, holding up a hand to block his eyes. "She's brighter than the sun."

Lucille gave him a Vanna White smile. "Hiya!" Then she snapped his picture.

"You reported a fire," Jack said. "Where is it?"

Concentrating on her phone now, messing with the camera setting, Lucille was distracted. "I realize this is going to sound so wrong, but..." She looked at them. "Could you all take off your shirts?"

Ian laughed.

But Jack wasn't finding the humor. "Put the phone down, Lucille."

"Aw. Please? Just one shirtless pic? You can't even imagine the online traffic boost we get from shirtless pics."

"The fire, Lucille," Jack said. "Where's the fire?"

"Oh. *That.*" She blew out a sigh. "It's all that fuddy-duddy Mrs. Burland's doing."

"She have another medical emergency?"

"Does being a pain in the behind count?"

Jack resisted pointing out that *she* was the pain in the behind. "Is there a fire or not?"

"My goodness, you're in an awful hurry today. I tell you, storytelling is a lost art nowadays. A real shame too, because—"

"Lucille."

"Fine!" She sniffed in irritation. "I wanted to make everyone my cheesy toast special. Except a little piece of bread got caught in the toaster and a tiny little flame popped up, and Mrs. B called you."

Jack turned to the toaster. No smoke. No flames.

"I tried to tell her she was overreacting," Lucille said. "That she at least needed to pass out or something to make it worth her while."

"Don't you mean *our* while?" Tim asked.

"No." She smiled at the rookie. "Because if she passed out, she'd have had a shot at CPR from one of you hotties."

For the first time ever, Tim looked relieved to *not* be point.

Chapter 11

At the end of the week, Leah stopped by the station with a box of fresh pastries. The big doors were wide open to the bright sun, and the trucks were out in the driveway, being washed by the platoon of Station #24.

Cindy and Hunter were on top of the ambulance. Ian and Sam were head deep in the open compartment. Tim was untangling some hoses. And Jack was on top of the fire truck, wearing his navy-blue firefighter BDUs and reflector sunglasses.

No shirt.

Leah tripped over her own feet but managed to catch herself.

"Aw," Tim said, getting to her first, quickly relieving her of the pastry box. "You're the best girlfriend ever."

Jack had straightened on the fire truck and was looking right at her. She could tell because her nipples got perky.

Tim leaned into her. "Hey, when you're done playing with the old guy, you let me know."

"Why?"

Tim grinned. "So I can show you what a young guy can do."

Leah laughed and waved at Jack.

He didn't smile or wave back, but he did hop down agilely. By the time he ambled over to her, he had to push his way through the crew. Leaning in, he looked into the empty pastry box.

"Two kinds of people here, LT," Tim said with mock sympathy. "The quick"—he flashed a grin—"and the hungry."

Jack slid Tim a look that might have had a smarter guy messing his pants. Pretty sure she was saving Tim's life, Leah pulled a white bag from her purse and handed it to Jack.

"What's this?" he asked as if she were handing him a spitting cobra.

"Look for yourself."

He opened the bag and peered inside, his expression not changing one iota.

"What is it?" Tim wanted to know. "You leave your tighty-whities at her place?"

Jack turned his head in Tim's direction. Leah couldn't see what Jack's expression was exactly, but Tim heaved out a sigh and headed back to the hoses.

"So," she said when they were alone. "Hi."

"What are you doing here?" he asked quietly.

"Pretend dating you," she said, watching him take a second look into the bag at the two cream cheese croissants she'd packed. "How am I doing at the pretend-girlfriend thing so far?"

"My girlfriends all greet me with sex," he said.

She laughed and his mouth twitched, and she knew she had him. The relief that hit her made her knees wobble. Or maybe that was just Jack and all that bronze skin stretching across the tough, sinewy muscles in his arms and chest that tapered to a set of abs that had her mouth watering.

"Don't do this," he said, and her smile faded. "Don't make it a spectacle."

"Is that what you think I'm doing?"

"I don't know what the hell you're doing, which is my point."

And oh, how he hated not knowing every little last thing. "Maybe I just wanted to bring you a treat," she said. "You telling me I don't remember your favorite?"

"I'm telling you that you no longer know me. And my mom isn't even here, so there's no point to this now."

"Fine." She reached for the bag to take it back, damn him, but he was much quicker than she, lifting it out of her range.

She wasn't a small girl. Never had been. From the fifth grade, she'd been taller than most of the boys in her life. But not Jack. Jack had a way of making her feel petite.

Feminine.

Sexy.

Damn him anyway.

He shoved his hand into the bag, pulled out a croissant, and took a large bite. Then he closed his eyes and groaned.

"Good?"

"Shh. I need a moment."

She found herself fascinated by his Adam's apple as he swallowed.

"Oh yeah," he said, voice thick and husky. Hypnotic. "This is the stuff. Save me the rest of these, whatever you have at the bakery. I want them all."

"Let me see if I have this right," she said. "No to the playing-the-girlfriend thing unless your mom's watching—" She broke off when he licked some sugar off his thumb, the sound of the suction making her quiver just a little bit. "But," she managed with what she hoped sounded like utter disinterest, "you want me to save you the rest of the cream cheese croissants."

He tilted his head down enough to eye her over his dark lenses. "Problem?"

She sent him a smile that had far more vinegar than honey. "Not even a little bit."

When the next episode of *Sweet Wars* aired, Jack and the rest of the platoon watched it in the station living room. Ben had come by with popcorn and a chew toy for Kevin. "Dee's good," he said to Jack before he could ask. "Made her soup and toast for dinner, which she ate. Lucille's with her. They've got *Magic Mike* on DVD for after *Sweet Wars*." Ben shuddered. "I vacated the premises."

Tonight's challenge was baklava, and Jack immediately relaxed. Granted, baklava was an incredibly difficult dessert to make because of the many layers of phyllo dough required, which he only knew because Leah said so whenever she made it. But the good news was that she did often make it for the bakery, and in his humble opinion, it was the best on the planet.

"She's got this one in the bag," Ben said, tossing Kevin a piece of popcorn, which he caught in midair with a snap of his huge jaws. "She tell you how she did?"

Jack turned up the volume. "Shh."

"He doesn't like to talk about her," Tim told Ben. "He's touchy as hell."

Jack turned up the volume even more. The camera loved her. Leah looked amazing as she made the challenge look effortless, even when Rafe got in her space and started questioning everything she was doing.

"Amazing," Ben said. "She's amazing." He nudged Jack. "Way too good for you."

"This is what I'm saying," Tim said, tossing up his hands and looking around for affirmation. "I totally have a shot at her, right?"

Jack, never taking his eyes from Leah on the screen, reached casually for more popcorn. "Take a shot and I'll end you."

Ian and Emily snickered.

Tim scowled. "I'm pretty sure you can't threaten me," he said. "It's sorta illegal. Tell him, Ben."

Ben slid him a look that was even more deadly serious than Jack's had been.

Tim pulled his hand back from the popcorn bowl and sank farther into his seat. "Whatever. I could totally have a shot. If I wanted one."

Jack was pretty damn sure that wasn't true. Actually, if he had to go off of Leah's behavior, there wasn't a guy in Lucky Harbor who had a shot.

Except maybe him.

At least until he'd blown that by being an ass. Not that he was sorry. Because he didn't want it to be real.

And maybe if he kept telling himself that, he'd believe it.

* * *

That night, Jack was sleeping like shit, wondering how the hell it was that Leah was permeating his dreams and pissing him off even there when a storm hit. The lightning flashed first, lighting up the large station bedroom like day.

Kevin leaped off his pallet and onto Jack's bed, landing right on Jack's stomach, knocking the air out of him as the dog buried his face in the crook of Jack's neck and whined like a baby.

Across the room, Sam sat straight up in bed with a "what the fuck—" just as the ensuing thunder boomed, rattling the windows and shaking the building on its axis.

"Holy shit," Tim said from his bed. "You think we'll get a good call out of this?"

He hadn't even finished the sentence when another bolt hit, followed by an immediate crack of thunder that nearly burst their eardrums.

"Yeah," Tim said, excited. "We'll get something good."

Kevin whined again and pressed tighter to Jack. Jack hugged the big oaf close and managed to sit up. Because Tim was right. Unless the storm planned on bringing moisture with it, those lightning strikes were dangerous as hell, and they were going to get action.

At the next bolt, Kevin whimpered and tried to climb Jack like a tree. Jack held the big baby tight and thought of Leah. She'd always hated thunder and lightning. During the craziest of storms, he always thought about her. Did she still get scared? Standing up with Kevin still in his arms, Jack transferred him to Tim's bed.

"Jesus," Tim complained but let the dog crawl under the covers. "Your paws are cold."

Jack strode to the window and shoved it open. The temp hadn't dropped much, but the wind had kicked up into high gear. Tumbling dark clouds churned up the sky like dark-gray wool blankets in a dryer, but not a single drop of rain fell.

"Precip?" Sam asked.

"No."

"Damn," Ian muttered.

"Yeah." Jack pulled out his cell phone and stared down at it as indecision warred with the need to know she was okay. Fuck it, he thought, and slid his thumb across the screen to access a blank text.

You okay?

Just as he hit SEND, another window-rattling bolt hit, and then, not all that surprisingly, the fire alarm sounded. A two-alarm, meaning two companies would be responding. Not good.

"Why are the fires always at three in the morning?" Ian wanted to know.

"Karma." Jack pulled on his clothes and shoved his feet into his boots. "For every time you've woken us up with those stupid late-night booty-texts you get."

"You're just jealous now that you're wearing a ball and chain," Ian said. "And how's that working out for you, by the way? 'Cause you're grumpy as hell, so I know you're not getting any. I thought that was the whole idea of an almost-fiancé."

"If you're tired of Leah, I'll take her off your hands," Tim offered.

Jack ignored this and got out of the room first. Tim,

knowing the last one out had to do the paperwork, swore, shoved Kevin off of him, and scrambled after Jack. They suited up, boarded the vehicles, and while heading to the scene, put on their air packs.

Each firefighter was assigned a very specific job, but that job shifted with each rotation. So sometimes Jack was the ladder, sometimes the engine. Sometimes he drove, sometimes he was tails. Everyone had their favorite position. Ian preferred driving. Emily liked the ladder. Some guys were just better at some jobs. Jack was good on the medicals with teenagers or old people, so he usually got that job instead of, say, Tim, who didn't have the experience needed and often came off as an impatient asshole.

On the way, they all dove into the bag of candy that Ian pulled out of his pocket, laughing at Tim when he dropped his and Kevin inhaled it before anyone could stop him.

"Candy's bad for him," Jack said. "Don't let him have any more."

Tim turned to Kevin. "You hear that? Candy's bad for you. Give it back."

Kevin licked his chops and wagged his tail for more.

The joking halted on a dime when they got to the fire.

Just outside of town was an older residential section. Hardworking, lower-middle-class families lived here, in a row of apartment buildings close together and in need of repair. In this particular complex, there were three floors of units, most likely full of sleeping families.

And flames were shooting out the roof.

The other station had responded and arrived at the same time. So did Ronald. As deputy chief and fire marshal and the highest ranking official there, normally he'd be incident commander, but he passed this off to Jack, who did a quick walk around of the perimeter while the ladder was positioned to open up the roof and let out the hot gases accumulating in the upper floor of the building.

Until that happened, the danger could only escalate.

Jack relayed by radio that they had fire out two windows of the first floor on the south side, extending up into the second floor and the attic. A third alarm was struck, and the coordinated attack began.

"Holy shit," Tim breathed, sounding awed as he stood still at Jack's side staring up at the flames. "Holy shit. Let's go! We'll head into the—"

Jack caught him up by the back of his gear. Firefighters were taught from day one to never enter a structure alone, but it was usually the first thing an excited rookie forgot. "You know you're on exterior with Emily." At LHFD, they practiced what was known as the two-in, two-out rule. Anytime someone entered a hazardous environment, there was an equal number of personnel available outside the hazard area to rescue those who entered in case they got into trouble.

Emily and a pissed-off-looking Tim moved into position on the exterior. Sam joined the ladder team and headed to the roof. Jack and Ian would clear the interior and make sure everyone was out.

Forcing the rear door, they hit the stairs, standing at the top floor, doing a sweep, banging on doors, getting people out. Panic and fear always made people clumsy and difficult to maneuver. Jack and Ian moved fast and efficiently together, searching each apartment, working in sync with the other platoons by radio.

By the time they'd finished the floor, the smoke was so thick they were working blind, even with their self-contained breathing apparatus.

When they finished they started again on the secondary search, even if everyone was confirmed out, because sometimes people forgot that Johnny had a friend sleeping over, or that Uncle Joe didn't work tonight, and so on.

They were on the stairs to the second floor when they heard it, the sound of the team on the roof. They used a pike pole to push down on the ceiling below, letting smoke and gases escape from above the fire. It was always a gamble working on a roof that may or may not be able to handle the weight of the guys, the gear, and all the equipment, and tonight the weather wasn't helping.

But from one moment to the next, the heat and smoke lifted, and everyone in the interior took a breath of relief. They worked to finish clearing the building, most people happy for the help. Of course, Jack and Ian came across the one cantankerous old guy who wasn't. Neither was his snarling poodle. The man was waving a baseball bat, yelling about his "constitutional right to remain put."

"You also have the constitutional right to die here," Jack said. "But do you really want to?"

The guy lowered his baseball bat. "Bum leg," he admitted. "'Nam. Me and Killer here are just guarding our valuables."

"What do you have that's worth more than you and Killer?"

The old man scratched his head. "Well, when you put it like that..."

In the end, Jack carried him and Killer out, the six-pound poodle snarling and yipping in his ear the entire time, and Jack decided a one-hundred-and-fifty-pound pesky Great Dane with an eating disorder wasn't so bad after all.

Then the radio crackled, and out came the words that struck terror in all their hearts.

"Northeast corner of roof collapsed. Firefighter down."

Ian whirled to face Jack, eyes wide. "Fuck!"

Jack ordered Tim and Emily to enter and finish evacuating, and he and Ian fought the flames back up to the third floor, smoke curling around them, thick and unforgiving.

At the top, they met Tim hitting the stairs, carrying Sam. "Got to him," he said.

"You were told to stay on evacuation," Jack said.

"Firefighter down," Tim said simply.

Jack held his temper because now wasn't the time or place, but not following directions was a good way to get someone hurt, or worse.

And Tim knew it.

Sam had fallen through the roof, landing perilously close to an air vent. If Tim hadn't gotten to him, he might have fallen another twenty feet to his certain death. He was bruised and bloody from a few fairly deep gashes, but mercifully nothing seemed broken.

Half an hour later, the flames were out and so was everyone who'd been inside.

They'd gotten lucky. Three hours from start to finish, and other than Sam, there'd been no injuries.

The building wasn't as lucky. The firefighters had all done their best not to destroy more than was necessary but they'd opened up the place to ventilate it, breaking windows and tearing down sheetrock to do so. Checking for hot spots was always messy, but it was just too dangerous not to do it. If they'd left any embers smoldering, the fire could renew itself hours and hours later.

So when it was all said and done, the roof was completely gone, the building had lost three units on the top floor, and there was extensive smoke and water damage.

Back at the fire truck, tensions were high among the crew. No one had liked what Tim had done, but neither could anyone argue with the results.

Ian shoved Tim out of the way. "Move."

"Jeez," Tim said, staggering. "Take a Midol."

"Shut up."

"What the hell is your problem, man?"

"You. You're my problem," Ian said.

Tim looked confused.

"You didn't follow procedures, and you ignored a command," Jack said.

Tim didn't look concerned. "I saved a guy's life. One of our guys. You're all pissed off because I got there first. What are you going to do, give me the shit jobs? Dishes? Send me to the senior center?" He laughed and shook his head. "Oh, wait. I already do all that. You're just jealous because I got to be the hero today."

"A hero wouldn't call himself a hero," Ian said.

"You guys are all assholes. Jealous assholes." He climbed into the truck. "Where's my candy?"

Kevin uncurled his big body from his sleeping spot in the driver's seat and blinked at them. "Woof."

Tim searched high and low, and swore. "Goddamn dog. Did you eat my candy?"

Kevin hunched over and yakked on Tim's boot, a slimy mess that was all that was left of Tim's candy.

Chapter 12

♥

By the time they debriefed, got back to the station, and deconned the masks and regulators and refilled the air tanks, dawn had broken and Jack was off shift. After a night like they'd just had, sleep would be impossible, no matter how tired he was. He had adrenaline coursing through him and needed…

Something. A hard run, a fast bike ride…

Sex.

Too bad he had a pretend almost fiancé who'd gotten all his options cut off in that department. He and Kevin stepped outside the station to head to Jack's truck, both man and dog stopping short at the sight of a woman leaning on it. Long, toned legs were shown off to perfection in low-riding jeans and leather boots, and the snug tank with an unbuttoned cropped sweater over it wasn't so bad on her curves either. She wore a baseball cap, but there was no mistaking that auburn hair falling to her shoulders, lit to a fiery gold by the rising sun.

Leah.

When had she gotten so damn beautiful?

She did her fair share of staring right back, which had his heart executing a funny little beat in his chest. Yeah, he thought, still keyed up.

Kevin recovered first with a joyous bark and rushed her. Leah wrapped her arms around the dog and gave him a big, warm hug that gave Jack a twinge.

Jealous of a damn dog...

Leah loved Kevin up, murmuring into his fur. "You big knucklehead. Scaring me like that. When the call went out that a firefighter was down, I..." She shut up and squeezed the dog tighter as Jack went still.

"You have a scanner?" he asked.

She lifted her head, and for the first time he got a good look at her. Eyes shadowed, face tense. "Grandma does," she said.

"No casualties."

"That part didn't get transmitted," she told him.

How many nights had his mom looked just like that, waiting on his dad to come home? Too many.

And then had come the night that his dad hadn't come home at all.

"Stop with the scanner," he said gruffly and tossed his bag into the back. He didn't want to ever see her waiting and anxious because of him. "Just turn the fucker off."

"Right." She let loose of Kevin, eyes flashing. "I'll just turn the fucker off. And my damn head and heart too. How's that, Jack? Is that how you do it?"

Well, hell. He was way too tired for this. "Leah—"

"Never mind. I get it."

"Do you?"

"Yeah. You don't want a relationship, pretend or otherwise. You never have."

He didn't bother to point out that he'd told her so, multiple times. "My life doesn't lend itself to one," he said instead.

"I wonder, Jack, if you've said that so often that you actually believe it." She shook her head. "Your staff at the station, all the other rotations…more than half of them are married. Have families even."

He was absolutely not doing this here, now.

Ever.

"Jack," she said, still sounding furious. "You could have the same thing. You don't have to cut yourself off like you do."

Did she think he didn't realize that other people managed the job and a life? Of course he knew it. Just as he knew, after watching his mom struggle all these years, that he personally wasn't capable of it. "I don't want anyone to care for me that way. I don't want to ruin anyone's life like—"

"Like your dad ruined your mom's?" Leah asked after a terrible beat of painful silence. "Oh, Jack." She rubbed her forehead and softened her voice. "You're not responsible for what happened to him, or her. And as for controlling anyone's feelings, that's the most asinine thing I've ever heard. You can't. You can't control my feelings any more than you can control how I breathe." She studied him for a beat, and then shook her head, looking as frustrated as he had. "And talking to you is like talking to a brick wall," she said, picking up a big purse at her feet. From inside, she came up with a smaller white bag that smelled like heaven. "Breakfast," she told him. "Don't ask me why, because honestly I don't know."

"Leah," he said when she'd whirled off. Jesus. "Leah, wait."

She stopped but kept her back to him.

"Thanks," he said to her stiff spine. "For the food." He paused. "And for...caring."

"Thanks right back at you," she said in what might have been a slightly grudging tone.

"For?" he asked, confused.

"For being too stubborn to get hurt."

This tugged a low laugh out of him, and she turned to face him, still in a temper given the light in her eyes. "Your knee okay?"

No, actually, it wasn't. It ached like a son of a bitch, but he'd live. "I'm good," he said.

She gave him an eye roll accompanied by a sound that spoke volumes on what she thought of his definition of "good." "You're such an idiot."

"In more ways than one," he agreed.

"Yeah?" She sounded greatly interested in hearing more of his idiocy. "What's more idiotic than turning down no-strings sex?"

He went still. "You never said no-strings sex."

"You should learn to read between the lines, Jack," she chided softly. "And you call yourself a ladies' man."

He laughed. "Oh, trust me. I'm well aware how little I know about the ladies."

He could admit that he'd had more than his fair share of meaningless attachments. But what she didn't seem to get was that nothing about her was meaningless to him.

"So what do you want to do?" she asked.

"About?"

"I know you're not going to sleep. You're going to go do something to let down all that adrenaline coursing through you. What's it going to be?"

The list of possibilities clicked through his head, each involving a different version on the same theme, her naked—except for those boots—and beneath him.

Or over him.

Or however he could get her.

In fact, he actually got hard standing there having it all flash through his head.

But this was Leah, he reminded himself for what felt like the thousandth time. Leah, who had always been fickle with her heart and its wants. If he let himself fall for her again, losing her this time would kill him. Which meant that he was going to go for Door Number Two—his motorcycle and the narrow and windy and isolated roads outside of town.

It would work.

It would have to.

"Jack?"

"A fast bike ride," he said.

She nodded and got into her car.

Well, that was that, he thought, and he and Kevin got into his truck. But as they pulled out of the lot, Jack realized Leah was following him.

Apparently, she was coming with.

And for the life of him, he couldn't have said whether he was relieved or terrified.

Leah pulled in behind Jack at his place, not at all sure what she thought she was doing. The whole "firefighter down" thing had rattled her much more than she'd thought, to the point that she'd needed to see him. Needed to be with him every bit as much as he needed to burn off his excess adrenaline.

She let out a breath and decided not to think beyond the fact that he was okay, and that she was grateful for the few mornings that Riley opened for her.

She got out of the car. It was going to be a lovely day, already nice and warm. The leaves were changing, slowly turning from green to every shade of gold, brown, and red under the sun and just starting to fall.

Someone had painted Jack's and Ben's duplex. Probably Ben, since she doubted that Jack had any spare time right now between his work and caring for Dee.

Leah was still pretty steamed at him, although she didn't examine why too closely as she got out of her car.

He was standing at the top of his driveway looking at her. Without a word, he let Kevin inside the house.

He was in jeans that were faded at all the stress points, and he had some *most* excellent stress points. His T-shirt said LHFD on the pecs and was stretched tautly across his broad shoulders. His hands were loose at his sides, his face carefully blank, but everything about him gave off a warning: *bad 'tude alpha alert*.

She didn't care.

Nor did she know what she thought she was doing.

Okay, that was a lie. She knew. She watched him walk toward her, clearly favoring his knee, which had her taking a deep breath. "You need to get off that leg," she said. "What did you do, jump out of a window? Carry someone? Run the stairs?"

"All of the above."

She knew this should reach right inside her heart and squeeze hard, and it did. Which was a good part of why she got even madder. Since he was now close enough, she poked a finger into his chest, hard. "You've paid your dues, Jack. You paid them a long time ago now."

"What are you talking about?" He grabbed her finger and pushed it away. "And ouch."

"Do you think the only way you can match your dad's legend is to die like he did?" Letting her fears finally escape, the ones that had been choking her ever since hearing those two terrifying words "firefighter down," she let him have it. "You have some sort of stupid martyr complex. You won't be happy until you die like your dad, is that it? You're not Superman, you know."

"Jesus, I know that."

"Do you? Do you really? Because we both know that the uniform comes with an expectation. Especially as the son of a hero."

He shrugged, like, *what am I supposed to do*, and she let out a sigh. "You don't have to follow the exact same path to honor his memory. You know that."

"I know that you don't know what you're talking about," he said.

"Don't I? You're always doing your duty, what's expected. In fact, you've never done anything unexpected in your life—"

He proved her wrong by cutting her off with a hard kiss.

And she learned something else—apparently a brain couldn't hold onto anger when unexpectedly pummeled by sheer lust, because she let out a gasp of desire and flung her arms around his neck. Letting out a low, very male sound of satisfaction, he took the kiss deeper, rougher, stroking his tongue to hers. Leah welcomed him with a shocking eagerness that she'd have to hate herself for later because she had no room in her brain for anything but the erotic, sensual feel of him against her. In fact, the heat of him burned through her clothing. She didn't know who was moving—maybe it was both of them—but she found herself grinding against him, and then he thrust a muscled thigh between hers and she greedily rode it. She might have drowned in him then, but from behind them a door opened.

Tearing herself from Jack, Leah's breath came out in ragged pants as she whirled to the duplex.

Ben stood on his stoop in nothing but navy-blue boxers, looking big, bad, and rumpled. "What the hell?"

"Go back inside," Jack told him.

"And miss the show?"

"We're just...working something out."

Clearly in no hurry, Ben leaned against the doorjamb. "That kind of 'working something out' could get you arrested for indecent exposure."

Jack gave him a look that would have had Leah needing to check her pants, but not Ben.

"Fine," Ben said. "But you have a bedroom. You might want to think about using it before pictures of you two jumping each other's bones ends up on Facebook."

The door shut behind him, and Leah let out a shuddering breath. There was a hum of something coursing through her veins, a combination of things. Fear, which had been present ever since she'd heard the "firefighter down" go out on the scanner. Aching regret, for starting this whole mess in the first place. And lingering anger, which she suspected was really misplaced worry.

And something more.

Need.

For him.

Whatever Jack wanted to believe, she knew him. Maybe she knew him better than just about anyone else, in spite of all the years they'd spent apart.

He was unhappy. Oh, the stubborn ass would never admit it. Hell, he'd deny it, and this sparked her temper all over again because he was standing there stoic and edgy, the adrenaline still pouring off him in waves.

It made her want to hug him, which was just about as smart as wanting to hug a caged leopard. But that was Leah. Drawn to things that were bad for her. And Jack was bad for her, always had been. Not to her physical well-being, of course. Nothing as simple as that.

Nope, he was lethal to something else—her heart.

Shaking his head, muttering something about needing to be alone now, Jack headed to his garage. Inside was his lovingly restored Indian motorcycle. Shoving on his helmet, he straddled the beast.

And Leah's heart hitched. After his father had died, there'd been a period of time when Jack had gone feral. Wild. She'd always known when he'd been about to go off and do something stupid because there'd been a certain energy to him, the kind he had now. And oh, how that wild side of him appealed to her. Back then, she'd always begged and pleaded to be a part of that trouble.

He'd never let her, not once.

Looking back, she knew why. He'd been protecting her, in the only way he knew how. And he was still doing it. That's what the other night had been about, his "rules" about no hurt feelings.

In light of that, she had no explanation for the kiss he'd just laid on her, absolutely none. This was probably because her brain hadn't kicked back on yet. God knew her body was still trembling in hopeful anticipation.

The thing was, though, she no longer needed protection. She handled herself. And she could handle him too. She wanted to, especially because he had that look in his eyes, the one he got when he was especially tired or angry. It made him seem especially rough around the edges and wary, as if maybe he knew he couldn't count on his normally sharp senses to keep him functioning. She'd never say so, but she liked him best this way because it proved he wasn't a superhero at all, but just a man.

Either the fire had gotten to him more than he'd let on or he was worried about his mom. Maybe both. Hell, maybe it was her too. Clearly, he'd intended to get out, go a little crazy, blow off steam. But this time, she wasn't going to be sent home. Stepping close, she put a hand on his arm. "Take me with you."

"Hell no."

Refusing to be left behind, she simply stepped close and got on the bike behind him. She felt him exhale deeply, but before he could make her get off, she slid her arms around his waist and pressed her face to his back.

And that was absolutely the undoing of the last of her anger because even though he'd showered, he still smelled faintly like smoke, and the reminder of what he did every single day only made her want him all the more.

"Leah." Gruff. Pissed. His muscles flexed beneath her cheek but she held on, her palms flat against his abs. A wordless response rumbled in his chest—most likely an oath—and then he was reaching up and pulling off his helmet, which he handed back to her.

"No," she said. "I'm not taking your helmet—"

"Wear it or get off."

She knew how to pick her battles so she took off her baseball cap, grabbed the helmet, and pulled it down over her head.

"Hold on," he said.

And then the bike leaped to life beneath his very capable hands. So she did as he'd ordered.

She held on…

Chapter 13

♥

In five minutes, Leah and Jack were out on the highway, going fast enough to make her heart pound as they leaned into the S-turns.

Or maybe that was from being plastered up against his back, her legs spread by his hips, every inch of her in contact with his body.

And his body. Holy cow. How had she never been affected by how tough and built he was? Combined with the rumble of the horsepower beneath her, his body had her in a state that only got more and more pronounced the higher they climbed.

There was a cliff on their right now, where far below the Pacific Ocean pitched and rolled, fog lingering in long, silver fingers on the frothy water. The Olympic Mountains stood on their left, tall, majestic, rugged, and wearing their pretty fall colors.

Ahead of them, the road wound its narrow way upward, and Jack steered into the sharp curves. A sign warned them to keep a lookout for unexpected animal crossings. Out here, that could mean deer, bears, anything really. But nothing crossed their path at all, and Leah could feel some of the tension slowly leave Jack.

Half an hour later, the sun was much higher in the sky, and they were up near Beaut Point. A fitting place, as Jack had been the first person to ever bring her here.

She'd been in eighth grade, and the day had sucked. In the girls' locker room after PE, she'd realized someone had hidden her clothes. Standing there in nothing but her undies, the five mean girls who always made her life a living hell had surrounded her. She'd been tall even back then and had developed breasts early, which she'd hated, just two more ways in which she'd been different from everyone else. She could still feel the heat of embarrassment and shame standing there nearly naked as one of the girls had shoved her.

Leah'd gone down on her ass. Before she could scramble back up again, there'd been the sound of the door slamming open, and the girls had scattered.

And then a shirt had been tossed over her.

When she'd looked up, Jack had stood there, shirtless, scowling at her. "I've told you," he'd said. "Just hit one, any one of them, *hard*. One time is all you need."

The next time the girls had surrounded her in the locker room, she'd done just that.

And had gotten suspended for a week.

But the punishment from her father had been far worse. He'd yelled and screamed at her until her ears had been ringing. She'd dared to interrupt the tirade, attempting to tell him that this wasn't her fault, and he'd slapped her.

Later that next night when she'd crawled out of her bedroom window and into Jack's, he'd been waiting for her. They'd sneaked into his garage and "borrowed" his mom's car. They'd come here and then had climbed down to the mouth of the caves and sat watching the stars swirl in the sky far above.

It still ranked as the best night of her teenage years.

Now Jack stopped the bike so they were overlooking the ocean far below. He turned off the engine, and they sat there a moment, still. Not speaking.

Hell, Leah was hardly breathing.

Still locked around Jack like white on rice, she didn't want to break the spell. Right now, right here in this moment, she wasn't worried about her grandma. About money. About the bakery. About her future and what the hell she was going to screw up next. She wasn't worried about anything, in fact. She felt...safe. And maybe content.

Although maybe "content" wasn't quite right, since her entire body was humming with a sort of anticipation and heat that spoke of the very opposite of content.

She was aroused.

Not sure exactly what Jack was feeling, she started to get off the bike, but he took one of his hands from the handlebars and gently squeezed her fingers, where they were resting low on his abs. "We have a rule in place," he said.

Right. No one gets hurt because this wasn't real. "Then why did you kiss me like that? Like you wanted me so badly you couldn't help yourself?"

He didn't answer for a long moment. "I don't want to ruin our friendship," he said.

"We've managed to not ruin anything so far." She pulled off the helmet and set it behind her. "And we've done some pretty stupid stuff."

"Not yet, we haven't."

Her arms went around him again, flattening her hands on his abs, which clenched. Lightly, she let her fingers drift up and down. "I know you, Jack," she murmured. "I know what you need right now."

He let out a long breath when her hands drifted up high on his chest, and then low again, just to the loose waistband of his low-riding jeans.

"Aren't you even the slightest bit curious?" she wondered. "To see what it'd be like between us?"

He made a very male sound, one that told her he'd given it more than a passing thought.

"It'd make our lie to your mom half true," she said.

"*Our* lie?" he asked so dryly that she laughed.

"You know what I mean."

He caught her wandering fingers in his and brought their joined hands up to his mouth, brushing his lips against her knuckles. "I have another rule."

She dropped her head to his back and laughed again. "Mr. Control. Fine. What's this new rule?"

"No promises."

Her heart caught. Once, a long time ago, she'd made him that promise, and she'd broken it. She'd never let herself believe that it had really mattered to him, but she could admit that he had reason to doubt her. "I'm good with no promises."

"Yes," he said. "You are."

Ouch. "I have a rule too," she said evenly, pulling her hands back and sliding off the bike.

He cocked his head, waiting.

"If there are no promises, at least keep your…options from your mom."

"Options?"

"Yeah. I'm not going to go to all this trouble only to have the whole thing messed up by one of your blond bimbos."

She'd expected him to smile. He didn't. "Who?" he said instead. "Who are your options?"

She shivered at his commanding tone. Sexy, in a caveman sort of way. "Maybe I have several."

He just leveled her with a narrow-eyed, steely stare and waited her out.

"Fine," she said, caving like a cheap suitcase. "I don't have any. Happy now?"

"I'm something, but happy isn't it." He studied her a moment longer, and she returned the favor. The exhaustion was shadowing his eyes. There was a rough, two-day growth on his square jaw and strain in those broad shoulders.

Drawn to him like a moth to the flame, she held out her hand to him. Without hesitation, he put his in hers, letting her pull him off the bike.

They climbed down to the caves and sat there, completely alone, watching the morning sun shimmer on the water three hundred feet below as it crashed into the rocky shore.

"Yes," he finally said, startling her.

"Yes what?"

Turning his head from the water, he looked at her, his eyes filled with enough heat to blow her hair back. "Oh," she breathed, and her nipples hardened. "You mean…"

Suddenly her mouth was dry, and all she could do was swallow hard. "Here?"

"You change your mind already? After all the convincing arguments and fact citing?"

No. Hell no, she hadn't changed her mind. This had been her idea, after all. Except...dammit. Some of that same old panic she'd felt that night long ago flooded her now.

Because this wasn't just any guy.

It was Jack, and expectations were at a lifetime high, at least for her. What if she didn't do it for him? What if she wasn't everything he needed? What if she screwed this up? "What if it doesn't work?" she whispered.

"What if what doesn't work?"

Not willing to let him see her fears, she went on the offensive. "Um...what if we don't turn each other on?"

He blinked, and she realized he was truly flummoxed by this question. Not getting turned on had never occurred to him. If this wasn't so deadly serious, she'd have laughed because he was such a guy.

"You get naked first," she decided.

"Why?"

Her heart was pounding, and her palms were slick with nerves, but she gave him a cool smile. "Well, what if you're ugly beneath all those clothes? I might have no choice but to rethink my options."

He narrowed his eyes again. "New rule."

"Oh my God. Now? You want to talk about your rules now? I don't want to discuss your other women right now, if you don't mind."

"No others," he said. "Not for me, and not for you. No options, period."

Her heart was at stroke level now. "So…an exclusive pretend relationship."

"That's right," he said, eyes surprisingly serious. "Tell me we have a deal, Leah."

This wasn't exactly a hardship for her, not that she was going to say so. "Deal."

He paused. "That felt too easy."

She smiled, trying to look innocent. Because he was getting off topic. And besides, they both knew he wasn't ugly beneath his clothes. He was perfect. Not wanting to lose control of this situation, she rose to her feet and pulled off her sweater.

He watched her, not moving a single, big muscle.

"Well?" she said.

"Well what?"

"Are you turned on?"

"Leah, I've been turned on since I kissed you over a week ago on the beach. But—"

"No. No more buts," she said quickly and kicked off the boots she'd gotten in Amsterdam, trying to look sexy while doing it.

Problem was, he still wasn't looking impressed, so she pulled off her tank top and then hesitated. She hadn't dressed for seduction, hadn't realized…and she was wearing a plain cotton, black sports bra that covered her more than a bathing suit would.

Worse, Jack didn't appear overcome with lust.

"Now you," she said desperately. "You have to lose something."

"But you're not finished." He leaned back on his elbows, all long, sprawled-out grace. The caged leopard at rest…

Good Lord. "Fine." She shoved off her jeans. Dammit.

To go with her sports bra, her panties were laundry day panties, faded yellow, and worse, they had "Thursday" printed across the butt.

It was Sunday.

Jack grinned.

"This isn't supposed to be funny." Mad, she bent over, reaching for her tank top, determined to get dressed again and somehow find her dignity while she was at it.

Somehow.

But Jack, moving silent and fast as a wild cat would have, stepped up behind her.

"Forget it, Jack—"

"Shh." With his big body snug at her back, his hands went to her hips, holding her in place.

She froze, thinking he'd heard or seen someone—but he didn't move. "What are you doing?" she hissed.

"I like this position."

Straightening up, she tried to push free, but he held her still, his hands sliding up from her hips to her breasts, his quick, clever thumbs rasping over her nipples. "And this one," he said low and husky. "I really like this position too."

He was hard—she could feel him pressing into her—and that went a long way toward soothing her bruised ego. Turning in the circle of his arms, she faced him so her breasts smashed into his chest.

"And this one," he murmured, his hands sliding down to cup and squeeze her ass.

The rest of her embarrassment and anger dissolved, and she felt a reluctant smile curve her mouth. "I'm getting the idea you like all the positions."

"Every single one," he assured her.

Chapter 14

♥

Around them, the day went on. Insects buzzed. The sun warmed. The wind, what there was of it, stayed outside the cave rustling only the very tips of the two-hundred-foot-tall pines surrounding them. The sounds were as familiar to Leah as her own breathing and brought comfort.

The man in front of her had always brought comfort too. But now, in this moment, he brought something entirely different.

Holding her gaze, Jack stroked a strand of hair off her forehead. "Still with me?"

"Yes," she said with far more confidence than she really felt.

Seeing right through her, he smiled. "We're going to do this, Leah," he said calmly. "We're going to take one for the team."

Oh God. *Yes.* It was what she wanted, desperately. But...had she coerced him into it? Into wanting her?

Of course she had.

If only she wasn't standing there in her plain cotton underwear. The *least* she could've done was arm herself with something really silky and lacy. No, wait. Armor. Yeah, armor would have been perfect. Something to protect her heart—

"I want you, Leah."

Some of her doubt must have still been visible because he cupped her jaw and met her gaze. "I want you," he repeated softly, his fingers sliding into her hair.

The words and his voice melted her. It was just that simple for him, she realized, as he stared her down, letting her see the hunger in his gaze. It'd been a long time since he'd looked at her like that. She'd have liked to savor it, but she couldn't resist the promise in every line of his body.

"You want me too," he said. "Bad."

She held the eye contact, trying to outlast him, but she was losing the battle and he knew it. His slow smile said so.

Yeah. She wanted him.

Bad.

He was looking at her with the absolute confidence he always seemed to carry. It might have been infuriating if she had room for anything but the need. The desperate need. But… "Here?" She looked around them. "Now?" The cave was secluded, and the area around it completely deserted. Their only company was the sun slanting through the trees, dappling the forest floor with dotted patches of shade. There were a few bees and other various insects, and hopefully no bears, but…

"Here," Jack said. "Now." He backed her to a huge, ancient wall of rock, trapping her there with a hand on either side of her face. "This was your idea," he reminded her. "And, as it turns out, a really good one." Showing none of his earlier resistance and certainly no mercy, he pressed into her, caressing her body with big, sure hands. "You're wet," he murmured with a hint of naughty accusation as his hand moved between her thighs.

"It's from when I was thinking about my options," she said.

He slid her a look as he let a finger stroke over her slowly. Purposefully. "Is that right?"

"A-absolutely."

"So it's not for me at all, is that what you're saying?" One of his long, callused fingers played with the edge of her panties, and she couldn't breathe for the need.

"N-nope," she managed.

"Liar." Then he laughed softly. Cocky. The bastard. His hand continued its wonderful torture, and she strained closer for more.

He'd never touched her like this before, never, and yet her body quivered as if it were recognizing a long-lost lover's touch. And far before it seemed possible, he had her writhing against him, breathing unevenly and desperate. "How," she managed, unable to get the rest out. *How did he know how to drive her crazy?*

He trailed his mouth along her jawline to her ear. "You're good at hiding," he murmured, his voice low and serious, no trace of teasing in it now as he lightly ran the pad of his finger just beneath her panties.

So close to where she needed him.

And yet so far…

"But your eyes," he went on. "They don't hide a thing, not from me. Neither does your body."

Had anyone ever known her so well? It was both a terror that he did, and a relief. She could let go, forget, forget everything but this. Her hands fisted in his hair and pulled until his mouth was a breath from hers. "Now," she said, hearing the desperation in her voice. "You said *now*." She pushed his shirt up his chest. It was a glorious chest, and her mouth watered with the need to lick him from sternum to his low-riding jeans waistband.

He took over before she could, tugging his shirt off over his head in that one smooth motion that guys always make look so easy, and her breath caught. He was all smooth, hard muscle, in perfect proportion.

He tossed the shirt behind him and reached for her. She pulled him in, a little clumsy and a lot eager, kissing him with all the pent-up frustration that the uncertainty and anxiety of being back in Lucky Harbor had brought. She opened for him, pressing closer, harder, kissing him with everything she had.

He let her be the aggressor a moment, stroking her back, her hips, teasing her by slowly stroking his fingers lightly down her ribs and stomach, the rough pads of his fingers drawing goose bumps to her skin. Grasping her bra, she began to tug it over her head, but he took control then too, pushing her hands away to do the job himself.

She watched his eyes as he tossed her bra the same way he'd tossed his shirt, watched as he stroked her bare breasts with one hand, the other sliding beneath her panties. She moaned at the contact, which made him let out a very male sound of pleasure.

Then he dropped to his knees in front of her and dragged her panties down her legs, leaving her completely exposed to his hot gaze.

"Jack," she murmured.

He scraped his teeth gently across her hip bones before moving lower. "Too late to run," he said, and stroked his fingers over her until she trembled. Then he leaned in and put his mouth on her.

Her fingers tangled in his silky hair as he took her, not with the same untamed ferocity that she'd kissed him with, but a doggedly patient precision that told her how much her pleasure meant to him. He found her rhythm with shocking ease and settled in, and suddenly the game was no longer a game at all, but something much more personal.

And satisfying.

When she came and her legs collapsed, he caught her.

"Now you," she managed. "Take off your pants." Without waiting for him, she tried to do it herself.

"Easy," he murmured, his large hands brushing hers aside to free himself.

Her breath caught again. She couldn't help it; he was so perfectly, beautifully made. "I don't have a condom," she breathed, disappointment a physical ache.

He pulled one from his wallet and she nearly whimpered in relief. Spreading his shirt on the ground, he lowered her onto it, following her down, moving over her, running hot, open-mouthed kisses over her body until she could have instantly combusted. "Jack."

He slid nine inches of perfection inside of her, and she did combust then, crying out, rocking into him as she came again. "Oh my God," she managed. "Did you feel that?"

"Leah, you're all I feel."

Undone by him, wanting to drive him as crazy as he'd

driven her, she lifted her hips so he could sink in even deeper.

He groaned. "Do that again."

When she did, he dropped his head back, throat and shoulders corded tight, pleasure etched in every line of his face. "Oh fuck, yeah." With surprising gentleness, he fisted his hand in her hair and tugged so she was looking directly into his eyes, which had gone dark with passion.

Her body throbbed, and unbelievably, the heat started to build within her again. "Jack."

He answered by thrusting into her hard and lowering his mouth to hers. "Right here."

Her nails dug into his skin as he moved; she couldn't help it. And staring into his eyes, she let him drive her right over the edge. Again. This time she wasn't alone; they came together with shuddering impact. It was the single most erotic, intimate moment they'd ever shared.

She came back to herself slowly, realizing she was plastered all over him. The sun was shining into the cave as Jack pulled her in closer, nuzzling at her temple, apparently perfectly content to lay with her in the morning sun.

He didn't move or speak. But after a while she was afraid she might be coming off as too clingy, so she tried to separate herself, but he tightened his grip.

"Not yet," he murmured.

Leah dropped her head to his shoulder and tried not to put too much into the fact that having sex with Jack had been better than every other experience of her life.

Combined.

Jack spent the rest of the day with Ronald going over the open fire reports.

Actually, that wasn't true. He spent the day lost in fantasies involving a naked Leah on a mountaintop...

But in between replaying that over and over in his head, he managed to do some work. In the afternoon, the station got a call saying a woman was reporting that she had a garter snake in her house, and they needed to come get it out. Jack, as the head of station, told dispatch to tell her that unless it was an emergency, they didn't remove snakes from homes. He referred her to animal control. He hung up and met Ronald's wide grin. "What?"

"You turned away a damsel in distress."

"Animal control handles snakes."

Ronald just kept grinning.

"It's their job."

"Uh-huh," Ronald said, sounding hugely amused. "Or...you hate snakes."

Jack rolled his shoulders because he would swear he could feel a snake crawling over him right now. It'd been twenty-something years since it'd happened but it still made him shudder. "Me hating snakes has nothing to do with it."

"I remember your dad telling me a story about a garden snake that got into your bedroom. It crawled through your bedroom window and dropped into your bed. You woke up with it on you. After that, you slept in your parents' bed for a month."

"I was seven."

Ronald just cracked up.

Two minutes later, another call came in, direct to Ronald's line, which he answered on speaker.

It was the mayor. "Listen, I need you to do me a favor. My neighbor is calling me at the office. She's got this snake in her house, and I can't get away to go help her out."

Ronald was still grinning widely when he looked at Jack as he answered. "She called you about a snake?"

The mayor blew out a breath. "Listen, she's new. She's hot. And I'd like to date her. I can't get away from the office, and animal control put her on hold. Can you go get the fucking snake or not?"

"I'll send someone to save your future sex life," Ronald said, and disconnected. He tossed Jack his keys. "Go get 'em, Tiger."

Jack grabbed Ian, the only other guy he knew of who was also terrified of snakes. Misery loves company and all that... They dressed in their bunker gear, with Ian bitching the whole way that Jack owed him big.

The woman looked shocked to see them in full gear but led them down the hallway to her bedroom.

Jack stood in the doorway, sweating like a whore in church. Ian pushed him into the room, where they began their search. Ian went to the closet. Jack swallowed hard and dropped to his knees to look beneath the bed.

And hell. There it was. A two-foot-long, harmless garter snake that was taking years off Jack's life just looking at him. Jack jerked back and fell to his ass.

Ian stared at the bed like it was a bomb. "It's under there?"

Jack could only nod.

Ian gulped, appearing frozen in place.

The woman's voice came from down the hall. "Did you find it?"

"Yes, ma'am," Ian said, his voice sounding like Mickey Mouse. He grimaced and cleared his throat.

Jack found his legs and went out to the engine, where he grabbed a pike pole. He shoved it at Ian, who shook his head adamantly. "You're head of shift," he said.

Jack considered using the pike pole on Ian's head, but there'd be a lot of paperwork afterward, so he resisted. And then, holding his breath, he went back to his knees and peered beneath the bed.

The snake was looking right at him with those obsidian eyes. Slowly Jack reached in there with the pike pole and snagged the motherfucker. Shaking like a leaf, he walked it outside.

The snake slithered off into the bushes and vanished.

And Jack had to lock his knees and gulp in air. Christ. He needed a new job.

Ian came out of the house, looking fully restored back to his good humor as he clapped his hand on Jack's shoulder. "We did good," he said.

Jack slid him a look. "We?"

"Hey, I had your back, man. If you'd dropped him, I'd have snatched him up for you."

"If I'd dropped him, you'd have shit your pants."

Ian grinned. "Well, now we'll never know."

At the station, Jack went back to the reports. He had the convenience store fire and auto shop fire reports side by side. Ronald wasn't convinced either was arson, but Jack couldn't get past the feeling that both points of origin had been buckets of rags, accidentally ignited. It just all felt far too pat, too convenient, and Jack didn't believe in coincidences.

Nor could he buy the vagrant's story of a Santa on crack theory, though that seemed more solid than the vagrant himself setting the fires since he'd been at the homeless shelter on the night of the auto shop fire.

And then Jack discovered something they hadn't known—the auto-parts store had been in escrow too. To a Mr. Rinaldi, the same man in escrow to buy the convenience store. Jack ran a search on him. The guy had a squeaky-clean record and a well-documented history of cleaning up and turning around downtrodden areas.

It didn't make sense. Not a lick of it made any sense at all.

That night, Leah made dinner for her grandma and was so distracted she burned the chicken and undercooked the rice.

Elsie, always a good sport, still ate everything with her usual gusto.

"Sorry," Leah said. "I can't believe I failed dinner so badly."

"I can." Elsie smiled. "Your mind is somewhere else."

This was very true, but she didn't want to go there. "I need to head into Seattle this week. I want to hit up that new restaurant supply warehouse. I need to borrow a truck."

"Ask Jack," Elsie said slyly. "I'm sure he'd take you wherever you wanted to go."

He'd taken her to heaven just that morning, not that she'd tell him so. His ego didn't need the boost.

"So what did you do today?" Elsie asked. "It's rare for you to take a day off. You left early and were gone until past noon."

Jack. She'd done Jack.

With effort, Leah pushed the tactile memory of his big,

warm, strong body wrapped around hers out of her head. "Nothing much."

"Really? You didn't see anyone exciting?"

"In Lucky Harbor?" She forced a laugh. "Who would that be?"

"Jack."

Leah's pulse skipped a beat. "Why would you think that I was with Jack?"

"Other than the two of you are dating?" Elsie asked, sounding amused. "Because someone saw you with him."

Leah dropped her fork and rice splattered everywhere as her heart kicked into gear. "Saw us? Where?"

"On Highway 219, on his bike."

"Oh." Feeling foolish, she relaxed. On the highway. On his bike. Good. That was really good. No one had caught them, exhibition-style, at the caves.

"That Jack," Elsie said. "He sure grew up nice, didn't he?"

Leah flashed to how he'd felt moving over her, his broad shoulders blocking out the sun, his voice a whisper against her ear, the fierce look in his eyes as he slowly, purposely took control and drove her right out of her ever-loving mind… "Yes," she said a little weakly. "He grew up real nice."

"And he's so responsible. He runs that entire station, and he uses his position to give back to the community. Last month, he came over and taught all us seniors how to do CPR. Of course that was right after Edward had his heart scare, which turned out to be a bad case of gas. But Jack made sure each and every one of us could revive someone if need be. So sweet."

"Sweet," Leah agreed. He did have his moments…

"And the town sure is talking about you two. Everyone's all aflutter that yet another of our eligible bachelors has been taken off the market."

Leah swallowed wrong and choked.

Elsie brought her a glass of water and smiled. "And you've made Dee so happy."

Leah caught her breath and sobered as guilt stabbed through her. "Yes."

Elsie's eyes were knowing as she squeezed Leah's hands. "You're sweet too," she said quietly.

Leah opened her mouth and then shut it again, not sure what to say. That she'd lied about being in a relationship with Jack? Or that she wasn't all that sorry to be pretending…?

Neither was something she wanted to discuss.

Elsie poured them each a second glass of wine, then lifted her glass to Leah. "To whatever Jack did to distract you so."

"Grandma."

"What? I'm old, not dead. And I haven't seen you look so dreamy-eyed since…well, ever."

"I'm not…dreamy-eyed."

Though she'd gone to the store for condoms…

"Honey," Elsie said slowly. "About the bakery."

"What about it?"

"I'm not sure how long I'm going to keep it going after you leave."

Leah set down her fork so she didn't drop it again. The bakery had been her grandma's first love for…well, for as long as she could remember. It wasn't just a shop, it was her grandma's identity. Warm apple pies and fresh sourdough bread and chocolate chip cookies. Hopes and dreams. Comfort. Leah couldn't even remember a time when Elsie hadn't smelled like vanilla or cinnamon. Oh God, she thought, her gut tight. Maybe her grandma was sick? "What do you mean? Are you okay?"

Elsie smiled. "Don't look at me like that. I'm fine. I'm more than fine. I'm actually…enjoying the time off. I'm old, honey."

"No—"

"I am. And I'm tired. And watching how hard you're working to keep my business going is making me more tired. You understand, don't you?"

"Of course," she said. "Maybe I could stay and help—"

"No. No way." Her grandma adamantly shook her head. "You're destined for bigger things, Leah. Way bigger things. *Sweet Wars* will be over soon enough."

Leah couldn't stop thinking about that as she helped her grandma to bed. How had the season of *Sweet Wars* gone so fast? She'd planned to be gone before the finals aired, and yet she was still here. More unsettling, how could she go? And when she did, what would it be like to come back to Lucky Harbor the next time and have there be no Grandma Elsie's bakery?

She couldn't imagine.

She watched some old movies on the couch. She must have drifted off because a sound startled her awake.

Elsie stood by the front door in bright-white tennis shoes, her favorite dress, and her purse clutched to her chest. "Oh," she said in surprise when Leah sat up. "Oh, honey. You startled me."

"Grandma? What are you doing?"

Elsie smiled. "Well, I thought I'd just go get us a paper."

Leah looked at the clock. "It's the middle of the night."

"Coffee. We need coffee for the morning."

Leah blinked the last of the sleep from her eyes and stood up. "I'll get it."

"Oh no, I can do it. I don't want you to have to get dressed, or—"

"Or know that you were sneaking out?" Leah asked.

Elsie grimaced. "What clued you in?"

"Well, you're about as clandestine as a bull in a china shop."

There'd been a few crazy teenage years when Leah had done her fair share of sneaking out. Her dad had always kept an extremely tight leash on her, so tight that she'd lived in perpetual danger of strangulation. It'd been painful. Beyond painful. She'd had to do all her homework immediately after school, then show it to him. And if she'd gotten anything wrong, he'd rip it up and she'd have to start over. "You can't get anything right," he'd snap. "Do it again. Do it perfect or don't bother at all." After homework, she had to put in three hours minimum at his dental office, helping with the filing and housekeeping, or whatever was needed.

That had been the worst part.

Spending time with him. She'd never been able to do anything right, and her self-esteem had suffered. This had all been made worse by the fact that she'd not really fit in at school either. She'd never been the girlie-girl, or the athlete, or particularly social, and then there'd been her ruthless 9:00 p.m. curfew, no exceptions.

So she'd sneaked out.

A lot.

She'd sneak out to walk the beach alone. Or go to

Jack's. But if the water was rough and Jack was out somewhere with Ben raising trouble, she'd gone to her grandma's.

Elsie had always seemed to expect her. She'd greet Leah with a warm hug and then they'd go into the kitchen and bake something. Elsie always let Leah take the lead there, allowing her come up with whatever concoction she wanted, no matter how crazy it sounded.

It'd soothed Leah's aching heart and fueled her creative soul. There'd been no recriminations, no judging, and blessedly, no yelling. Elsie had never questioned her need to run away, had never so much as hinted at the worry she surely must have felt knowing that Leah had walked two miles in the dark to get to her.

And now it was Leah's turn to swallow *her* urge to ask the questions, to express the worry, and there was a lot of both. What the hell was her grandma planning to do out there in the middle of the night? "What if your knee gives out?" Leah asked her. "What if you get tired?"

"Well goodness, honey, I'm not that old."

"Of course not," Leah said. "But it's not safe."

"I've got my smartphone and a backup battery, along with my tablet and a can of hairspray. If anyone comes at me, all I have to do is swing my purse at them and I'll knock the perp right on his ass." She demonstrated by giving her purse a broad swing and knocked the lamp off the foyer table. "See?" she asked.

Leah picked up the lamp and righted it. Elsie was the most calm, rational, logical person in her life. In fact, Leah had counted on that calm, rational logic more times than she could count.

But this didn't seem calm or rational. Could it be the

start of dementia? Alzheimer's? Is that why Elsie had mentioned giving up the bakery? Leah's heart clutched at the thought of losing the most important person in the world to her. "Where do you really need to go? I'll take you."

Elsie sighed. "I really thought you'd be sleeping."

This was not an answer and didn't assuage Leah's worry in the slightest. "Okay, what's going on?"

"I didn't want to tell you, but I...have a date."

Leah just stared at her. Years ago, her grandma had been married for only a short time before her husband had died of lung cancer, leaving Elsie pregnant and alone. She'd never remarried. Nor, as far as Leah knew—and despite Elsie's claims to having had a "wild streak"—had she appeared to ever date. "A date," she repeated.

Elsie smiled. "I know. Hard to believe, right?"

"No," Leah said, shaking her head. "You're fun, and sweet, and smart. And pretty."

Elsie laughed now, the sound light and musical. She was pleased. "Oh, aren't you the one. And the same goes. Leah..." Her smile was warm. Caring. And utterly without judgment. "I'm fine. My life is exactly what I want it to be. Can you believe that?"

"Well...sure."

"Can you say the same about *your* life?"

Leah opened her mouth and then closed it.

Elsie gently patted Leah's cheeks. "Don't *ever* wait around for your life. Go get what you want. Because believe me, no one's going to give it to you. You should know that by now." She moved to the door. "Don't wait up, honey."

And then she was gone.

Leah watched out the front window as Elsie got into her car and drove off.

"What the hell just happened?" she asked the quiet living room. But she already knew. Her grandma had proven that she had better social life than Leah did.

Chapter 15

♥

It's your day off," Ronald said the next day when Jack walked into his office. "What the hell are you doing here?"

"You get anything back from forensics on the convenience store or auto shop fires?"

Ronald studied Jack for a long beat. "Not yet. Why?"

"I've been thinking."

"Uh-huh. With head number two, I hear. You've caught yourself a girl."

Jack didn't bother to sigh. "Whatever you've heard, it's greatly exaggerated."

"Well, that's a damn shame," Ronald said. "I was hoping it was true." He paused. "Your daddy wouldn't have wanted you to be the job, Jack. And you are. You're working full-time firefighting and taking up the slack for me."

"About the forensics—"

"Saw your baseball game, you know." Ronald leaned

back, hands behind his head, sighing with pleasure as he put his feet up. "You sucked ass."

"I had an off week. Listen, about the—"

"You couldn't hit worth shit. And you lost that fly ball. I've never seen you choke like that before."

Jack leaned forward and thunked his head on Ronald's desk.

Ronald laughed. "Son, go home. Go take that girl of yours out. Have some fun."

Fun. If fun was having Leah beneath him, panting out his name in that breathy way she had of making him feel superhuman, then yeah. He could use some more fun. He lifted his head. "In the report for the convenience store, we recorded that footprint in the mud along the west wall. Men's size thirteen. Sneaker."

"Yes. The one the vagrant claimed was his."

Jack opened his mouth, but Ronald cut in. "I know, he was barefoot when we found him, but he admitted that he'd been wearing sneakers earlier, remember? He'd gotten hot and kicked them off."

"We never located the shoes," Jack said, knowing if they matched that print to the actual footwear the vagrant had been wearing, he was as good as sunk in court. But it wasn't the right direction. Jack could feel it. "You were working on the tread to name the brand. Did you get that?"

Ronald frowned. "Not yet. I had it sent out. That could take a few weeks. We don't have it on urgent, since we're not sure we have arson here."

"A size thirteen isn't a standard size," Jack mused.

"No."

"And the vagrant's foot is size ten."

Ronald was already shaking his head. "You know as well as I do that he doesn't have his own shoes. He wears whatever he took out of someone's trash or what someone gave him. He claimed to not remember where he'd left the shoes."

"Did you ask him if they were too big for him?"

Annoyance crossed Ronald's face. "Before or after he said he saw Santa on the roof smoking crack, Jack? We both know those shoes weren't his. The question is, was there an arsonist and was the print his?"

"The print showed heavy tread loss," Jack said. "Especially on the outside of the shoe."

"Yeah? So our guy is a runner. So what?"

"So that's also an unusual wear. It's a guy who doesn't roll his ankles inward enough, tending to stride on the ground with the outside edge of his feet. Walking or running on the outside of the foot like that puts a lot of pressure on the legs. Possibly causing shin splints or stress fractures."

"So we're looking for a big-footed runner with a shin splint or stress fracture. Perfect. That narrows it down."

"It's a start." Jack moved to the door, then looked back. "We didn't find any prints at the auto shop fire."

"Not size thirteen, no. And nothing to lead to a perp. Just the bucket of rags."

Jack stood up. "I'm going back to the convenience store site. Check the grounds with a fine-toothed comb."

"You're off duty."

"I have the time."

Ronald took off his glasses and swiped at them with the hem of his shirt. "How's your mom?"

"Better. A lot better," Jack said.

"I asked her out. She tell you that?"

Jack sat back down. "No."

"She said she wasn't ready," Ronald said.

"It's been twenty years."

"Maybe you could put in a good word for me," Ronald said. "Tell her I have a lot more time these days because there's some big, fancy hotshot on my heels, trying to take over my job."

Jack rolled his eyes and strode out the door.

A few nights later, Jack watched the next episode of *Sweet Wars*. The challenge was to create a tart. Jack found himself soaking up the sight of Leah working on a rum sponge tart, once again working calmly and efficiently while everyone else was running around like chickens with their heads cut off.

"How's she doing?" Ben asked, letting himself in and plopping onto the couch next to Kevin, who immediately crawled into his lap.

"You're looking right at her," Jack said.

"I mean here. In Lucky Harbor." Ben had brought another bag of popcorn and smelled like a movie theater. "With her boyfriend."

"You know it's not real. And if you plan to feed that shit to Kevin, you walk him. The last time you gave him popcorn, it required three doggie bags."

Ben tossed Kevin a kernel just to be an asshole. "Not real, huh? I guess that's why you bought condoms."

Jack slid him a look.

"Your receipt's right here, man." Ben nudged the piece of paper on the coffee table with his foot. "A twelve pack, which is either a really impressive one-night stand, or you're thinking long term." He cocked his head and squinted to read that far. "Yep, twelve extra-large condoms *For Her Pleasure*. Aw, that's real considerate."

Jack rolled his eyes and went back to the show.

"So which is it?" Ben asked.

"What?"

"An impressive one-night stand or long term?"

"Shut up."

"Long term," Ben decided. "Quite a commitment, a twelve pack…"

Jack snatched the popcorn and shoved some into his mouth, his gaze on Leah. Which did he want? Hell, all he knew for sure was that he craved her. She was easy on the eyes. And easy to hang out with. She was smart and funny and kind, and he never got tired of being with her.

This thought brought him up a little since it was entirely different from any thought he'd ever had about a woman. But it was true. When he wasn't with Leah, he thought about being with her again. And when something cracked him up or made him think, or *anything* really, he wanted to tell her about it.

Like now. On screen, she was talking, smiling, and kicking ass. No one on the cast came even close to her easy talent. And he wanted to tell her so.

"See that?" Ben asked, pointing to the screen. "That host guy—the one who dated that hot chick from *Big Brother* last year—he's into Leah big time. You notice?"

Jack watched as Rafe Vogel kept finding excuses to end up at Leah's station, twice bumping up against her.

Leah didn't seem to mind all that much, smiling up at him, laughing into the camera while everyone around her was sniping and yelling at each other as the clock counted down.

"You think Leah's two-timing her fake boyfriend?" Ben asked casually.

Jack slid him a look. "Why are you here?"

Ben grinned and grabbed back the popcorn. "You have the bigger TV."

The next morning, Jack got up at the crack of dawn and nudged Kevin. "Let's go."

Kevin did his imitation of a dead dog.

"We're running to the station, dude. Gotta work off all the shit we ate last night."

Kevin squeezed his eyes shut tighter, and Jack shook his head. "If you stay here, I'm going to let the little girls next door dress you up like their pony again."

Kevin opened a single eye and assessed Jack for his level of seriousness. With a loud sigh, he lumbered out the door with Jack.

Kevin wasn't a great running partner. In fact, he was a downright horrible running partner, trotting along at best, stopping to smell every flower, rock, and imaginary foe between home and work. Halfway, he was nearly unmanned by a cat that popped out of the bushes and snarled at him. Kevin, always a lover, not a fighter, tried licking the cat's face, which earned him a bitch-slap. Bewildered and hurt, he ducked behind Jack, where he stayed until they got to the station.

There, Jack grabbed the first hot shower of the day. The first guy to shower always made out because the building's plumbing was cranky. If you didn't get the first shower, you weren't guaranteed hot water. They were a

family at the station, and they did as family did—they
bugged the shit out of each other. Normally, it was acceptable for the first one up to use as much of the hot water
as possible, just because. But today Jack hurried, dressed,
and then grabbed the keys to the supervisory unit, heading out the door only to bump into Tim, who'd clearly just
come in from his own run. In shorts and a damp T-shirt,
he reached for keys as well. "Hey," he said with a nod to
Jack. "Going for donuts."

They typically took turns going to the bakery every
morning, grabbing a box of whatever Leah had fresh, and
bringing it back for the other guys. And it was definitely
Tim's turn.

But Jack didn't want Tim to go to the bakery. *Jack*
wanted to go to the bakery. He'd told Leah that nothing
would change between them, but that'd been before
they'd had the hottest sex of his life up on a mountaintop.

Now he wasn't so sure that *everything* hadn't changed.
Because now he knew how she kissed, how she
tasted…the sexy little sounds she made when she came.
"I'm going to get the donuts," he said.

"It's my turn," Tim said.

"No, it's not."

"Yeah, don't you remember? Sam went last time
and—"

"I got it," Jack said.

Tim stared at him, then let out a slow smile. "Right.
Because you and Leah are a thing. You see the show last
night? Her and that Rafe guy? Some serious chemistry
there."

"The show was filmed six months ago."

"So they're not together?"

Jack headed to the door. "Let it go."

"I don't know, man. Maybe you've been dumped and you don't even know it."

"Tim?"

"Let me guess. The senior center?" But Tim was cracking his ass up as Jack slammed the door and stalked to the truck. An idiot. He was a fucking idiot.

And he didn't mean Tim.

Chapter 16

♥

Jack tied Kevin's leash to the bench in front of the bakery. "Stay."

Kevin immediately hopped up onto the bench like he owned the thing.

"Down," Jack said.

Kevin indeed went down. He laid down, across the entire bench.

Since there was no one else around, Jack shook his head and walked into the bakery. The bell above the door tinkled, and the usual delicious scents assaulted his nose. Vanilla, sugar, cinnamon, and a hundred others that made his mouth water and his brain go straight to Leah.

And his other body parts as well.

Like Pavlov's dog, he thought, with a shake of his head.

There were people seated at the tables, and a few more at the counter still eyeing their selections, among them Lucille and Mrs. Burland. Mrs. B had been Jack's second-grade teacher, and he still twitched whenever she gazed at him with those hawklike eyes that saw everything.

Leah came out from the back carrying a huge tray. She was wearing two tank tops layered over each other, a short denim skirt, and high-heeled ankle boots that had a bunch of cutouts in them and were so damn sexy it made it difficult to put a thought together. Her arms were tanned and toned, carrying her burden with ease as she bent and began reloading the shelves of her glass-front display.

She served a couple of customers before glancing his way. Lucille and Mrs. B were down at the other end of the counter, and Jack scrambled for something clever to say but the only thing he could think of wasn't clever at all.

He wanted to ask about the "fuck me" shoes.

Instead, he kept his mouth shut. Or he tried. He blamed his caffeine-deprived brain. "Nice shoes."

He heard Lucille chuckle, but when he glanced at her, she was busy looking at donuts.

"What's this new thing you have about my shoes?" Leah asked.

"I don't know." But he wanted to see her in those boots and nothing else. He leaned over the counter and caught a whiff of whatever she'd washed her hair with. Something with coconut, which made him hungry and not for food. "You smell good too."

"You're in a bakery," she said dryly. "Everything smells good."

He was a little stymied by her tone, but before he could ask her about it, someone tapped him on the arm. Turning, he looked down at all four feet of Mrs. Burland.

"Hey, you hoodlum, no cuts."

There'd been a time when her voice had struck terror

in his heart. And he supposed that if she was still judging his character on his "little hoodlum" eight-year-old self, the one who'd painted her desk chair with superglue and let the hamsters free in the ventilation system, then she had good reason to call him a hoodlum.

"He's not a hoodlum," Lucille said.

"Really?" Mrs. B asked snidely. "I take it he didn't rearrange your Christmas reindeer lawn ornaments every year so they were…copulating."

Lucille fought a grin and lost. "No, he didn't."

Jack sighed, gestured Mrs. B ahead of him, and waited while she curtly snapped her order at Leah.

"And make sure the cannoli is vanilla," Mrs. Burland told her. "You don't make good chocolate cannoli."

"Yes she does," Jack said.

Mrs. Burland turned an eagle eye on him. "She's already yours, Harper. No one likes a kiss-ass."

"I'm not *his*," Leah said. "I'm my own woman." She thrust a bag of baklava at Mrs. Burland. "It's made with phyllo dough, which is much lower in fat than the cannoli."

"I want cannoli. I am paying you for the cannoli." Mrs. Burland waved a few bills.

Leah pushed them away. "And Dr. Scott paid me to give you something low-cholesterol instead."

Mrs. Burland snatched the baklava and huffed off.

Leah turned to Lucille, who smiled. "Jack can go first," she said.

Leah gave Lucille a look. "So you can eavesdrop?"

Lucille grinned. "Well, of course. But also the good men don't wait around. You don't know that yet because you're still a spring chicken."

"You're not worried about him waiting around for me," Leah said. "You want your daily dose of gossip."

Lucille had the good grace to look slightly guilty. "People like to know what's going on, that's all."

"What's going on," Leah said, "is that you're both holding up my line."

Both Lucille and Jack turned and looked behind them.

There was no one else in line.

Lucille looked up at Jack. "Seriously," she said. "You can go first."

"Seriously," he said. "No thank you."

"Because you and Leah have to talk?" Lucille asked hopefully.

"If I say yes, will you get the hell out?"

"Jack," Leah said admonishingly.

Lucille didn't seem bothered in the slightest. She pointed to a coffee éclair. "Anyone ever mention that those look like a one of them toys you can buy at the dirty stores? What are they called, dildos?"

Jack laughed, but Leah looked horrified. "Lucille!"

"Hey, this is the modern ages, honey," Lucille said. "Women don't have to hide the fact that they buy devices for themselves. After all, that's what a nightstand drawer is for, right?"

Jack didn't want to know what Lucille kept in her nightstand drawer, but the thought of looking in Leah's was giving him a whole bunch of fantasies.

Leah packed up a bag and thrust it at her.

Lucille just grinned. "You're my favorite," she said to Jack.

"Favorite?" Jack asked.

"Yeah, you've got some competition, you know." At

Jack's expression, she laughed. "So you *don't* know…"

Jack looked at Leah. "That host guy?"

Leah blinked. "Who?"

"I noticed that too," Lucille said. "The whole town noticed. What?" she said at Jack's long look. "We gather to watch it at the bar. Anyway, that's not what I'm talking about."

"Lucille," Leah said, "I think your phone is ringing."

"Oh, I don't have my phone on me." She looked at Jack. "And you. You have no one to blame but yourself. You haven't put a ring on it, so she's got some real good options."

"Lucille," Leah said again, more tightly. "How much do you like my pastries?"

"More than George Clooney's sexy tushie."

"Then you'll stop talking now," Leah said.

"Honey, a man should know what he's up against." With that, she patted Jack's arm and left.

Jack met Leah's gaze.

"I'm sorry," she said.

"No worries. I can't think past wondering what's in your nightstand drawer anyway."

"You're bad."

"So bad I'm torn between begging you to let me watch you use whatever you have in there or offering my services to replace it."

She went pink as Lucille poked her head back into the bakery. "Oh, and don't forget about the Facebook poll, Jack. You might want to round yourself up some votes. Tim's out in front right now, with Ben right behind him."

Jack looked at Leah, but she was suddenly very busy wiping down counters. "A poll," he said.

"Honestly, don't you ever go online?" Lucille shook her head. "You young people." She vanished again.

Without a word, Leah began loading up a box for the fire station. She closed the box and handed it over. "I added a few old-fashioned glazed donuts for Tim. I was out of them the other day, and he had to help me change some fuses and said I owe him."

"Tim's on your list of options?"

"Not *my* list," Leah said. "Facebook."

"And Ben's on it too."

"Apparently."

"And I'm…third."

"Actually, I think you're fifth," she said. "Someone put Rafe on there."

"Rafe."

Leah shrugged.

Jack wasn't actually worried that she was involved in something with Rafe. Six months was a long time, and long-distance relationships weren't Leah's strong suit. Plus, one of the very best things about her was how loyal she was, to her very core. If she'd had something going on with anyone else, she wouldn't have slept with him. Logically, Jack knew this. But he wasn't feeling all that logical at the moment. "Where would *you* put me on the list?" he asked softly.

"Does it matter?" She met his gaze, her own suddenly hooded. "No promises, remember? And this is just pretend."

Well, hell. He'd walked right into that one. Reaching over the counter, Jack settled a hand on her wrist.

Quicker than he, she pulled free. Then she vanished into the kitchen.

He looked around. No one was paying them any mind at all. Outside on the bench, he could see Kevin, sitting in Mr. Lyons's lap now. Since Mr. Lyons had his bony arm wrapped around the huge dog, Jack assumed they were both amenable to the arrangement, so he hopped over the counter and followed Leah into the back.

She was hauling a fifty-pound bag of flour to her work station, arms straining. He reached for it, and she gave him a don't-you-dare look. Ignoring that, he took the bag and carried it for her, setting it down where she pointed.

"Leah," he said to the back of her head as she worked at getting the bag open. "We need to talk."

"So talk." She was struggling, dammit, and he reached around her to help just as the bag opened and flour poofed out in a big white cloud.

She went still, then slowly turned and faced him, face and hair and chest covered in flour. "Look what you did."

"Me? I was trying to help you."

"Then why aren't *you* white?"

They both looked down at his firefighter uniform. Navy-blue BDUs, navy-blue T-shirt with the firefighter logo on his left pec. Radio on his hip. Not a speck of flour on him. He solved that by hauling her up against him and wrapping his arms tightly around her. He felt her freeze for a beat, then her arms came around him with a soft sigh of acquiescence that made him instantly hard. Lowering his head, he took a nibble of her neck, absorbing her quiver as she rocked against him. "And good enough to eat," he murmured.

She laughed, the sound music to his ears even as she pushed him away. "Now look at you," she said.

He had a full imprint of her down his front, including two round white spots on his chest where her breasts had been, and then there was the patch of flour right over his crotch, where hers had pressed nice and snug like it belonged there. He grinned, his first of the morning.

"You're a nut," she said with a shake of her head and a helpless half smile. "And everyone's going to think we went at it in here."

"So?"

Her smile faded. "So we already did that."

He let his smile fade too, let her see how serious he was. "You said that wouldn't change anything, Leah."

"It hasn't."

He caught her as she tried to move away and reeled her back in. "Then why are you changing right before my eyes?"

Her gaze slid over his features, landing at his mouth, where she lingered for a beat too long.

"Leah. Talk to me."

There was a flare of heat in her eyes before she dropped her head to his chest. "It's my body. It's not listening to my brain."

He knew what her body was saying because it was plastered to his, soft and warm and pliant. "And your brain's saying...?"

"That we are *not* going to do it again. It was wrong and awful and...wrong."

This was news to him. "Awful," he said carefully, trying to reconcile the word with the woman who'd had at least three orgasms in that cave on the mountaintop. In fact, he'd gone to sleep every night since remembering exactly how it'd felt to hear her breathily pant, "Oh, please, Jack, oh yes, Jack, omigod, *yes!*" He took a deep breath. "Awful," he repeated stupidly.

She lifted her head from his chest and took in his expression. Whatever she saw had her eyes darkening, and she bit her lower lip. "You think you can prove my brain wrong?"

"Oh yeah."

She paused, glancing around as if to make sure no one was listening. "How long do you have before you're missed at the station?" she whispered.

Not much shocked him, but this did.

"There's our bathroom," she said. "It's small, but—"

"We're not doing it in the bathroom."

"You're right," she said, nodding, turning away. "The storage closet. There's even some props in there—"

He tugged her back and wrapped his hand in her ponytail, tipping up her face so he could look into her eyes, all the possibilities playing havoc with his common sense. "Much as it kills me, not the closet either. At least not until we get a few things straightened out."

"More rules?"

"Yes."

She sighed. "Great. I'm so not good at rules."

No kidding. "You'll be good at mine."

"What's that supposed to mean?" she asked, and then her eyes widened. "Oh my God. You're not one of *those* guys, are you? Like a…dom?"

He just stared at her. "What?"

"Someone who ties up their sub and…dominates them."

"I know what a dom is," he said slowly. "I meant *what the hell*?"

"It's very popular right now," she said. "And okay, maybe I've always had a little teeny-tiny fantasy about being tied up. Just to try it. And a light spanking might be all right, but if you think I'm going to call you sir and bend to your every whim, *you're* going first."

On his hip, his radio went off, but he just stared at Leah. He'd completely lost all coherent, cognizant thought.

"Jack?" she said. "Earth to Jack."

He blinked.

"I think you're being called." She actually looked pretty relieved as she pointed to his radio. "Right? Isn't that you? I think you've got to go."

She was right, his radio was squawking, and he considered retiring from the job right there on the spot so he didn't have to leave.

As if reading his mind, she shook her head and let out a low laugh. "Go."

He pointed at her. "We're coming back to this."

The bakery phone rang and she turned toward it, but he caught her hand and pulled her back around. "I'm serious, Leah. We are going to finish this."

She gnawed on her lower lip some more. "I—"

"Do *not* forget where we were."

"Um—"

"Never mind," he said. "I'll remember enough for the both of us."

Chapter 17

♥

Leah was just closing up the bakery that night when Ali came in the back door. "Need cookies," she said.

Leah was used to people coming into the bakery all stressed out and desperate for a sugar fix. Without breaking stride, she opened a bag and began stuffing some cookies into it. She was halfway through that task when the back door opened again, and in came Aubrey.

Aubrey pointed at the white bag. "Whatever she's having, double it."

Leah flipped the OPEN sign to the CLOSED side, shut off the lights in the front room, and pulled out a couple of chairs. She poured three serious mugs of milk and dumped all the day's leftovers onto a tray.

Finally, she sat, getting off her feet for the first time since five that morning. She shoved a blueberry tart into her mouth, drank down half the mug of milk, and leaned back with a sigh. "Okay. Who's going first?"

"I'm fine," Ali said, stuffing in a cookie. She was wearing jeans and a tank top. She had dried clay on her jeans and a few flower petals in her hair, and what looked like some paint on her chest. Her hair was piled on top of her head, with a lot of it escaping in wild, frizzy tendrils, but she did indeed look fine. And happy. "I was just hungry," she said, mouth full.

"I'm fine too," Aubrey said. "If you count 'fine' going through that dusty old bookstore, where the newest book I have in inventory was printed back in 1959 and is a list of rules for a woman's place in society—which include the grocery store and laundromat. The shelves are rusty and everything's claustrophobic in there. It's a mess."

Both Leah and Ali looked Aubrey over. She was in white jeans and a red tee, and there wasn't a speck of dust on her. "It must have been awful," Leah said dryly.

"It was. I'm tossing everything."

"So you taking on the project then?" Leah asked.

Aubrey shrugged. "The shop needs me. And it also needs new bookshelves and new furniture, including big, fat, comfy couches where people sit and talk about books and knit and drink tea."

"Tea?" Leah asked.

"Tea," Aubrey said. "People who read like tea. I'll sell coffee too, damned good coffee." She paused. "Not that I want to put you out of business with my own awesomeness," she said to Leah.

"I'm not worried," Leah said.

Aubrey nodded. "I'm going to sell ebooks too, though that's going to require some serious updating of the building's electrical, and then some fancy Internet setup."

Both Ali and Leah laughed.

"What?" Aubrey said with a scowl.

"In this building you can't run the toaster and flip on a light in the bathroom at the same time without blowing fuses," Leah said. "Have you talked to your uncle?"

"He's not willing to put a penny into the building because it's in escrow," Aubrey said. "But the new owner promised upgrades. So fingers crossed this thing goes through. It'll mean good things for all of us."

"Well, except for Leah," Ali said. "She's going to be leaving soon."

Leah looked at her. "Tired of me already?"

"You going to tell us that you didn't win *Sweet Wars*? That you aren't only an episode away from starting up your own pastry shop with a hundred grand in your pocket?"

Leah got very busy rearranging the pastries on the tray in front of them. "I signed a contract," she started. "I can't talk about—"

"Fine," Ali said agreeably. "Let's talk about Jack instead."

Leah slid her a wary look. "What about him?"

"How's it going?"

Leah squirmed a little bit and glanced at Aubrey, who was looking eager to hear her response. "Fine."

"Fine?" Aubrey asked. "You're dating the hottest firefighter in town, and it's going 'fine'? What's the matter with you?"

"I don't really want to discuss it."

Ali snorted and Aubrey divided a look between the two of them. "What am I missing?"

"Nothing," Leah said quickly.

Aubrey looked to Ali, who lifted her hands. "Not my tale to tell."

Leah sighed. "You're a big help."

"I want to hear the tale!" Aubrey said. "What is it? Does he wear women's underwear? Snore? Oh! Does he have a small d—"

"Oh my God," Leah said, and stood up.

"Hey, aren't you at least going to answer any of the questions before you storm out of your own place?" Aubrey asked.

Leah turned back. "No, no, and most definitely no." She picked up the tray of pastries and hugged it close as both Ali and Aubrey hooted with laughter. "You're both cut off."

"Aw, don't go away mad," Ali said, laughing.

"I don't care if you go," Aubrey said. "But leave the pastries."

Leah moved back to the table. "I have a question."

"No answers until you put down the tray," Aubrey said.

Leah set the tray down and bit her lip.

"Spill it," Aubrey said, mouth already full as she gave her a go-ahead gesture with her hand.

"Okay." Leah took a deep breath. "Have either of you ever secretly started to like someone, and then you sort of blow it, and I don't know, say, vanish for a while? Like for years. And then you come back, and it turns out you still feel something for him, but now he's over you and also a little wary. So you then blow it again by making it so you're together but it's pretend. Only you don't want it to be pretend…"

They were both staring at her, goggle-eyed.

"You know what?" Leah said. "Never mind." She started to turn, but Aubrey caught her and pointed to a chair. "Sit," she said.

"I'm such an idiot," Leah said, and sat.

"Yes." Aubrey patted her hand. "But the good news is that I know all about being an idiot."

"Me too," Ali said, raising her hand. "I'm quite the experienced idiot."

Leah's phone vibrated. Her grandma. "Hey," she answered. "I'll be out of here in just a few—"

"Are you listening to the kitchen scanner?"

Leah glanced at it. She'd turned it off as Jack had asked. "No."

"Town Hall's on fire."

Leah hurried down the street, Ali and Aubrey at her side. It was only a two-block walk, but they heard the sirens and saw the ominous plume of smoke the minute they'd stepped outside the bakery.

It was dark outside now, but commercial row was well lit. And if it hadn't been, the flashing strobes and the glare of headlights made it easy to see the scene.

The entire block was cordoned off, and yellow police tape stretched everywhere, holding the crowd back. Police officers were standing guard. Fire trucks and emergency vehicles were angled between police cars, lights flashing.

The spectators were multiplying, spilling onto the street and clogging up the sidewalk. Leah moved as close as she could and stood there in shock. Ali found Luke and came back to Aubrey and Leah with news. "It started as a car fire in the back lot," she said. "Possibly set purposely. The car exploded and the building caught."

"Oh my God," Aubrey said. Up until six weeks ago, she'd worked inside the building as an admin to the town clerk. "Did everyone get out?"

"Yes."

"Except for the firefighters," Dee said from right behind them, looking pale and shaken. "They're still inside, including Jack." She reached for Leah's hand and gave her a smile that didn't quite meet her eyes. "But it's okay. It's going to be okay."

She was talking to herself, and knowing it, Leah pulled her in for a hug. "Of course it's going to be okay. Hell, this is your crazy son's idea of fun."

Dee let out a watery laugh and hugged Leah so tight it hurt to breathe. "Oh, Leah, you're so good for him, you know that?"

Again she felt that now-familiar stab of guilt.

Dee held on to her. "You're just so much stronger than I could ever hope to be."

If only that were true.

Chapter 18

Several hours later, the fire had been put out. There was still a police presence, but the crowd had dwindled.

Jack was supervising the cleanup and going through the scene with Ronald. Town Hall had been saved, though there was some fairly extensive damage to the second floor and the roof, both of which had caught when the car exploded.

They'd found a few cigarette butts in the alley, which had an excellent view of the back of the Town Hall building. And beneath the burned wreckage of the car, the same incendiary device that they'd found at the auto parts store—a bucket of oily rags.

This was no vagrant.

It was 2:00 a.m. before Jack got back to the station. By the time dawn arrived and he dragged his tired ass—and Kevin's—home, he was gritty-eyed and exhausted. Far too exhausted to be surprised when he found his mom and Ben waiting for him.

They dragged him out to breakfast, and then they went with Dee to her doctor's appointment, where they got good news from the results of her last tests.

The treatment was working.

It was nearly noon by the time Jack got home, with bed firmly on his mind.

Leah was sitting on the top step of his porch in a sundress, another of her cropped sweaters, and strappy, high-heeled sandals that had a bow around her ankle. Kevin bounded over to her like he hadn't seen her in years. She gave him a full body rub that had the dog sinking to the ground in boneless ecstasy, rolling onto his back, with his legs straight up in the air, tongue lolling.

Leah smiled and shook her head at his antics. "You boys are all the same," she said. "You just want to show off your junk." She pulled a doggie biscuit from her purse, and Kevin wriggled like a beached whale trying to right himself in a hurry.

"Sit," she said firmly.

"He doesn't sit," Jack said.

Kevin sat.

"Good boy! Oh, what a *very* good boy," Leah said in that high, silly voice that all women used with dogs and gave Kevin another big, warm hug.

Kevin glanced back at Jack, who would have sworn the dog was grinning at him. "Careful," he said. "Or I'll let you adopt him."

"No thank you," she said. "I don't have big enough baggies."

Jack moved to the top step and sat next to her. He told himself it was because she always smelled so good and he wanted to get the scent of the fire out of his nostrils.

And also because his legs were so tired he didn't think he could keep standing up. "So."

She pulled her bottom lip into her mouth. "So…"

"Where were we?"

She flushed. "I don't remember."

"Seriously," he said. "How is it that your nose isn't a foot long by now?"

She smiled and handed him a small white bag. "Happy birthday."

He should have known she would remember. She always remembered. "What is it?" he asked cautiously. And with good reason. One year, she'd gotten him a gift certificate for a spa treatment that had turned out to be for a male Brazilian wax. He'd never cashed that one in… Another year, she'd left him a pair of really huge women's underpants on his truck antenna out in front of the station along with a "love note" from a secret admirer. That one had taken a while to live down.

"Open it," she said, sounding far too innocent.

"Do I need insurance first?"

"Maybe it's just what you wanted," she said.

What he wanted was her in his bed wearing nothing but those sexy shoes. He started to open the bag, and Kevin moved in close, licking his chops hopefully.

"You already got yours," Jack told him.

Kevin whined.

"I'll tell you what," Jack told him. "If you sit, maybe I'll share."

Kevin offered a paw.

"No, I said sit."

Kevin barked.

Leah laughed, the sound going a long way toward reviving Jack. Shaking his head, he opened the bag. Cream cheese croissants. "I like the lack of public humiliation with this one," he said as he pulled the first one from the bag.

She smiled. "I figured it was time to grow up just a little bit. Aren't you going to go inside to eat?" she asked.

"Nope." He downed the croissant in two bites and pulled out number two. "Can't wait that long." He swallowed. "You made these when the cast from *Sweet Wars* guested on the *Today Show*."

"Yes."

"And you fed one to that host guy, whatever his name is."

They both knew damn well that he knew Rafe's name. Leah didn't respond, just pulled something else from her big bag. A thermos.

Milk, which as it turned out was gloriously, icy cold. He washed down the croissant, filling his stomach with something more than adrenaline and acid. "God, you're good."

"That's what they tell me." She waited until he'd taken a big, long gulp. "As for Rafe." She paused until he looked at her. "I did sleep with him," she said quietly.

The milk went down the wrong pipe, and he choked. When he could breathe again, he swiped his face with his forearm. "I didn't want to know that."

"Yes you did. But it was only once. I didn't like him enough to repeat the experience."

Their gazes met again and held as he wondered if she liked *him* enough to repeat *their* experience. In his pocket, his phone vibrated. He ignored it. "Go on," he said.

"There's nothing else to tell." Standing up, she moved to the porch railing and leaned on it, staring out into the bright morning. "He got pissed off and made a big stink about how if I didn't sleep with him again, I was going to blow the chance of a lifetime."

Jack narrowed his eyes. "He threatened you?"

"He was just blowing off steam after getting rejected. I could have handled it better." She shrugged. "He wasn't my type. We weren't a thing. You'll see that in the finals, where he ignores me completely."

Feeling a whole lot better, he looked at her and realized she wasn't feeling better at all. She was tense. "You okay?"

She let out a low, mirthless laugh that told him she wasn't, and why.

It hit him then, like a bucket of ice water. She'd been watching the fire last night with everyone else in town. Watching and worrying. He remembered those years his mom had made herself sick with the strain and stress and fear of waiting. Just the thought of having a woman do that for him had always been enough to keep himself from letting anyone get too close. Lots of other people managed to do the job and have families, and it all seemed to work out. But after watching his mom fall apart when his dad had died, Jack had known he'd never be one of them.

He set the bag and the thermos down and stood up. Turning her to face him, he stepped into her, his boots on the outside of her pretty shoes, his hands gliding up her arms to her face, which he tilted to his. "I'm really good at what I do, Leah."

"Yes," she agreed. "I know."

"I'm not my dad."

"I know that too."

"I'm trying to honor his memory," Jack said. "Trying to live up to what he believed in, but trust me, I have no intention of being a hero. Not like he turned out to be."

She set her hands on his biceps and looked into his eyes. "There was a time that wasn't true," she reminded him. "When you were wild and reckless."

"I'm past that," he assured her. "*Long* past. And knowing what my mom went through, how she suffered, it's made it easy to say no to any sort of deep relationship."

"To *any* relationship."

He lifted a shoulder. "Fine. Yeah. I stay away from them."

"Except for one," she said, and drew in a deep breath. "Me."

This was true. His relationship with her had stood the test of time—although not without its share of bumps and bruises along the way.

"Because we've been friends," he said. "Not lovers."

She arched a brow.

"Until recently," he allowed.

She took in his expression. "Let me guess," she said quietly. "We're going back into negotiations on our rules." She pulled out her phone. "Go ahead," she said. "I'll take notes."

"This isn't funny."

"Well, give the man an A."

Irritation bubbled at the base of his skull. His very tired skull. "Tell me this, Leah. Where do you see this charade going? Or ending?"

Something flashed across her face that he couldn't quite interpret. Maybe guilt.

"I don't know," she admitted. "I didn't think that far.

It's not like this was premeditated," she said, voice heavy with regret. "I only meant to make your mom happy—"

"I know." And he did know. "It's worked. She's eating. Getting up and out." He shook his head in marvel. "She's happy. But…"

"You're not," she said softly. "Happy."

"You want to know what I think?"

"Probably not."

"I think you're using this opportunity to avoid whatever the hell you're running from this time."

She stared at him for one stunned beat before pushing at him. "I've got to go."

"Shit," he muttered, catching her, pulling her around, and pinning her to the railing. "I'm right, aren't I? You ran from whatever happened. Was it Rafe?"

"No." In his arms, she squirmed. Her hair tickled his nose, caught on the stubble of his jaw. It smelled good. She felt good too, and like always when it came to being with her, she both aroused and frustrated the shit out of him. "So are your plans to run from me, Leah? Because that's next, right? And how are you going to explain that?"

She sighed and dropped her forehead to his chest. "I don't have plans to go anywhere, Jack. Does that make you feel any better?"

When he didn't respond, she lifted her head and let out a mirthless laugh. "I see that makes you feel worse," she said. "Since it means you're stuck with me. Aren't we a pair? Look, I really do need to go. Apparently I can only pretend to like you in small doses."

Ignoring the fact that they were visible to anyone coming down the street, he pressed into her again, plastering himself to her from chest to thigh.

An electric charge zinged between them, heating the air. She didn't move, not a single muscle.

He couldn't say the same since he went instantly hard.

"Jack," she whispered, gaze on his mouth. "Don't. We're too bad at this."

"So let's go back to something we're good at," he said, and kissed her, long and hard and wet. It wasn't enough. Fisting his hands in her hair, he held on to her and plundered. With a moan that soothed his soul, she wound her arms around his neck. "Damn you," she murmured against his mouth. "*Damn you.*"

With a growl, he backed her into his front door, unlocking it, pulling her inside.

They staggered like drunks into his living room, still kissing while attempting to strip each other.

Kevin, thinking they were playing, was jumping up and down on his back legs like Scooby-Doo, trying to get in on the fun.

"Sit," Jack told him.

Kevin barked. *Jesus.* "Kevin, bark."

Kevin sat.

Leah was shaking with laughter when Jack once again took her mouth with his. The urgency hadn't abated. She got his shirt unbuttoned and off one arm. He kicked off one boot while ripping off her sweater. She tripped over the boot, and they both went down onto his couch.

She landed on top, forcing the air out of his lungs with her bony elbow. Hell, she very nearly unmanned him completely with an ill-placed knee. None of it mattered as he continued to kiss her like she was better than air.

And in that moment, she was.

Chapter 19

♥

Leah sat up to take in the glorious sight of Jack sprawled beneath her on the couch. He wasn't like any other man she'd ever been with. Even when he was in a hurry, he never let anything rush him.

She'd watched him at the fire. Calm, level-headed, never losing his cool.

Now he lay still with deceptive languor, deceptive because she could feel him, thick and hard between her legs as she straddled him. Weaving her fingers in his, she slowly slid his arms up, resting them above his head on the back of the couch. Holding him like that, she rocked against him.

He groaned, simmering heat radiating from his big body. "Leah, kiss me."

Oh yes, she'd kiss him, but first she let go of his hands to shove his shirt up. "Mmm," she said, and stared down at what she'd exposed. Warm skin and ridged muscle.

He looked up at her, gaze hot and unapologetically

sexual. His pants had ridden low, revealing the way his obliques were cut at his hips. She wanted to taste him there. So she did just that, humming in pleasure while he gave a low growl.

At the sound, Kevin bounded over and thrust his huge head between Jack's and Leah's, trying to see what he was missing. "Lay down," Jack commanded.

If he'd used that voice on her she would have done anything he commanded, but Kevin only whined.

"Horse factory," Jack grated out.

Kevin heaved a sigh and trotted off.

"Do you have birthday plans?" Leah asked Jack softly, unbuttoning his pants. She ran her fingers down the center of his chest and lower abdomen, following the line of dark hair to where it vanished into his opened pants.

"Yes," he said, his voice sounding as strained as the waistband of his boxers. "I have plans to make you scream my name."

"I'm not much of a screamer."

"I have my ways."

Leah shivered because she knew it to be true. She'd seen firsthand what happened when Jack was...determined. Her body quivered again as she took in the sight of him beneath her, taut, ripped, waiting with mock patience. "Ah," she said, "but it's *your* birthday. Maybe you'll scream *my* name."

He slid his hands to the backs of her thighs and then up her skirt to cup and squeeze her bottom. Then he tore away her panties.

"Jack!" she gasped in shock.

"Hmm. That's a good start." He nudged her bra straps from her shoulders. "Take this off," he said, then put his attention to shoving up her skirt. His gaze followed his fingers, and at the sight of her, he growled out her name.

She unhooked her bra and let it slip down her body, and then kissed him again, a soft touch of lips to lips before pulling back slightly.

His warm brown eyes were heavy-lidded as he watched her watching him. Reaching for her hands, he guided them down his chest and farther until she'd wrapped her fingers around his hard length.

She squeezed, and a slight tremor ran through him. Practically vibrating with pleasure, she kissed her way down the same path her hands had taken. "Happy…" She gave him a long, slow lick. "Birthday…"

With a low, long groan, his fingers slid into her hair. Not pulling, not guiding…more like he needed a handhold.

Against him, she smiled. He'd been her neighbor. Her protector. Her greatest friend. But her favorite thing was what they were now. Lovers. They fit together as if they were made for each other. Knowing it, reveling in it, she took him into her mouth. Beneath her, hands still tangled tight in her hair, his hips bucked, control slipping. "Fuck, Leah."

"Later," she said, and made him snort. And then she made him sweat. And pant. And swear like a sailor.

And then finally, she made him come, hard.

Afterward, he hauled her up his body to kiss her with enough heat to let her know he'd liked the birthday gift.

Then he flipped them so he was on top, his arms bracketing her body. Every part of him slid against every part of her, and she wrapped her arms and legs around him, anticipation swimming through her.

As she'd done to him, he slid his hands to hers and

slowly guided them above her head to the armrest of the couch. He squeezed her fingers and met her gaze, his message clear. *Leave them there.*

She drew one breath before he took possession of her mouth, and it was like she'd never been kissed before. She'd never even dreamed that a kiss could be so...soul searching.

Perfect.

It was different from their earlier kisses, which had all been just as hot, but also flirty. No end destination.

This was different. This was...intense, demanding everything from her, and her heart started to pound against her ribs.

Lifting his head, he stared into her eyes, trailing his fingers down her jaw, his mouth following, along her throat, where he stopped at the pulse point.

His thumb lightly glided over the spot. "You're either having a heart attack or I'm really doing it for you," he murmured.

"Both. Jack—"

"Shh," he said, his gaze hot enough to scorch. "It's my turn now." And then he lightly nipped her throat before soothing the sting with a kiss. Her collarbone was next, and then her breast. He took her nipple into his mouth and laved, nipped, and teased until she was writhing beneath him. Then he switched sides, taking his sweet-ass time about it too, until she whispered his name. And then said it again in a rather commanding tone that matched the frantic rock of her hips.

This only encouraged further torture on his part. He slid to his knees on the floor as he finally, God *finally*, kissed his way down her stomach.

Her skirt was still shoved up to her waist, and he seemed to really like the look as he stroked a hand over one thigh, urging her to open for him, to hook her leg on his shoulder. His other hand rested low on her belly, so low his thumb could lightly scrape over her. And then not so lightly. "I have condoms," she managed. "An entire box of them. In my purse."

He looked up at her, his eyes dark and intense with concentration, though now there was also a light of humor. "That's a big box."

She felt herself flush. "Well, I thought maybe we weren't done yet."

Turning his head, he rubbed up against her inner thigh with a day's worth of scruff on his jaw.

She nearly came. "Jack—"

"I bought some too. Also a big box. Because I was *sure* we weren't done yet." He glided his thumb over her again and followed it up with his tongue, eyes still on hers.

A man had never looked at her like that, not in her entire life. And okay, so she wasn't all that experienced, but she was feeling things, so many, many things, and she could tell that he was feeling them too. She breathed more than said his name, and he let his eyes drift closed as he went back to what he was doing—driving her out of her ever-loving mind. He was quite thorough about it too, and she lost it completely, coming with a shuddering cry that rocked her to her very core.

Jack staggered to his feet. "Bed," he said firmly.

"I can't feel my legs."

"I've got you." Bending over her, he stilled when she slapped a hand to his chest.

"You're not going to carry me like I'm some silly

girly-girl in the movies all romantic-like," she said. "It always brings me out of the scene because I worry about his back, and— Hey!"

He'd scooped her up and over his shoulder into a fireman's hold.

"*Jack*." She laughed and squirmed to get free, but then realized that she had a most excellent view of his most excellent backside as he strode down the hall as if she were light as a feather. "Put me down."

"I'm dragging you off to my cave."

Well then. Willing to play, she tried to bite his ass. Since she couldn't quite reach, she settled for low on his back, but the bastard didn't have an ounce of fat on him so she couldn't really get a good hold.

He swatted her butt. "Behave."

She tried to bite him again, but then she was flying through the air and landing on his bed. Before she could bounce twice, he'd pulled a condom from his bedside drawer and was on top of her.

And then in her.

He stilled and pressed his face to her neck. "I'm a dead man," he murmured, and then, holding her right where he wanted, he began to thrust, pulling out with each stroke, rolling his hips, and then grinding back in. She could feel him hot and hard, deep inside every time he moved. He gripped her thighs and pushed them forward slightly so he slid in more, pressing a spot deep inside of her. She'd never experienced anything like it. When he groaned her name, she knew neither of them were going to last. Everything about him was causing sensations in her body that she didn't even know what to do with. Squeezing her legs around his waist, she clutched him, crying out.

They came together. Or at least she thought they did. She couldn't be sure because she lost track of all her senses.

When she came back to herself, they were damply entangled and she was breathing like a lunatic. Holy cow… She tried to roll free and found she couldn't move. She was pinned by one-hundred-and-eighty solid pounds of muscle, and he was breathing just as hard as she, the small of his back slick with sweat. And her only coherent thought was, if they kept at this whole naked friends thing, they were going to kill each other…

Eventually Jack got up to get them some water and sustenance, and Leah managed to roll over and shove her hair from her face. His bedside drawer was open, the box of condoms torn into and spilling out over a colorful stack of envelopes—

Leah went still, then reached out and brushed the condoms away, even though she didn't need to. She knew what that stack of cards was.

Her own cards, sent to Jack when she'd first left Lucky Harbor. Christmases, birthdays, Valentine's Days…she'd used them all as excuses to keep in touch, her own way of hoping he would keep her in mind.

He still had them. Every one of them, by the looks of things. Her throat tightened as she wondered what it meant. But she knew. It meant that she'd been important to him.

And she'd hurt him.

She could have had something here with him, something real. Instead, she was now stuck in this…*fake* relationship that was quickly turning not so fake at all.

And it was all her own doing.

* * *

The next morning, Jack knew the minute Leah woke up because, like Kevin always did, her entire body tensed without moving a muscle.

He wondered if she expected him to do what he did with Kevin: point to the floor and say, "Get down." The truth was, he was far more likely to roll over and expose his vulnerable underbelly.

Instead, he let her have the moment of pretense as he watched her in the early morning light. God, it felt good to wake up with her, which begged the question—how long was she sticking around? She seemed to be settling into Lucky Harbor, though this didn't make any sense at all if she'd won *Sweet Wars*. And surely she had won. This meant she had the prize money to start her own pastry shop and was financially stable, probably for the first time in her entire adult life.

Maybe she'd continue to revamp her grandma's bakery. Surely she wouldn't have started this thing between them if she'd been in a hurry to go anywhere. He tried to figure out what that might mean but couldn't. "Morning," he said quietly.

She didn't move.

This didn't surprise him. If he knew her, and he sure as hell did, he knew she was panicked right about now and reviewing her options.

And most likely the closest exit.

He could feel her heart kick into high gear, and he had some sympathy. She wasn't alone in this. This whole new lover intimacy they had going between them now was going to affect their friend intimacy, no matter what they said or did.

"I know you're awake," he said.

She cracked open one eye. "How? How do you always know?"

"You stopped breathing."

She sighed. "What time is it?"

They'd called in for pizza late last night, ravished it in the same manner in which they'd ravished each other, and then fallen asleep, the heavy sleep of the dead—or two people who'd fucked their brains out. "Eight," he said.

"Eight…" With a gasp, she sat straight up. "*Eight*? Omigod, we fell asleep? The bakery—"

"I thought today was your day off."

"No! I told Grandma she could have the day for herself. I've gotta go." Rolling to her feet, she staggered until she got her sea legs, and then she whirled to look for her clothes.

Jack tucked his hands beneath his head and enjoyed the view of her, all naked and rosy and… "Damn," he said, sitting up. "Sorry about that whisker burn."

She glared at him and then strode—still bare-ass naked—to the mirror over his dresser. She took in the sight of her reddened neck and growled. "Is it too hot for a turtleneck?"

He bit his lower lip to hold in his grimace.

She looked at him, narrowed her eyes, and then looked down at her body.

The whisker burn extended to her breasts, belly, and inner thighs. "You suck," she said.

"Actually, you're the one who—"

"Stop!" She clapped her hands over her ears but did let out a low laugh that pretty much made his heart swell too big for his ribs. "Where the hell is my bra?"

He got out of bed, tripped over Kevin, and headed down the hall to the living room. The dog happily trotted along after him, thrilled to have his people awake, even more thrilled because he could tell time and knew it was *way* past time to eat. To remind Jack, he put his icy nose on Jack's ass, goosing him.

Jack picked up Leah's clothes from the living room floor and handed them over. She began to jerk them on, doing that whole not-quite-making-eye-contact thing that he recognized. It was what she did right before she did something stupid, and some of his glow faded. "That was quick," he said.

"What?"

"The regret."

"Don't start." She whirled for her shoes and purse. "This is all your fault."

"Mine?" He laughed. "You gave me a birthday blow job, which started the whole thing. How was that my fault?"

"Because you came home looking edgy and rumpled and...hot. And then I took your clothes off and...and you looked even hotter."

He grinned. "You think I'm sexy."

"The entire female race thinks you're sexy." She sighed. "Okay, Mr. Rules, Mr. Gotta Be In Charge... we're going to have to renegotiate some things."

"Such as?"

"That," she said, and pointed to the bed. "What the hell are we going to do about *that*?"

"If you're referring to the amazing orgasms, then I vote for more as soon as possible."

"At least that part isn't pretend," she said.

He frowned at her. "What does that mean?"

"Look, forget it. But we need to remember your first rule: this isn't real and there are no hurt feelings." She whirled away and began digging through her purse for her keys. "When people are bitching that I don't have any fresh bread or donuts available today at the bakery, I'm going to blame you."

"Sure," he said, a little distracted by her reiterating his own rule. Which was ridiculous of him. "My reputation could use the boost."

She rolled her eyes, headed to the door, then stopped, sighed, and came back to him. "You're still naked."

"Yeah," he said. "Just in case you want to give me any more birthday presents."

"Look, Jack," she said and then paused.

Uh-oh. "You going to dump me on my birthday?" he asked softly.

"It's the day *after* your birthday." She closed her eyes. "And I don't know what I'm doing here, Jack. I feel antsy. I feel like…"

"You have to run?"

Her silence was answer enough, and he felt the age-old temper for her father rear its ugly head. "You're letting your past rule you again. It's your life, Leah. Own it. Do with it what you want."

"It's not that."

They both knew it was a lie. She sighed and put a hand to his chest and then dropped her head to it. "I'm having trouble with this pretend thing."

His heart kicked hard. "What do you mean?"

"I mean, dammit, you're messing with my head." She lifted hers. "We *have* to go back to pretend, Jack.

All pretend. It's a rule! And it's for my own mental health!"

He thought of what they'd done to each other in the name of sheer lust over the past twenty-four hours, how she was saying what he already knew. They were skating on thin ice. Thin, cracked ice. "What about for *my* mental health?" This came out completely unbidden, and if he had a do-over card, he'd have taken it back. He didn't want to discuss his mental health, or lack thereof. Hell no.

"What are you saying?" she asked.

"Nothing. Forget it." He turned away, stopping to look down when he felt her hand on his arm.

"Jack," she said softly.

"Throwing in the towel now makes sense," he heard himself say. "My mom's getting better. The treatment's working."

"Oh, Jack, that's wonderful. I'd hoped..."

He nodded. "She's still got some treatments left, but the bottom line is that it's working." He paused, his throat feeling like he'd swallowed broken glass. "So I suppose it's best to break her heart sooner than later and tell her the truth." Feeling hollow, he took a step back. "You're late," he reminded her.

"But...are we...okay?"

"Aren't we always?"

She looked at him for a moment, then nodded and headed toward the door, and he let her go.

Had to.

She was in denial, and he wasn't going to call her on it because...well, hello, Pot, meet Kettle.

Still, he hauled her back against him, using the stolen

moment to adjust the collar on her sweater so it covered as much of her throat as possible. For her.

And then he kissed her one last time, long and wet and deep.

For him.

Chapter 20

♥

Leah raced home, changed, then continued on her rush to the bakery, definitely *not* thinking about all that had just happened in the past twenty-four hours: being in Jack's bed—and then later on his couch, his table, his bathroom counter… Everything about it had been magical.

And then the not-so-magical morning after.

She had to park down the street, and she ran to the back door and the bakery, only to skid to a shocked stop.

Her grandma was in the middle of the kitchen, surrounded by the day's baked goods.

"But," Leah said, staring around. Fresh bread. Muffins. Pies… "You made all this?"

Elsie grinned and poured Leah a big mug of burn-the-hair-off-your-tongue, straight-black coffee.

Leah took a few gulps and let the caffeine sink in. But she was still boggled. "Did the pastry fairy visit?"

Elsie laughed, soft and musical. "Funny thing about not having to get up at four in the morning to start baking every day…you don't mind doing it once in a while. In fact, I had the time of my life this morning." She gestured to the recipes Leah had been working on, spread across the counter. "Your stuff is amazing, honey. Utterly amazing."

"It's all in the hands of the baker," she said.

"No," Elsie said. "It's all in the heart of the person putting together the recipes."

Leah didn't know what to say. The praise, coming from her grandma, meant so much and embarrassed her at the same time, and she checked her watch.

Elsie laughed softly. "You can just say thank you."

"Thank you."

"You never did learn how to take a compliment."

Leah thought of how Jack had looked at her when he'd told her she was beautiful. How she'd wanted to close her eyes from the look in his warm gaze, the one that told her he meant it, down to his soul. She *had* closed her eyes, even as she'd wanted to hear him say it again…

But she'd blown that, hadn't she?

Lord. She needed therapy.

"So…," Elsie said. "Big day yesterday?"

Leah winced. "Sorry I didn't come home. I—"

"Don't you dare apologize. You have a life. I'm so happy for you, Leah."

"It's not what you think, Grandma. Jack and I are…" She broke off, not sure how to continue.

"Honey, anyone with eyes can see exactly what you and Jack are." She smiled. "Now I'm going up front to see to our customers."

Alone, Leah worked in the kitchen. She was nearly done when her phone rang. She jumped for it, hoping it was Jack. But of course it wasn't, she'd made sure of that.

"Hey, Sweet Cheeks." Rafe. "Finally able to give you a call. Got your email a few weeks back. Thought you'd forgotten about me there for a little while."

"Not likely, since you're on my TV every week."

He laughed softly, an easy, contagious laugh. If one could make a mold of pure infectious charm and charismatic wit, it was Rafe. He knew how to make you forget everything but him. He knew how to get the best out of anyone. He knew how to get what he wanted.

And he had no soul.

"I thought about your offer," she said.

"Which offer?"

He knew damn well which offer, so she remained quiet.

He laughed again. "Aw. You miss me. Who'd have thought?"

"I want the job."

"But maybe it's no longer available."

Leah ground her teeth but kept her voice light. "Okay. Then I'll go to the Food Network. They were interested as well."

"Well, there's no need to get your panties in a twist," he said. "I was just messing with you. You used to have a sense of humor."

"And you used to at least be a good guy."

"I still am," he said, a little more stiffly now. He had great illusions of being the perennial boy next door and didn't like his faults pointed out to him. "The job offer stands."

"You're going to let me have my own reality show, following a group of fledgling pastry chefs in their final semester of school?"

"I'm going to let you have your own reality show, following *you* in *your* last semester of school."

She stared at her phone. "That wasn't the deal."

"It's been six months. The deal changed."

"Rafe—"

"Look, Leah," he said, not quite as jovial and friendly as before. "The ratings have been pouring in. You're the little media darling now. The camera loves you, and the viewers love you. They all think you're about to win this baby."

She grimaced. "I haven't said a word—"

"Of course not, or we'd have sued your sweet ass off."

"I can't just go back for my last semester," she said, feeling a little panicky at just the thought of it. "I left there. They don't take people back."

"Of course they do. For a price. And we're willing to pay it. Yes or no, Leah?"

You never finish a damn thing, Leah. Not one damn thing. And you never will...

Her father's words echoed in her head and gave her an instant jaw ache from clenching it so tight. It used to be that her father's words were in her head all the time, but she'd managed to block them more and more. Now she heard a different voice in her head. She heard Jack, brave, confident Jack.

You're letting your past rule you again. It's your life, Leah. Own it. Do with it what you want.

Oh how she wanted to be more like Jack, strong of body and spirit, sure of herself. But her mind raced. Leaving here would be leaving him.

You've already done that.

Besides, she knew the truth now. She had to make

something of herself. She had to prove to herself that she could before she could let him in.

But going back to school in front of a camera? Good God. Failing herself was one thing, but failing in front of an audience? Torture.

So don't fail...

"I'm in," she said.

"Good." She heard some clicking, as if his fingers were racing over a keyboard. "The semester starts October first."

Her heart clutched. Was she really going to do this? "That's in three weeks."

"Don't be tardy, Sweet Cheeks. Or you won't be the teacher's pet."

Somehow she went through the motions for the rest of the day. She baked. She sold. She took Elsie shopping for some "hot shoes." She'd planned on an early night to crawl into her bed and crash, but Ali and Aubrey dragged her to the Love Shack, during which she managed to avoid any and all questions about her personal life by keeping her drink near her mouth.

"She's deflecting," Aubrey noted.

"Think that's a bad sign?" Ali asked.

"I know it is," Aubrey said.

"I screwed up," Leah admitted.

"Oh good," Aubrey said. "I love to hear stories of other people's screwups. It's such a refreshing change from reliving my own hundreds of screwups."

"You have hundreds?" Ali asked.

"Maybe thousands," Aubrey said.

"I've just got the one for now," Leah said. "But it's a biggie."

"We're all ears," Aubrey said, and waved for another round of drinks.

Much later, the three friends left the bar together. "Am I the only one who's on a merry-go-round?" Leah asked, world spinning.

"Yes," Ali said, hugging her. "But that's because you did all the drinking." She looked at Aubrey. "Who's driving Tipsy Girl home?"

"I can," Leah said, raising her hand.

Aubrey rolled her eyes and snatched Leah's keys. "*You're* Tipsy Girl," she said.

"Oh." Leah sighed. It was true. Her tongue was numb and her toes tingled, and she wasn't entirely sure but it felt like she had two heads.

She was more than tipsy.

They said good night to Ali, and then Aubrey shoved Leah into her car. Leah looked out the window as Aubrey drove through a quiet and sleeping Lucky Harbor. The shops were dark, the streets deserted. After traveling around the globe, this place should have seemed far too…quiet.

But the opposite was true. She felt like herself here. She was happy here.

And now she was leaving…

A pang hit her right in the center of her chest, but she knew it wasn't a heart attack. Nope, nothing as simple as that.

It was the thought of walking away. Again.

And yet she hadn't given herself much of a choice, had she? She'd been in such a damn hurry to get the hell out before she could prove that she was nothing but a screwup. And now she'd broken up with her pretend boyfriend—

The pang hit again. It might have been indigestion from the chili cheese fries she'd inhaled at the bar along with the alcohol, but she was pretty sure it was a certain tall, dark, and sexy-as-hell firefighter.

Yeah. This was all Jack's fault. Leah pulled out her phone.

Aubrey reached over and snatched it from her fingers.

"Hey," Leah said.

"Trust me, when it's this late and you're toasted, the only call you ever make is to do something monumentally stupid. You can thank me tomorrow. Where do you live?"

"Maybe I just want to see what time it is." Leah sighed. "Okay, so I was going to do something monumentally stupid." She gave Aubrey the address.

Aubrey didn't speak, just drove, for which Leah was grateful. She really needed to go to bed. After all, she had only four hours before she had to be up again…

Aubrey pulled up to the address Leah had given her and parked.

"You don't have to walk me in," Leah said. "I'm not that drunk."

Aubrey gave Leah a long look. "Yeah you are. And this isn't your grandma's house."

Leah bit her lower lip. "How did you know?"

Aubrey didn't answer for a long moment, just stared at the duplex. "Let's just say you're not the only one who's done something monumentally stupid in this lifetime."

Leah's stomach sank. "You and Jack…?"

"No," Aubrey said. "No. Not Jack."

Which meant… *"Ben?"*

"It's not what you think," Aubrey said cryptically and got out of the car.

Leah knew she wanted to follow this conversation, but at the moment she didn't have the brain capacity. So she got out of the car. "I'm good from here," she said.

"Oh, I know."

Leah watched Aubrey head toward the porch. "Then what are you doing?"

"I don't want to miss the monumental mistake."

Leah sighed and followed. She knocked softly on Jack's front door in case he was sleeping and was startled when Ben's front door opened instead.

Ben stood there in faded jeans, a T-shirt, and bare feet.

"Sorry," Leah said. "Did I wake you?"

His hair was rumpled but his eyes were sharp and on Aubrey. "No."

Aubrey met his gaze evenly. "Hello, Ben."

Ben didn't say a word, but his eyes were saying plenty. Leah just couldn't tell *what* they were saying plenty of, though the tension was thick enough to cut with a knife.

Then a *huge* shadow shoved its way past Ben.

A bear.

A bear that was white with black spots and looked like Kevin, greeting Leah with a snuffle and a warm, wet nose that he pushed into her belly.

She fell backward to her butt on the porch.

"Shit," Ben said. He scooped Leah up and set her back on her feet, pausing to peer into her eyes. Still holding on to her, he turned to Aubrey. "She's drunk."

"Tipsy," Leah said.

Aubrey shrugged. "Not her keeper."

Ben shook his head, eyes accusatory. "You okay?" he asked Leah.

"Yep." She put her hands on her butt. "I've got plenty of padding. Where's Jack?"

"Out back in the hot tub," Ben said. "Take Kevin the killer guard dog here. He just drank my last beer, and we're no longer friends."

Kevin burped.

Leah smiled at the dog, then turned to Aubrey. "Thanks for the ride—"

But Aubrey was halfway back to her car. Ben was watching her go, eyes dark and unreadable.

"I'm going to go visit Jack now," Leah said. But her feet didn't move.

Ben sighed as he took her hand and began to lead her around the back of the house.

"You don't have to walk me," she protested. "I can find my own way—"

"Humor me."

"But I don't want to intrude." She paused. "And I'm not at all sure why I'm here. He's not going to be happy to see me, you know. He's tired of pretending."

Ben smiled in the dark. She could hear it in his voice. "You think he's pretending to like you?"

"I think he's pretending that he doesn't want to wring my neck."

This gave her the rare pleasure of hearing Ben laugh. By this time they were around the side of the house and coming up on the back deck, Leah could hear the drone of the hot tub's jets running. Ben guided her up the wood steps to the edge of the tub.

Jack was in it; big body sprawled out, an arm on the

edge on either side of him, head back, eyes closed. There were ear buds in his ears, leading to an iPod on the bench behind him.

Also on the bench—three empty beer bottles.

"He's probably tipsy too," she whispered to Ben.

"You two are a pair," Ben agreed.

"No," she said. "That's the thing. We're *pretending* to be a pair. Or we were. I screwed that up too."

Ben shook his head and let out a sound of amusement. "Like I said, you're a pair."

"A pretend pair," she said. Jeez. And she'd always thought Ben was so smart. "And I don't want to really be his girlfriend anyway."

"No?"

"No. He's bossy. And he likes to have his way. And he thinks I'm just playing with him." She sighed, not taking her eyes off Jack's form.

Jack's very fine, very built, very wet form.

She couldn't see much below the bubbles, and she wondered if he was wearing a bathing suit. She hoped he wasn't. "Can't blame him," she whispered. "I've played with him before, you know. Just last night in fact."

Ben laughed again. "And I'm sure he hated every minute of it. Listen, Leah, you have to wake him up before I leave. I can't leave two drunks out here alone."

"Tipsy. I'm just *tipsy*."

"Right," he said and gave Jack a nudge. Actually, it was more like a shove.

Jack didn't jump. He didn't react at all except for the one eye that cracked open.

"Drunk Goldilocks here wants to crash your party," Ben said.

"*Tipsy*," Leah said, irritated.

Jack's other eye opened, both landing unerringly on Leah.

Leah gave him a little wave, trying to look like the best thing to happen to him that night. She wasn't sure she was successful, but he did reach up and pull out his ear buds. "You got her drunk?" he asked Ben with a hint of disbelief.

"Not me," Ben said. "She managed that all on her own."

Leah sighed. "Tipsy!" Though why she bothered, she had no idea. She kicked off her shoes and dropped her purse to the deck.

"What are you doing?" Ben asked.

She pulled off her sweater. "I'm about to seduce my pretend boyfriend. Go away, Ben."

Ben turned to Jack, who'd risen to his feet in the hot tub. "You need to stop her."

"I'm going to exercise my right to remain silent," Jack said.

Which worked, because Leah had no intention of stopping. She let her sweater fall. She was disappointed to note that Jack was indeed wearing black swim trunks, but at least they clung to his every inch. She *really* liked his every inch… "Go away, Ben."

"Jack," Ben said warningly.

"You heard the woman." Jack never took his eyes off Leah. "Go away, Ben."

Ben tossed up his hands. "You two deserve each other," he muttered and walked away.

When they were alone, Jack looked at her. "What are you doing here?" He sounded wary, which in a distant part of her brain she recognized was probably wise of him.

But she kept stripping. "I'm just realizing that the only time my pretend boyfriend and I get along is when we're not pretending. I want to not pretend, just for a little while." She pulled off her top.

"Leah…seriously. *What are you doing?*"

"Seriously? You're the investigator. You figure it out." She shimmied out of her denim skirt, letting it fall to her ankles. She took a peek at herself and sighed in relief. *Not* her laundry day underwear this time, thankfully. A red lace thong.

Jack's gaze raked down her body, slowly and thoroughly. "Stop."

She shivered at his commanding tone and then stepped right into the tub and plastered herself against his big, wet, warm body. "You sound all official and in charge."

"In charge?" His arms closed around her, and he sank with her into the deliciously hot water. "I have no delusions of being in charge of you."

She smiled. "You saying I have all the power?"

"You always have," he murmured and nipped at her throat, working his way south. "What are we doing, Leah?"

She let her head fall back to give him room to work as steam and bubbles and Jack surrounded her. "I thought we'd wing it."

Chapter 21

When Jack woke up, he knew without opening his eyes that Leah was gone. She had to get up early for the bakery, but he hadn't even heard her leave. Still, he reached out to the spot where she'd been in his bed and…came in contact with fur.

Kevin lifted his head and panted a happy smile. Not quite the smile he'd hoped for.

"We've had this discussion." Jack gave him a shove. "You have your own damn bed."

Kevin licked his chin.

Definitely not the kiss he'd been hoping for.

As for what that meant, both that he was disappointed to be alone and that Leah had sneaked off, he had no idea.

He got up, made Kevin run with him, then spent the entire day digging through the rubble of the Town Hall fire. By dinnertime he was filthy, exhausted, and ready to eat his left arm.

Not officially on duty, he stopped by the station to

shower off the ash and filth and was surprised to find an off-duty Tim at Jack's desk. "What are you doing?"

"Research. Hey, can anyone take that arson certification that you and the deputy chief have?"

"You have to be recommended."

"So…" Tim flashed a grin. "Recommend me?"

"Why?"

"Can't let you have all the fun." He logged off, gathered some papers off the printer, and headed to the door.

Jack put a hand out to stop him. "Why do you want to take the class?"

"Maybe I'm aspiring to take your job." Tim waggled a brow. "Come on, man. Don't be a TBBD."

"TBBD?"

"Typical big boss dick." He paused and smiled again. "No offense intended, of course. So…can I take the class?"

Jack met Tim's earnest gaze. "It's not up to me. I'll check with the deputy fire chief."

"You and he go way back. He was your dad's BFF."

"It doesn't work like that."

"No? How does it work?"

"You earn it," Jack said.

Tim nodded. "Earn it," he repeated. "I can totally do that."

He left, and Jack stood there a moment, wondering if he himself had earned anything at all, or if once again, he'd simply followed the career path laid out for him.

The bakery's new ovens came that afternoon, and it was quite an event. It required a handful of really big installation guys, which brought their neighbors out of their shops to watch.

Elsie had accepted the change and seemed excited, handing out free cookies to all the workers. The ovens were still being set when Max Fitzgerald came by. The guys had just opened up the wall to install the new ventilation hoods, and Max just about had a seizure.

"You're tearing down a hundred-and-fifty-year-old wall like it's nothing." He leaned on his cane, a hand on his heart like he was having a heart attack.

"The wall's going right back up," Elsie told him. "You know it is. You represented the historical society as a part of the permit process Leah got from the building department." She smiled. "And hell, maybe the wall will even be plumb this time around."

Max didn't smile. He was staring in horror at the broken bricks at his feet. "Do you have any idea how *old* these bricks are?"

"One hundred and fifty years?" Leah asked.

He pointed his cane at her. "No one likes a smartass, missy."

Elsie's good-natured smile faded. "Actually," she said slowly, linking her arm in Leah's, "I do."

Max narrowed his pale-blue, rheumy eyes in her direction. "I'm disappointed in you, Elsie. Very disappointed."

"So am I," she assured him. "I'm disappointed that I spent eighty bucks on a hot new dress for the Firemen's Ball since I won't be going with you after all."

Max shook his head and left, and Elsie sighed. "Damn, I really wanted to wear that dress."

"You will," Leah said. "You'll get another date."

Elsie laughed. "Honey, in my world, men don't just grow on trees."

There came a knock at the opened back door. Mr.

Lyons stood there with a small bouquet of lilies. "Hello, ladies. Elsie…" He hesitated. "Ah, hell. I'm no good at this. I was next door at the florist shop collecting the rent when I heard you yelling at Max."

"I'll get you our rent too," Leah said.

"No, I— That's not why I'm here." He thrust the flowers at Elsie. "I bought these for you from Ali. Or I *will* buy them. I sort of just grabbed them and ran out of there, so hopefully she doesn't call the cops. Elsie…"

"Yes," she said firmly, taking the flowers. "Most definitely yes."

He blinked. "Yes?"

"Yes, I'll be your date. That is what you were going to ask, right?"

He blushed to the top of his bald dome. "To start."

Leah watched her grandma beam at him. Mr. Lyons was two inches shorter than her, and twice as round—not that Elsie seemed to notice as she smelled the flowers and then leaned in to kiss him.

There was a sweetness to them that tightened Leah's heart. Happiness always seemed so…mysterious. So elusive. But looking at Elsie and Mr. Lyons, it didn't seem so elusive at all. It seemed as simple as just choosing to be happy. She could do that, right? She deserved that. Didn't she?

Baby steps, she decided. One thing at a time. Getting her grandma set up so everything would run smoothly in her absence was one of those steps, no matter what Elsie decided to do.

Getting her own life in line would be step two. Whichever direction that step took her…

By the end of the day, the ovens were in, the wall

patched, and the kitchen cleaned up. Leah looked around with a huge sense of accomplishment. The place had really turned around, and business was up. Way up. She'd had a big hand in that, and she felt pride. And relief. She could really go and things would be okay.

Everything would be okay. The bakery. Elsie. Lucky Harbor. Jack.

And if she wasn't so sure about herself yet, well, that would come.

Jack spent the morning hours scouring the evidence gathered so far on the Town Hall fire. He pulled out everything they had on the other possible arsons. His gut said he'd missed something, something big.

When he couldn't find it on the page, he hit the fire sites again. He walked each of them as if it were the first time. Nothing stuck out at him.

What were they missing?

He pulled out the notes again. The footprint at the convenience store site didn't match any footprints at the other two sites. Which, if the vagrant had been wearing "acquired" shoes, didn't necessarily mean a thing. Jack turned to the tread forensics and realized they'd never gotten any back for the auto shop fire. He called Ronald.

"Doing my job again?" Ronald asked.

"No." Jack blew out a breath. "Okay, maybe. We're missing forensics on—"

"The auto parts fire. I know, it's coming. I'll forward it as soon as I get it. Also, I'm sending a recommendation for you to be my replacement."

"What?"

"I have a bucket list."

Jack felt his heart stop. "You're sick?"

"No. I'm healthy as an ox. I just want to get to my bucket list while I can still zip-line in Costa Rica and eat the spicy food in Thailand. And I want to be fit enough to walk through Scotland. There's some castles there that someone in my life wants to visit."

His mom. He was talking about Dee.

"I'm not asking your permission," Ronald said. "But it'd be great if you didn't object."

"My mom isn't in a good place, Ronald."

"No shit. But she's getting there. And I intend to help her. To be there for her. To love her. For real, Jack. None of this *pretend* bullshit."

Jack grimaced. "You know?"

"I'm an investigator, as you're about to be. And if you're half the man I think you are, you'll fix things up right with your girl. She's a cutie, and she's good for you. It's been fun seeing you knocked off your high and mighty horse for a change."

"What the hell does that mean?"

But Ronald had disconnected.

Chapter 22

♥

The next day, the town came alive as it prepared for the annual arts and crafts fair at the pier. Every year Leah's grandma set up a booth and sold goodies for people to eat as they walked the fair and made merry.

This year, Jack's mom had a booth right next to theirs to sell her scarves and blankets and other knitted wares. Knowing Jack was working and unable to help, and that Elsie wanted to run their booth and had Riley to help her, Leah went to be there for Dee.

"How are you?" Leah asked, always the first question of the day.

Dee smiled. "I'm better today."

"Today?" Leah's senses sharpened. "What happened?"

"Oh, it's silly," Dee said. "A few weeks back one of my meds got changed, and I like to read all the paperwork with each prescription. Anyway, one of the side effects was paralysis, of all things. And I swear to God, my legs and arms just stopped working."

Listening to the story, Leah felt like her heart stopped working. "Oh my God. What did you do?"

Dee laughed softly. "Well, Jack has picked up my meds ever since, and now all the paperwork is always mysteriously missing."

Leah's throat tightened, even through the urge to laugh along with Dee. *Jack...*

As she worked on setting up Dee's booth, she caught sight of him a few times in his uniform and dark sunglasses. He was standing in for Ronald today, walking the length of the booths and checking out everyone's setup.

As if he felt the weight of her stare, he turned and met her gaze. They hadn't spoken since she'd left his bed the other morning after the Jacuzzi event, and it most definitely *had* been an event. Even now, flashes of Jack holding her, his hands tight on her hips as he thrust into her, his head back, face in a mask of pleasure, gave her a hot flash.

Dee sighed dreamily. "You two are so romantic."

Leah tore her gaze off Jack and went back to work setting up Dee's canopy. It was a collapsible thing, and it did not want to work. "You've been reading too many romance novels," she said, struggling.

"Careful with that. It'll catch your fingers. And I like the happy endings. We should all get a happy ending."

"Those are illegal in some states, you know."

Dee laughed. "I'm serious. Would an HEA be so bad?"

Leah stopped and looked at her. "If you want one, all you have to do is get it."

"Oh. Well." Dee brushed that off with a wave of her hand. "I'm too old. But you're not. Your HEA is right there in front of you."

"Hmm." Leah fought with the stupid canopy for a moment, then realized Dee was sitting there smiling widely at her. "What?" she asked. "Am I doing it wrong? Do I have toilet paper on my shoes? Something disgusting in my teeth?"

"No, you're perfect. You're perfect for him."

"Perfect?" Leah laughed. "Dee, I'm just about as far from perfect as a woman can get."

"You're warm, caring, smart, and you always put him first."

"I—"

"You'll make a great wife, you know."

Oh boy. This had been all Leah's idea, this whole her and Jack façade, but every day that it went on made her feel worse and worse. Now, with her heart pounding dully, it was hard to speak, but she knew she had to find the words. She had to tell the truth because she wasn't going to be Jack's wife anytime soon.

Or in this lifetime. "Dee."

"I know, I'm just a silly old woman. But it makes my heart soar to see my son look so happy. It just seems like a wedding should be the next step. And then…" Dee laughed musically. "Grandkids." She clapped her hands together. "Can you imagine?"

All too easily… Oh God, this was bad. How could she do it; how could she crush Dee and tell her that they'd only been pretending? The answer was simple.

She couldn't.

"Look at you," Dee said to someone behind Leah. "You look just like your dad. So handsome."

Leah turned and came face-to-face with Jack.

Reaching above her, he took over her hold on the canopy.

"I could have gotten it," she said.

"I know." Then he locked it into place with annoying ease, smelling ridiculously amazing while he was at it. "Just trying to help," he said, and leaned in and kissed his mom on the cheek. "You doing good?"

"Yes, sweetheart, I'm great. Thanks for the cookies. The nurses all think you're the sweetest thing. They actually believe you made those cookies." She flashed a smile at Leah. "Even though he can't bake to save his life."

"I can so," Jack said.

"Yeah?" Leah asked. She'd never seen him cook anything. "What do you bake?"

"Frozen cookie dough."

Leah burst out laughing.

Dee laughed too. "Well, now the nurses want you to make some for *them*, whatever they were."

Leah eyed him. "You going to make the nurses cookies, Jack? Up the numbers of your fan club?"

"It'd help you out on that Facebook poll," Dee said. "You're still lagging behind Ben, Tim, and that TV cutie. What's his name? Rafe?"

Jack swore beneath his breath, something about "damn options" before turning to Leah. He rubbed his jaw, looking a little unsure of his welcome. She sighed and gave him a smile. "You going to be in the firemen's dunking booth today?"

He glanced in the direction of where the booth was being built just across the pier and grimaced. "I'm first up, actually."

Leah pulled a ticket from her pocket. She'd gotten it with her entrance fee and could have used it to ride the Ferris wheel or play an arcade game. But she was saving it to dunk Jack. "I'm all ready."

"Good thing you throw like a girl."

"You're going to eat those words," she promised him.

He leaned in and put his mouth to her ear. "Make me." Then he swatted her on the ass and strode off.

Oh, hell no. "Dee," she said. "I've got to—"

"Go dunk him." Dee nodded and handed over her free ticket. "Get him for me too."

Leah stalked over there and got in line behind Ben.

He turned and looked at her, and his mouth quirked. He handed her a string of five tickets and then nudged her ahead of him.

"You don't mind?" she asked.

"I'm only going to mind if you miss."

She stepped up to the white line and met Jack's gaze. He'd stripped out of his BDUs, beneath which he wore navy board shorts. His legs were so long that his toes nearly touched the water of the tank as he sat there looking relaxed and at ease, swinging his feet. Not a care in the world.

He didn't think she could dunk him.

Determined to prove him wrong, she wound up and threw. The ball went wide.

"Shake it off," Ben said from behind her, and she adjusted her stance.

From inside the dunking booth, Jack narrowed his gaze at Ben.

Ben didn't look concerned. "You see the thing you want to hit, right? That round target that's like fifteen feet wide?"

"I see it," she grumbled. *Jeez*. "And it's only a foot wide, max."

"Pretend it's your almost fiancé's face."

"Thanks, man," Jack said.

But Leah did just that. And missed again. She went through two more balls, and then her last, and someone tapped her on the shoulder.

Aubrey.

Leah narrowed her eyes. "You're on my Do Not Acknowledge list after letting me go to Jack's house inebriated."

"You weren't inebriated. You were shit-faced." She handed Leah three more tickets. "Truce?"

"*You let me go to Jack's house*," Leah repeated.

"You were…determined."

"You did it for your own amusement," Leah said.

"Well, of course I did," Aubrey said. "It's Lucky Harbor. It wasn't like I had any other entertainment available. And how'd it work out for you?"

Leah met Jack's gaze and sighed. It'd worked out pretty damn good. She used Aubrey's tickets and… missed some more.

In the tank, Jack leaned back, hands behind his head now, definitely relaxed.

"Jesus," Ben muttered, and pushed Leah up past the throwing line, halfway to the dunking tape.

"Hey," Jack said, straightening up. "Cheating."

The crowd behind her cheered. They didn't care. They loved Jack, but they definitely wanted to see their favorite firefighter dunked.

Leah wanted Jack dunked too. She wound up and threw the ball. No one was more surprised than her when it found its target, and with a loud splash, Jack hit the water.

Leah took a lot of fist bumps and pats on the back, and

then, before Jack could get out of the tank, she hightailed it out of there, racing back to Dee's booth. Breathless, she scooped up her purse. "Gotta go, Dee."

"I know." Dee grinned. "You'd better run fast, honey. He was all-state track, remember?"

No one knew better than Leah just how fast Jack could be when he put his mind to something. She headed straight for Ali's booth, where she found Ali and Luke kissing. And not just any little kiss either, but a full-bodied lip-lock. She waited, glancing at her watch, tapping her foot. Finally, she tossed up her hands. "Hello! On a schedule here."

Ali tore her mouth from Luke's and grinned at Leah. "You're not on a schedule. You're running scared because you dunked Jack."

"Oh and nice job, Ace," Luke said, an arm slung around Ali. "You can play on our baseball team anytime."

"Really?" Leah asked, pleased.

"Hell no," Luke said.

Leah sighed and turned to go, and she ran smack into a brick wall.

A brick wall that was Jack's wet chest. Big hands closed on her arms and held her there. "Going somewhere?" he asked smoothly.

She gulped. "Well, I have to—"

"Later," he said and tugged her along with him.

Both Ali and Luke grinned and waved good-bye. Big, fat lots of help there. "Hey." Leah tried to dig her heels in, but Jack was determined. And she already knew that trying to deter a determined Jack was about as easy as trying to stop a train in its tracks. "Jack—"

"Shh."

Oh no. He didn't just— But before she could even finish that thought, Jack had pulled her down a set of stairs and onto the beach. He was a sight, standing in front of her with his board shorts riding low on his hips, making him look dangerous, alluring, and hotter than sin as he tugged her under the pier.

"Jack—"

He pressed her up against a pylon. Water slapped against the wood and on the rocky shore. Somewhere a seagull squawked, and another answered.

All of that barely registered, nothing mattered except Jack's hot, hard body up against hers. "You're all wet," she complained, feeling her sundress getting soaked from his drenched board shorts.

"Whose fault is that? You were playing with me." His mouth was near her ear, and he nipped at it. "Dangerous." He sank his teeth into the column of her throat, and she gasped.

"You c-can't take it personally," she managed. "It was for a good cause."

"Yeah? What cause was that?"

Yeah, Leah, what cause was that? "Well…it made me happy," she said.

Lifting his head, he met her gaze. "I've got other ways to make you *happy*." Proving it, he threaded his hand through her hair and tilted her head back for his kiss. Parting her lips, he slowly stroked her tongue with his own until she couldn't remember her own name. And then he kissed her some more, until all her bones were gone, and certainly her resistance.

From up above, the sounds of the fair drifted down to them, music, laughter… It surrounded them like a bubble, their own intimate bubble, and as Jack groaned and tightened his grip on her, she knew she was in trouble. "Okay," she murmured, all hot and damp and ready. "But we have to be quick."

He pressed a kiss to her temple and sucked in some air. "We're not doing it beneath the pier, Leah."

"Dammit, you always do that. You get me all revved up and say no. You can't just leave me like this."

"I never say no," he said, his thumb rasping over a nipple. "And I can't leave you like what?"

She arched into his touch. "All hot and bothered. It's rude, Jack."

He laughed softly against her hair and slid his free hand down her body. "Just how hot and bothered are we talking?" That hand snaked beneath her sundress. Up the inside of her thigh.

"Very hot and very b-bothered— God!" she stuttered when his fingers slipped into her panties.

He let out a low groan, a sexy sound that pushed her to the very edge. "You remember what I told you, Leah?"

"Um—" She gasped when he nuzzled the sweet spot beneath her ear at the same time his fingers grazed over her heated, wet flesh. "I'm not sure—"

He stopped stroking her.

She wanted to cry. "Jack—"

"Think about it."

She was thinking about his fingers, those work-roughened, callused fingers that were driving her slowly out of her mind. "You said it was dangerous to play with you—" One of those fingers slid into her, and her knees buckled.

"And yet it didn't stop you," he said against her collarbone, nipping her.

Oh God, those fingers. "Oh, Jack. *Please*—"

He dragged his mouth back to hers and took her lips on the exact right side of rough as he worked her with his fingers until she was grinding against him, panting for air. "Jack." Her toes were curling. "Jack, we have to stop, I'm going to—"

"Come," he murmured, absolutely not stopping. "I want to feel you come for me." He kissed her again, absorbing her cry as she burst, shuddering wildly in his arms.

"I never get tired of that," he said, slowing his fingers, softening his hold, bringing her down gently until she sagged against his chest.

She could feel him hard against her and reached for him just as he pulled his hand away and stepped back. While she stared up at him in a dazed afterglow, he lifted his fingers to his mouth and sucked them clean.

Her knees wobbled.

He gave her a smile that was so wicked she nearly came again, and then he was gone.

Leah sagged against the pylon, still trying to catch her balance in a world that was spinning more and more out of control every day.

She'd assumed they were done with this. Apparently not. In any case, whatever they were—or weren't—Jack knew her body even better than she did.

And, she was pretty sure, he also knew her thoughts. Which meant that he knew her feelings were becoming real. She thought maybe his feelings were just as real, but the problem with that was she'd had her shot at his heart. A long time ago. She'd had her shot, and she'd blown it.

Jack had a lot of really great qualities. He was smart,

and loving, and strong of both mind and body. He would do anything for someone he cared about.

Anything.

Including going along with a hare-brained plan like pretending to be in a relationship just to please his ill mom. But unlike her, Jack actually learned from his mistakes and rarely, if ever, repeated them.

Which meant that for him, loving her was off the table.

This left her hanging out here with these emotions all on her own. And it was time to face the facts. There were emotions, lots of them, because she'd gone and broken yet another promise to him. She wasn't pretending.

This *was* real, and she *was* hurt.

Chapter 23

♥

After the arts and crafts fair, when everything had been broken down and hauled off, Jack ended up at the Love Shack with Ben.

Ben ordered while Jack checked his email and then stared down in shock at the forwarded message from Ronald.

DNA results had come in, adding a hard fact to the arson case. The DNA from the cigarette butts found near the convenience store and Town Hall fires matched. The same person had stood within watching distance of the fires and...watched? Unfortunately there was no known ID or record, which meant that their arsonist was either new...or smart enough to not have gotten caught.

Yet.

Ben came back to the table with a basket of chili fries and two beers, and Jack didn't even look up. "Must be good porn," Ben said.

"It's work. DNA came back on the cigarette butts found at two of the three questionable fires."

"And?"

"Smoked by the same person."

"Son of a bitch."

"We'll nail him."

"We?" Ben asked. "You on the arson team now?"

Jack shrugged. "I've been working with Ronald. I like this end of things." He paused. "A lot."

"You going to give up firefighting?" Ben asked. "The job you were pretty much born to do?"

"Actually," Jack said. "I think I was born to do this."

Ben looked at him for a long beat and nodded. "Then do it."

"You're relieved," Jack said, surprised.

"Fuck, yeah. Don't get me wrong, taking over as deputy fire chief and fire marshal is going to be hell on wheels, and in some ways much harder than the firefighting, but…"

"But what?" Then he read Ben's expression and leaned back, shaking his head. "Jesus, not you too. I'm not going to die on the job. Tens of thousands of firefighters are on the job at any given moment and most of them manage to stay very alive."

"Your dad didn't."

"I'm not my dad."

"You're kidding me, right?" Ben asked. "'Cause the apple's practically still on the tree, man."

"Look who's talking," Jack said. "Your job takes you to third-world hellholes for months at a time. When you're gone, the rest of us can only hold our breath until we see or hear from you again."

Ben lifted a shoulder. "Guess you're not the only one influenced by your dad's hero complex."

"Yeah." Jack nodded. "But I'm making this choice to get off the front line based on my own needs for the future. It has nothing to do with my dad's influence or memory."

"Nothing wrong with that. What does Leah think of your new job?"

"Haven't told her yet."

Ben stopped with his beer halfway to his mouth. "Why not?"

When Jack didn't answer, Ben swore and set down his beer. "Don't ask me how you can be the smartest guy I know and the most stupid at the same time."

"You know we're not a real thing."

Ben gave an impressive eye roll.

"You thought it was stupid that we pretended," Jack said.

"No. I thought it was stupid that you didn't just go for it."

Jack took a long pull of his beer. "You're going to have to repeat that because I think you just suggested I should be with Leah for real. *Leah*."

"Yeah, you keep saying that. Yeah, it's Leah, who you've had a thing for since…well, ever."

Jack shook his head. "What is this? It's not like you're exactly a relationship king. You haven't been in a relationship since Hannah died five years ago. You're no better at getting yourself into this shit than I am."

Ben shrugged. "At least when it came my way, I went for it."

Jack stared at him and then laughed. "Let me get this straight. You're saying if the right woman came your way, you'd take a shot at another relationship?"

Ben's attention drifted to the bar. Jack followed his cousin's gaze to a beautiful blonde sitting there alone, nursing something clear out of a shot glass.

Aubrey.

"Well, there's a bad idea," Jack said with a shake of his head. "Tangling with her."

"Yeah?" Ben asked lazily. "Why's that?"

"She's got claws." Jack looked at him. "You know this. Remember how she was in school?"

"I also remember how we were."

"We were wild, not mean."

Ben didn't look concerned as he rose, dropped cash on the table, and headed out into the night.

"Gee," Jack said, getting to his feet as well. "Guess we're done here."

He left the bar too, but Ben was nowhere in sight. This wasn't so unusual when it came to his cousin, but it was still irritating. Jack grabbed Kevin from where he'd been happily sleeping in the truck. Kevin's favorite thing—after eating or taking a shit on the neighbor's lawn—was going for a walk on the beach.

After that, inexplicably, they ended up standing in front of the bakery. It was closed, of course. But Jack could see a light on in the back, and with a frown, he walked around to the alley. The back door was ajar, and he stepped close to hear a voice muttering softly.

Leah.

She had her back to him as she stood at the cooking island whipping something into a froth. "Okay, cookie dough," she said, "listen up. Just because I'm giving you to Jack doesn't mean I'm giving a piece of *me* to Jack." She added something from a smaller bowl and went back to whipping. "Because I'm not. I might be a little broken, but no one's getting any of my pieces. Not even if…" More from yet another bowl. "A piece of me—or two—really wants to be given."

Jack wasn't sure how to acknowledge the emotion that went through him at her words, uttered with good humor but also with a sort of grim truth. He'd known she cared about him deeply. Just as he'd known that she didn't know how to deal with those feelings. He'd known all of it, and he'd even known why. He'd accepted it. Hell, he was responsible for the rules in the first place. But hearing her talk about her broken pieces killed him. "Leah."

With a shriek she whirled around, her whisk held out in front of her like a weapon. "Jack!" she gasped. "You scared me."

"Stay," he said to Kevin, and to make sure he did, Jack tied the leash to the back porch railing before entering the kitchen. "What are you doing here this late?"

"Making black-and-white cookies." She paused and then shrugged. "For your mom's nurses."

Again emotion swelled, and he stepped into her, taking the bowl from her hands and setting it aside. "Why?"

Leah met his gaze. Her heart was still pounding, but not from fright. "That's what people who care about each other do," she finally said. "They help each other out."

"People?"

She drew a deep breath and let it out. She wasn't exactly sure what was wrong between them, but she knew it was her fault. "Friends," she said.

Jack expressed polite, doubtful surprise with one quirk of his dark brow.

"We are friends," she said, then hesitated. "Aren't we?"

"Naked friends."

"We're more than naked friends," she said and then bit her lip, because why had she said that? Why had she gone there?

Jack studied her for a long moment, and she knew he could see her nerves. "Talk to me, Leah."

"I'm a bit of a mess. No surprise there though, right?" She turned from him, and wiping her hands on her apron, walked to her purse hanging on a hook by the door. From it, she pulled out the stack of cards she'd sent him throughout the years, the ones she'd found in the night-stand by his bed.

He looked down at them for a beat. "What are you doing with those?"

"The question is, what are *you* doing with them?"

"You sent them to me," he said simply.

And to him, it *was* that simple.

In fact, the only person who'd ever complicated this, the most important relationship in her life, was herself. She ran her fingers over the envelopes postmarked from all the places she'd been. She could still remember where she'd bought him each and every card, how she'd felt when she'd signed it and sent it off.

Homesick.

For him.

In the past she'd always shrugged that part off because *she'd* left Lucky Harbor. *She'd* been the one to go. So how could she get homesick for a place, a man, she'd willingly walked away from? "You missed me," she said.

He shrugged, and her gaze flew to his, catching the light of teasing in his. "Maybe a little," he said.

"I missed you," she admitted. "More than I wanted to."

He gave a slow head shake. "Leah, you don't have to do this."

"I don't want it to be pretend," she whispered in a rush, the words tumbling out of her. "I know I said I did, that I promised that it was just that, but I lied. When I'm here in Lucky Harbor, it all feels right. I love it here. In this place, in this bakery. I love it here with you."

He closed his eyes. "Leah—"

"I was just a stupid teenager, Jack. Too immature to know what I was running away from."

He let out a long, slow breath. "You weren't the only one."

"What did you run from?"

"What I want. I always have." He paused. "Ronald's retiring."

She blinked. "What?"

"Yeah, and he's recommending me as his replacement. I have a formal interview for the job next week."

She stared at him and felt a slow smile curve her mouth. "Oh, Jack," she breathed. "It's perfect for you. Just what you've always wanted."

He stared down at her for a long beat, saying nothing, then he laughed real low and quiet. "Hell if you don't drive me absolutely crazy, even as you get me like no one else."

She still held the whisk. Her other arm wound around his neck. "I drive you crazy? In a good way, right?"

"No," he said, but he smiled a little, hooked an arm around her waist, and pulled her in.

"Hi," she whispered.

"Hi." Lifting her up, he set her on the counter. Holding

her there, he reached out and dipped a finger into the bowl of batter at her hip.

"You want some chocolate?" she whispered.

"Yes." He sucked it into his mouth and then took the whisk from her hand, setting it aside. And then he grasped the hem of her sweater and lifted it up over her head.

"What are you doing?"

Instead of answering, he dipped his finger back into the chocolate. Just as she might have said something about him double-dipping, he painted a streak of chocolate across her collarbone.

"Uh—" she started, but then he flicked open her bra and finger-painted her already hardened nipples.

And then he licked every inch of the chocolate off her, by which time she was attempting to tug off his clothes.

"Not here," he said, holding her off.

"Oh my God," she said. "You and your *not here*." But he was right; they were in the bakery kitchen, for God's sake. Panting, she looked around. "The office."

Lifting her up, he walked with her wrapped around him to the office. He set her down on the desk, right on top of the stack of bills she had to pay. "Lift up," he said, and tugged down her leggings, taking everything off, including her boots and panties.

"Jack—"

He cupped her face and tipped it to his for a hot kiss as he nudged her legs open. Then he dropped to his knees and slid his palms up her inner thighs.

She could feel his breath against her and she slid her fingers into his hair, unable to look away as he put his mouth on her. When he did something cleverly diabolical with his tongue, her breath hitched and her head fell back.

Jack never failed to take her right out of herself, out of everything she knew, detonating the careful distance she liked to put between herself and what she was experiencing.

With Jack, there was no distance. He didn't allow it. He had her right where he wanted her, legs splayed by his broad shoulders, hands gripping her possessively, his tongue making her writhe. She couldn't be more vulnerable to him, and in that moment, on the very edge of a steep, slippery precipice, she couldn't care.

"You taste better than the chocolate," he murmured against her and gently sucked in exactly the right spot at exactly the right rhythm, essentially flinging her off a cliff. As her release washed over her, she felt him press a kiss to her inner thigh before rising to his feet. Towering over her, he scooted her back a little and crawled up her body, making her moan as her achingly sensitive nipples grazed his chest. She clutched him to her and kissed him. Somewhere along the way he'd lost his clothes and put on a condom. Taking over the kiss, he slid inside her. "Leah."

She opened her eyes and looked into his, feeling his heart pounding in tune with hers. She knew there wasn't much that could make Jack's heart race and felt a rush of feminine power.

And then, as he began to move, his hips pushing against hers, she felt the rush of another power entirely as the earth moved.

A few beats later, the earth moved for him too.

They lay there on the hard desk in the small, hot room,

breathing hard, working at getting their pulse back from near stroke levels, when her phone rang startlingly loud in the quiet night.

It'd fallen out of her pocket and was on the floor.

"Late for a phone call," Jack said, and they both peered over the desk and looked at the screen.

The ID said: *Dickhead.*

Jack raised one dark brow.

"Rafe," she said.

He stood up and offered her a hand to do the same. "You should answer it."

"Oh, I don't—"

Jack crouched low and hit SPEAKER, and Leah grimaced, reaching for her discarded clothes. "Rafe," she said, self-consciously, scrambling into her leggings and top sans underwear. Ridiculous, since he couldn't see her.

Clearly feeling no such self-consciousness, Jack still stood there butt-ass naked.

"Way to call me back, babe," Rafe said.

"I've been..." She met Jack's gaze. *Why wasn't he putting on his clothes?* "Busy."

"Doing what? Making donut holes because no one in Podunk knows the difference between *pasticiotti* and *tarte au citron*? Whatever, babe. Lucky for you, the network still wants you back. We've agreed to your terms. You said you wanted out of there before the finals, and your wish is our command. I've emailed your flight confirmation."

She'd closed her eyes halfway through this, and when she opened them, Jack had pulled on his jeans and shrugged into his shirt. "Rafe—"

"Oh no," he said. "Hell no, babe. You're not backing

out. You set these plans in motion. You're playing it cool, but I know you're desperate. My favorite state. The tickets, Leah. Use them." And then he disconnected.

Without a word, Jack headed to the door. Leah caught his arm. "Jack, wait."

He paused. He hadn't buttoned his shirt. His hair was tousled from her fingers. He looked big, bad, and ticked off. "Why?"

"It's not what you think."

"Really? Because I'm experiencing a painful déjà vu here, Leah. A minute ago you were telling me Lucky Harbor feels right. I think you were also telling me that I felt right."

"Yes," she said. "I was."

He shook his head. "And yet you were planning to go. You wanted out before the next show aired."

"I made that call to him weeks ago, Jack."

"When?"

"I don't know exactly."

"Yes, you do," he said. "*When*?"

She couldn't tear her eyes off his. They were filled with things, things she'd dreamed of seeing from him, but she was blowing it faster than she could gulp in air.

Nothing new there.

"Before or after you told my mom we were together?" he asked.

She hesitated. "After."

"Are you kidding me? The whole façade was your idea!"

"I know." She paused again. "It's not you, Jack. It's me."

He laughed harshly. "Oh, Christ. Really? You're going

to use the breakup line, Leah? The one *I* taught you? What's next? You have to 'work on yourself'?"

Her throat burned with shame and misery because it was true, it was happening, her biggest fear—screwing this up with him—was coming true right before her eyes. And the worst part? She'd done it all herself. "This time it's actually true. I'm not good at this stuff. You know that."

She could see that he wasn't buying this. "You don't have to be good at it, Leah. Jesus. Do you think I care what words you use to show me how you feel? I don't need words. I have the actions. You watch out for me. You watch out for my mom. And my oversized, drool-manufacturing dog. You care so much about everyone else and their life, but when it comes to yours, you give up. I know your dad made you feel that you were never good enough, but he was a dick, Leah. And he's gone, so why do you still let him do this to you, let his memory keep you from finishing…everything?"

"That's not what I do."

He ticked items off on his fingers. "Our relationship the first time, college—all four times—culinary school—"

"Okay," she said tightly. "I get it. So I have a little follow-through problem."

"Little?" He spun her around to face the steel refrigerator, where their reflections stared back at her. Her own face, pale, pinched with strain. And Jack's, his expression serious, so deadly serious.

"Your parents didn't deserve you," he said, "but at some point you have to grow up and realize you're not a product of your environment. You are who you want to be. You're *you*, Leah. You're a daughter. A friend. A lover. A sweet, warm, smart, beautiful, talented, successful pastry chef. You're anything you want to be. Figure it out and then own it."

She desperately searched her reflection for the woman he saw. "I don't see me that way," she whispered, throat tight.

"Why not?"

It was a most excellent question, one for which she did not have an answer.

"When do you leave exactly, Leah?"

"I don't—I don't know exactly."

"You always know."

Touché. "Soon," she admitted.

He turned her to face him. "How soon? Truth, Leah."

"Truth?" She forced the words out. "I should have left already."

"Why haven't you?"

"You know why."

He shook his head. "Don't. Don't say you stayed here for me."

She bit her tongue rather than say exactly that. And then she gave him the truth he wanted. "I'd planned to go before the finals."

"Were you going to tell me?"

She wanted to turn away from the look in his eyes. The recriminations. The hurt. But she couldn't tear her eyes from his. "I'm going because I need to. I want to finish school. I want to finish something to prove to myself that I can. I was going to tell you, yes, but I didn't know how," she managed.

He gave one curt nod and reached for the door.

She ran after him and slipped between him and the wood, arms spread as if she could really stop him if he chose to leave.

He scrubbed a hand over his face. "Move, Leah."

"No."

"Listen," he said, a grim set to his mouth. "New rule."

"Jack—"

"No big, drawn-out good-bye." At the look on her face, he let out a long breath. "All my life, you've been my Almost." He softened slightly, his gaze touching over the features of her face as if memorizing her. "I want you, Leah. I've always wanted you. But wanting isn't enough. You have to fight for it too, and you're not going to."

"Jack—"

"I'm cutting my losses on this one, Leah. Pulling the plug. Call it another rule if you want. No more intimacy. I'm ending this now before either of us gets hurt."

And then he gently set her aside, walked out the door, and was gone.

She stood there in shock. "How is walking away fighting for it?" she asked the night.

The night didn't answer.

"Dammit." She searched for her usual state of denial, for her temper, for anything that might allow her to rationalize what had just happened as not being her own fault.

Nothing came except pain.

And guilt.

And more pain.

There was no way around this. However it had happened, it had happened. And worse, for the first time in her life she hadn't been the one to walk away. Jack had beaten her to the punch.

Chapter 24

Jack left the bakery, hitting the highway at one in the morning at speeds designed purely for adrenaline. He got halfway up to Beaut Point before he saw the red-and-blue lights whirling in his rearview mirror. "*Shit.*"

The cop turned out to be Sheriff Sawyer Thompson. Sawyer had been about five years ahead of Jack in school, but Sawyer's wildness was still legendary. How the guy had ended up on the right side of the law was a mystery to Jack, but one thing about Sawyer—he didn't sugarcoat anything.

"Christ, Harper, I clocked you at ninety-five." The sheriff leaned in past Jack to pat Kevin on the head. "The paperwork's going to piss me off."

"So don't do it."

Looking disgusted, Sawyer went hands on hips. "I'm only out here tonight as second-string because the flu's hit the station. I didn't hear a fire call go out."

"There isn't a fire." Except the one in his gut. "You could pretend you didn't see me."

"Or you could slow the fuck down." A full moon was just peeking over the inky black silhouette of the Olympic peaks in front of them, and Sawyer gestured to it. "See what happens when you slow down? You get to enjoy shit."

They both watched the moon. Kevin went back to sleep.

"Yeah, that's real pretty," Jack said after a minute or two. "We going to make out now?"

"Temperamental," Sawyer noted. "And pissy too. You know what temperamental and pissy plus a lead-foot equals? *Sorry-ass dumped.*"

Jack slid farther down in his seat.

"Got it in one," Sawyer said. Clearly enjoying himself now, he leaned against the truck like he had all night. "I haven't been keeping up with your social calendar, Harper. Who dumped ya? That cute flight nurse? Or the teacher? Oh wait. I know. The cutie pastry chef who moons over you when you're not looking."

"Maybe I was the one who left."

Sawyer nodded. "Good. Go with that. That bitchy 'tude works. So…who was it?"

Jack sighed.

"Aw, come on. You know how quiet it's been tonight? I'm bored. Tell me, and maybe I won't ticket you."

"Just give me the fucking ticket."

Sawyer grinned. "It's the pastry chef. Right?" He pulled out his ticket pad and started writing.

"Hey. You said you wouldn't give me a ticket."

"I said *maybe…*"

Twenty minutes later, Jack was in possession of a speeding ticket to go along with his stupid broken heart. He pulled into his driveway, waited for Kevin to do his business, and then headed straight to the fridge for a beer.

He was on his second when Ben came in the back door. Without a word, he took the third and last beer in the fridge and tossed it back. Setting the empty down on the counter, he swiped his mouth and looked at Jack. "What are we drinking to?"

"Women. They suck."

The smallest of smiles appeared on Ben's mouth. "If they're very bad they do. Or very good…"

"Why are you here?" Jack asked. "It's two in the morning."

Ben shrugged. "You seem like maybe someone kicked your puppy."

From his huge bed in the corner of the kitchen, Kevin lifted his big head. "Woof."

Jack craned his neck and stared at Ben. "You're not that good. How did you hear?"

"Maybe I *am* that good."

"No you're not."

Ben flashed a rare smile. "Okay, I'm not. Sawyer told his wife, Chloe, that he wrote you up, and Chloe happened to be at the Love Shack with her sisters, one of whom is friends with one of the ER nurses. Mallory. She's married to Ty Garrison, who's on flight care with…wait for it…Danica. It's all on Facebook," he explained.

Jack just stared at him. "It's like a bad sitcom."

"Except it's your life." Ben's amusement faded. "You okay?"

"Is that concern or gruesome curiosity?"

"Definitely the latter."

Jack swore and moved toward the door, but Ben shoulder-checked him. "Okay, Jesus. It's concern. Put your vagina away."

"Fuck you."

"We're related, so that's illegal in most states." Ben put his hand on Jack's chest when Jack started to push past him. "So it's true then? You and Leah? You're done?"

"We were never *not* done."

"Bullshit," Ben said. "Admit that much at least. It was never a pretend game, and we both know it. What the hell happened?"

"She took a job with that asshole producer."

"Rafe Vogel," Ben said, and at Jack's narrowed-eyed look, shrugged his shoulders. "So I like trash TV; sue me."

"She's going back to school in France, and it's being filmed for a new show," Jack said.

"Nice gig."

He gave Ben a long look.

"And...I'm missing something," Ben said. He thought for a moment. "When did she take it?"

"Shortly after telling my mom that we were dating."

Ben let out a low whistle. "And you think she's running."

"Again. She's running again."

"Maybe she didn't think she had an option."

"There's *always* an option."

Ben studied him. "Oh Christ. She didn't dump you. *You* dumped *her*. You love her and yet you dumped her." He shook his head in disgust. "You sure have a God-given

talent for pushing people who really care as far away
from you as possible."

"Yeah?" Jack asked, getting pissed off all over again.
"Then why are *you* still here?"

"Because someone has to be in your corner, even when
you're being a complete dumbass."

"Thanks."

Ben clapped his shoulder. "Anytime." He headed to the
door.

"And I don't love her."

"Okay. But you totally do."

Well, hell. It was shockingly, horrifyingly true.

Sleep didn't come to Leah until somewhere just before
dawn, when she was woken up by a call from Dee. "You
okay?" Leah asked quickly, her heart racing, thoughts
jumbled from both the lack of rest and being startled
awake after what felt like only a few minutes of sleep.
"What's wrong?"

"Oh sorry, honey. Did I wake you? I figured you got up
at this time to get to the bakery."

"It's okay; I do need to get up." She shoved a hand
through her hair and sat up, flicking on the light. "What's
wrong? Are you—"

"I'm fine."

"Jack—"

"Is fine too. Or so I assume," Dee said. "You know
what today is, right?"

The first day of the rest of her screwed-up life. "Uh…"
She struggled to remember.

Dee laughed. "It's Firefighter Car Wash Day."

Firefighter Car Wash Day was practically a national

holiday in Lucky Harbor. It occurred monthly during the summer and early fall and was more highly attended than the Fourth of July parade.

"I want to get my car washed," Dee said. "But I'm not really okay to drive. I was hoping you'd drive my car to Jack for me."

"You want to make Jack wash your car?"

"I want to contribute to the cause. If I tried to just hand him money to put into the till, he wouldn't take it."

This was undoubtedly true, but Leah wasn't going to be high on the list of people Jack wanted to see today. She kept picturing the look on his face after Rafe's call.

I want you, Leah. I've always wanted you, but you have to fight for it too…

She wanted to hate him for that, but how could she when it was the truth? She'd never fought for anything in her life.

She'd always walked away. Or run. She'd always been a quitter, doing her damnedest to prove her father right. That was going to change.

"You don't mind, do you, honey?" Dee asked.

"Of course not," Leah said, which was how later that day, after eight hours at the bakery, she ended up with Dee—and Grandma, who "didn't want to miss the hotties"—waiting in line at the fire station lot for a car wash.

All three shifts of firefighters had shown up for the gig and were good-naturedly out there doing their part in dark-blue swimsuits and little else except charm and charisma.

Grandma Elsie pulled out her phone to access her camera.

"Grandma!"

"It's not my fault," she said unperturbed. "Lucille pays us for the really great shots."

"Oh my," Dee said and put a hand to her chest. "Look at them all."

But Leah's gaze was on only one. Jack. Unlike most of the other guys, he wore a dark-blue T-shirt as well as his board shorts, with his official badge on a pec. He was standing in front of a Vespa, which had a beautiful red-head in it. She was talking animatedly to him, her hands moving as she told some story that made Jack burst out laughing.

He'd gotten wet at some point because his shirt was clinging to him. His hair was tousled, like he hadn't bothered with a comb. And when he laughed, Leah's chest ached.

"He looks tired," Dee murmured. "Poor baby."

"Yeah," Leah said, watching him lean into the redhead for a good-bye hug before she rode off. "Real tired."

"You know who that is, right?" Dee asked. "Chloe Traeger. Well, she's really Chloe *Thompson* now that she married the sheriff. She and Jack are just friends, honey. You don't have to be jealous—"

"I'm not," Leah said. "Of course I'm not." But she totally was. "Jack can do whatever he wants."

Dee turned to her. "I hope you two aren't going to have some sort of new age open relationship—"

"Dee." Leah blew out a breath and knew it was time to face the music. She reached for Dee's hand. "Jack and I, we're not a thing. I lied to you. I'm sorry. So sorry. I was just trying to help, but I ended up making it worse." She hesitated and then admitted the rest. "I did it to try to make you feel better, or that's how it started anyway. But the truth is, a part of me wanted it to be true between me and Jack. I shouldn't have ever said it though, or tried to deceive you."

"Oh, Leah," Grandma Elsie murmured from the back-seat.

Dee was quiet a moment, taking in the emotion in Leah's eyes. Then she leaned in and hugged Leah hard.

Leah squeezed her eyes shut and squeezed her back. "I never meant to hurt you. I—"

"I know." Dee pulled back, keeping her hands on Leah's arms as she looked her in the eyes. "And I *know*. I always knew."

Leah stared at her. "What?"

Dee sighed. "I was so touched, *am* so touched, that you wanted to help so badly. I'd hoped that you wanting it as much as you did would make it true."

Leah felt her eyes fill and she covered her face, but Dee gently pulled her hands free. "You weren't the only one in on the subterfuge, Leah. Jack isn't a man who bows to pressure. He doesn't do anything that he doesn't want to. He went along with it, and that brought me great hope." She paused, laughter in her voice. "And great amusement as well. Goodness, you two are fun to watch."

Leah groaned in misery.

"I wish you could have seen the way you two danced around each other, slowly coming to realize that it wasn't pretend at all."

"But it's not real," Leah said. "Last night we— He—" She shook her head. "It's not happening, Dee. It's over. Whatever it was that we were doing, it's over."

"Oh, honey," Dee said. "Running isn't the answer."

Leah opened her mouth to tell her that this time, this

one time, it was Jack doing the running, but the simple truth was she'd let him go. She'd taken the easy way out before he could discover her real secret—she loved him.

Hopelessly.

"It's my fault," she said. "I should've told him—"

"What, baby," Dee said. "That he's the one? That he's always on your mind?" She smiled, a wealth of knowledge in her gaze. "I remember what it's like, you know. Being afraid to let go. It's like that silly game you play when you're kids, falling backward and letting your friends catch you. It's all about trust, isn't it? Such a hard thing to do."

"So how did you finally do it?" Leah asked.

"My mom told me that I should trust the man who could see the sorrow behind my smile, the love behind my anger, and the reasons behind my silence."

Elsie was nodding. "Those are good ones. And you had that with Jack Senior, Dee. You surely did."

"He was the one and only," Dee agreed, and her gaze tracked across the parking lot to Ronald.

He met her gaze and lifted a hand.

Dee blushed and returned the wave.

"Dee," Leah said softly. "It's been so long. Don't you think maybe it's time for another one and only?"

"Oh, honey. No one's going to be interested in my old bones. Look at me." She gestured to the kerchief she had on her head, covering up the fact that she'd lost her hair. "I'm a mess."

"Dee Harper," Elsie said sternly. "You're thirty years younger than I am. I'd trade this old body for your skinny ass any day of the week, you just say the word."

Dee pulled down the visor to look at herself just as

Ronald knocked on the window. "Oh!" she said, jumping.

Leah powered the window down for him, and he nodded politely to Elsie and Leah. "The finals run tomorrow night," he said to Leah. "You going to win?"

"She can't tell you," Elsie said. "But yes, she's going to win."

"Grandma," Leah said and sighed.

Ronald smiled and turned back to Dee. "You look beautiful today."

She blushed some more. "You look busy out there."

"It is busy," he said. "Which is great. The money we're collecting today goes to the teen center." He was leaning on the car door by now, and craned his neck, taking in their bird's-eye view of the firefighters working hard. "You enjoying the scenery?"

Dee shocked Leah by looking right into Ronald's eyes. "Yes," she said.

And then it was Ronald's turn to blush a little. He cleared his throat and straightened. "You know, I've got two New York steaks in my fridge. Planning on barbecuing them tonight. Thought maybe you could use some protein."

"Are you asking her out?" Elsie wanted to know. "Because you might have to be more forward than that, Ronald. Our girl here is slower than a three-legged turtle in peanut butter when it comes to these things. You can't be obtuse."

"Grandma," Leah said again, but Ronald just nodded. And didn't take his eyes off Dee. "I'm asking you out," he clarified. "To my place."

"Yes," Elsie said. "She'd love to."

The corners of Ronald's mouth twitched. "Dee?"

Dee's smile had faded. "I...can't," she said and unhooked her seat belt. "Excuse me." She pushed open the
door and headed to the stands, where others were gathered, waiting for their vehicles to get washed.

Elsie got out and patted Ronald's hand. "You did good.
Real good," she said gently. "She's just gun-shy."

Leah helped her grandma to the stands to wait with
Dee.

"I can't believe you passed that man up," Elsie said to
Jack's mom.

Dee shook her head and made herself busy cleaning
out her purse.

Elsie sighed and rose to her full four feet, eight inches.
"It's a sad day when *I'm* the risk taker."

"Grandma," Leah said. "Where are you going?"

"To the seniors." She jabbed her cane in the direction
of the other end of the stands, where a group of seniors
sat together, joking and laughing. "They might be old, but
at least they know how to kick it."

Chapter 25

♥

At a lull in the car washing, Jack pulled Ronald aside. "I wanted to talk to you about the forensics."

"Never mind that," Ronald said. "I've got something more important."

"There's something more important than the only serial arsonist in Lucky Harbor's history?" Jack asked.

Ronald blew out a sigh. "Said a guy who still has his entire love life ahead of him."

Jack paused. "Huh?"

"I want to retire, goddammit!" Ronald burst out. "I want to retire so I can spend some time with someone I care about while sex is still more fun than bingo, or before I need a little blue pill to—"

"Jesus! I get it, okay?" Jack resisted the urge to cover his ears like a little kid and go running.

"I want that with your mom, Jack. I'm in love with her."

Jack shoved his fingers through his hair. "I don't know what to say to you."

"How about that you'll talk to her and tell her that she's been a widow longer than she was a wife. That it's time to look around and see there are other fish in the sea. That she should keep the smile you put on her face with the whole you and Leah thing. That she could have it for herself if she wanted, and it sure as hell wouldn't be pretend."

Jack looked into Ronald's eyes. He was solemn and quite serious, and...not at all nervous. Ronald was a steady, stand-up sort of guy who didn't do things frivolously or without merit. If he said something, it was so.

And he wasn't asking for Jack's opinion on his feelings, or for Jack to necessarily approve. "You know she's not...well."

"You're enabling her."

"She's been through a lot," Jack said tightly.

"And she's survived. She's going to keep surviving." He gave Jack one last long look and moved off.

More cars pulled into the lot. Jack washed two cars on autopilot, then looked up when he realized Danica was standing there talking to him. "I'm sorry," he said, shaking his head. "What?"

She was in a skimpy little white sundress that showed off her curves to perfection, and she sent him a smile that said she knew it. "I said I heard that you and Leah are over, and that you should let me help you commiserate."

"I can't."

"Aw." She hugged him before he could stop her. "You're so brave," she said. "So hurt. You call me when you're ready. I can help, Jack. I promise."

Jack caught sight of his mom and managed to disentangle himself. "Sorry," he said. "I've got to go," and he strode over to Dee. "Hey," he said.

"Son."

Not a happy tone. But then again, other than when Leah had told her he was in a relationship, he hadn't heard a happy tone from her in so long he'd nearly forgotten what it sounded like. "You okay?" he asked. "Why are you here?"

"To support my son," she said and lowered her voice. "The one who felt he had to lie to me."

Having no idea how she'd found out, he pulled her aside for privacy. "Mom—"

"Oh no. Don't you 'mom' me in that tone. Jack—" She cupped his face. "I didn't want you to make my mistakes. I didn't want you to wallow. I'm so deeply ashamed that you saw me give up like I did. And then to make you feel like you had to fake a relationship to make me happy... No." She inhaled deeply. "This isn't about me. It shouldn't be about me. It's your turn, Jack. Your turn to be happy."

"I *am* happy." Or he had been, until about 0100 hours last night.

She stared up into his eyes. "You aren't. Lie number two. Good Lord, Jack. What else have you lied about?"

"Remember that time Jack told you that someone hit-and-ran your car? Not true. He ran over Mr. Lyons's mailbox."

They both turned to face Ben, who raised his hands in surrender. "Not funny yet? Sorry, my bad." He started to back up, but Dee reached out and snagged him by the front of the shirt. "Did you know?"

"Uh..." He slid a glance at Jack. "Hard to tell. Did I know what exactly?"

"That Jack and Leah were faking their relationship just to make me happy."

"Uh…," Ben repeated, shoving his hands in his pockets and hunching his shoulders. He'd faced hell itself with a shocking fearlessness, but his beloved Aunt Dee in a mood simply terrified him.

"Benjamin Matthew Kincaid," she said sternly. "Look at me."

Ben met her gaze unflinchingly. "Yes, ma'am."

"Don't you 'ma'am' me!" Dee threw her arms around him. "I love you so much, you big, cranky, adorable sweetheart. So much more than your idiot cousin."

Ben had winced at the "adorable sweetheart" but his arms closed around Dee, as over her head his amused gaze met Jack's. "Of course you do," he murmured to Dee.

Jack flipped Ben off.

Ben returned the gesture without letting go of Dee.

Dee pushed free and looked up at Ben. "Thank you."

"You're welcome," Ben said.

"You have no idea what I'm thanking you for."

"None," Ben agreed.

Dee laughed and smacked him lightly on the chest. "For letting Jack pretend to be with Leah. Thank you."

"Let?" Ben asked. "Dee, no offense, but no one lets Jack do shit. He does whatever he wants, when he wants."

Dee beamed. "Exactly."

When both Jack and Ben just stared at her, she shook her head. "Honestly, do I have to spell everything out? You don't see? Neither Jack nor Leah pretended anything."

Jack shook his head, seeing where she was going with this. "Mom, listen—"

"No, Jack. *You* listen. You've been so good to me. And

I've had a good life. All I wanted for you is the love of a great woman, someone who would treat you right and take care of you. And then I could die happy."

Jesus. "Mom—"

"And when I'm gone," she said. "I—"

"Mom. Stop."

"I'm not done, Jack."

"Hell no, you're not done. You're not dying."

"But—"

"You're *not*. I'm not going to let you," he said very seriously.

At his side, Ben nodded just as solemnly. "No one's dying," he agreed. "Especially you. You're the glue, Dee. We need the glue."

"Oh." She breathed and sniffed noisily, searching her pockets, presumably for a tissue. "Oh, you boys are just the sweetest things."

Again Ben winced at the "sweet" moniker but offered her the hem of his T-shirt for her to swipe at her eyes.

"And as for Dad," Jack said. "You've waved the widow's weeds for long enough. I know you loved him; we all know it. And I know you miss him, but that doesn't mean you're half human. Live, dammit. It's worth it."

She stared at him, and then, horrifying him, her eyes filled with tears again.

"Ah, Mom. No." He pulled her in and hugged her, pressing his jaw to the top of her head. "I'm sorry."

"Don't you dare be sorry." She sniffed and pressed her face to his chest. "I shouldn't have let everything overcome me as much as I have." She lifted her head. "I taught you boys better than that."

"You did," Ben said quietly. "You taught us to go for what we wanted, and we each did."

Jack didn't say anything because in Ben's case it was absolutely true. Ben had wanted to design and build stuff, and he had. He'd wanted to fall in love and get married, and he'd done that too, until it'd been taken from him.

But Jack had let his future be guided by his past. Exactly what he'd accused Leah of, which made him a hypocrite.

He wasn't much for regrets, but that one was starting to weigh on him now.

"Jack," his mom said, cupping his face. "If I have to get over myself and go for what will make me happy, promise me you'll do the same." She pulled Ben in by the hand as well. "Both of you."

"Mom—"

"Promise me," she said fiercely.

Jack nodded. Ben did the same.

And then Dee smiled her queen bee smile, squeezed them both one last time, and pulled back. "Now, if you'll pardon me, I have to RSVP to a steak barbeque."

They watched her walk toward Ronald with great purpose.

"Imagine if she harnessed her powers for good," Ben said.

Jack started to respond, but then Dee went toe to toe with Ronald. Putting her hands on his, she pulled him to her and kissed him like she meant it. "Shit."

"Yep," Ben said. "She's tonguing your boss."

Jack grimaced and then rubbed a hand over his face. When that didn't clear his head, he gave Ben a shove. That helped only marginally.

"Your maybe, sort of, pretend ex-fiancé is next in line, man." Ben shoved him back. "Time to get to work."

Jack turned and looked. Sure enough, Leah was in his mom's car. She'd come around to the hoses and buckets of soapy water and had just hefted one of the hoses in her hand.

Leah stood there in white short shorts and a dark-blue LHFD T-shirt that he was pretty sure was pilfered from *his* closet. It was tied at her belly button, and she looked like a cross between his greatest fantasy and his biggest heartache.

She met his gaze, her own hooded.

Jack handed Ben his sponge and headed toward her. "You're not supposed to be here," he said when he got close.

Her eyes flashed. "Look, you might be right about everything you said last night. I am a complete screwup. I'm a lot of things. But I am still a contributing member of society here in Lucky Harbor, so—"

"I meant you aren't supposed to be *here*, behind the line, with all the gear." He gestured to the madness around him. "It's some sort of insurance liability."

"Oh." In the bright sunlight she blushed. "Right."

He caught her arm just as she turned away, not sure what he planned on saying, only knowing that seeing her was like a punch to the gut. But the next thing he knew, he was doused with water right in the face.

"Whoops," Tim said from the next car over, where he was hosing off the soap. "Sorry, kids!"

He'd also managed to hose down Danica, who was standing next to her car behind them. That snug, thin white sundress was now turning the family car wash into an X-rated wet T-shirt contest. She turned on Tim and nailed him in the face with a soapy sponge.

And just like that, the water fight was on. No one escaped unscathed. And in fact several people ganged up on Jack, including Tim and Ian, and he was pretty sure that it was Danica who'd jumped on his back and smashed a wet sponge in his face. The craziness went on for a while. People were soaking wet and having a good time. Lucky Harbor residents were nothing if not opportunistic and resilient.

When Jack finally pried free and swiped his eyes clear, Leah was gone.

Chapter 26

♥

On the night of the *Sweet Wars* finals, it was Elsie's turn to make dinner. "So," she said over meatloaf and potatoes. "Back to school, huh?" She smiled. "I'm so happy for you."

"It's only for one quarter."

"And then you'll go run a pastry shop, probably somewhere really exciting like Paris or New York, right?"

"I don't know," Leah said. She hadn't gotten that far in her head yet.

Elsie laughed a little. "Why am I asking? Three months out is about as far as you ever plan."

Leah went still, then reached for her grandma's hands. They were dry and callused. A baker's hands.

They matched Leah's.

"Grandma, you knew this was temporary."

Elsie nodded. "Of course, honey. I knew. I understand. If I were thirty years younger and half as talented as you, I'd be off making the most of it too. You have a lot out in front of you. I hope you know that."

"I know it," Leah said. "And I know it because of you."

"Oh. Well." Elsie's eyes filled, but she shook her head. "You'd have figured it out sooner or later."

"No, Grandma, it was all you. You and Jack." Her own eyes filled. "Always loving me unconditionally. Beating me over the head with it all until it sank in."

The doorbell rang.

It was Max Fitzgerald. Leah stared at him in surprise. "Mr. Fitzgerald. What are you doing here?"

"I need to speak to your granny."

"She's busy."

"I'm right here," Elsie said, coming up next to Leah. "What do you want, Max?"

"You convinced Lyons to pull out of escrow? You can't do that."

"Can and did," Elsie said and went to shut the door on him, but Max stuck his foot in it.

"Why?" he asked. "Why the hell would you get him to back out of a deal like that?"

"Why do you care?"

"Because believe it or not," Max said, "I care about you. It was a great offer. He would've gotten good, fair-market value on that piece-of-shit building. So what the hell?"

Leah stared in shock at Elsie. "You talked Mr. Lyons into keeping his building?"

"Yes." Elsie tilted her nose up to nose-bleed heights. "Yes, I did."

"Why, Grandma?"

"Because…" Elsie turned to Leah and softened her gaze. "Because you've reminded me how much I love that damn shop. I made that place, from the bottom up.

I know it's nothing fancy, and I'll probably have to hire some more help after you leave, but…" She shrugged and broke eye contact with Leah. "I'm not ready to let go."

"You didn't have to let go!" Max said. "No one was going to kick you out."

"But the new guy will be making changes. Updating, renovating. At the end of the year, the lease will go up. Everything will change."

Max couldn't deny this. He sighed. "Look, one thing I've learned…it's the way of things, Elsie. Change happens."

Elsie looked at Leah as she answered. "But I know," she said softly. "Except this at least, this one thing, didn't have to."

"You don't think Lyons will raise the lease?" Max asked. "Because he will."

"Not mine," Elsie said confidently, causing Max to toss up his hands and stomp off.

Leah parked at the bakery. She'd made her excuses to Elsie, and to Ali and Aubrey as well.

She didn't turn on any lights as she let herself into the kitchen and hopped up on the counter with a tub of left-over cookie dough and a wooden spoon.

And there, with her iPad and her impending sugar rush, she watched the *Sweet Wars* finals.

Alone.

The challenge had been deceptively simple. Make a five-tiered wedding cake large enough to serve two hundred people.

Except a cake that size was never simple, as Rafe so cheerfully pointed out to the camera. Unlike a smaller cake, frosting wasn't just spread onto traditional wedding cakes. Rather fondant covered each cake tier to give a smooth look. Fondant was made from a sugar syrup that took up to forty minutes of constant stirring to get to the correct consistency. And then after applying it to each painstaking layer, there were still many hours of decoration needed.

Leah could remember the buzz of the adrenaline flowing her through her veins as she'd worked fast and steady, tuning out the sounds and scents and overwhelming air of panic around her.

Now in the quiet kitchen she watched, as with twenty-five seconds left on the clock, the enormity of the situation caught up with her. She could see it so clearly on her own face. The self-doubt reaching up and grabbing her by the throat as she carried her beautiful, perfect, five-tiered wedding cake to the judging table and…

Dropped it.

She watched as it hit the floor with a splat, watched herself go pale and bring shaky hands to her mouth. Watched as everyone else on the cast turned to take in the disaster, shocked horror on their faces.

Each of them had been playing for second place, and everyone had known it.

Except Leah had dropped the cake.

The show cut to an ad break, and there on the counter, Leah closed her eyes. *What had she been thinking?*

But she knew what she'd been thinking. She'd stood there on the set, the win literally within her reach, and it'd hit her like a ton of bricks.

It was hers. The win was hers. She was about to be given everything she needed to open her own pastry shop—with the world watching.

You're never going to amount to a damn thing, Leah.

The anxiety had ridden up and grabbed her by the throat.

And suddenly the very best thing that could happen had become the worst.

The commercial break ended. The show came back on, and Leah forced herself to watch. Forced herself to take in her own misery at being sent home when she knew damn well she'd had first place if she'd only been brave enough to take it.

But she wasn't brave.

She let out a careful breath and turned off her iPad. And since her phone was buzzing like it was having a seizure, she turned that off as well.

That's when the bakery phone started going off.

"Oh my goodness, Leah," came Dee's disembodied voice from the answering machine. "Honey, I'm so sorry you tripped and dropped the cake."

Click.

The phone immediately rang again.

"Leah?" It was Ali. "You tripped? Do you need me? I mean, I realize you've known you tripped for six months, but…damn. Call me."

And so on.

Leah closed her eyes and tuned it out. It wasn't hard to do when the messages were all the same. Lucille said it looked like she'd been tripped by another cast member. Aubrey offered to drive the getaway car.

Leah dug into the bowl of cookie dough with renewed energy, inhaling the rest of it—which was delicious. Gee, maybe she should do this for a living…

Why hadn't she left already?

She hadn't left because of Elsie, she reminded herself. In spite of her grandma's assurances, Leah wasn't at all sure that she could go back to handling the bakery by herself.

And then there was the fact that Leah was all Elsie had.

No, wait. That was backward. Elsie was all *Leah* had. Leah had nearly forgotten what it felt like to be with family, to be unconditionally loved...

And that wasn't all, a little voice inside her head reminded her. There was more holding her to Lucky Harbor, and she knew it.

There was Jack. He was family too, in a very different way. Jack was...

Everything.

As if she'd conjured him up, he appeared at the back door looking superficially neutral. Letting himself in, his gaze settled on hers as he shut and locked the door behind him.

He was in a T-shirt that said JUST DO IT and a pair of old Levi's that lovingly contoured his body, intimately cupping parts of him that she missed. He smiled at the sight of her on the counter, bowl under one arm, wooden spoon in her other hand. But the smile didn't meet his serious eyes.

He'd seen the show.

"I'm not going to talk about it," she warned him. "So if that's why you're here, go away."

He didn't respond to this.

"I mean it, Jack. You said no big good-bye. You said it. It was your rule. I'm leaving tomorrow. Let's just let it go."

He came closer, until his thighs bumped hers. He looked into the bowl and then ran a finger along the bowl's edge and sucked it into his mouth.

"Double fudge," he said.

"You're good."

His eyes met hers, and the things she saw in them dried up her mouth. Because he was also bad. Perfectly, wonderfully *bad*. Not wanting to acknowledge the tightening in her gut—God, she hated knowing she'd let him down along with everyone else she knew—she licked the wooden spoon and said nothing.

He leaned against the counter and waited her out. He always could.

"Still not going to talk about it," she finally said.

He just looked at her.

Dammit. "Listen, just being on that show was a big deal for me, okay? Who could have expected me to get as far as I did, much less win it?"

More nothing from the big, bad, attitude-ridden firefighter, and this pissed her off. "Your expectations for me have always been too high," she snapped.

"You dropped the cake. You fucking *dropped* the cake."

"I know," she said. "I was there."

"Leah, you could make a wedding cake when you were thirteen years old. I know it. I ate it. You'd carry it across my mom's kitchen to the table with pride and grace. You never dropped it."

"Well I did this time."

He shook his head. "Why?"

In the heavy silence, her breath caught audibly. "I don't want to discuss it. I screwed it up, that's all. I'm not going to be a star pastry chef and that's that. Get over it."

He closed his eyes and dropped his head to his chest for a beat before looking at her again, his eyes filled with exasperation and frustration. "I don't give a shit about what you do for a living, Leah. It's not about that. It's about you."

The storm that had been brewing inside her broke open. "I'm not perfect, all right? We both know it. So you, and everyone else who thinks I should be, need to back off. I'm only me."

"Well finally," he said, his voice not quite as low and controlled as usual. "Something real out of your mouth."

She pointed her chocolate-covered spoon at the door. "Get out."

"Oh hell no. We're just getting somewhere."

She clamped her mouth shut. She'd chosen to stay here in Lucky Harbor until the bitter end, so she had no one to blame for this confrontation but herself. She was going to own it. "I lost, okay? I'm not going to make excuses for not being the best."

"Are you going to make excuses for not letting yourself be happy? For thinking you don't deserve it?"

"I'm not going to open a pastry shop in New York City. Big deal. How many people get to do that anyway? I've got other stuff going on. I'm happy."

"If only you believed that," he said very seriously. Way too seriously.

"Don't start with me, Jack. I am happy."

"Are you?"

"Yes."

He looked around, and she followed his gaze, taking in everything he saw. Elsie's favorite bowls stacked up along the counter. Elsie's utensils and cookery. Elsie's everything.

"There's nothing of you here," he said.

"It's Grandma's bakery. Not mine."

"I've been at the house. There's nothing of you there either."

"Again," she said. "Not my place."

"Yeah? Well then, where *is* your place, Leah?"

"You know I don't have one right now. I've been a little busy. And now I'm leaving anyway, so—"

"Bullshit." He caged her in with a hand on either side of her hips. "I'm calling bullshit, Leah."

"No, it's true. I leave tomorrow night."

"Not that," he said. "Yeah, you're leaving. No one knows it better than me. I'm talking about you not letting anyone too close or they'll see your flaws."

Her breath hitched. Dammit. He knew her far too well.

He ducked a little to look into her eyes. "But I've always seen you, all of you, flaws and all. I know you, so I can say this. You're not perfect. But you're perfect for me. And it pisses me off that you won't let that happen. Let us happen. I'm tired of watching you implode, Leah. Tired and done."

"Then get the hell out," she said. "I've asked you twice now."

He did just that. He got the hell out.

Leah covered her face and tried to tell herself he was an ass. A pushy, unforgiving ass. But she knew exactly who was at fault here.

"Knock, knock."

Leah jerked and opened her eyes.

Aubrey stood in the doorway holding a flask and a bag

of potato chips. "Thought one of these might be of some help about now."

"Alcohol and chips?"

"It's my emergency 'Just Fucked Up Again' kit."

Leah sighed. "You heard."

"Everything," Aubrey agreed. "Thin walls." She came in and helped herself to two glasses. She poured a splash of something amber into each and then handed one to Leah, keeping the other for herself. "Cheers."

"Cheers?" Leah choked out.

"You're right," Aubrey said. "How about…to fucking up? I mean, let's face it, we're both pretty good at that."

"What have you ever fucked up?"

Aubrey laughed a little coldly, and yet somehow the sound held volumes of loneliness. "You grew up here. You know my rep."

"You have a rep for being unflappable and gorgeous."

Aubrey took another shot. "And…"

"Okay," Leah said. "And maybe a little untouchable."

"Bitchy," Aubrey corrected. "Mean. Cold."

"I don't think you're mean or cold," Leah said.

Aubrey laughed again, this one much more real. "Just bitchy? Okay, I can live with that."

There was a soft knock, and Ali appeared at the doorway. She saw the glasses and immediately her mouth went into a pout. "Hey. I want to join."

"Can't," Aubrey said. "*You* aren't a fuckup."

Ali paused a beat, taking this in, clearly thinking hard. "You're wrong. I've been a fuckup before."

Aubrey smiled. "Is that the first time you've ever said fuck?"

"Maybe," Ali said. "Let me join the club and I'll say it as much as you want. Look— fuck, fuck, fuck—"

"Stop," Aubrey said on a laugh and got out a third glass, filling it with a few fingers straight up.

Ali knocked it back, coughed, and swiped at her mouth. "So are we drinking to the *Sweet Wars* final or something else?" She divided a gaze between them, clearly assuming it could have been either of them equally to be the screwup.

Leah raised her hand. "The finals. I'm this week's idiot."

"No you're not," Ali said, loyal to the end, but she bit her lower lip because she loved Jack too. "It can't be unfixable, it can't. You both care so much about each other."

"And isn't that just it," Leah said softly and scrubbed her hands over her face. "How can you fall for the person who knows you better than anyone else?"

"The question is," Aubrey said just as quietly, "how can you not?"

"He knows everything about me," Leah said. "All my secrets. There's no hiding with him, no holding back." She stood up, restlessly turning in a circle before coming back around to stare at her friends. "Do you have any idea how terrifying it is to be laid bare before someone like that?"

Both Ali and Aubrey were looking at her with eyes that assured her that they knew exactly, and she sighed. "I'm afraid," she whispered.

"Jack wouldn't hurt you," Ali rushed to say. "He'd rip off his own arm first."

Leah nodded. She knew this, she did. "It's just that I've never needed a man before to make my life complete. Never. But…"

"But what?" Ali demanded when Leah trailed off, a little overwhelmed by her own epiphany. "But what?"

"But…I need *that* man," Leah said. "I need Jack."

Jack lost himself in his drug of choice—work. It was late, and he was off duty, and yet he was at his desk staring at his computer screen. Around him, the station was quiet and dark.

Inside him, there was no quiet to be found as he picked up the phone.

"Do you know what time it is?" Ronald grumbled.

"And do you know that Mr. Rinaldi, that new developer in town, isn't new at all?"

Ronald blew out a long breath, sounding like he was struggling to come awake. "What are you talking about?"

"He's Max Fitzgerald's brother."

"Well, hell," Ronald said.

"Yeah. Well, hell."

The next morning, Leah was surprised to find her grandma already up and dressed to go to work.

"I'm baking with you this morning," Elsie said. "Our last day. No sadness," she said at the look on Leah's face. "And anyway, yes it's an ending, but it's also a new beginning as well. I'm feeling great. Turns out, having a man's better than Metamucil."

"I'd have to agree," a man said, and to Leah's utter shock, Mr. Lyons walked into the kitchen using his cane, looking as dapper and cheery as Elsie. He gave her a smacking kiss on the lips, winked at Leah, and then limped to the door. "I'll see you soon, chickie," he said to Elsie, and was gone.

"Isn't he the sweetest thing?" Elsie asked.

Twenty minutes later, they were at the bakery. And Leah had a bitch of a headache, which she tried to ignore. It was her last day, and she was stressed. That was all.

It had nothing to do with the hole in her damn heart.

An hour passed and she was elbow deep into the early morning baking when it happened.

The power flickered and went out.

"Dammit," Leah muttered. She had a searing hot poker of pain behind one eyeball. Her headache had upgraded to migraine level, and she was feeling lightheaded to boot.

Not enough sleep.

Dawn hadn't quite broken, so she felt for the junk drawer and fumbled for the flashlight and some new fuses. "Grandma," she called to the front room, where Elsie had been cleaning the display shelves for the new day's goods. "Have a seat for a few minutes; I'll get this."

"Already sitting," Elsie called back. "I might have been a little overzealous on the knee."

"You shouldn't be bending down and cleaning those displays."

"That's not what I got overzealous about," Elsie said.

Leah winced and rubbed her temples. "TMI, Grandma."

Elsie laughed in delight. "Go. I'm fine."

Leah paused to flick the beam of light into the little glass window of the new oven.

Her soufflé was going to be ruined. And hell if it hadn't been one of the most amazing batches ever too. Frustrated, she left the heat of the kitchen and stepped outside, closing the door so she didn't let out the bought air.

Ali wasn't in yet, and the bookstore was closed like

always. Dawn was breaking, the light a brilliant kaleidoscope of oranges, reds, and purples. The air was chilly
and seemed to clear her head. There was a tang of salt
from the ocean and…

She went still and sniffed again.

Sulfur?

In the alley, she turned in a slow circle, something
crunching beneath her shoe.

A scattering of cigarette butts.

That was odd. Extremely odd. The only reason for
anyone to be back here was if he belonged in one of the
three shops that made up the building.

But no one who did belong here smoked.

She glanced at the back door to the bakery and at the
glass window there. Right now, with the sun's rays stab-
bing through the early morning, the reflection on the glass
nearly blinded her, and she couldn't see in. But as of only
a few minutes ago, it would have still been dark outside.
Inside the kitchen, she'd have been like a fish in a fish-
bowl to anyone in the alley, and knowing it, goose bumps
rose on her skin.

Someone had stood right here in this spot, smoking
and watching her.

Hugging herself against the chill that raced down her
spine, she reentered the kitchen and shut and locked the
door. And then bolted it. "Grandma," she called out.
"Make sure the front door's still locked, okay?" Her
headache was killing her, and adding that to the exhaustion of not sleeping was making her dizzy. All this broken
heart stuff was hell on her immune system, she thought,
realizing she felt weak too. And…sick. Dammit. She sat.
Just for a minute, she told herself, and set her head on her

arms. Whew. She was seriously woozy. In the back of her mind, it occurred to her that her grandma had never responded to her.

She heard footsteps. Not her grandma's uneven, shuffling gait but someone with a more steady stride. A man, she thought. But her head was too heavy to lift, and her eyelids wouldn't open...

Chapter 27

♥

Jack was deeply asleep, dreaming of being smothered when someone started banging on his door. By the time he sat up and shoved Kevin off his chest, Ben had let himself in and stood in the doorway in a pair of unbuttoned jeans. "Get up," he told Jack, shrugging into a shirt. "Now."

There was little that ever made Ben rush, and knowing it, Jack immediately rolled off the bed and reached for pants.

"Luke called," Ben said. "There's a problem downtown."

Jack knew damn well that Luke wouldn't call about just any problem. "What is it?"

"The bakery. Someone called in a report of seeing an older woman unconscious inside the closed bakery. He didn't know more; the call had just come in. Let's go."

Jack was already out the door, calling dispatch while Ben drove. Emergency responders were just arriving on scene. Nothing to report yet.

Jack ended the call and leaned forward in the passenger seat, like that could get them to the scene faster.

"You think it's Elsie?" Ben asked.

"Don't know." Jack hit Leah's number.

No answer.

If it was Elsie in trouble—and who else could it be—then he wondered what she'd been doing alone at the bakery. Where was Leah? Under different circumstances, she might have been in Jack's bed, but he'd screwed that up pretty good.

He tried her cell again but it still went straight to voice mail. "Leah," he said. "Call me." He disconnected and stared at the road. Had she avoided a good-bye altogether and left town early? He had to work on not having heart failure when Ben went straight instead of left at the pier. "What the hell are you doing?"

"Driving you to the bakery," Ben said.

"By way of Africa? Why the hell didn't you turn on Harbor Boulevard?"

"They're tearing up Harbor. Repaving."

When they got caught at one of the only three stoplights in town, Jack could actually feel a stroke coming on and had to put a finger to his twitching eye. "There's no one in the intersection. Go through it."

Ben didn't move.

"Ben."

"You already have a ticket this week."

"But you don't!"

The light turned green, so in the end Jack didn't have to kill his cousin. And twenty-five hundred years later, Ben pulled up behind the ambulance and fire unit. Both men got out of the car and ran toward the scene.

Luke stepped away from a group of uniforms and into Jack's path. "Tim was driving by before dawn and saw the front light on in the bakery," he told them. "He said he got excited that Leah had opened early and parked. But the door was locked, and through the window he could see Elsie slumped at a table. He knocked but got no response. He broke in and hauled her out. She's come to briefly, but she's woozy and confused. Incoherent. It's a possible CO_2 poisoning, so we're testing for that now."

Carbon monoxide poisoning was known as a silent, viciously fast killer, and he got cold to the bone. "Leah?"

Luke shook his head. "Haven't seen her, but you're literally only two minutes behind us. Still clearing the building."

Hunter and Cindy were rolling the gurney toward the ambulance, where an agitated Elsie struggled with Hunter, who was trying to fit her with an oxygen mask. Her hands were fluttering, her eyes wide with confusion and shock.

"Shortness of breath and chest pains," Hunter told Jack.

Jack leaned over a confused Elsie, taking her hands in his. "You're safe, Elsie." Gently he placed the oxygen mask over her nose and mouth. "Lie still a minute. Just breathe."

Her hand came up, clutching at his wrist. She tried to say something, striking terror into his heart with one word.

"Leah," she whispered.

He gripped her hand. "Is she inside?"

Elsie's head lolled, and her eyes drifted shut.

"Elsie," Jack said firmly, watching her try to snap back into focus. "Elsie, is Leah still in the building?"

"Leah. Get Leah."

Jack whipped around and bumped directly into Luke. "Leah's here," Jack said. And then he ran toward the building, heading around the back via the alley. He got to the porch in time to see the back door crash open and Tim step out, Leah in his arms.

Chapter 28

♥

"Leah."

At the low but commanding male voice, Leah startled. *Jack.* She tried to look at him, but it was dark. Very dark.

"Leah, stay with us. Don't you dare leave me."

Oh, how she loved that tone, the way he could be demanding and so alpha she just wanted to eat him up.

His familiar grip settled around her hand and held on like a lifeline. "Open your eyes, Leah."

Oh yeah, she liked that tone too, the one he used when he was letting his emotions get the best of him. Like when he was buried deep inside her, telling her all the things he planned to do to her.

But she wanted to see his face, so in spite of a bitch of a headache, she struggled to open her eyes.

That's when she realized she was flat on her back. Jack stood by her side, his expression grim as he clutched her hand. She was on a gurney, with an oxygen mask on her face, but she did her best to give him a faint smile.

It was enough to bring some light to his gaze. "You're okay," he said.

"What—"

"Possible CO_2 poisoning."

She struggled to sit up. Jack wasn't alone. Tim and Ben and Luke were right there too, and a sea of others. Behind them, there were flashing lights and a crowd gathering.

And it started to come back to her. Being in the bakery, feeling sick, so sick— "Grandma," she managed. "Where's—"

"Being transported to the hospital," Jack said. "She was coming to as they pulled away. She's okay, Leah. Stay still."

She pulled off the mask, shaking her head as Jack started to object. "I'm fine. I..." Whoa. Her world swam, and there was a little man with an icepick behind her eyes, hacking away. An inch from throwing up, she decided maybe Jack had a point and went very still. "I want to go see her."

"Take another minute," Jack said firmly, holding her down when she would have hopped off the gurney. "Dammit, Leah. Give yourself a minute."

"How did I get out of the bakery?"

"Me." On the other side of the gurney, Tim smiled grimly. "I found you unconscious in the kitchen. You were crumpled right at the door on the floor, like maybe you'd crawled there to get out but hadn't made it. I had to break the door down."

"The power went out," Leah murmured, struggling to remember. Everything felt so confusing and fuzzy. "And I got tired..." She trailed off, images coming back to her.

Jack's face when Tim had brought her to him—not his usual calm, nothing even remotely close.

He'd been afraid. For her.

"If I hadn't driven by," Tim said, "God knows what would have happened."

Leah shuddered, and Jack squeezed her hand. She met his gaze, the both of them knowing exactly what would have happened. She and her grandma would've gone to sleep and never woken up. She sucked in some oxygen, and after a few minutes, she retained all her faculties. She insisted on being released at the scene, promising everyone she'd go straight to the hospital and get herself checked after seeing Elsie.

"Hell no," Jack said, taking her arm when she turned to her car. "I'm driving you."

"I'm fine—"

"I'm driving you to the damn hospital, Leah."

They didn't speak on the ride over. Jack was in his zone, and Leah's ice picker had graduated to using a jackhammer inside her head, rattling her brain. She drifted off a little bit, not stirring again until she felt a warm hand cup her face.

"Leah."

She opened her eyes to Jack's concerned ones. He was crouched low at her side in the opened door of his truck. She sat up. "I'm fine."

Reaching in, he clicked open her seat belt and then held her in place a moment. "You know, for a minute back there, I thought—" He broke off and closed his eyes, dropping his forehead to hers.

It was one thing to think the worst, another entirely to have the nightmare come true. He'd had that happen too many times in his life. "I'm okay," she murmured, cupping his stubbled jaw. "Really."

"I'm not." He drew in a long, unsteady breath, his eyes shadowed. "I'm not ready to lose you, Leah. Even when you're pissing me off."

She gave a little laugh and pressed her face against his throat. His arms immediately came around her, pulling her in. "We're still friends, right?" she whispered, needing to hear it. "You still love me, forever?"

He let out a barely there sigh. "Forever."

Her eyes burned. "I'm sorry I'm such a pain in the ass," she said against his warm skin, squeezing him tighter.

"You are a pain in my ass," he agreed. "I just want you breathing, Leah. For a damn long time."

He helped her out of the car, then tightened the grip he'd retained on her when she wobbled. Just outside Elsie's hospital room he stopped her, waiting for her to catch her breath. She could hear his phone vibrating, but he gave no sign that he cared about anything other than being here with her. He had her back. Always. No matter how much either of them screwed things up, they'd still have this. Each other. It was enough, she told herself. It was.

All she had to do was learn to believe it.

"Don't expect much," Jack said to Leah before letting her go into Elsie's room. "She's sedated and drowsy."

Leah nodded her understanding. Even with his warning, he could tell it was a shock to see her grandma prone on the bed, still as stone, eyes closed, skin waxy and pale. Elsie looked tiny and entirely too vulnerable, and Leah put a hand to her mouth.

Jack slipped an arm around her waist and nudged her in.

Tim was taking a chair bedside, clearly having just arrived. He was looking quite serious but also still in cocky hero mode. Next to him was Max. And next to Max was Mr. Lyons.

Leah let out a breath and a reluctant smile. "I hope she knows you're all here because she'd love this, three men at her beck and call."

Elsie's eyes fluttered open and they landed first on her audience, then on Jack. She struggled to say something to him, but Leah rushed to her side. "Shh, Grandma," she murmured softly. "It's okay. You're okay."

Jack pulled out a chair for Leah and gently pushed her into it. Then, feeling the tiny tremors wracking her, he pulled off his sweatshirt and wrapped it around her. Delayed shock. He wanted to get her warm and looked at, and then he wanted to pull her in and hold on.

And never let go.

Leah picked up Elsie's hand. "That was way too close of a call, Grandma."

Elsie let out one light chuckle but her eyes drifted shut.

"I love you," Leah whispered to her, her voice soft. "I love you so much."

Elsie's other hand came up and pulled the oxygen mask from her face. "Ah, honey, and you didn't even choke on it."

Leah let out a half sob, half laugh and dropped her head to her grandma's bed.

"No worries, it gets easier each time now," Elsie said, and over Leah's head she gave Jack a look that had him moving to her side.

"You're going to be okay," he said. "They want you to stay quiet for a little while and rest—"

"Yeah, yeah." She stared up at him. "I hear you, but…sometimes you can't stay quiet. Sometimes…" Her expression was pained, and her eyebrows kept waggling, as if she were having a seizure.

"Are you okay?" Leah asked, straightening to call for help. "Hang on—"

"Oh good Lord," Elsie muttered. "I'm fine. I'm trying to tell Jack something here. I'm saying that sometimes things aren't as they seem. Sometimes people, they act irrationally." She paused, her eyes not moving from Jack. "Do you know what I'm trying to tell you?"

"Oh, Grandma," Leah said, sounding exasperated now. "Just concentrate on getting better. You can go back to meddling into our lives later—"

Jack put a hand on Leah, quieting her. Because he knew exactly what Elsie was saying. He'd put it together the minute he'd seen who'd been waiting at her bedside with anxiety and adrenaline rolling off them in waves.

It made sense, horrible, sickening sense, but he kept his gaze on Elsie. "I do understand," he said, and because the entire energy in the room had changed, he had no choice but to act now. Pulling out his phone, he made a call. "Need backup," he said, and slipped the phone away again.

With clear relief, Elsie lay back and closed her eyes.

Leah craned her neck and stared up at Jack. "What are you doing? What's going on?"

She broke off when Max jerked suddenly to his feet. "Look at the time!" he said, his voice unnaturally jovial. "I've got to go."

Leah stood up and stepped into his path, halting him, eyes narrowed. "You smell like cigarettes."

"Since when is smoking a crime?"

"Oh my God," she breathed. "It was you."

"I didn't do anything!"

"Except maybe try to scare off the new developer from buying up the buildings for sale in town. What I can't figure out is why you were so upset when my grandma convinced Mr. Lyons to pull out of escrow."

Max sighed deeply. "It's complicated."

"Why?" she pressed.

"Because…"

"Because Vince Rinaldi is your brother?" Jack filled in helpfully.

Max looked at him and nodded. "My half brother, actually." He turned back to Leah. "So if what you're really doing is accusing me of setting those fires and then nearly killing you and your granny today out of greed, be very careful, missy."

"You should go, Max," Jack said.

"But—" Leah broke off when Jack slid her a look, and waited with what looked like barely restrained frustration as Max walked out of the hospital room.

Tim was going as well, apparently without a single word, until Jack stepped in his path. "Leaving?" he asked the younger firefighter softly.

"Yeah," Tim said, shoving his hands in his pockets. "Being the big hero really takes it out of a guy."

"Wait." Leah paled suddenly and put a hand to her head. "I remember you being there today," she said slowly. "You were in full firefighter gear."

Tim laughed. "You were out cold, Leah. You don't

know what or who you saw." He started to brush past them, but Jack blocked him.

"Hold on," Jack said.

"Why?"

"You grimaced when you stood up. You hurt?"

"My shins," Tim said. "From running."

"Shin splits?"

"A stress fracture, actually."

Jack nodded. "It's because you don't roll your ankles inward enough. Instead you hit the ground with the outside edges of your feet. Walking or running like that puts a lot of pressure on your legs."

"Okay," Tim said, trying to get around Jack. "That was real informative, thanks."

Jack blocked his path. "Tell me again how it is that you just happened to be at the bakery?"

"I was hungry. The place was still closed, which was weird. I just happened to be there at the right time to help."

"In full gear."

"No. Yes." He laughed a little. "Just my mask. You're trying to trip me up. I was at the front, and then the back." He glanced at his watch. "Seriously. Gotta go."

Sneaky. And cocky. He didn't think he could get caught. Jack leaned in and sniffed at him. "Why do you smell like cigarettes?"

"Dude, that was Max. You getting senile, old man?"

"No, it's you. You stink."

"Aw, you smell good too, LT. Like a fire. It's sexy as hell."

"Thought you quit smoking."

Tim gave up the pretense with easy grace and a shrug. "I quit every day. It doesn't always take."

"Use the damn patches."

"Says the nonsmoker." Tim's affable smile faded. "Doing my best, man."

Jack poked his index finger against Tim's pec pocket and cellophane crinkled.

Tim knocked Jack's hand away. "Knock it off. It's none of your business what I do when we're off the clock."

"We're never off the clock."

"Yeah," Tim said. "As proven by my actions today." He'd been wearing his cockiness like a shield, but there was something new there now, hovering just behind it. An edge of fear.

"Jack?" Leah asked behind him, uncertain. "What's going on?"

Jack held Tim's gaze. "So are we going to do this easy or hard?"

Tim just stared at him, his mouth a little tight now.

Great. The hard way then. "Tim and I are going to go outside and talk."

Leah opened her mouth, glanced at Tim, and then shut it again, giving him a nod that he hoped like hell meant she'd stay put.

Less than a minute later, with her head still spinning and her brain not firing on all circuits, Leah heard a shout in the hallway and then a thump. She let go of her grandma's hand and rushed to the door to find Jack holding a struggling Tim against the wall. They were surrounded by hospital staff, including Dr. Josh Scott and an ER nurse who was on the phone presumably to 9-1-1 because she had one finger in her ear and was yelling about location.

But though it was chaos, Jack's movements were sure

and controlled as he contained Tim. "It's over, Tim," he said. "It's done."

"I want my lawyer," Tim yelled, still struggling. "You can't pin the fires on me, and you sure as hell can't pin the carbon monoxide poisoning on me either. That ancient gas heater they have in there must be faulty."

"No one ever said it was the heater, Tim," Jack said. "But I'm sure that if you're right, a court of your peers will find it interesting that you knew exactly where the leak was."

Tim went still, then dropped his forehead to the wall, no longer fighting. "You fucker," he said. "You think you're better than the rest of us because your dad was some sort of hero. Well, I'm a hero too. I've saved countless people. In that apartment building fire, Sam would have died if I hadn't gotten him out of there. And then the auto parts store fire. Christ, that was beautiful... No one would have gotten there in time to save anyone if I hadn't called it in."

Jack let out a breath. Unbelievable. "Are you kidding me? If you'd managed to start that fire, do you know what would have happened in combination with the gas leak? The whole fucking street would have blown up. People would have died, Tim."

"I wouldn't have let that happen." Tim shook his head, eyes flashing temper. "You should have just let me train to follow in your footsteps. Or let me have a shot at Leah. You have it all, and you wouldn't share. I deserve everything you have, I'm just as good. Hell, I'm better."

Jack stared at him, stunned by the sick and twisted hero complex. "You should shut up now," he said. "Wait for your lawyer. You're going to need him."

Tim turned his head, pressing his cheek to the wall as his gaze locked with Leah still standing in the doorway. "She was next. Your woman was next."

Leah staggered back into her grandma's hospital room and sat heavily in the chair by the bed.

"Leah," her grandma murmured. "Are you okay, honey?"

Before she could answer, Jack strode into the room and tugged her up to her feet and into his arms, as if he needed to hold her every bit as much as she needed to be held by him.

"Yes, Grandma," Leah murmured, gripping him tight, proud that her voice didn't wobble. She tightened her grip and breathed in the safeness and solidity that was Jack. "I'm okay."

Leah was trying to sleep and having no luck when she felt someone slip into bed behind her. Warm, strong arms came around her.

"Jack," she murmured. "You came."

He kissed her shoulder, her neck. "Not yet. You first."

She smiled, then moaned when his hand slid beneath the covers and under the T-shirt she wore. It was his; she'd stolen it years ago and worn it so often it was threadbare.

Jack cupped her bare breast and let out a low, inherently male sound of approval, when she arched into his touch. He didn't say anything but she could feel the tension in him.

Immediately after Tim's arrest, he'd had to go back to the scene. They'd gotten word through Luke that Max and his half brother weren't involved with any of the arsons and cleared as suspects. Max had slunk out of town.

Tim wasn't going to get so lucky. He'd smoked the cigarettes left outside the fire sites as he'd waited for his opportunities. He wore the same size shoes as the footprints found. And, according to what he'd admitted in interrogation, he'd done it all solely for the glory of being a hero.

Leah had been checked out by Dr. Scott—at Jack's insistence, she'd discovered—and then had stayed with Elsie until visiting hours had ended. She'd called Rafe to say she needed a few extra days. Then Ali had taken her home, where she'd showered, crawled into bed, and...stared at the ceiling.

"You okay?" she asked Jack now.

"Tim's being held on evidence that we presented to the judge."

Not an answer to her question. She couldn't imagine how hard it had been, arresting one of their own, and she glanced over her shoulder at him, finding his face shadowed with exhaustion and worry. His hands were touching as much of her as he could reach, gently roaming over every inch of her. "Are you wearing my shirt?"

"Maybe," she said.

When he spoke again, there was a whisper of a smile in his voice. "You stole my shirt."

"Maybe." She tried to turn over, but his arms tightened on her and he buried his face in her hair. "Talked to Dr. Scott," he finally said, his lips brushing the curve of her ear as he spoke. "You were treated for mild shock. How are you feeling?"

He was still touching her. His fingers brushed the front of her panties and she forgot the question.

"Leah?"

His front was plastered to her back. She fought the urge to turn and burrow into him, to inhale his scent and hold on forever. "I just can't believe it was Tim," she whispered with a shudder.

Jack stroked a hand up her arm, the warmth of him chasing the chill that wracked her. "You did good, Leah. You took a bad situation and held it together." He was still tense, but she was pretty sure that was pride she heard in his voice. He was proud of her. He was also hard. "Jack?"

He pulled her tighter, his fingers trailing over her skin. "Yeah?"

"The rule," she said softly. "The one where we're done?"

He paused, clearly choosing his words carefully. "I was pissed off and butt hurt. And I was wrong. You've never misled me or tried to be someone you weren't. Life is short, Leah. Too fucking short. It took me a while to catch on to that. I'm not going to make that mistake again."

"What about the no big good-bye."

His teeth closed over her earlobe and bit down lightly, and heat spiraled through her belly.

And lower.

"I remember," he said.

"So…what are we doing?"

"New rule just for tonight," he said. "I'm going to fuck you until you forget about what happened the bakery," he said. "And then I'm going to make love to you until you scream my name again. I really like it when you do that."

She nearly came from just the words.

His fingers slid under the edge of her panties. "Still with me?"

"Y-yes."

"I want you, Leah."

Her heart squeezed at the words, given so freely. "Even though I hurt you? Even though I'm leaving? Even though—"

"Even though," he said, voice low. "I don't always agree with you, but I always understand. I want you in my life, Leah. That's never going to change."

Her breath hitched. Unconditional acceptance. It washed through her, heated her.

His cheek brushed against hers, sandpaper rough. "I know you don't want a good-bye, and hell if I do either. So this isn't good-bye. It's an until. Until our paths cross. It's happened before. It'll happen again."

Not a promise, and that was of her own making. She closed her eyes and took in the feel of him surrounding her, his heart beating at her back, his breath on her jaw. Did it matter?

His mouth was on the nape of her neck, his hands gliding over her body, stirring the desire, the all-consuming need. With a moan, she rocked back against him.

No promises. None were needed, she realized, and whispered his name entreatingly.

He dragged her panties down her legs and then his hand slid back between her thighs. She shivered as his fingers stroked, moving in a pace designed to drive her wild.

Or make her beg. Which at the moment she was perfectly willing to do. "Jack."

He pulled free and she heard him open a condom, replacing his fingers with something even better. Sliding into her to the hilt, he bit lightly into the junction of her shoulder and neck, and she came.

"More." His voice was gruff, and he thrust again, deeper. "Again."

She could barely hear him over the rushing in her ears, though she did hear her own whimper when he pulled out. Lifting his weight off her, he rolled her onto her back. "This way," he said. "I want to see you."

"You're so beautiful," she whispered.

"No, that's you," he murmured. Staring down at her, his gaze dark, determined, intense, he tugged her shirt over her head and slid back into her, making her cry out as he thrust right where she needed him. She rocked against him, her eyes fluttering closed with ecstasy.

"Leah, look at me." When she did, he thrust again. His eyes seared into her. "Remember this."

Did he think she wouldn't? He was all she remembered. Always. "Jack—"

His hand slid between their bodies and found her, and she nearly arched off the bed. She met his every move as another wave washed over her, and through it all she kept her eyes open, let him watch as everything inside her peaked and convulsed.

She took him right along with her. His control snapped and he shuddered, groaning out her name. Shifting his hips, he grinded against her, sending more tremors rippling through her. "This, Leah. I'll remember this. You. Always."

Unraveling at his words, she wrapped her arms around him, her legs, and then, she was pretty sure, her heart as well.

Chapter 29

Two days later, Leah stood at her parked car, surrounded by…everyone.

So much for a quiet good-bye.

Jack had spent most of the past two days at work dealing with the Tim fallout. They'd had no private time at all, and now their good-bye was going to be a public deal in front of Ben, Elsie, Dee, and half the town. Nothing she could do about that, she thought, not surprised when Jack took her hand and pulled her aside.

"Not fair," Lucille called out. "We can't hear you."

Jack's amused but solemn gaze met Leah's. "So," he said.

"So." She sucked in some air. "Love me forever?"

"And ever," he said. No smile.

Shaken, she stepped into him for a hug. "It really doesn't matter to you that I didn't win *Sweet Wars*, does it?" she whispered, holding on to him tightly. "Or that I screwed up. You really don't care about any of that. You know the core of me, of who I am, and you still put up with me."

"Leah." He slid his fingers into her hair, cupping the back of her head as he pressed his mouth to her temple. "You know all of my dark places, and you accept them. You accept me. So why is it so hard for you to believe that I know yours and accept them as well? You've been a part of my life for so long, one of the most important parts. That's what I care about. Not you quitting some TV show, but that you don't quit me."

Her breath caught. Her heart hitched. "But I have to go do this."

"I know. It's okay. Whatever you want to do, school, open a pastry shop, or nothing at all… That's not why I love you. And I do love you, Leah. I want you to know that before you leave. Not to change your mind, but to take with you."

The marvel of it washed over her and was better than the straight shot of the oxygen mask had been. That he felt this way was no surprise, not really. He'd been showing her how much he loved her in one form or another since the day she'd moved in next door to him.

Having grown up as she had, she knew the expression of emotions was all in the actions, not the words.

But the words…oh, the words. They were the most amazing words she'd ever heard. Getting into her car and driving off was the hardest thing she'd ever done.

As the dust settled from Leah's car, Lucille patted Jack on the arm.

"I'm fine," he said.

"Of course you are. You're an idiot, but you're fine."

Ben, at his side, choked out a low laugh.

When Jack slid him a look, Ben lifted a shoulder. "She's right, you know. You are an idiot."

"Yeah? And how's that?"

"You let her go."

Jack buried himself in work, and when he wasn't snowed under by all the work Ronald had left him, Luke and Ben dragged him out. They ate and drank so much he had to increase his workouts, which turned out to be for the best.

Exhaustion was the only way to sleep.

Leah wrote him. She sent emails, texts, and even a few greeting cards that made him smile.

He wasn't as good with the written word, so he called. The time difference was a bitch, but they spent hours on the phone talking about...hell if he knew.

He just liked the sound of her voice.

She often asked about his mom, who was doing well, thanks to Ronald. She asked about her grandma, who was also doing well. She asked about Jack's work, and how the transition to deputy fire chief and fire marshal was working out for him, better than he could have hoped for.

"Leah," he said halfway through her last semester. "I miss you."

There was a thick silence, and then her shuddery sigh sounded across the airwaves. "Miss you too."

"Wow, you didn't choke on it," he said, teasing her by mimicking her grandma's words.

"Or this," she said, and drew in a deep breath. "I love you, Jack."

He let a stunned beat pass, and then he had to swallow hard. "We pretended to be a couple for an entire town, you nearly died by the hand of a serial arsonist who wanted to date you, and then there was the big, dramatic good-bye we didn't want, and you never said a word. Now you're, what, twenty million miles away and you say it?"

"Five thousand miles." She laughed a little. "And timing was never my strong suit."

No kidding.

Leah did what she'd promised and committed to doing. She finished school. And surprising even herself, she enjoyed it.

She didn't have to be the best to be *her* best. All she had to do was be herself.

Rafe made her an offer.

"I've been asked to get you to renew your contract," he said. "The network wants to keep you on board. You're a natural in front of an audience, and the camera loves you. The network wants to follow you as you open up your own pastry shop."

It was a sweet offer. But the last time she'd truly been happy had been in Lucky Harbor, with Jack. He loved her, and she understood what that meant now.

How had she walked away from that? "No," she said to Rafe. "Thank you, but no."

"No?" Rafe sighed. "Fine. What's it going to take?" A ten percent raise?"

"Again, thank you. But I can't." She had something she wanted to do. Needed to do. For the first time in her life, she had a plan. She had revisited that plan in her mind every day for three months—knowing exactly the life she wanted for herself, and she was going for it.

"Listen," Rafe said. "I get it, okay? We're prepared to double your contract, but that's our last, cold, hard line, Leah. Take it or leave it. And let's be clear, we expect you to take it."

She shook her head, pushed his big, fancy contract back at him, and walked away.

"Where you going?"

"Home."

"You don't have one."

Maybe not. But that was simply a technicality. She knew where home was. Truthfully, she'd always known.

A day and a half later, she pulled into Lucky Harbor. It was dusk. It'd rained, making everything shiny and wet. The strings of white lights on the storefronts and in the tree-lined sidewalks glistened in the fading light...

Home.

She drove by the senior center and slowed. The lot was completely packed, but what caught her eye was the fire truck, front and center.

She recognized that fire truck and knew exactly who'd be inside. Heart already thumping in anticipation, she parked and entered the building beneath a huge sign: SAFETY AWARENESS NIGHT.

The main room was packed to the gills, and up front stood Jack and Kevin. The former was giving a safety speech. The latter was snoozing at Jack's feet, sprawled on his back, feet straight up in the air like a three-day-old carcass.

Unlike when Leah had once come to the senior center to give a cooking lesson, none of the seniors were napping or playing on their phones. In fact, everyone was riveted. Elsie was there, sitting next to Mr. Lyons.

Leah gave her a big hug. "I'm sorry," she whispered. "But there's something I have to do before I can talk to you."

"Go get him, honey," Elsie said.

Leah realized the room had gone so silent she could have heard a pin drop.

Kevin gave one exuberant, joyous bark and leaped at her, knocking her back a step in his exuberance.

"Good boy," she said, giving him a hug too.

Jack stood still at the front of the room, watching her with an unreadable face.

She waved at him.

His smile came slow and warm, and everyone craned their necks like they were watching a tennis match. "You're home," he said.

Some of the tension left her, but not all, because he still wasn't giving much away. Not that she expected him to in front of their captive audience. Plus, it was her turn to give it all away. To give him everything. "I'm home."

He gave her a finger crook, the universal sign for "come here." She glanced at the crowd avidly soaking up her every move.

"Ignore them," Jack said. "You're only surrounded by fifty of Lucky Harbor's finest gossips. Everything you say here will be repeated and posted on Facebook."

"And tweeted," Lucille called out. "I've found the Twitter."

"I thought 'tweet' was a female body part," one of the seniors said, sounding confused.

Anxious but holding her gaze steadily on Jack, Leah walked up the center aisle toward him.

"Damn," she heard Lucille whisper. "Siri, remind me to download the bride's march song on my iPhone."

"Wait. She's back?" someone else asked, sounding confused. "I thought she ran off."

"She didn't run off, you moron." This from Elsie. "She went back to school. Don't any of you read Facebook?"

Leah stopped at the foot of the stage and looked up at Jack. "I was wrong," she said.

Jack curled a hand around his ear, like he hadn't caught her words.

"*I was wrong*," she repeated.

"Oh, I heard you." He smiled. "I just like the sound of the words on your lips."

The crowd tittered at this. Ignoring them, Jack reached down and gripped Leah by the wrist, easily lifting her to the stage. "And not that I don't love those words, but what were you wrong about?"

"Walking away from you." She stepped into him. "I'm done with that, by the way. I'm walking straight at you from now on."

Around them came a collective "aww," and Jack's smile spread to his eyes as he finally pulled her into his arms.

Over his shoulder she could see her grandma beaming, and Kevin sitting in Lucille's lap. Lucille was handing over money to Mr. Lyons.

"They were betting on whether you were going to break my heart or not," Jack told her. "The stakes got so high I even put in my own bet."

"Which way did you bet?" she asked.

Mr. Lyons walked to the front of the room and slapped some twenties into Jack's palm and then stomped back to his seat.

"Let's just say I won," Jack said easily. And then he

bent and kissed her to the whoops and hollers of their delighted audience.

"I wouldn't mind a kiss like that," Leah heard Lucille say.

"Me either," Elsie said, and then squeaked in delighted surprise when Mr. Lyons pulled her close and gave her a smacking kiss right on the lips.

Against her, she could feel Jack shake with laughter just as he scooped her up and slung her over his shoulder in a fireman's hold.

The crowd ate this up, especially when Jack turned and flashed them a grin. "Excuse us," he said. "We need a minute in private."

"Well that's no fun," Lucille complained as Jack strode out of the room, down a hall, and into the first room they came to—the dining room.

He set her down on the counter that ran along one wall, pinning her there with a hand on either side of her hips as he looked into her eyes. "Hey."

Everything within her flooded with affection, need... love. "Hey." She cupped his face. Beneath her fingers, his face was rough with at least a day's growth. She wanted to feel it against her bare skin. "Last time I was home you asked me when I was going to realize that I deserve to be happy." She paused. "Now," she said. "I realize it now. I deserve it," she said softly.

The very corners of his lips curved, and what might have been pride came into his expression. "Yeah?"

"Yeah. And I know something else I deserve," she told him.

"What?"

"You. I'm in love with you, Jack. And you're in love with me too."

There was a very slight quirk at the corners of his mouth. "You sound pretty sure."

"I've never been so sure of anything." She gave him a nudge, hopped down off the counter, and pushed him into a chair. "So you might as well give in now."

"You think so, huh?"

She climbed into his lap. "I really do."

Someone knocked on the door.

"Lucille," Jack called out, not taking his gaze off Leah. "This conversation is off limits. Go practice your safety techniques. There's going to be a quiz."

"Oh!" She squealed in delight through the door. "I love quizzes."

And then there was blessed silence.

"So," Jack said. "Back to this you love me thing."

She pressed closer and slid her fingers into his hair. "I do love you, Jack. I don't want to be without you."

"Neither do I."

Hearing the true emotion in his voice, in the grip he had on her, she felt herself begin to let loose of the last of the tension in her gut.

"New rule," he said. "No more rules."

She smiled. "And if I agree to this 'no more rules,' what's in it for me?"

"Me."

She felt the smile burst full bloom across her face. "Well, if that's not the best offer I've ever had," she said.

He was grinning as he kissed her until she was dizzy.

"Come on," he said, and then stood up with her still wrapped around him.

"Wait!" she said, panicked, when he headed toward the door.

"Oh no you don't," he said, tightening his grip on her. "Not now, not when I finally have you where I want you."

"And where is that?"

"With me." He stepped back into the front room, and everyone clapped until he held up a hand for silence, letting Leah slide down his body. "We have an announcement."

"We do?" Leah said, her world spinning out of control, like a dream. The best dream she'd ever had.

"We do." He brought their entwined hands up and brushed his mouth across her knuckles as everyone in the room leaned forward in unison, straining to catch his next words.

"What?" Lucille finally demanded. "What's the announcement?"

Jack smiled at Leah. "We're taking this relationship off the radar."

"Well dammit," Lucille said as the rest of the room groaned.

Ignoring all of them, Jack tugged Leah into his side, kissed her softly, and smiled into her eyes. "Class dismissed," he said.

And then kissed her again.

And again…

About the Author

New York Times bestselling author **Jill Shalvis** lives in a small town in the Sierras full of quirky characters. Any resemblance to the quirky characters in her books is mostly coincidental. Look for Jill's bestselling, award-winning books wherever romances are sold and visit her website for a complete book list and daily blog detailing her city-girl-living-in-the-mountains adventures.

You can learn more at:
   JillShalvis.com
   Twitter @JillShalvis
   Facebook.com/JillShalvis